Awakening in Germany

It was probably the German people, the Volk, which surprised me most of all. I really did everything humanly possible to destroy the foundations for a future existence on this soil, this soil which the enemy had desecrated. Bridges, power stations, roads, railways – I gave instructions for every last one to be obliterated. I have since checked when this order was issued – it was in March – and I believe I had made myself perfectly clear. All supply facilities were to be razed, waterworks, telephone systems, resources, factories, workshops, farms, all material assets – everything, and by that I did mean absolutely everything! These matters must be approached with care and precision; a directive such as this can leave no room for doubt. For we all know of the ordinary soldier at the front who, contained within his own particular sector, understandably lacks an overview of the general situation, knowledge of the strategic, tactical necessities. The soldier who comes and says, "Do I really have to set light to this . . . this . . . [let's say] kiosk, too? Can't we let it fall into enemy hands? Is it really so bad if the kiosk falls into enemy hands?" Bad? Of course it's bad! The enemy reads newspapers, too, doesn't he? He will use the kiosk to conduct business, he will turn the kiosk against us, everything he finds will be turned against us! Every material asset – let me underline this once more – every single material asset must be destroyed. Not just houses, but doors too. And door handles. Then the screws, and not only the long ones. The screws must be unscrewed and then ruthlessly bent out of shape. The doors must be ground into sawdust. And then burned to cinders. Else the enemy will show no mercy; he will walk in and out of these doors as it pleases him. But present him with a broken door handle, bent screws and a heap of ashes – well, Mr Churchill, be my guest! At all events these requirements are the brutal consequence of war – of this I have always been aware – and thus the instructions I gave could not have been worded differently, even though the background to my directive was different.

To begin with, at any rate.

It could no longer be denied that the German Volk had ultimately proved itself inferior in the epic struggle against the English, against Bolshevism, against imperialism, thereby – and I will not mince my words – forfeiting its future existence, even at the most primitive level as hunter-gatherers. Accordingly, it lost its right to waterworks, bridges and roads. And door handles, too. This is the reason I issued my directive. It must be said that I also did it in part for the sake of thoroughness, for when I took the odd stroll outside the Reich Chancellery I had to concede that with their Flying Fortresses, the Americans and the English had already relieved us of a substantial volume of the work. Naturally, after the directive was issued, I did not monitor in every minute detail how it was executed. The reader will appreciate how much else I had to do: grappling with the Americans in the West, resisting the Russians in the East, planning the development of the world's capital city, Germania. In my opinion the Wehrmacht should have been able to cope with any remaining door handles. And this Volk should no longer exist.

As I have now established, however, it is still here.

A fact I find rather difficult to comprehend.

On the other hand, I am here too, and I cannot understand that either.

I remember waking up; it must have been early afternoon. Opening my eyes I saw above me the sky, which was blue with the occasional cloud. It felt warm, and I sensed at once that it was too warm for April. One might almost call it hot. It was relatively quiet; I could not see any enemy aircraft flying overhead, or hear the thunder of artillery fire, there seemed to be no shelling nearby or explosions, no air-raid sirens. It also struck me that there was no Reich Chancellery and no Führerbunker. I turned my head and saw that I was lying on an area of undeveloped land, surrounded by terraces of houses. Here and there urchins had daubed the brick walls with paint, which aroused my ire, and I took the snap decision to summon Grand Admiral Dönitz. Still half asleep, I imagined that Dönitz must also be lying around here somewhere. But then discipline and logic triumphed, and in a flash I grasped the peculiarity of the situation in which I found myself. I do not usually camp out.

My first thought was, "What did I get up to last night?" Seeing as I do not drink, I could rule out any overindulgence in alcohol. The last thing I recalled was sitting on a sofa, a divan, with Eva. I also remembered that I was – or we were –

feeling rather carefree; just for once I had decided to put the affairs of state to one side. We had no plans for the evening. Naturally there was no question of going out to a restaurant or to the pictures – entertainment in the capital was gratifyingly thin on the ground, largely as a result of my directive. How could I be sure that Stalin would not be arriving in the city in the coming days? At that point in the war such a turn of events could not be dismissed out of hand. What was absolutely certain was that he would be as unlikely to find a picture house here as he would in Stalingrad. I think Eva and I chatted for a while, and I showed her my old pistol, but when I awoke I was unable to recall any further details. Not least on account of the bad headache I was suffering from. No, my attempts to piece together the events of the previous evening were leading nowhere.

I thus decided to take matters into my own hands and get to grips with my situation. Over the course of my life I have learned to observe, to reflect, to pick up on even the smallest detail to which many learned people pay scant heed, or simply ignore. Thanks to years of iron discipline, I can say with a clear conscience that in a crisis I become more composed, more level-headed, my senses are sharpened. I work calmly, with precision, like a machine. Methodically, I synthesise the information at my disposal. I am lying on the ground. I look around. Litter is strewn beside me; I can see weeds and grass, the odd bush, a daisy, and a dandelion. I can hear voices shouting – they cannot be far away – the noise of a ball bouncing repeatedly on the ground. I look in the direction of these sounds, they are coming from a group of lads playing association football. Not little boys anymore, but probably too young for the Volkssturm. I expect they are in the Hitler Youth, although evidently not on duty. For the time being the enemy appears to have ceased its onslaught. A bird is hopping about in the boughs of a tree; it tweets, it sings. Most people will simply interpret such behaviour as a sign of happiness. But in this uncertain situation the expert on the natural world and the day-to-day battle for survival exploits every scrap of information, however small, and infers that no predators are present. Right beside my head is a puddle which appears to be shrinking; it must have rained, but some time ago now. At the edge of the puddle is my peaked cap. This is how my trained mind works; this is how it worked even then, in a moment of confusion.

I sat up without difficulty. I moved my legs, hands and fingers. I did not appear to be injured, my physical state was encouraging; but for the sore head I was in rude health. Even the shaking which usually afflicted my hand seemed to have subsided. Glancing down I saw myself dressed in full military uniform. My jacket had been soiled, but not excessively so, which ruled out the possibility of my having been buried alive. I could identify mud stains and what looked like bread or cake crumbs, or similar. The fabric reeked of fuel, petrol perhaps; Eva may have used too much solvent to clean my uniform. It smelled as if she had emptied a whole jerrycan of the stuff over me. Eva was not to be seen, nor did any of my staff appear to be in the immediate vicinity. As I was brushing the most conspicuous specks of dirt from the front of my coat and sleeves, I heard a voice:

"Hey guys, check this out!"

"Whooooa, major casualty!"

I seemed to have given the impression that I needed help, and this was admirably recognised by the three Hitler Youths. Even though they were off the mark with my rank. They stopped their game and approached me respectfully. Understandably so – to find oneself all of a sudden face to face with the Führer of the German Reich amongst daisies and dandelions on a patch of wasteland generally used for sport and physical training is an unusual turn of events in the daily routine of a young man yet to reach full maturity. Nonetheless the small troop hurried over like greyhounds, eager to help. The youth is the future!

The boys gathered around me, but kept a certain distance. After affording me a cursory inspection, the tallest of the youths, clearly the troop leader, said:

"You alright, boss?"

Despite my apprehension, I could not help noticing that the Nazi salute was missing altogether. I acknowledge that his casual form of address, mixing up "boss" and "Führer", may have been a consequence of the surprise factor. In a less confusing situation it might have been unintentionally comic – after all, had not the most farcical events occurred in the unremitting storm of steel of the trenches? Even in unusual situations, however, the soldier must have certain automatic responses; this is the point of drill. If soldiers lack these automatic responses, then the army is worthless. I stood up, which was not easy as I must have been lying there for a while. But I straightened out my jacket and attempted a makeshift dusting of my trousers with a few gentle slaps. Then I cleared my throat and asked the troop leader, "Where's Bormann?"

"Who?"

Unbelievable!

"Bormann! Martin!"

"Don't know who you're on about."

"Never heard of him."

"What's he look like?"

"Like a Reichsleiter, for pity's sake!"

Something was very amiss. I was obviously still in Berlin, but I appeared to have been deprived of the entire apparatus of government. I had to get back to the Führerbunker – urgently – and it was as clear as daylight that the youths around me were not going to be a great deal of help here. The first thing I needed to do was orient myself. The featureless piece of land where I now stood could have been anywhere in the city. I had to get to a street; in this protracted ceasefire surely there would be enough passers-by, workers and motor-cab drivers to point me in the right direction.

I expect my needs did not appear sufficiently pressing to the Hitler Youths, who looked as if they wanted to resume their game of association football. The tallest of the lads now turned to his friends, allowing me to read his name, which his mother had sewn onto a brightly coloured jersey.

"Hitler Youth Ronaldo! Which way to the street?"

The reaction was feeble; I am afraid to say that the youths practically ignored me, although as he shuffled past one of the two younger ones pointed limply to a corner of the wasteland. Peering more closely I could see that there was indeed a thoroughfare in that direction. I made a mental note to have Rust dismissed. The man had been Reich Minister for Education since 1934, and there is no place for such abysmal sloppiness in education. How is a young soldier supposed to find the victorious path to Moscow, to the very heart of Bolshevism, if he cannot even recognise his own supreme commander?

I bent down, picked up my cap and, putting it on, walked steadily and purposefully in the direction the boy had indicated. I went around a corner and made my way between high walls down a narrow alleyway towards the brightness of the street. A timid and bedraggled cat with a coat of many hues sloped past me along the wall. I took four or five more steps and then emerged into the street.

The violent onslaught of light and colour took my breath away.

The last time I had seen it I remembered the city being terribly dusty and a kind of field-grey, with heaps of rubble and widespread damage. What lay before me now was quite different. The rubble had vanished, or at least had been removed, the streets cleared. Instead there were numerous, nay innumerable brightly coloured vehicles on either side of the street. They may well have been automobiles, but were smaller, and yet they looked so technically advanced as to make one suspect that the Messerschmitt plant must have had a leading hand in their design. The houses were freshly painted, in a variety of colours, reminding me of the confectionery of my youth. I admit, I began to feel faintly dizzy. My eyes sought something familiar, and on the far side of the carriageway I spied a shabby park bench on a strip of grass. I ventured a few steps, and I am not ashamed to say that they may have seemed quite tentative. I heard the ring of a bell, the screeching of rubber on asphalt, and then somebody screamed at me:

"Oi! What's your game? Are you blind or what?"

"I . . . I'm terribly sorry," I heard myself say, both shaken and relieved. Beside me was a bicyclist, this at least was an image I was comparatively familiar with. Added to that, the man was wearing a protective helmet, which appeared to have sustained some serious damage given the number of holes in it. So we were still at war.

"What the hell do you think you're doing, staggering around like that?"

"I . . . pardon me . . . I . . . need to sit down."

"I suggest you take a lie down, pal. And make it a nice long one!"

I found sanctuary on the park bench; I expect I was somewhat pale when I slumped onto it. This young man did not seem to have recognised me, either. Again, there was no Nazi salute; from his reaction one would have thought he had almost collided with any old passer-by, a nobody. And this negligence seemed to be common practice. An elderly gentleman walked past me, shaking his head, followed by a hefty woman pushing a futuristic perambulator – likewise a familiar object, but it offered no help out of my desperate situation. I stood up and approached her with as much outward confidence as I could muster.

"Excuse me, now this may come as something of a surprise, but I . . . I urgently need to find my way to the Reich Chancellery."

"Are you on the Stefan Raab Show?"

"I'm sorry?"

"Or Kerkeling? Harald Schmidt?"

It may have been nervousness which triggered my impatience; I grabbed her by the arm.

"Pull yourself together, woman! As a fellow German you have your duties and obligations! We are at war! What do you think the Russians would do to you if they got here? Do you honestly think a Russian would glance at your child and say, 'Well, what a fine young German girl we have here, but for the child's sake I will leave my baser urges in my trousers?' At this very hour, on this very day, the future of the German Volk, the purity of German blood, indeed the survival of humanity itself is at stake. Do you wish to be responsible for the end of civilisation merely because, in your extraordinary stupidity, you are unwilling to show the Führer of the German Reich the way to his Reich Chancellery?"

The lack of a helpful response had almost ceased to be a surprise. This imbecilic woman shook her sleeve from my grasp, glared at me dumbfounded, and tapped the side of her head with her index finger: an unequivocal gesture of disapproval. I had to accept the truth of the matter; something here had spiralled completely out of control. I was no longer being treated like a commander-in-chief, like a Reichsführer. The footballers, the elderly gentleman, the bicyclist, the perambulator woman – this was no coincidence. My first instinct was to notify the security agencies, to restore order. But I curbed this instinct. I had insufficient knowledge of my circumstances. I needed more information.

With ice-cool composure my methodical brain, now functioning again, recapped the situation. I was in Germany, I was in Berlin, even though the city looked wholly unfamiliar to me. This Germany was different, but some of its aspects reminded me of the Reich I *was* familiar with. Bicyclists still existed, as did automobiles, so probably newspapers still existed too. I looked around. And under my bench I did find something resembling a newspaper, albeit printed far more lavishly. The paper was in colour, something new to me. It was called *Media Market* – for the life of me I could not recall having given my approval to such a publication, nor would I ever have approved it. The information it contained was totally incomprehensible. Anger swelled within me: how, at a time of paper shortage, could the German Volk's valuable resources be squandered on such mindless rubbish? As soon as I got back to my desk, Funk was going to get a proper dressing-down. But at that moment I needed some reliable news, a *Völkischer Beobachter*, a *Stürmer*; Why, I'd have settled for the local *Panzerbär*, which had only been going for a few issues. I spotted a kiosk not too far away, and even from that distance I could make out an extraordinary array of papers. You could have been forgiven for thinking we were deep in the most indolent peacetime! I got up impatiently. Too much time had already been lost – now order must be restored as rapidly as possible. Surely my troops were awaiting orders; it was quite possible my presence was sorely needed elsewhere. I hurried to the kiosk.

Even a cursory look furnished me with some useful information. Myriad colourful papers hung on the outside wall – in Turkish. A large number of Turks must now be living in this area. I must have been unconscious for a significant period of time, during which waves of Turks had descended on Berlin. Remarkable! After all, the Turk, essentially a loyal ally of the German Volk, had persisted in remaining neutral; in spite of all our efforts, we had never been able to get him to enter the war on the side of the Axis powers. But now it seemed as if during my absence someone – Dönitz, I imagine – had convinced the Turk to lend us his support. Moreover, the comparatively peaceful atmosphere on the streets suggested that the deployment of Turkish forces had brought about a decisive turning-point in the war. Yes, I had always harboured respect for the Turk, but would never have imagined him capable of such an achievement. On the other hand, a lack of time had precluded my having followed the development of that country in any great detail. Kemal Atatürk's reforms must have given the nation a sensational boost. This seemed to have been the miracle on which Goebbels had always pinned his hopes. Full of confidence, my heart was now pounding. My refusal to abandon faith in ultimate victory, even in the deepest, darkest hour of the Reich, had paid off. Four or five Turkish-language publications, all printed in bright colours, were unmistakable proof of a new, triumphant Berlin–Ankara axis. Now that my greatest concern, my concern for the welfare of the Reich, appeared to have been assuaged in such a surprising manner, I had to find out how much time I had spent in that strange twilight on the patch of waste ground. Unable to see a *Völkischer Beobachter* anywhere – obviously it had sold out – I cast about for the most familiar-looking paper, which went by the name *Frankfurter Allgemeine Zeitung*. It was new to

me, but unlike some of the others displayed there, I was heart-
ened by the reassuring typeface of its title. I didn't bother with
any of the news reports; I was looking for the date.

It said 30 August.

2011.

I gaped at the number in amazement, in disbelief. I turned
my attention to a different paper, the *Berliner Zeitung*, which
also displayed an exemplary German typeface, and sought out
the date.

2011.

I tore the newspaper from its bracket, opened it and turned
a page, then another one.

2011.

The number began to dance before my eyes, as if mocking
me. It moved slowly to the left, then back again more quickly,
swaying like a group of revellers in a beer tent. My eyes tried to
follow the number, then the paper slipped from my grasp. I felt
myself sinking; in vain I tried to clutch at other newspapers on
the rack. I slid to the ground.

Then everything went black.

ii

When I regained consciousness I was still lying on the ground. Something damp was being pressed against my forehead.

"Are you O.K.?"

Bent over me was a man who may have been forty-five, or even over fifty. He was wearing a checked shirt and plain trousers – a typical worker's outfit. This time I knew which question to ask first.

"What is today's date?"

"Ermm . . . 29 August. No, wait, it's the thirtieth."

"Which year, man?" I croaked, sitting up.

He frowned at me.

"2011," he said, staring at my coat. "What did you think? 1945?"

I tried to come up with a fitting riposte, but thought it more prudent to get to my feet.

"Maybe you should lie down a little longer," the man said. "Or at least sit. I've got an armchair in the kiosk."

My first instinct was to tell him that I had no time to rest, but I had to acknowledge that my legs were still shaking. So I followed him into the kiosk. He sat on a chair near the vending window and stared at me.

"Sip of water? How about some chocolate? Granola bar?"

I nodded in a daze. He stood up, fetched a bottle of soda water and poured me a glass. From a shelf he took a colourful bar of what I took to be some sort of iron ration, wrapped in foil. He opened the wrapping, exposing something that looked like industrially pressed grain, and put it in my hand. There must still be a bread shortage.

"You should have a bigger breakfast," he said, before sitting down again. "Are you filming nearby?"

"Filming . . . ?"

"You know, a documentary. A film. They're always filming around here."

"Film . . . ?"

"Goodness me, you're in a right state." Pointing at me, he laughed. "Or do you always go around like this?"

I looked down at myself. I didn't notice anything out of the ordinary apart from the dust and the odour of petrol.

"As a matter of fact, I do," I said.

Perhaps I had suffered an injury to my face. "Do you have a mirror?" I asked.

"Sure," he said, pointing to it. "Right next to you, just above *Focus*."

I followed his finger. The mirror had an orange frame, on which was printed "The Mirror", just for good measure, as if this were not obvious enough. The bottom third of it was wedged between some magazines. I gazed into it.

I was surprised by how immaculate my reflection appeared; my coat even looked as if it had been ironed – the light in the kiosk must be flattering.

"Because of the lead story?" the man asked. "They run those

Hitler stories every three issues nowadays. I don't reckon you need do any more research. You're amazing."

"Thank you," I said absently.

"No, I really mean it," he said. "I've seen *Downfall*. Twice. Bruno Ganz was superb, but he's not a patch on you. Your whole demeanour . . . I mean, one would almost think you were the man himself."

I glanced up. "Which man?"

"You know, the Führer," he said, raising both his hands, crooking his index and middle fingers together, then twitching them up and down twice. I could hardly bring myself to accept that after sixty-six years this was all that remained of the once-rigid Nazi salute. It came as a devastating shock, but a sign nonetheless that my political influence had not vanished altogether in the intervening years.

I flipped up my arm in response to his salute: "I *am* the Führer!"

He laughed once more. "Incredible, you're a natural."

I could not comprehend his overpowering cheerfulness. Gradually I pieced together the facts of my situation. If this were no dream – it had lasted too long for that – then we were indeed in the year 2011. Which meant I was in a world totally new to me, and by the same token I had to accept that, for my part, I represented a new element in this world. If this world functioned according to even the most rudimentary logic, then it would expect me to be either one hundred and twenty two years old or, more probably, long dead.

"Do you act in other things, too?" he said. "Have I seen you before?"

"I do not act," I said, rather brusquely.

"Of course not," he said, putting on a curiously serious expression. Then he winked at me. "What are you in? Have you got your own programme?"

"Naturally," I replied. "I've had one since 1920! As a fellow German you are surely aware of the twenty-five points."

He nodded enthusiastically.

"But I still don't recall seeing you anywhere. Have you got a card? Any flyers?"

"Don't talk to me about the Luftwaffe," I said sadly. "In the end they were a complete failure."

I tried to work out what my next move should be. It seemed likely that a fifty-six-year-old Führer might meet with disbelief, even in the Reich Chancellery and Führerbunker; in fact he was certain to. I had to buy some time, weigh up my options. I needed to find somewhere to stay. Then I realised, all too painfully, that I had not a pfennig on me. For a moment unpleasant memories were stirred of my time in the men's hostel in 1909. It had been a vital experience, I admit, allowing me an insight into life which no university in the world could have provided, and yet that period of austerity was not one I had enjoyed. Those dark months flashed through my mind: the disdain, the contempt, the uncertainty, the worry over securing the bare essentials, the dry bread. Brooding and distracted, I bit into the foil-wrapped grain.

It was surprisingly sweet. I inspected the product.

"I'm rather partial to them, too," the newspaper vendor said. "Want another one?"

I shook my head. Larger problems faced me now. I needed

a livelihood, however modest or basic. I needed somewhere to stay and a little money until I had a clearer perspective. Perhaps I needed to find a job, temporarily at least, until I knew whether and how I might be able to seize the reins of government again. Until then, a means of earning money was essential. Maybe I could work as a painter, or in an architect's practice. And I was not above a bit of labouring, either – not at all. Of course, the knowledge I possessed would be more beneficial for the German Volk if it were put to use in a military campaign, but given my ignorance of the current situation this was an illusory scenario. After all, I did not even know which countries the German Reich now shared a border with. I had no idea who was hostile towards us, or against whom one could return fire. For now I had to content myself with what I could achieve with my manual skills – perhaps I could build a parade ground or a section of autobahn.

"Come on, be serious for a moment." The voice of the newspaper seller rang in my ears. "Don't tell me you're still an amateur. With *that* routine?"

This was the height of impertinence. "I am no amateur!" I said emphatically. "I'm not one of those bourgeois parasites!"

"No, no," the man assured me. He was beginning to come across as a thoroughly honest individual at heart. "I mean, what do you do for a living?"

What indeed? What ought I to say?

"I . . . well, at present I am partly . . . in retirement," I said, cautiously outlining my situation.

"Don't get me wrong," he said. "But if you really haven't . . . well, that's incredible! I mean, they pass by here all the time, the place is teeming with agents, film types, telly people. They're always delighted to get a tip-off, discover a new face. If you haven't got a card, how am I going to get hold of you? What's your phone number? E-mail?"

"Er . . ."

"Where do you live, then?"

Now he really had hit a nerve. But the man did not appear to be attempting anything underhand, so I decided to risk it.

"At present, the question of my billeting is . . . how should I put it? . . . somewhat unresolved . . ."

"O.K. So are you staying with a girlfriend?"

I thought briefly of Eva. Where might she be?

"No," I mumbled, feeling unusually disconsolate. "I have no female companion. Not any longer."

"Oooh," the newspaper seller said. "Got you. It's all still a bit fresh."

"Yes," I admitted. "Everything here is really quite fresh for me."

"Wasn't really working out towards the end, eh?"

"That would be an accurate assessment of the situation." I nodded. "Steiner's army group offensive never got off the ground. Inexcusable."

He looked confused. "With your girlfriend, I mean. Who was to blame?"

"I don't know," I said. "Ultimately Churchill, I expect."

He laughed. Then he gave me a long, thoughtful stare.

"I like your style." Then his voice changed as he growled, "I'm going to make you an offer you can't refuse."

"Offer?"

"Listen, I don't know what your standards are. But if you haven't got any particular requirements then you're welcome to spend a night or two here."

"Here?" I looked around the kiosk.

"Can you afford the Adlon?"

He was right. I looked at the floor with embarrassment.

"You see me – virtually penniless . . ." I conceded.

"Well then. And it's no surprise, seeing as you don't put your talent out there. You shouldn't hide."

"I have not been hiding!" I protested. "It was because of the relentless bombing!"

"Whatever," he said dismissively. "O.K. Let's say you spend a day or two here, and I'll have a word with one or two of my customers. The latest issue of *Theatre Today* arrived yesterday, along with one of the film magazines. One by one they'll come and buy their copies. Maybe we can fix something up. I'll be absolutely honest with you: the uniform is so spot on it wouldn't even matter if you weren't much of a performer . . ."

"So, I'm going to stay here?"

"Just for now. During the day you'll stick around here with me. That means if anyone comes I can introduce you to them straight away. And if no-one comes then at least I've something to make me giggle. Or have you got somewhere else to go?"

"No," I sighed. "I mean, apart from the Führerbunker."

He laughed. Then he paused.

"Listen, mate, you're not going to clean me out of all my stuff, are you?"

I gave him a look of disgust. "Do I look like a criminal?"

He looked at me. "You look like Adolf Hitler."

"Exactly," I said.

iii

The next few days and nights were to be a real test for me. Humiliated by my circumstances, billeted in makeshift accommodation, cheek-by-jowl with dubious publications, tobacco, confectionery and tinned drinks, at night bent double in a passably (but not particularly) clean armchair, I had to catch up on the past sixty-six years without arousing unfavourable attention. Whereas others would have no doubt spent hours and days fruitlessly agonising over scientific explanations, hunting in vain for a solution to this time-travel conundrum, which was as fantastical as it was unfathomable, my trusty methodical reasoning was well placed to adapt itself to the prevailing circumstances. Instead of wallowing in self-pity, I accepted the facts of the new situation and focused on reconnaissance. Especially as – to anticipate events briefly – the changed conditions seemed to offer considerably more and better opportunities. It transpired that in the last sixty-six years the number of Soviet soldiers on the territory of the German Reich had fallen substantially, particularly in the Greater Berlin area. The current figure was between thirty and fifty men; in a flash I could see that this afforded the Wehrmacht a far better prospect of victory compared to the last estimate from my general staff of around 2.5 million enemy soldiers on the Eastern Front alone.

I toyed, albeit momentarily, with the idea that I had been the victim of a plot, an abduction, in which the enemy's intelligence service had concocted an elaborate hoax, circumventing my iron will to prise from me key secrets. But the technological demands of creating an entirely new world in which, after all, I could move about freely – that variation on reality was even more inconceivable than the one I found myself in, with the ability to grasp things with my hands and see with my eyes. No, I had to wage the struggle in this bizarre here and now. And the first step in any struggle is always reconnaissance.

The reader will not find it hard to imagine that obtaining new, reliable information without the necessary infrastructure posed considerable difficulties. The premises were extremely inauspicious: as far as foreign affairs were concerned, I had neither military intelligence nor the foreign ministry at my disposal; with regard to domestic affairs, establishing contact with the Gestapo was, given my circumstances, no simple matter. Even undertaking a library visit seemed too hazardous for the time being. I was thus reliant on the content of numerous publications, whose trustworthiness I was of course unable to verify, as well as on utterances and scraps of conversation from passers-by. The newspaper seller had very kindly supplied me with a wireless set, which on account of technological advances in the intervening years had shrunk to unbelievably tiny proportions; but the standards of Greater German radio had nosedived since 1940. As soon as I switched it on I heard a hellish din, frequently interrupted by utterly incomprehensible gibberish. I continued to listen, but the content never changed; the only difference was that it began to alternate more frequently between the racket and the gibberish. I made a number of futile attempts, each lasting several minutes, to decrypt the noise issuing from this technological marvel, then switched it off in horror. I must have sat there absolutely still for a quarter of an hour, virtually paralysed by shock, before deciding to postpone my efforts with the wireless. So I was left with the periodicals. It had never been their top priority to provide a true historical account; I was almost certain nothing had changed on that front.

An initial review, which could not, of course, provide a complete picture, pointed to the following conclusions:

1. The Turk had not come to our assistance after all.
2. In light of the seventieth anniversary of Operation Barbarossa, there were numerous reports about this episode in German history painting a negative picture of the campaign. The unanimous view was that Barbarossa had not been a victory; indeed, the whole war had ended in defeat, or so these papers said.
3. I was reported to be dead. They said I had committed suicide. In truth I do recall having discussed this contingency – purely theoretically – with my confidants, and my memory was definitely lacking a few hours of what had been a terribly difficult time. But, in the final analysis, I only needed look at myself to see the facts.

Was I dead?

We all know, of course, what to make of our newspapers. The deaf man writes down what the blind man has told him, the village idiot edits it, and their colleagues in the other press houses copy it. Each story is doused afresh with the same stagnant infusion of lies, so that the "splendid" brew can then be served up to a clueless Volk. In this instance, however, I was prepared to be somewhat lenient. So rarely does Fate intervene this strikingly in its own workings that even the smartest minds must find it difficult to comprehend, let alone the mediocre intellects serving our so-called opinion sheets.

4. My brain required the stomach of an ox to digest the other information I managed to unearth. One had to disregard the press's miscalculations on matters military, historical, political – on every topic, in fact, including economics – the result of either ignorance or malicious intent; otherwise, faced with such reams of foolishness, a thinking person would simply go mad.

5. Or one would develop an ulcer from reading the scribblings of the syphilitic, degenerate minds within the gutter press who, manifestly freed from all state control, were at liberty to publish the sick and profane view of the world they had dreamed up.

6. The German Reich appeared to have given way to what was called a "Federal Republic", the leadership of which resided with a woman ("Federal Chancellor"), although men had been entrusted with this position in the past.

7. Political parties existed again, with all the infantile, counter-productive squabbling this entails. Social Democracy, that ineradicable pest, was making merry

mischief once more at the expense of the long-suffering German Volk. Other organisations were sponging off the wealth of the people in their own way; amazingly, perhaps, I found little appreciation of their "work", not even in the dishonest press, which otherwise seemed so benevolent. By contrast, N.S.D.A.P. activity had ceased altogether. If one were to believe the view that the Reich had been defeated, it was possible the Party's work had been impeded by the victorious powers. Alternatively, the organisation may have been driven underground.

8. The *Völkischer Beobachter* was not available everywhere; at least the kiosk belonging to this vendor – patently a radical liberal – did not have it on display. In fact he had no German-national publications for sale at all.

9. The Reich seemed to have shrunk, despite the fact that our neighbouring states were by and large the same ones. Even Poland was still there, living out its artificial existence unchecked, and partly on Reich territory! Now, I may be a level-headed man, but at this point I was unable to suppress my indignation; I found myself screaming out into the darkness of the kiosk, "I might as well have handed them the war on a plate!"

10. The Reichsmark was no longer legal tender, even though others – probably some clueless dilettantes on the side of the victorious powers – had clearly adapted my plan to turn it into a European-wide currency. At any rate, transactions were now being carried out in an artificial currency called "Euro", regarded, as one would

expect, with a high level of mistrust. I could have told those responsible that this would be the case.

11. A partial peace seemed to be in place, although the Wehrmacht was still at war. Now known as the "Bundeswehr", it was in an enviable state, no doubt on account of the technological advances that had been made. If the statistics in the newspapers were to be believed, one would have to conclude that German soldiers in the field were practically invulnerable; these days casualties were few and far between. You can imagine my anguish when with a sigh I thought of my own tragic fate, of those bitter nights in the Führer-bunker, hunched in grief as I brooded over maps in the operations room, battling a hostile world as well as Destiny herself. Back then, more than 400,000 soldiers bled to death on countless fronts, and that was in January 1945 alone. With this astonishing modern outfit there is no doubt I could have swept Eisenhower's armies into the sea, and crushed Stalin's hordes in the Urals and Caucasus like insects within just a few weeks. It was one of the few truly encouraging pieces of news that I read. With this new Wehrmacht the future conquest of Lebensraum in the north, east, south and west appeared as bright a prospect as it had with the old one. The consequence of recent reforms introduced by a young minister who must have been of the highest calibre, but who was forced to step down following a conspiracy hatched by resentful and small-minded university professors. Little seemed to have changed

since my time, when once I had hopefully submitted my designs and drawings to the Vienna Academy. Devoured by envy, mediocrities continue at every turn to obstruct the lively genius who parades his talents undeterred. They cannot stomach the fact that his brilliance easily outshines the feeble glow of their own pitiful aura.

Oh well.

My new circumstances certainly needed getting used to, but with some satisfaction I was able to conclude that, for the moment at least, there was no acute danger, even though there were inconveniences. As is normal with creative minds, my recent tendency had been to work for long periods, but also to take long rests, so as to preserve my habitual freshness and speed of response. The newspaper seller, however, would open up his kiosk at the crack of dawn, which meant that I, despite the fact that I frequently continued with my studies into the early hours of the morning, could not count on any restorative sleep thereafter. What made it worse was that this gentleman had an irritating need to talk in the mornings, whereas at that time of day I usually required a period of reorientation. Even on the very first morning he swept jauntily into the kiosk with the words, "So, mein Führer, how did you sleep?"

Without waiting for a second, he opened his vending window and allowed a particularly bright light to dazzle the interior of the kiosk. I moaned, screwed up my tormented eyes, and endeavoured to recall where I found myself. I was not in the Führerbunker, this was as clear as the daylight flooding into my makeshift lodgings. Had we been at headquarters I would have had the oaf court-martialled and shot there and then; this early-morning terror was undermining morale – why, it was practically sabotage! I retained my composure all the same, took on board my new situation, and reassured myself that this cretin probably had no alternative, given his livelihood; indeed, in his own blundering way I expect he was even trying to do his best by me.

"Time to rock and roll," the newspaper vendor announced cryptically. "Come on, give us a hand!" He nodded towards a number of portable magazine racks, and dragged one of them outside.

Still exhausted, I sighed and struggled to my feet to help him. What irony: yesterday I was repositioning the 12th Army; today it was magazine racks. My gaze fell on the new issue of *Hunting and Hounds*. Some things had not changed, then. Although I had never been one for hunting – on the contrary, I had always looked upon it rather critically – at that moment I was gripped by the desire to flee this unfamiliar environment and roam the countryside with a dog at my heels, observing at close proximity the comings and goings of the natural world . . . I snapped out of my reverie. Within a few minutes the two of us had set up his kiosk for the day. The newspaper seller fetched two deckchairs and put them out in the sun. He invited me to sit, took a packet of cigarettes from the breast pocket of his shirt, flicked a couple through the aperture and offered me one.

"I don't smoke," I said, shaking my head. "Thanks anyway."

He put a cigarette to his lips, took a lighter from his trouser pocket and lit it. Drawing in the smoke and exhaling with great pleasure, he said, "Ahhh – now for a coffee! Would you like one? I've only got instant, I'm afraid."

The British must still be blockading the seas. It was a problem I'd had to deal with often enough, so it was hardly a surprise that, in my absence, the new Reich leadership – whatever form it now took or whichever name it went by – continued to be vexed by this predicament and was still searching for a solution. The brave, stoic German Volk had been forced to make do with substitutes for so long. I recalled that this alternative to coffee had been known as "ersatz", and immediately I thought of the sugary grain bar which now took the place of good German bread. This unfortunate newspaper seller was embarrassed in front of his guest because the stranglehold of the British vermin allowed him to offer nothing better. It was an outright scandal. I was overcome with emotion.

"It's not your fault, my good man," I assured him. "In any case, I'm not much of a coffee lover. But I would be very grateful for a glass of water."

And so I spent my first morning in this strange new epoch shoulder to shoulder with the smoking newspaper vendor, bent on analysing the population and gaining new insight from their behaviour until such a time as my host, through the contacts he had mentioned, might be able to secure me some sort of employment.

For the first couple of hours it was humble workers and pensioners who patronised the kiosk. They bought tobacco and the morning papers, but said little. A newspaper by the name of *Bild* seemed to be highly popular – particularly with older people. I assumed this was because the lettering was so extraordinarily large that those with poor vision would still be able to digest the news. An excellent idea, I was forced to concede, one that not even the zealous Goebbels had thought of. Just think of how much more enthusiasm it would have sparked for our cause amongst the elderly! In the last days I could remember of the war, it was chiefly the older members of the Volkssturm who lacked the drive, the determination and willingness to sacrifice themselves for the German nation. Who would have thought that a simple device such as larger lettering could have such an effect?

In mitigation, there had been a paper shortage during the war, but when all is said and done that Funk chap had been an utter moron.

My presence outside the kiosk began to cause a stir. There was the occasional outburst of gaiety, especially amongst the younger workers; more often it was recognition, conveyed by the words "cool" and "epic" – totally incomprehensible, I know, but from their facial expressions I inferred a definite respect.

"Isn't he great?" the newspaper seller beamed to one of his customers. "Practically no difference, is there?"

"Nope," the customer said, folding his newspaper. He was a worker, mid-twenties probably. "But are you allowed to do that?"

"What?" the newspaper vendor said.

"You know: the uniform and all that."

"What objection could possibly be raised against the coat of a German soldier?" I asked suspiciously, a hint of irritation in my voice.

The customer laughed, to silence me, I expect.

"He's really good. No, I mean, obviously you do this professionally, but don't you need some sort of special licence to wear that in public?"

"Well I never!" I replied, incensed.

"All I'm saying," he said, a touch intimidated, "is what would the authorities think if they saw you looking like that?"

This made me ponder. His intentions were honourable, and he was right: my uniform was no longer in the best condition; it was barely presentable.

"I agree, it is a bit dirty," I said, somewhat crestfallen. "But even soiled, a soldier's coat is forever nobler than the spotless dinner jacket of a fraudulent diplomat."

"Why would it be forbidden?" the newspaper vendor asked soberly. "He's not wearing a swastika."

"What the devil is that supposed to mean?" I yelled in anger. "Everyone knows damn well which party I'm in!"

The customer left, shaking his head. When he was out of sight, the newspaper seller invited me to sit down again.

"He's got a point," he said in a friendly tone. "My customers are giving you funny looks. I know you take your work seriously, but couldn't you wear something different?"

"Am I to deny my life, my work, my Volk? You cannot ask that of me," I said, leaping up. "I will go on wearing this uniform until the last drop of blood has been spilled. I will not, as Brutus did to Caesar, commit a wretched act of betrayal; I will not stab in the back for a second time those who have given their lives for the Movement . . ."

"Do you always have to get in such a lather?" the vendor said with a hint of impatience. "It's not just what your uniform *looks* like . . ."

"What then?"

"It stinks, too! I don't know what it's made out of – was it one of those boiler suits they wear at petrol stations?"

"In the theatre of war the infantryman cannot change his coat, and I myself refuse to indulge in the decadence of those who live in comfort behind the front."

"Whatever . . . but just think about your programme!"

"How do you mean?"

"Listen, you want to your programme to do well, don't you?"

"Yes, and?"

"Just think about it: someone comes by wanting to meet you, and there you are, reeking so strongly of petrol that they don't even dare light up within ten metres!"

"*You* did," I replied. But my words lacked their customary edge; reluctantly I had to concur with his arguments.

"I'm brave, you see," he laughed. "Come on, why don't you pop home and fetch some more clothes."

The tiresome accommodation problem.

"I told you, it's difficult at the moment."

"Sure, but your ex must be at work now. Or out shopping. Why are you being so cagey?"

"You see," I said hesitantly, "it's all very difficult. My home . . ." My logic was now in a bit of a tangle. But it was a humiliating situation, too.

"Don't you have a key, or what's the problem?"

This time I couldn't help laughing at such naivety. I had

no idea whether or not there was a key to the Führerbunker.

"No, er, how should I put it? Somehow contact was . . . er . . . cut off."

"Are you under a restraining order?"

"I can't even explain it to myself," I said. "But it's something like that."

"Heavens above, you don't give that sort of impression," he said. "What on earth did you do?"

"I don't know," I said, truthfully. "I've lost all memory of the intervening period."

"You don't seem like the violent type to me at any rate," he said thoughtfully.

"Well," I said, running my fingers over my parting, "I am a soldier, of course . . ."

"O.K., soldier," the newspaper vendor said. "Let me make another suggestion. Because you're ace and because I've got faith in obsessive types like you."

"Of course you have," I said. "Like any sensible person. We must spare no effort, indeed we must be obsessive in the pursuit of our goals. Lily-livered, two-faced compromise is the root of all evil and—"

"Yes, O.K.," he interrupted me. "Now look. Tomorrow I'll bring you some of my old things. No need to thank me, I've put on a bit of weight recently and can't do up the buttons anymore. But they might fit you," he said, looking rather unhappily at his stomach. "I mean, you're not working as Göring, are you?"

"Why would I do that?" I asked, confused.

"And I'll take your uniform straight to the dry cleaner's . . ."

"I will not part with my uniform!" I said adamantly.

"As you like," he said, suddenly looking weary. "You can take your uniform to the dry cleaner's yourself. But you do understand, don't you? That it has to be cleaned?"

It was an outrage – I was being treated like a child. But I realised that nothing would change as long as I went around looking as grubby as a child. So I nodded.

"The shoes might be a problem, though," he said. "What size are you?"

"43."

"Mine will be too small, then," he said. "But I'll come up with something."

The reader must be shown some sympathy if, at this or any other point, he is flabbergasted by the speed with which I adapted to my new circumstances. How can the poor reader, who during the years, nay decades, of my absence has been drowning in the Marxist broth of history from the soup kettle of democracy, be capable of peering over the edge of his own bowl? I have no intention of casting any reproach upon the honest labourer or farmer. How should the simple man protest when so-called professionals and academic nonentities have, for six decades, been proclaiming from the lecterns in their "temples of knowledge" that the Führer is dead? Who would hold it against the man who, amidst his daily struggle for survival, cannot find the strength to say, "Where is he then, the dead Führer? Show him to me!"

Or the woman, for that matter.

But when the Führer suddenly reappears in the place where he always was, in the capital of the Reich, the confusion and disorientation which strikes the Volk is as paralysing as the astonishment. And it would have been perfectly understandable had I, too, spent days, weeks even, in utter bewilderment, crippled by the incomprehensible. But Fate decreed that it

37

should be different with me. That as a result of a vast amount of effort and enormous deprivation over harsh yet instructive years, I should be able early in life to form a reasoned outlook, forged in theory, but hardened into a finished weapon on the battlefield of practice, an unwavering viewpoint which had consistently governed my life and work ever since. Even now, there was no need for newfangled or casual tinkering; on the contrary, my grounded perspective helped me achieve an understanding of both the old and the new. And so it was the Führer principle which ultimately liberated me from my fruitless hunt for explanations.

Having spent one of the first nights tossing and turning in my armchair, unable to sleep after those strenuous hours of reading, and ruminating on my plight, all of a sudden I was struck by a flash of understanding. I sat up bolt upright, my eyes wide with enlightenment as they surveyed the large jars of colourful confectionery and everything else inside the kiosk. It was crystal clear: in her own inscrutable way, Fate herself had intervened in the course of events. I slapped my forehead; it was so obvious that I reproached myself for not having realised it earlier. Particularly as this was not the first time that Destiny had taken hold of the rudder. Had it not been exactly the same in 1919, at the nadir of German misery and hardship? Did not an unknown corporal rise from the trenches in that portentous year? Despite being afflicted by poverty, abject poverty, did not a brilliant orator emerge from the desperate multitudes, from where one might have least expected? Did not this orator also reveal a rich hoard of knowledge and experience, amassed during those darkest of days in Vienna and born of an insatiable curiosity which, from early childhood, spurred this young man, keen of mind, to devour everything relating to history and politics? The most valuable information, stored seemingly at random, but in fact carefully accumulated morsel by morsel within one man? And did not this man, this incon-spicuous corporal, upon whose lonely shoulders millions placed their hopes, did he not smash the shackles of Versailles and the League of Nations, withstand with God-given ease the conflicts forced on him with Europe's armies, against France, against England, against Russia? Did not this man, who was said to possess no more than a mediocre mind, lead the Father-land to the highest peaks of glory in the face of unanimous judgement by self-professed experts?

This man, of course, was none other than myself.

My ears were pounding. Each single event, each single occurrence from back then was by itself more improbable than everything which had befallen me over these past two or three days. Now my razor-sharp gaze pierced the darkness between a jar of bulls-eyes and one of sugar drops, where the bright light of the moon soberly illuminated my brainwave like an icy torch. Of course, for a lonely warrior to lead an entire people out of a slough of errors is a wondrous talent, which could appear only every one hundred or two hundred years. But what was Fate to do if she had already played this priceless trump card? If, amongst the human material available, there was not a single soul with sufficient presence of mind?

Then, for good or evil, he must be snatched from the clutches of the past.

And although this was unquestionably a miracle of sorts, it

was comparatively easier to achieve than the task of fashioning a sharp new sword from the inferior metal at hand. Just as this stream of insight began to calm my erratic thinking, a new concern swelled in my alert mind. For this conclusion brought with it another, like an uninvited guest: if Fate had been forced to play a cheap trick – there was no other way to describe it – the situation, however tranquil it may seem at first glance, must be even more cataclysmic than before.

And the Volk in even greater danger!

This was when I understood that now was not the moment to waste time on academic arguments, to agonise pedantically over the "how" and the "whether", seeing as the "why" and the "that" were by far the more important considerations.

And yet there was still one question that remained unanswered: Why me? Given that so many heroes of German history were waiting for a second opportunity to lead the Volk to new glories.

Why not a Bismarck, or a Frederick the Great?

A Charlemagne?

An Otto?

After brief deliberation the answer came so easily that I almost chuckled at how flattered I felt. For the Herculean task that was waiting to be undertaken here truly seemed as if it would put even the bravest men, the great and greatest Germans in their place. All on his own, without party apparatus or executive power, one man in particular was being entrusted with the job, the man who had already demonstrated that he was capable of cleaning out the Augean stables of democracy. But did I want to put myself through all those painful sacrifices a second time? Swallow all the privations and derision again, nay, gulp them down with disdain? Spend my nights in an armchair beside a water urn in which sausages are heated up during the day for human consumption? And all this for the love of a people which, in the struggle for its destiny, had already left its Führer in the lurch once before? Whatever happened to the Steiner offensive? Or Paulus, that ignominious blackguard?

At this point I needed to keep my rancour in check, to separate reasonable anger from blind rage. Just as the Volk must stand by its Führer, so the Führer must stand by his Volk. Under the right leadership the simple soldier has always done his best – how can he be upbraided if he is unable to march loyally into enemy fire because cowardly, neglectful generals surrender his opportunity to die an honourable soldier's death?

"Yes!" I cried, into the darkness of the kiosk. "Yes, I want to! And I will! Yes, yes, and three times, yes!"

The night answered with black silence. Then, close by, a lonesome voice hollered, "Exactly! They're all a bunch of arse-holes!"

I should have taken this as a warning. But if, back then, I had known of the ceaseless efforts, the bitter sacrifices that I would ultimately have to make, the sheer torment of the unequal struggle – I would have merely sworn my oath more heartily, at twice the volume.

The first steps were hard work. There was no question of any physical weakness on my part; the fact was, I felt like an imbecile in the newspaper vendor's borrowed clothes. Trousers and shirt were just about passable. He had brought me a clean pair of blue cotton trousers, which he called "genes", and a clean, red-checked cotton shirt. I had rather been expecting a suit and hat, but when I took a closer look at the newspaper seller I had to admit that my reasoning had been deluded. This man did not wear a suit in his kiosk and, from what I had observed so far, there was little of the bourgeois about the dress of his clientele, either. Hats, just to complete the picture, seemed to be uncommon. With the modest means at my disposal, I decided to lend as much dignity as I could to the ensemble by eschewing his bizarre habit of wearing the shirt loose outside the trousers, instead pushing it as far down my waistband as possible. The trousers were slightly too big for me, but with my belt I was able to fasten and hitch them up tightly. Then I fixed my strap over the right shoulder. It was no German soldier's uniform, but the overall look was at least one of a man who knows how to dress decently. The shoes, on the other hand, were a problem.

Having assured me that he knew nobody else who took my size, the newspaper vendor had brought along an outlandish pair belonging to his adolescent son. Whether they could rightly be called shoes was a matter open to debate. They were huge, white, with massive soles: I felt like a circus clown. I had to resist the impulse of throwing them straight back into the face of that halfwit.

"I'm not wearing these," I said. "Why, they make me look like a buffoon!"

No doubt insulted, he made a remark to the effect that he disapproved of the way I wore the trousers, but I ignored this. I wrapped the legs of the genes tightly around my calves and pushed them into my boots.

"You really don't want to look like other people, do you?" the newspaper vendor said.

"Where do you think it would have got me if I had always done everything like so-called 'other people'?" I retorted. "And where would Germany be?"

"Hmm," he said, silenced by my comment. He lit another cigarette and said, "You could see it that way, I suppose."

He folded up my uniform and put it in an interesting-looking bag. What struck me was not just the material, synthetic and very thin, clearly much more durable and flexible than paper. I was also intrigued by the words that were printed on it: "Media Market". The bag must have served as packaging for that cretinous newspaper that I had spotted under the park bench. This proved that, deep down, the newspaper seller was a sensible man – he had kept the serviceable bag, but thrown away its infantile contents. Handing it to me, he explained the way to the cleaner's and said perkily, "Hasta la vista, baby!" This modern German would take some time to accustom myself to.

I set off, albeit not directly to the cleaner's. First I went back to the patch of ground where I had woken up. In spite of my fortitude, I could not deny I harboured a faint hope that someone from my past had accompanied me into the present day. I found the park bench where I had taken my first rest, then crossed the street – very carefully this time – and made my way between the houses to the waste ground. It was late morning and all was quiet. The Hitler Youths were not playing; they were probably at school. The place was empty. Bag in hand, I gingerly approached the puddle beside which I had awoken. It had practically dried up. Everything was so quiet, or at least as quiet as it can be in a big city. There was the muted drone of automobiles in the distance, and I could also hear the buzzing of a bumblebee.

"Psst," I said. "Psst!"

Nothing happened.

"Bormann," I called out softly. "Bormann! Are you there?"

A gust of wind whooshed across the terrain, an empty can knocked against another. Otherwise nothing stirred.

"Keitel?" I said. "Goebbels?"

But there was no answer. Fine. In fact, it was better this way. The strong man is mightiest alone, an axiom as true now as it ever was. Indeed it was truer than ever; I had greater clarity now, after all. It was my task and mine alone to save the Volk. Mine alone to save the earth and humankind. And the first step along this path led to the cleaner's.

Full of resolve and bag in hand, I returned to my roots, to

the place where I had learned the most valuable lessons of my life: the street. I carefully followed the directions I had been given, comparing terraces of houses and streets, checking, considering, cogitating, chancing. My preliminary survey was rather positive: the country, or the city at least, seemed free of rubble and in good order; overall one might certify it satisfactorily pre-war. The new Volkswagens seemed to be performing reliably; they were quieter these days, albeit an acquired taste aesthetically. What stood out to my keen eye were the mystifying slogans covering every wall. Yes, I was familiar with this technique; in Weimar, especially, the communist accomplices used to daub their Bolshevist claptrap all over the place. And I myself had learned from this. But at least back then you could read the words painted by either side. Now, I noted, a large number of the messages – their authors evidently regarded them as sufficiently important to deface the houses of honest citizens with them – were simply impossible to decipher. I could only hope that this was the brainchild of illiterate left-wing vermin, but as I kept going I observed that the legibility of the slogans did not change from house to house, and therefore had to assume that important messages such as "Germany, awake" or "Sieg Heil" were possibly hiding amongst them too. Confronted with such ubiquitous dilettantism, I felt my blood boil. It was plain for all to see that what was missing here was firm leadership, tight organisation. What made this particularly irksome was the fact that many of these writings had been produced with substantial colour and apparent effort. Or had the world in my absence developed a specific style of writing for political slogans? Determined to get to the bottom of the matter, I approached a lady who was holding a child by the hand.

"Please excuse me for bothering you, madam," I said. Pointing to one of the inscriptions, I asked, "Could you tell me what that says?"

"How should I know?" the lady said, giving me an odd look.

"So you find this writing rather strange, too?" I enquired further.

"Not just the writing," the lady said hesitantly. "Are you alright?"

"Worry not," I said. "I'm on my way to the dry cleaner's."

"You'd be better off going to the barber's!" the woman said.

I turned my head to the side, bent to the window of a new-fangled automobile and took a good look at myself. Although not impeccable, my parting appeared fine, and although my moustache would need a trim in a few days' time, for the moment a visit to the barber's was not essential. I took the opportunity to calculate that the following evening would be the most strategically advantageous for a more thorough body wash. Setting off again, I passed more of the same propaganda slogans, which might as well have been written in Chinese. The other thing that struck me was how many people seemed to be equipped with wireless receivers – an admirable number. Radar dishes were attached to windows everywhere, for receiving radio transmissions, no doubt. Were I to have the opportunity to speak over the radio waves, then winning over a new horde of staunch comrades amongst the Volk would be as easy as marching into Denmark. I had, after all, listened fruitlessly to a broadcast on the wireless, which sounded as if drunken musicians were playing, and announcers were babbling the very words that were smeared so illegibly on these walls. All I had to do was speak comprehensible German, surely that would suffice? – child's play. Full of confidence and with a spring in my step, I strode on. Then, a short distance away, I saw the sign for YILMAZ BLITZ CLEANER'S.

This came as something of a surprise.

Yes, all those newspapers had implied that there must be a large Turkish readership in the city, even if the circumstances of their arrival remained something of a mystery. And during my stroll I had also noticed the occasional passer-by whose Aryan ancestry was questionable, to put it mildly, and not only four or five generations back, but right up to the last quarter of an hour. Even if it was still a mystery what exactly these racial aliens were doing here, at least they did not appear to be playing a leading role. Which made it unlikely that businesses were being annexed by foreign types on a large scale and their names changed accordingly. As far as I was concerned – even for the purposes of economic propaganda – it was hard to comprehend why anyone should want to christen a "Blitz Cleaner's" with the name "Yilmaz". Since when did "Yilmaz" represent the guarantee of clean shirts? At most, "Yilmaz" represented the guarantee of a serviceable donkey cart. The only problem was that I had no alternative to this cleaner's. And given that rapidity of action was of the essence, to allow me to exert pressure on my political opponents, I needed a Blitz cleaner's. Plagued by doubts, I marched in.

I was greeted by a distorted glockenspiel. The place reeked of cleaning fluid, and it was sweltering – far too hot for a cotton shirt, but the splendid Afrika Korps uniform was unavailable at present, alas! On the counter was one of those bells one often sees in hotel receptions.

Nothing happened.

I could make out some sort of plaintive oriental music; perhaps, in a back room of the shop, an Anatolian washer-woman was lamenting her faraway Heimat – queer behaviour indeed, especially if one had the good fortune to live in the capital of the German Reich. I perused the items of clothing which hung in rank and file behind the counter. They were wrapped in a transparent material, not dissimilar to the sub-stance my bag was made of. In fact, everything seemed to be wrapped in this stuff. I had once seen something similar in a laboratory, but I.G. Farben must have come a long way with it in recent years. According to what I knew, the production of this material was highly dependent on a ready supply of crude oil; correspondingly it came at great expense. But the way in which synthetic materials were used here – indeed, the extent to which automobiles were driven – suggested that crude oil was no longer a problem. Had the Reich somehow kept posses-sion of the Roumanian deposits? Unlikely. Had Göring ultimately discovered new sources on home soil? A bitter chuckle rose within my chest. Göring! That incompetent morphine addict! He would sooner find gold up his own nostrils than oil in Germany. I wonder what had become of him. It was more probable that we had fallen back on other resources, and . . .

"Been waiting long?"

A southern European man with Asiatic cheekbones peered out from a passageway at the back of the shop.

"Absolutely!" I said impatiently.

"Why not ring?" He pointed to the bell on his counter and tapped it gently with the palm of his hand. The bell rang.

"I did already ring – *here*!" I insisted, opening the door to the shop. The strange glockenspiel rang out once more.

"Must ring *here*!" the cleaner said dismissively, hitting the bell on the counter again.

"A German only rings once," I said, prickly.

"Then *here*," the half-breed of indeterminate lineage said, ringing with his palm a third time. I was seized by the urge to send round the S.A., and have them lacerate this cretin's eardrum with his cursed bell. Or even better, both eardrums. He could then explain to his customers to wave when they entered his establishment. I sighed. Being deprived of even the most basic auxiliary staff was downright annoying. A number of things would have to be put straight in this country before I could settle this matter to my satisfaction, but I started to compile a list of traitors sabotaging the future of the German Volk, and "Yilmaz Cleaner's" was at the very top. In the meantime all I could do was scowl and remove the bell from his grasp.

"Tell me," I said harshly, "do you clean things, too? Or where you come from is the cleaning industry just about bell-ringing?"

"What you want?"

I placed my bag on the counter and took out my uniform. He took a sniff, said, "Aha – you work at petrol station," and calmly picked up the bundle.

I ought to have been indifferent to the opinions of a

non-voter from an alien race, and yet I could not ignore what he said altogether. Granted, the man did not hail from here, but could I really have fallen into such obscurity? On the other hand, most of the German Volk knew me from press photographs only, and these generally showed my countenance from a favourable angle. Meeting someone in the flesh is often surprisingly different.

"No," I said assertively. "I do *not* work at the petrol station."

I then turned my head upwards and to the side, offering the more photogenic angle to give the half-breed a clearer view of just who this was standing before him. The cleaner looked at me, more out of politeness than any apparent interest, but I received the impression that I was not entirely unknown to him. He leaned over the counter and studied my trousers, tucked impeccably into my high boots.

"I dunno . . . You famous fishing man?"

"Just try a bit harder, man," I said forcefully, though feeling slightly deflated. Even with the newspaper seller, no genius himself, I was able to build on some prior knowledge. Now this! How on earth would I make it back to the Reich Chancellery if nobody had a clue who I was?

"A moment, please," the non-native fool said. "I get son. Always watch T.V., always look at Intanet, know everything. Mehmet! Mehmet!"

The Mehmet in question soon appeared. A tall, moderately neat-looking youth shuffled to the front of the shop together with a friend or brother. The seed of this family was not to be underestimated; both boys wore clothes that must have once belonged to brothers who were even taller – they must be truly

50

gigantic. Shirts like bed sheets, unfathomably large trousers.

"Mehmet," his progenitor said, pointing at me. "You know this man?"

I could detect a spark in the eyes of this boy whom one could hardly call a boy any longer.

"Hey, man, yeah, of course! That's the bloke who always does the Nazi stuff . . ."

Something, at least! There was no denying that his manner of expression was rather sloppy, but what he said was not altogether incorrect. "It is called National Socialism," I corrected him sympathetically. "Or National Socialist policy, you could also say." My identity validated, I cast "Cleaner Yilmaz" a look of satisfaction.

"It's that Stromberg," Mehmet said confidently.

"Epic," his friend said. "Stromberg in your laundry!"

"No," Mehmet corrected himself. "It's the other Stromberg. The one from the send-up."

"No way!" the friend said "The other Stromberg! In your laundry."

I was keen to come back with a response, but was simply too exhausted. Who was I again? Petrol-pump man? Fishing man? Strom-man?"

"Can I have an autograph?" a delighted Mehmet asked.

"Yeh, me too, Herr Stromberg," the friend said. "And a photo!" He waved a tiny instrument at me as if I were a dachshund and it a canine treat.

It was infuriating.

I took the receipt for my uniform, consented to have a souvenir photograph taken with these strange companions and

51

left the cleaner's, but not before I had signed two sheets of tissue paper with the colour pen I was handed. A brief crisis followed the autographing, when complaints were aired that I had not signed "Stromberg".

"Look, it's obvious," the friend said reassuringly, although it was unclear whether he was trying to placate Mehmet or me. "That's not Stromberg!"

"You're right," Mehmet agreed. "He's not Stromberg. He's the other one."

I must concede that I had underestimated the enormity of the task facing me. Back then, after the Great War, at least I was the anonymous man from the heart of the Volk. Now I was Herr Stromberg – not the first Stromberg, but the other one. The man who always did the Nazi stuff. The man who did not care which name he put on a sheet of tissue paper.

Something had to happen.

Fast.

vi

Fortunately something *had* happened in the meantime. When, lost in thought, I returned to the kiosk I noticed two men in sunglasses talking to the newspaper vendor. They were wearing suits, but not ties; they were youngish, around thirty perhaps. The shorter of the two may even have been younger, but because of the distance between us I could not quite tell. I was surprised that, despite his manifestly good-quality suit, the older man was unshaven. As I neared them, the newspaper seller beckoned me over excitedly.

"Come here, come here!"

Turning to the men he said, "That's him! He's brilliant. He's mad! Puts all the others in the shade."

I refused to allow myself to be rushed. The true Führer senses at once when others attempt to seize control of a situation. When others say, "Quick, quick," the true Führer always endeavours to forestall an acceleration of proceedings and avoids being hurried into an error. How does he achieve this? By displaying prudence while others scuttle around like headless chickens. Of course, there are moments in which speed is necessary, for example when caught inside a blazing house, or when essaying a pincer movement to encircle a large number of English and French divisions and grind them down to the last man. But these situations are rarer than one might imagine, and in everyday life prudence – always closely allied with keen resolve – holds the upper hand in the overwhelming majority of cases, just as in the horror of the trenches the survivor is often the man who strolls along the line with a cool head, puffing away on a pipe, rather than bustling back and forth like a washerwoman, snivelling all the while. Pipe-smoking is naturally no guarantee of survival in a crisis; pipe-smokers have been killed in world wars, too. Only a simpleton might assume that smoking a pipe would offer some sort of protection. On the contrary, survival is perfectly possible without a pipe, even without any tobacco at all. I, who have never smoked, am testament to that.

Such were my thoughts as the newspaper vendor approached me impatiently. He practically shunted me like a mule over to the small "conference". I may have appeared somewhat hesitant; although not insecure, I would have felt more confident in my uniform. But nothing could be done about that now.

"Here he is," the newspaper seller repeated with uncustomary excitement. "And these," he said, indicating the two men, "are the people I told you about."

The older man was standing at one of the high tables. With one hand in his pocket, he was drinking coffee from a paper cup, a receptacle I had frequently seen used by workers over the past few days. The younger of the two put down his cup, pushed his sunglasses up to just below his short hair, which was styled with an excessive volume of cream, and said, "So you're the boy wonder. Well, you need to work a bit at the uniform."

I gave him a brief, superficial glance and turned to the newspaper seller. "Who is this?"

The vendor went red in the face. "These gentlemen are from a *production company*. They make programmes for all the major channels. MyTV! R.T.L.! Sat 1! Pro Sieben! All the private ones! That's about right, isn't it?" This last question was aimed at the two gentlemen.

"That is about right," the elder man said patronisingly. Then he took his hand from his trouser pocket and offered it to me. "Sensenbrink, Joachim. And that's Frank Sawatzki, he works with me at Flashlight."

"I see," I said, shaking his hand. "Hitler, Adolf."

The younger one smirked, a rather haughty smirk to my mind. "Our mutual friend has just been raving about you. Go on, say something then!" With a grin he put two fingers to his top lip and said in a strangled voice, "Ve hav been returning fire sinz qvarter to six!"

I turned to the man and scrutinised him closely. Then I permitted a short period of silence to descend on proceedings. Silence is often underestimated.

"So," I said. "You wish to talk about Poland. Poland. Fine. What exactly do you know about the history of Poland?"

"Capital: Warsaw. Invaded 1939, divided with the Russians . . ."

"That," I interrupted him "is merely what the books say. Any old halfwit could root that out. Answer the question!"

"But I . . ."

"The question! Do you not understand German, man? What! Do you! Know! About! The history! Of Poland!"

"I . . ."

"What do you know about Polish history? Do you know the contexts? And what do you know about the Polish racial mix? What do you know about Germany's so-called Poland policy after 1919? And seeing as you mention returning fire, do you have any idea where?"

I paused briefly to allow him to regain his breath. One must choose the apposite moment to crush one's political opponent. Not when he has nothing to say. But when he is attempting to say something,

"I . . ."

"If you heard my speech, then surely you must know how it continues."

"The . . ."

"I'm sorry?"

"But, I mean we're not . . ."

"Let me help you: 'Henceforth . . .' – now do you know how it goes?"

". . ."

"'Henceforth bomb will be met with bomb.' Write it down, maybe someday you will be interrogated again about great quotations in history. But perhaps you are better in the field. You have 1.4 million men at your disposal and thirty days in which to conquer an entire country. Thirty days and no more, for in the West the English and French are feverishly preparing for war. Where do you begin? How many army groups do you create? How many divisions does the enemy have? Where do you expect to meet the greatest resistance? And what do you do to prevent the Roumanians becoming involved?"

56

"The Roumanians?"

"Oh excuse me, General, I'm most terribly sorry, *sir*. You are, of course, perfectly right. Who gives a fig about the Roumanians? Naturally, Herr General here will always march to Warsaw, to Cracow. He does not look left, he does not look right, and why should he, by Jove? The Polack is a pushover, the weather is fine, the troops exceptional . . . but whoops! What is that? All of a sudden the shoulder blades of our troops are shot through with tiny holes, and out flows the noble blood of German heroes. And why? Because out of nowhere millions of Roumanian bullets have peppered the backs of hundreds of thousands of our infantrymen. But how can this be? How did this happen? Did our young general here maybe, possibly, perchance forget the military alliance between Poland and Roumania? Were you ever in the Wehrmacht, man? With the best will in the world I cannot picture you in the field. You could not find the way to Poland for any army on earth; you cannot even find your own uniform! I, on the other hand, can tell you at any hour, any minute, where my uniform is." I thrust my hand into my breast pocket and slapped the receipt on the table. "At the cleaner's!"

A curious noise came from the older man, Sensenbrink, and two jets of coffee shot from his nostrils onto my shirt, the newspaper vendor's and his own. The younger man sat there in bewilderment while Sensenbrink began to cough.

"That," he wheezed, bent double under the table, "that was unfair."

He felt in his pocket, pulled out a handkerchief and painstakingly liberated his respiratory passages. "I thought," he gasped, "I thought at first it was going to be some sort of military skit, a bit like that Instructor Schmidt character. But the remark about the cleaner's, that just killed me."

"What did I tell you?" the newspaper seller said in jubilation. "Didn't I say the guy's a genius? And he is."

I was unsure how to interpret the coffee fountain and the comments that followed. Although I was not keen on either of these broadcasting types, the situation had been no different in the Weimar Republic. It was unavoidable that I would have to put up with weasels like these for a while. Besides, thus far I had not said anything, at least not anything of what I had to say and was minded to say. Despite this I detected a significant degree of approval.

"You've grilled that burger to perfection," Sensenbrink said. "Classic. Set it all up, then wallop! – out with the punchline. And it comes across as über-spontaneous! But you prepared the routine in advance, didn't you?"

"Which routine?"

"The Poland routine! You're not going to tell me you did that off the cuff?"

This Sensenbrink fellow actually seemed to possess a more profound understanding of the issue. One does not produce a Blitzkrieg off the cuff, either. Why, maybe the man had even read his Guderian.

"Of course not," I said. "The Poland routine had been planned down to the finest detail by June '39."

"Well?" he asked, examining his shirt with a mixture of regret and amusement. "What other clubs have you got in your bag?"

"What do you mean, 'other'? What clubs? What bag?"

"You know, a programme," he said, "or other texts."

"I have written two books!"

"Extraordinary," he marvelled. "Why didn't we pick you up on our radar years ago? How old are you, actually?"

"Fifty-six," I said soberly.

"Of course," he laughed. "Have you got a make-up artist, or do you do it yourself?"

"Not usually, only when filming."

"Only when filming," he laughed again. "Excellent. Look, there are one or two people in our company I'd like to introduce you to. Where can I touch base with you?"

"Touch what?" I asked.

"Where can I get in contact with you?" he explained.

"Here," I said firmly.

The newspaper vendor interrupted me, adding, "I told you that his personal circumstances at the moment are a little . . . unsettled."

"Oh yes, that's right," Sensenbrink said. "You are, how should I put it, currently homeless . . . ?"

"For the time being I am indeed without fixed abode," I conceded. "But I am certainly not without a Heimat!"

"I understand," Sensenbrink said, and turned to Sawatzki. "Well, that's no good, is it? Sort something for him. The man needs to sharpen his pencils. I don't care how good he is, if he turns up in front of Frau Bellini looking like that he'll be scrap metal before he can open his mouth. It doesn't have to be the Adlon, does it?"

"A modest dwelling will suffice," I said in agreement. "The Führerbunker was not exactly Versailles."

"Excellent," Sensenbrink said. "Do you really have no manager?"

"No what?"

"Forget it," he said, flapping his hand. "That's settled, then. Now, I don't want to let the grass grow long on this one; we should try and diarise it this week. You're going to get your uniform back soon, aren't you?"

"Maybe this evening," I reassured him. "It is a Blitz cleaner's, after all."

Sensenbrink fell about laughing.

vii

Even taking into account the dramatic events I had already experienced, the first morning in my new quarters was one of the most arduous in my life. The great conference at the production company had been delayed, which did not bother me. I was not so presumptuous as to deny that I had much work to do in familiarising myself with this present era. By chance, however, I came across a fresh source for such information: the television set.

The structure of this apparatus had changed so substantially since its initial development in 1936 that at first I simply failed to recognise it. To begin with I assumed that the dark, flat plate in my room must be some bizarre work of art. Then, taking into consideration its shape, I speculated that it might serve as a means of storing my shirts overnight without them creasing. There were many things in this modern world to which I had to accustom myself, based as they must be on new discoveries or a passion for outlandish design. Now, for example, it was deemed appropriate to install a kind of elaborate washing galley for guests in place of a bathroom. There was no longer a bathtub, but the shower – a glass cabin – was more or less housed in the room itself. For several weeks I took this to be a sign of the modesty, nay, squalor of my billet, until I learned that in contemporary architecture circles these sorts of things are regarded as creative and remarkably progressive. Likewise, it was another coincidence which alerted me to the television set.

As I had forgotten to hang the DO NOT DISTURB sign on the door to my room, a cleaner entered just as I was attending to my moustache in the washing galley. I turned around in surprise, she apologised, promising to return later and, as she was leaving, she caught sight of the apparatus my shirt was hanging in front of.

"Is there something wrong with the telly?" she asked, and before I could reply she picked up a small box and turned on the device. An image appeared at once, which changed each time she pressed the buttons on the box.

"No, it's working," she said, satisfied. "I just thought . . ."

Then she went, leaving me full of curiosity.

Carefully I took the shirt from the screen, then reached for the little box.

So this was a modern-day television set. It was black, with no switches or knobs, nothing. Holding the box in my left hand I pressed button number one, and the apparatus started up. The result was disappointing.

The picture was of a chef, finely chopping vegetables. Unbelievable! Having developed such an advanced piece of technology, all they could feature on it was a ridiculous cook! Admittedly, the Olympic Games could not take place every year, nor at every hour of the day, but surely something of greater import must be happening somewhere in Germany, or even in the world! Shortly afterwards a woman joined the man and provided an admiring commentary on his knife skills. My jaw dropped. Providence had presented the German Volk with this wonderful, magnificent opportunity for propaganda, and it was being squandered on the production of leek rings. I was so furious that I could have hurled the entire apparatus out of the window, but then it occurred to me that there were many more buttons on the little box besides the simple on/off one. So I pressed number two. The chef vanished at once, only to be replaced by another chef, who was grandiosely discussing the differences between two varieties of turnip. This one had a floozy standing next to him too, who marvelled at the pearls of wisdom that fell from the lips of this "Turnip Head". In irritation I pressed number three. I had not imagined the modern world would be like this.

Turnip Head disappeared in favour of a thickset woman who was also standing by a stove. Here, by contrast, the preparation of food was peripheral to the scene, nor did the woman announce what was on the day's menu. Instead she complained that she had far too little money. This at least was good news for a politician; the social question had not been resolved in the past sixty-six years. Might one have expected anything better from those democratic windbags?

I found it astonishing, however, that the television should afford this trout such prominence; compared to a 100 metres final, the performance of the hefty whiner was terrifically uneventful. On the other hand I was grateful to be watching a transmission where nobody was fussing over the cuisine, least of all the fat woman herself. Her concern was for a scruffy young character, who now slouched up to her, muttered something that sounded like "grmmmshl", and was introduced by a narrator as Manndi. Manndi, he explained, was the obese woman's daughter, and she had just lost her apprenticeship. As I sat there, wondering how anybody could have possibly given this Manndi an apprenticeship in the first place, I heard her categorically rejecting every meal she was offered as "filth". As unsympathetic a character as this urchin must be, one could hardly be surprised at her lack of appetite, given the indifference with which her elephantine mother opened a box and carelessly tipped its contents into a pan. It came almost as a surprise that the box was not tossed in as well. Shaking my head, I switched again, to find a third chef chopping meat into small pieces and holding forth about how he held the knife and why. He, too, had a young blonde bint at his side, who nodded in admiration. Exasperated, I switched off the television set and resolved never to watch the thing again. I decided to hazard another attempt at the wireless instead, but after a thorough reconnaissance of my room I established that there was no receiver present.

If these modest quarters housed a television set but no wireless receiver, one had to conclude that the television had become the more important of the two media.

Nonplussed, I sat on the bed.

I grant that once I had been very proud of my ability, after years of independent study, to unmask with lightning clarity the Jewish lies concocted for the press, in no matter what guise they appeared. But here my skill in that area was of no help. Here were only gibberish radio and cookery telecasts. What kinds of truths were being hidden?

Were there lying turnips?

Were there lying leeks?

But if this was the medium of the age – which was indisputably the case – then I had no choice. I had to learn to understand the content of this device, I had to absorb it, even if it was as intellectually challenged and loathsome as the plump woman's boxed food. Full of resolve, I filled a jug of water at the washing galley, poured myself a glass, took a gulp and, thus steeled, sat in front of the apparatus.

I switched it on again.

On the first programme the leek chef's preparations had come to an end; in his place a gardener, marvelled at by a nodding strumpet, was discussing snails and the best way to combat them. Of considerable importance to the nutrition of the nation, true, but did it need to be the subject of a television transmission? Perhaps the reason it appeared so gratuitous was that, just a few seconds later, another gardener delivered the same speech almost verbatim, but on a different programme, this time in place of the turnip chef. My curiosity was now aroused as to whether the stout woman had also moved into the garden to take up the fight against snails rather than against her daughter. But this was not the case.

Evidently the television set had realised that I had been watching other broadcasts in the meantime, for a narrator now summarised what I had missed. Manndi, the narrator recapitulated, had lost her apprenticeship and did not want to eat her mother's food. The mother was unhappy. The same pictures I had seen only a quarter of an hour earlier were shown once more.

"Alright, alright!" I said, loud enough for the television set to hear. "There's no need to do it at such length. I am not senile, for goodness' sake."

I switched programmes again. And in fact I encountered something new. The meat chef had vanished, and there were no preaching allotmenteers; instead they were showing the adventures of a lawyer, which seemed to be one of a series of telecasts. The lawyer had a beard like Buffalo Bill's, and all the actors spoke and moved as if the silent film era had barely ended. A very jolly piece of buffoonery all in all, which made me laugh out loud on a number of occasions, even though in hindsight I was not entirely sure why. Perhaps it was mere relief that for once nobody was cooking or engaged in the defence of their salads.

I switched over, now feeling almost confident in my mastery of the apparatus, and stumbled across more feature films. Apparently older, and with variable picture quality, they depicted farm life, doctors, detectives. But in none of them did the actors have the same bizarre quality as the Buffalo Bill lawyer. The general aim seemed to be to offer unadulterated daytime entertainment. Which surprised me. Of course, I too was delighted when in 1944 *The Punch Bowl* was released, a wonderfully cheery film which enchanted and diverted the public at a particularly difficult time in the war. But this comedy had been consumed in the evenings, at least in the overwhelming majority of cases. How grievous the situation must now be, then, if the Volk was being offered up such a featherweight muse in the *mornings*. In shock, I continued my exploration of the device and was stopped dead in my tracks.

Before me now sat a man who was reading from a text, which in content appeared to be a news bulletin, but this was hard to say with absolute certainty. For while the man presented his reports, banners ran across the picture, some with figures, some with phrases, as if what the announcer was saying were so negligible that one might as well follow the banners instead, or vice-versa. What was certain was that one would suffer a stroke if one tried to follow everything. My eyes burning, I switched over again, only to find myself presented with a channel doing precisely the same, albeit with banners in another colour and a different announcer. Mobilising every last ounce of my inner strength, I spent several minutes attempting to grasp what was happening. A matter of some importance seemed to be the focus; the current German chancellor had obviously proclaimed, announced or decided something, but it was impossible to understand *what*. On the verge of despair, I crouched in front of the machine and tried to cover the inconsequential swarm of words with my hands so I could concentrate on the spoken word. But more gobbledygook was shifting, constantly, in almost every corner of the screen. The time, the stock prices, the price of the American dollar, the temperature of the remotest corners of the earth – oblivious to all this, the announcer carried on broadcasting news of world events. It was as if the information were being retrieved from a lunatic asylum.

And as if these nonsensical antics were not enough, interruptions for advertisements, as frequent as they were abrupt, declared where the cheapest holiday could be obtained, a claim, moreover, which a large number of shops made in exactly the same way. No sane person would be capable of remembering the names of these outlets, but they all belonged to a group called W.W.W. My only hope was that this was nothing more than "Strength through Joy" in a modern guise. Mind you, it was inconceivable that a man as intelligent as Ley could have created something which sounded like a frozen runt clambering out of a lido with chattering teeth: W.W.W.

I do not recall how I was able to summon the strength to compose my own thoughts. And yet I was struck by a flash of inspiration: this organised lunacy was a sophisticated propaganda trick. It was plain to see – in the face of even the most dreadful news, the Volk would not lose heart, for the never-ending banners gave the reassuring message that it was legitimate to dismiss what had just been read by the announcer as insignificant, and concentrate on the sports headlines instead. I gave a nod of approval. In my time we could have used this technology to inform the Volk of many things parenthetically. Not Stalingrad, maybe, but definitely the Allied landing in Sicily. And conversely, when one's Wehrmacht won great victories, one could promptly remove the text banners and announce from a static screen: TODAY, HEROIC GERMAN TROOPS GAVE THE DUCE BACK HIS FREEDOM!

What impact *that* would have had!

In need of a rest, I switched from this frenzied broadcasting and, out of curiosity, back to the fleshy mother. Had she sent her degenerate daughter to borstal? What did her husband look like? Was he one of those lukewarm supporters who hid himself away in the National Socialist Motor Corps?

The programme immediately recognised that I had

returned to it, and began hastily to outline events for me yet again. Sixteen-year-old Manndi, the narrator recounted, now in a voice full of gravity and urgency, had lost her apprenticeship, and when she came home did not want to eat the food her mother had lovingly prepared for her. The mother was unhappy and had turned to a neighbour for help.

"You haven't got very far," I scolded the reporter, but promised to look in again later on, when more had happened. On my way back to the news channel I paid another brief visit to Buffalo Bill, homage to the silent film. Another narrator greeted me there and informed me what the supposed "lawyer" had been up to till that point in the programme. It seemed that moral improprieties had taken place at the educational establishment frequented by sixteen-year-old Sinndi. The search for the culprit, a pedagogue, led to a polyphony of excruciating nonsense. So ridiculous was this shoddy effort that I laughed heartily once more. Surely it needed an unctuous Jew to render this haphazardly cobbled-together hogwash even half credible. But where might one find a Jew these days? On this count, at least, Himmler had been as good as his word.

I switched back to the chaos of the news and then switched further. I saw gentlemen playing billiards, which was now regarded as a sport, a fact which could be deduced – as I had discovered – from the name of the channel, which was fixed in an upper corner of the picture. Another channel was showing sport, too, but here the camera captured people as they played cards. If this was modern sport, it made one fear for the fitness of the men undertaking military service. For a moment I wondered whether someone like Leni Riefenstahl could have conjured more from such tedium, but even the art of the greatest geniuses of history has its limits.

It may be that the manner of filmmaking had changed. During my search I came across a few channels which were broadcasting something that superficially reminded me of the animated films of old. I still had a good recollection of the adventures of Mickey Mouse, but what I saw on the screen here was good for nothing more than inducing instant blindness. An endless succession of the most incoherent scraps of conversation was interrupted by an even more frequent injection of powerful explosions.

In fact the channels became ever queerer. There were some which broadcast only explosions, without the animations; for a short while I even suspected that this may be something like music, before coming to the conclusion that their sole aim was to sell an utterly mindless product called a ringtone. It was inexplicable to me why one should need a particular ring. As if everyone now worked in sound effects departments for talking films.

Having said that, selling via the television set seemed to be a fairly common practice nowadays. Two or three other channels were continually transmitting the sales pitches of hawkers, the likes of which one finds at every market fair. Here too the claptrap was casually overlaid with text in every corner of the screen. The dealers themselves broke every basic rule of serious oration; indeed they made not the slightest effort to give an impression of trustworthiness, and even the older ones wore ghastly earrings, like your average Gypsy. Their role-playing called upon the worst traditions of confidence trickery. One of them would spout forth the most preposterous lies, while another stood beside him, exclaiming "Hey!" and "No!", or even, "That's unbelievable." A complete farce which filled me with the urge to turn an 8.8 Flak on the assembled vermin, and have the untruths splattered from the scoundrels' guts.

My anger was partly induced by a mounting fear that I would go mad in the face of such collective lunacy. When I tried to switch back to the oversized woman, it was a sort of escape. I got stuck, however, on the channel where the amateurish lawyer had been up to such frightful mischief. Now a courtroom drama was playing, whose lead actress I at first mistook for the chancellor I had seen on the news. It soon turned out, however, that she was merely a courtroom matron who closely resembled the chancellor. The case being tried was that of a certain Sanndi, who seemed to have been charged with a variety of irregularities at her educational establishment.

The sixteen-year-old girl had only committed these offences, however, on account of her fondness for a boy called Anndi, who was entertaining relations with three female students at the same time, one of whom was evidently an actress, or wished to become one. Due to inexplicable circumstances, however, she had put this career on hold in favour of a side-line in the criminal world, and now was part-owner of a betting shop. More utter nonsense along similar lines was reeled off, while the courtroom matron nodded keenly, her face a picture of utter seriousness, as if these absurd tales were the most normal thing in the world and actually happened on a daily basis. I simply could not fathom it.

Who would choose to watch rubbish like this?

Untermenschen, perhaps, who can barely read and write, but besides them? Practically deadened, I switched back to the rotund woman. Since my last visit her adventure-filled life had been interrupted by a programme of advertisements, the end of which I just caught. Then the narrator insisted on explaining to me for the umpteenth time that this wretched bint had lost all control over her bastard halfwit excuse for a daughter, and all she had managed to accomplish in the last half-hour was to prattle on to a chain-smoking neighbour about throwing the little cretin out. "This entire coterie of hopeless cases belongs in a labour camp," I declared vociferously to the television set. "The apartment should be renovated or, even better, demolished along with the rest of the house, and a parade ground built in its stead, so as to expunge for good these calamitous goings-on from the wholesome minds of the German Volk. Exasperated, I hurled the control box into the waste-paper basket.

What a superhuman task lay ahead of me!

To subdue my fury I decided to step outside. Not for long, for I did not wish to be far from the telephone, but long enough to dash to the Blitz cleaner's to fetch my uniform. I entered the shop with a sigh, was greeted as "Herr Stromberg", picked up my surprisingly immaculate soldier's coat and briskly made my way back. I could scarcely wait to face the world again in familiar clothing. Naturally, the first thing the receptionist said when I returned was that there had been a telephone call for me.

"Aha," I said. "Of course. It would have had to happen while I was out. Who was it?"

"No idea," the receptionist said, staring blankly at her television set.

"Did you not make a note of the name?" I shouted impatiently.

"They said they'd ring back," she said, in an attempt to excuse her misconduct. "Was it important?"

"The future of Germany is at stake," I said in disgust.

"Whatever," she said, returning to gawp at her screen. "Got no mobile?"

"Mobile?" I spat.

"Yeah," she said. "It's like, handy."

"Like Hanndi?" I screamed in a rage. "Is this another tramp who's gone running to court because she lost her apprenticeship?" I turned on my heel and marched to my room to resume my study of the television.

viii

It was remarkable how much more recognisable I was in my usual clothing. When I entered the cab the driver greeted me sulkily, but with a definite air of familiarity.

"Alright, governor? Back then, are we?"

"Indeed," I replied, nodding to the man. I gave him the address.

"Right you are!"

I leaned back. I had not ordered any specific type of cab, but if this were an average model it was an excellent ride.

"What type of automobile is this?" I asked him nonchalantly.

"Mur-say-dees."

I was suddenly overcome by a wave of nostalgia, a wonderful feeling of security. I thought of Nuremberg, the magnificent rallies, the journey through the delightful old town, the latesummer, early-autumn wind, which would prowl around the peak of my cap like a wolf.

"I had one of these once," I said dreamily. "A convertible."

"And?" the driver asked. "Drive well?"

"I do not have a licence myself." I said. "But Kempka never voiced any complaints."

"So you're a Führer who's never in the driving seat?" The man burst out laughing. "Good joke, eh?"

"It's an old one."

There was a brief pause in the conversation. Then the driver started up again.

"Well? Still got it – the car? Or did you sell it?"

"To tell you the truth I have no idea what became of it," I said.

"Shame," the driver said. "So, what are you doing in Berlin? Winter Gardens? The Red Cock?"

"Red Cock?"

"You know – what theatre? Where are you appearing?"

"First of all I intend to speak on the radio."

"I knew it," the driver said. "Got grand plans again, have we?"

"Destiny forges plans," I said firmly. "I am merely doing what needs to be done, both now and in the future, for the preservation of the nation."

"You're really good!"

"I know."

"Fancy a little detour to your old haunts?"

"Perhaps later. I should hate to be unpunctual."

This, after all, was the reason for having ordered a cab. Given my limited means, I had offered to walk to the firm's headquarters or take the tramway, but anticipating possible traffic congestion or other imponderables, Sensenbrink had insisted on my taking a cab.

I peered out of the window to see if I could still recognise parts of the capital. It was no simple task, especially as the driver was avoiding the main thoroughfares to save time. Seeing very few old buildings, I nodded with contentment. It appeared as though almost nothing had been left behind for the enemy. What I still had not fathomed was how, after barely seventy years, such a large metropolis could be standing again. Did Rome not scatter salt in the earth of vanquished Carthage? Had it been down to me, I would have dispersed trainloads of salt in Moscow. Or in Stalingrad! Berlin, on the other hand, was no vegetable garden. The creative man can build a coliseum even on saline earth; as far as construction technology and engineering are concerned, of course, a tonne of salt in the soil is actually quite irrelevant. Moreover, it was quite probable that the enemy had been as awestruck when faced with the rubble of Berlin as the Avars had been before the ruins of Athens. And then, in a desperate attempt to preserve the culture, they had rebuilt the city only as well as second- and third-class races are able. For there was no doubt about it: even at first glance the trained eye could see that the vast majority of structures erected here were inferior. A frightful mishmash, compounded by the fact that wherever one looked the same shops appeared. To begin with I thought we were driving around in circles until I realised that Herr Starbuck owned dozens of coffee houses. The diversity of bakeries had gone, a chain of butchers was every-where, and I even spotted several YILMAZ BLITZ CLEANER'S. The houses, too, were built to a very unimaginative design.

The edifice that accommodated the production company was no exception. It was hard to believe that in five hundred or a thousand years people would stand here, marvelling at this insipid block of concrete. I was heartily disappointed. The building resembled one of those former assembly plants; perhaps this all-encompassing "production company" was not all it was cracked up to be.

A young, blonde, rather heavily made-up lady met me at reception to escort me to the conference room. I shudder to describe this place, with its bare, concrete walls, broken up occasionally by exposed brickwork. There was scarcely a door in sight; here and there one could see into large rooms where a number of people were working at their television sets beneath bright fluorescent tubes. The impression one gained was that the munitions workers had left but a few minutes ago. Telephones rang incessantly, and all of a sudden I realised why the Volk had been obliged to spend a fortune on ringtones: so that in this labour camp one could at least tell when one's own phone was ringing.

"I assume that everything here is down to the Russians," I said.

"Well, sort of," the young lady said with a smile. "But you must've read that in the end they didn't come in. Unfortunately. All we've got now are American locusts."

Locusts. I sighed. It was as I had always feared. No Lebensraum, no land to produce bread to feed the Volk. So now Germans were resorting to eating insects like negroes. Gazing at the poor young thing, I was moved as she strode steadfastly beside me. I cleared my throat, but I fear that she may have picked up on my emotion when I said to her, "You are a very brave girl."

"You bet," she beamed. "I don't want to remain an assistant for ever."

Of course. An "assistant". She was undertaking ancillary work for the Russians. Offhand I was unable to explain how such an arrangement could have come to pass in this modern world, but it bore all the hallmarks of those Russian vermin. I could not bear to contemplate what these "activities" under the yoke of Bolshevism might consist of, but I stopped abruptly and grabbed her arm.

"Look at me!" I said, and when she turned her head, somewhat startled, I stared her straight in the eye and said solemnly, "I make you this promise: You will live the future that your background deserves. I personally will do all I can so that you and every other German woman no longer have to serve these Untermenschen! You have my word, Fräulein . . ."

". . . Özlem," she said.

I still recall how unpleasant this moment was. For a fraction of a second my brain searched for an explanation as to how an honest German girl like her could come to have a name like Özlem. Of course, I failed to find one. I removed my hand from her arm, turned, and continued walking. I felt so deceived, so betrayed, that I wished I could leave this bogus woman behind. But I did not know where I was going. So I followed her in silence, resolving to tread more carefully in this new era. How extraordinary: these Turks were not only in the cleaning industry; they seemed to be everywhere.

When we arrived at the conference room, Sensenbrink came to meet me and led me inside. A group of people was sitting around a relatively long table, assembled from a number of smaller parts. I recognised Sawatzki, too, the fellow who had made the hotel reservation; besides him there were half a dozen young men in suits and a woman who must be "Bellini". She was around forty years old, with dark hair, and probably came from the South Tyrol. As soon as I entered the room I sensed that this woman was more of a man than all the other nincompoops here put together. Holding my arm, Sensenbrink tried to take me to the other end of the table, where, as I could see out of the corner of my eye, they had improvised some sort of stage or podium. With a subtle twist of my body I left him grasping thin air, marched up to the woman, removed my peaked cap and gripped the underside of her arm.

"This is . . . Frau Bellini," Sensenbrink said, quite unnecessarily. "Executive Vice President of Flashlight. Frau Bellini – our promising new discovery, Herr . . . er . . ."

"Hitler," I interjected, to put an end to his futile stammering. "Adolf Hitler, former Reich Chancellor of the Greater German Reich." She offered me her hand, which I raised to my lips as I bowed my head, but not too deeply. Then I stood upright again.

"I am delighted to make your acquaintance, madame. Together we can change Germany!"

She smiled, somewhat uncertainly I thought, but I knew from past experience the particular effect I have on women. It is virtually impossible for a woman to feel nothing when in the presence of the commander-in-chief of the most powerful army on earth. To forestall any unnecessary embarrassment on her part, I said "Gentlemen!" to the company around the table, and finally turned back to Sensenbrink.

"So, my dear Sensenbrink, where had you envisaged that I should sit?"

He pointed to a chair at the far end of the table. I had thought as much. This was not the first time that so-called industrialists had presumed they could gauge the importance of a future German Führer. Well, I was certainly planning to demonstrate my importance, but it was doubtful whether they would be able to handle it.

"O.K.," said Sensenbrink. "Sprinkle your magic. What are you bringing to the table?"

"Myself," I said.

"No, I mean, what are you going to say to us today?"

"I promise not to mention Poland again!" Sawatzki exclaimed with a grin.

"Good," I said. "That is progress indeed. I think the question is obvious: How can you help me to help Germany?"

"How do you intend to help Germany?" Frau Bellini asked, giving me and the others a strange wink.

"In your heart of hearts, I believe all of you around this table know what this country needs. On my way here I have seen the rooms in which you are obliged to work. These warehouses in which you and your comrades are forced to perform compulsory labour. Speer was not squeamish when it came to the efficient deployment of foreign workers, but these cramped conditions . . ."

"These are open-plan offices," one of the men said. "You find them everywhere."

"Are you trying to tell me that this was your idea?" I probed.

"What do you mean, 'my idea'?" he said, laughing as he looked around at the others. "All of us here decided it."

"Look here," I said, getting up and turning to face Frau

Bellini. "This is precisely my argument. I am speaking of responsibility. I am speaking of decisions. Who installed these massive cages? Was it him?" I pointed to the man whose idea it had not been. "Or him?" Now I glared at Sensenbrink's neighbour. "Or Herr Sawatzki? But I have grave doubts. I do not know. Or, to put it better: these gentlemen here do not know themselves. And what are your workers supposed to do if they cannot comprehend their own words in their workplace? If they have to spend a fortune on ringtones, just so that they can distinguish their telephone from that of their neighbour? Who bears the responsibility? Who will help the German worker in his time of need? To whom can he turn? Will his superior help? No, for he sends the worker to that man there, and that man there in turn sends him to another! And is this an isolated case? No, it is no isolated case, but a disease creeping stealthily throughout Germany! When you buy a cup of coffee today, do you know who is responsible for it? Who makes the coffee? This gentleman here," I said, pointing once more at the man whose idea it had not been, "this gentleman here naturally believes that it is Herr Starbuck. But you, Frau Bellini, you and I both know that Herr Starbuck cannot make coffee everywhere at the same time. Nobody knows who brews the coffee, all we know for sure is that it was not Herr Starbuck. And when you go to the cleaner's, do you know who cleaned your uniform? Who is this supposed Yilmaz? Do you understand? This is why we need change in Germany. A revolution. We need responsibility and strength. A leadership which takes decisions and stands by them with body and soul, with everything. If you wish to attack Russia you cannot say, as your colleague would like to: Actually, we all decided this together. Shall we encircle Moscow? I know, let's sit around a table and decide with a show of hands! It's all so jolly convenient, and if the whole thing goes wrong then all of us are to blame, or even better: the people are to blame because they elected us. No, Germany must be told once more about Russia. Russia was not Brauchitsch, it was not Guderian, it was not Göring – it was me. The autobahn – that was not any old clown – it was the Führer! And this must be the case throughout the country! When you eat a roll in the morning, you know it was the baker. When you march into rump Czechoslovakia tomorrow, you know it was the Führer!"

I sat down again.

There was silence around me.

"That's . . . not funny," Sensenbrink's neighbour said.

"Scary," said the gentleman whose idea it had not been.

"Told you he was good, didn't I? Über-good!" Sensenbrink said proudly.

"Mad . . ." Hotel Reserver Sawatzki said, although it was unclear what he meant by this.

"Impossible," Sensenbrink's neighbour said firmly.

Frau Bellini leaned forward. All heads turned to her at once.

"Your problem," she said, "is that you're all conditioned by these modern stand-up routines."

Shrewdly, she allowed her comment to hit home before continuing. In any case no-one else dared say a word.

"You lot think good comedy is when the guy up on stage laughs more than those in the audience. Look at the comedy scene today. Nobody can deliver a punchline anymore without laughing their bloody head off, just so everyone knows it's the punchline. And if one of them keeps anything like a straight face then we switch on the background laughter."

"Successful formula, though," said a man who had not spoken until then.

"Maybe," the lady said. She was beginning to make a considerable impression on me. "But what's going to follow that? I think we've reached the point where the public are taking that sort of stuff for granted. The first person to adopt a completely new approach will leave the competition for dead. Isn't that right, Herr . . . Hitler?"

"Propaganda is crucial," I said. "You need to send out a different message from the other parties."

"Tell me," she said. "Did you prepare all this?"

"Why would I?" I said. "I fashioned the cornerstone of my ideology a very long time ago. It enables me apply my knowledge to every single aspect of world affairs and draw the correct conclusions. Do you really think you can learn how to be a Führer in your universities?"

She slapped her hand on the table.

"He's improvising," she beamed. "He just comes out with it! And doesn't even pull a silly face! Do you know what that means? It means he's not the type who runs out of things to say after a couple of programmes. Or whimpers that we need to give him more writers. Am I right, Herr Hitler?"

"I do not like so-called writers meddling in my work," I said. "When I was writing *Mein Kampf,* Stolzing-Czerny frequently . . ."

"I'm beginning to understand what you mean, Carmen," said the man whose idea it had not been. He laughed.

". . . and we'll use him as a foil," Frau Bellini said, "where he'll make the biggest impact. We're going to give him a permanent slot on Ali Gagmez!"

"He's going to love us for that," Sawatzki said.

"He ought to take a look at his viewing figures," Frau Bellini said. "The figures now, where they were two years ago – and where they'll be soon."

"The other channels had better get all their ducks in a row," Sensenbrink said.

"There's just one thing I want to get straight," Frau Bellini said, suddenly looking at me very seriously.

"What is that?"

"We're all agreed that the Jews are no laughing matter."

"You are absolutely right," I concurred, almost relieved. At last here was someone who knew what she was talking about.

ix

Nothing is more dangerous for a fledgling movement than meteoric success. One has taken one's first steps, acquired a few supporters here, given a speech there – maybe even annexed Austria or the Sudetenland – and it is all too easy to think one has reached an interim stage from where the final victory is more easily in one's grasp. And, in truth, I did achieve some astonishing things in a very short period of time, which only confirmed that I had been the choice of Fate herself. When I think of all those battles I had to fight in 1919 and 1920, how the press blew up a storm in my face, how the bourgeois parties drivelled, how I painstakingly tore apart the web of Jewish lies, strand by strand, only to watch the glands of that noisome pest spin even stickier deceptions around me once again, and all the while the enemy, hundreds or thousands of times superior, sprayed new, ever more abominable poisons. Yet after only a handful of days in this modern epoch, I had gained access to the broadcast media, a vehicle for propaganda which the political opposition seemed to have entirely neglected. Why, it was too good to be true! What had the enemy learned of the art of public communication over the past sixty years? Precisely nothing.

In their shoes I would have made all manner of films! Romances in far-off countries aboard vast "Strength through Joy" ships, crossing the South Seas or cruising up the awe-inspiring Norwegian fjords; tales of young Wehrmacht soldiers courageously essaying their first ascent of towering cliffs, only to die at the foot of a rock face in the arms of their true love, a section leader in the League of German Girls, who, devastated yet hardened by the tragedy, devotes her life to National Socialist women's policy. In her belly she carries the brave scion of her dead lover, and with such a love affair one might even disregard the fact that they were unmarried, for where the voice of pure blood speaks, even heaven must remain silent. At all events, she cannot forget his final words as she steps into the valley at twilight, watched by a herd of admiring dairy cows. The sky gradually fades into a mighty swastika flag. Now what films those would be! I swear that the very next day they would run out of application forms for the League of German Women at every branch headquarters.

Her name should be Sieglinde.

Anyway, the political opportunities of this medium had been completely ignored. According to my television set, all the government appeared to have done for the Volk was to enact a measure which was called the "job seeker's allowance". Everyone loathed it. Nobody seemed able to utter its name without sounding offended. I could only hope that these people were not representative of society as a whole, for even mobilising the last reserves of my imagination, I could not envision any sort of flag parade on the Nuremberg Zeppelinfeld with hundreds of thousands of whiners like them.

My negotiations with Frau Bellini could likewise be considered a success. From the outset I had made it absolutely clear that besides money I would need a party apparatus and a party headquarters. At first she looked somewhat taken aback, but then she assured me of her wholehearted support, as well as an office and a typist. There was a generous expenses budget to cover clothing, propaganda trips, research materials to bring me up to date with current events, and many other things besides. Money did not appear to be a problem, but there was little understanding of the requirements of a prestigious party leader. So although I was promised several "historically accurate" suits from a bespoke tailor's as well as my beloved hat, which I always used to wear in the mountains and on the Obersalzberg, an open-top Mercedes with a chauffeur was turned down flat on the basis that it would look terribly silly. I gave in, reluctantly, but only for appearances' sake – after all, I had already achieved substantially more than I could have hoped for. In hindsight, this was without question the most dangerous moment in my new career. Another man might well have sat back in his chair at this point, and in so doing ended up a failure. Not I. Perhaps owing to the maturity of my years, I alone subjected all developments to the coldest, most ruthless analysis.

My supporters were fewer in number than ever before. And, mein Gott, there had been times in the past when they were in terribly short supply. I have a clear recollection of that occasion back in 1919 when I paid my first visit to what was then still the German Workers' Party: seven people were present. Now I was able to count myself, perhaps Frau Bellini at a push, and the kiosk owner, but it was doubtful whether the two of them were ready to fill out their party cards, let alone start counting membership subscriptions or act as stewards, brandishing chair legs at assemblies. The newspaper seller seemed to be a particularly liberal soul, even left-leaning, although he was unquestionably in possession of an honest German heart. I continued to dedicate myself to the iron discipline of my daily routine. I rose at eleven in the morning, had the hotel staff bring me a slice or two of cake, and then I would work until late into the night.

That is to say, I would have risen at eleven, had not the telephone rung out at the crack of dawn, around nine. On the line was a lady with an unpronounceable name of Slavic origin. Jodl would never have put someone like that through to me, but Jodl, alas!, was German history. Still woozy with sleep, I hunted for the receiver.

"Hrmm?"

"Good morning, Frau Krwtsczyk here," a mercilessly cheerful voice sang out. "From Flashlight!"

What irritates me most of all about these morning people is their horribly good temper, as if they had been up for three hours and already conquered France. Particularly since the vast majority of them, in spite of rising so appallingly early, have performed anything *but* great deeds. In Berlin I have time and again met people who make no secret of the fact that their only reason for stirring at such an ungodly hour of the morning is so that they can leave the office earlier in the afternoon. I have suggested to several of these eight-hour logicians that they ought to start work at ten o'clock at night, thereby allowing

88

them to leave at six in the morning and perhaps even arrive home before it is time to get up. Some even took this for a serious suggestion. In my opinion, only bakers need to work early in the morning.

And the Gestapo, of course – that is self-evident. To tear the Bolshevist rabble from their beds, so long as they are not Bolshevist bakers. For they would already be awake, and thus the Gestapo, for their part, would have to get up even earlier, and so on and so forth.

"How can I help you?"

"I'm calling from the contracts department," the voice exulted. "I'm just preparing your documents and I've got a few questions. I don't know, should we do it over the phone . . . ? Or would you rather come in?"

"What sort of questions?"

"Oh, you know, very general ones. Social insurance, bank details, that sort of stuff. For example, what name should I put on the contract?"

"What *name*?"

"I mean, I don't know what your name is."

"Hitler," I groaned. "Adolf."

"Yeah," she laughed again with her blood-curdling morning enthusiasm. "No, I meant your *real* name."

"Hitler! Adolf!" I said, indignant now.

A brief silence followed.

"Really?"

"Yes, of course!"

"Well, that's . . . I mean, that's a coincidence."

"A coincidence? How so?"

"You know, that you're called . . ."

"For goodness' sake, woman, you have a name too. But I am not sitting here, wide-eyed, and screeching, 'Oooh, what a coincidence!'"

"I know, but you look like it too. Your name, I mean."

"And? So you look quite different from your name, do you?"

"No, but . . ."

"Well then! In God's name get those damned papers finished," I barked, slamming down the receiver.

Seven minutes later the telephone rang again.

"What now?"

"Yes, it's me again. Frau . . ." and then came that queer oriental name which sounded like someone scrunching up a Wehrmacht report. "I . . . I'm afraid it's not going to work . . ."

"*What* is not going to work?"

"Look, I don't want to be unfriendly, but . . . it'll never get through the legal department, I can't . . . I mean, when they look at the contract and see 'Adolf Hitler' there . . ."

"Well, what else would you want to write?"

"Please excuse me for asking you again, but . . . is that really your name?"

"No," I said, tortured. "Of course not. My real name is Schmul Rosenzweig."

"I knew it," she said with audible relief. "How do you write that – Schmul? With a 'c'?"

"That was a joke!" I screamed into the receiver.

"Oh. Damn. Pity."

I could hear her crossing something out several times. Then she said, "I . . . please . . . I think it might be better if you did pop by after all. I need something like a passport. And your bank details."

"Ask Bormann," I said curtly into the receiver, and hung up. Then I sat down. This was irritating. And complicated. Feeling sorry for myself, indeed on the brink of despair, I let my thoughts wander back to loyal Bormann. Bormann, who always organised feature films for me so that I could enjoy a little evening relaxation after a hard day's warmongering. Bormann, who had arranged everything so smoothly with the residents of the Obersalzberg. Bormann, who had also dealt with the income from my book sales. Bormann, the most loyal of them all. With him by my side I was confident that many, most things in fact, were in the best possible hands. He would have sorted out contracts like this without the tiniest hitch. "This is your last warning, Frau Catarrh-Throat. You will issue these contract documents at once or you and your family will find yourselves in Dachau. And I'm sure you are aware of just how many people come back from there." Bormann's empathy and sensitivity, his ability to deal with people, were greatly under-estimated. He would have found me an apartment in a flash, as well as an impeccable set of personal documents, bank accounts, everything. On second thoughts it might be more accurate to say that he would have ensured nobody requested such bureaucratic niceties a second time. But now life had to go on without him. And somehow the matter of my papers had to be settled. How I would have handled this in the 1930s was anybody's guess, but now – for better or worse – I had to follow present-day convention. I set my keen mind to the problem.

I imagined I would have to register with the authorities.

And yet I had neither fixed abode nor proof of identity. The evidence for my existence was effectively based on my lodgings at the hotel and the production company's recognition of me, but on paper I had no proof to offer. I clenched my fist in fury and shook it at the ceiling. Papers – German bourgeois official-dom with its petty, mean-spirited rules and regulations. Once more this perfidious millstone around the neck of the German people was throwing a spanner in the works. My situation seemed utterly hopeless – I could see no way out – and then the telephone rang again. Only the iron resolve and quick-wittedness of the former front-line soldier allowed me to home in on the target. I picked up, sure of finding a solution, but still uncertain as to how.

"It's Frau Krwtsczyk from Flashlight again."

The simple answer came to me at once.

"Listen here, woman," I said. "Put me through to Sensen-brink."

X

It is a popular misconception that a Führer needs to know everything. He does not have to know everything. He does not even have to know most things; indeed it can be the case that he need not know anything at all. He can be the most ignorant of the ignorant. Yes, and blind and deaf too in the tragic wake of an enemy bomb blast. On a wooden leg. Or even without arms and legs, rendering the Nazi salute impossible at parades, and when the German anthem is sung only a bitter tear runs from a lifeless eye. I will even postulate that a Führer can be without memory. A total amnesiac. For a Führer's unique talent is not the accumulation of dry facts – his unique talent is rapid decision-making, and assuming responsibility for those decisions. Critics love to make light of this, citing the old joke about the man who – when moving house, for example – chooses to carry the "responsibility" rather than any crates. But in the ideal state the leader ensures that each man is effective in just the right capacity. Bormann was not a leader, but rather a master of thought and memory. He knew everything. Some referred to him behind his back as "the Führer's filing cabinet", which I always found rather touching as I could not have hoped for a more telling endorsement of my policy. At any rate, it was a far greater compliment than I ever heard paid to Göring: "the Führer's hot air balloon".

Ultimately it was this knowledge, this ability to separate the useful from the pointless, which allowed me, notwithstanding the absence of Bormann, to perceive the new opportunities offered by the production company. Given the precarious situation caused by my lack of papers, it was pointless to try to solve the problem of official registration by myself, so I assigned this task to someone who no doubt had greater manoeuvrability in his dealings with the authorities – Sensenbrink. Straight away he said, "Yeah, we'll park that one for you. You worry about your programme and we'll fix everything else. What do you need going forward?"

"Ask that Frau Krytchthingummy. An identity card, I assume. And more besides."

"Don't you have a passport? No I.D. card? How's that possible?"

"I never had need of one."

"Haven't you ever been abroad?"

"Well, obviously: Poland, France, Hungary . . ."

"O.K., they're inside the E.U."

"And the Soviet Union."

"You got in *there* without a passport?"

I thought about it for a moment.

"I cannot recollect anybody having asked me for one," I replied confidently.

"Strange. But what about America? I mean, you're fifty-six. Haven't you ever been to America?"

"I did, very seriously, plan to go," I said. "But unfortunately I was stopped in my tracks."

"O.K., so all we need are your papers, then I'm sure one of us can operationalise the registration and health insurance for you."

"This is the problem. There are no papers."

"No papers? None at all? Not even at your girlfriend's? I mean, at home?"

"My last home," I said sadly, "was devoured by flames."

"I see – oh – you're being serious now?"

"Have you seen the Reich Chancellery of late?"

He laughed. "That bad?"

"I do not see what there is to laugh about," I said. "It was devastating."

"Fine," Sensenbrink said. "I'm no expert, mind, but we're going to need some sort of papers. Where were you registered before? Or insured?"

"I always had something of an aversion to bureaucracy," I said. "I preferred to make the laws myself."

"Hmmm," Sensenbrink sighed. "Well, I've never had a case like this before. We'll see what we can leverage, O.K.? But at the very least we're going to need your real name."

"Hitler," I said. "Adolf."

"Listen, I've got every sympathy for your situation, don't get me wrong. That Schröder chap is exactly the same; away from the stage he loves his peace and quiet. And given how contro-versial your topic is you need to be careful as an artist – but I'm not sure the authorities will see it the same way."

"I have no interest in the details."

"I bet you don't," Sensenbrink laughed, a touch too con-descendingly for my liking. "As far as I'm concerned you're the consummate artist. But it really would make things easier. You see, there's no problem with tax. The finance office is the only one that doesn't give a damn; if necessary they'll tax illegal immigrants and negotiate cash payments. And if you want, we can arrange all the payments and help you manage your money, so I don't expect it would be the long pole in the bank's tent. But I'll bottomline for you: it'll be like putting socks on an octopus with the registration office or social insurance. We'll be chipping out of the bunker with no green to work with."

I had no idea what the man was saying, but sensed that he was in need of moral support. The troops must not be over-extended. After all, it is not every day that a Reich chancellor believed long dead parades himself through the country as fresh as a daisy.

"It must be difficult for you," I said, indulging him.

"What?"

"Well, I imagine you seldom encounter people like me."

Sensenbrink laughed.

"Of course we do – it's our job!"

His composure came as such a surprise that I had to probe further: "So there *are* more like me?"

"Come on, you know as well as I do that there are all sorts in your line of work . . ."

"And you arrange for them all to be broadcast?"

"Can you imagine the work we'd have on our plates? No, we only contract those we believe in."

"Excellent," I said. "One must fight for the cause with fanatical belief. Do you have Antonescu as well? Or the Duce?"

"Who?"

"You know: Mussolini."

"No!" Sensenbrink said so firmly that I could see him shaking his head down the telephone wire. "What would we do with an Antonini? He's low-visibility; no-one knows who he is."

"Or Churchill? Eisenhower? Chamberlain?"

"Oh, now I know which direction your arrows are firing in!" Sensenbrink roared into the telephone. "No, no. Where would the humour be in that? We'd never gain any traction. No, you're perfect as you are. We're going to stick with one character, we're going to stick with our Adolf!"

"Very good," I said, then immediately delved deeper: "What happens if Stalin turns up tomorrow?"

"You can forget Stalin," he said, pledging his allegiance. "We're not the History Channel."

This was the Sensenbrink I wanted to hear! Sensenbrink the fanatic, awakened by his Führer.

And here I cannot overemphasise the importance of a fanatical will. This was most clearly demonstrated by the course of the last world war, which was not always unproblematic. No doubt some will say, "Was it really a lack of fanatical will which resulted in the Second World War ending as unfavourably as the First? Was there not perhaps another reason, maybe an insufficient supply of manpower?" All of this is feasible, even possibly correct, but it is also the symptom of an ancient German disease, namely that of hunting for mistakes in the small details while ignoring the larger, clearer picture.

Naturally, one cannot deny that we suffered from a certain numerical inferiority of troops in the last world war. But this inferiority was not decisive; on the contrary, the German Volk could have coped with a greater superiority of enemy numbers. Indeed, on a number of occasions in the early 1940s I even regretted that the enemy did not have more troops. Just look at the inferiority enjoyed by Frederick the Great: twelve enemy soldiers to each Prussian grenadier! Whereas in Russia it was three or four Bolshevists per Aryan warrior.

It is true that after Stalingrad the superiority of the enemy was far more befitting to the honour of the Wehrmacht. On the day of the Allied landings in Normandy, the enemy advanced with 2,600 bombers and 650 fighter planes. If I remember rightly, the Luftwaffe resisted with two fighter aircraft – a truly honourable ratio. And yet the position was not hopeless! I wholeheartedly endorse the words of Reich Minister Dr Goebbels, who demanded that if the numerical disadvantage could not be rectified, then the German Volk must compensate for it in other ways, whether this be with better weapons, smarter generals or, as in this case, the advantage of superior morale. At first glance, the simple fighter pilot may consider it a near-hopeless task to take three bombers out of the sky with every shot, but with superior morale, with an unwavering, fanatical spirit, everything is possible!

This holds as true today as it did back then. And now I came across an example of fanaticism that even I would have thought impossible. And yet it was perfectly genuine. I observed a man – an employee of my hotel, I presume – who was engaged in a fascinating new activity. In fact, I cannot be absolutely sure that this activity *is* new; it is just that I remember it being performed differently, that is to say, with a broom or a rake. This man wielded a completely new type of portable leaf-blowing machine. A mesmerising apparatus with extraordinary blowing power, which I expect had become necessary to confront the more resistant forms of foliage that evolution must have given rise to over the intervening years.

I was able to infer from this that the racial struggle is far from over; on the contrary, it continues to surge in nature with greater intensity. Not even today's bourgeois-liberal press dares to deny it. One reads of the American grey squirrel supplanting the indigenous red species, so beloved of the German Volk; of tribes of African ants marching across the Iberian Peninsula; of Indo-Germanic balsams naturalising and spreading in this country. This last development is to be welcomed, of course; Aryan plants have every right to colonise the space which is their due. Now, I had not seen this novel, more combative foliage at close quarters – the leaves on the hotel's motor park seemed perfectly normal to me – but the blowing apparatus could just as easily be deployed against traditional leaves. After all, when driving a Königstiger tank you do not restrict yourself to taking on T-34s; if necessary you engage the old BT-7s too.

When for the first time I observed the man I was indignant. I had been woken that morning – it may have been around nine-thirty – by an infernal din, as if my pillow were nestling against a Soviet rocket launcher. I rose in a fury, hurried to the window, glared out and spotted that very man busily operating his blowing device. My wrath was only multiplied when I looked at the surrounding trees and saw that it was gusting. How absolutely preposterous it was to blow leaves from one place to another on a day like this! My first instinct was to race outside, vent my anger and give him a proper dressing-down. But I thought better of it. For I was in the wrong.

The man had been issued with an order. And he was executing the order. With a fanatical loyalty my leading generals would have done well to imitate. A man was following orders – it was as simple as that. Was he complaining? Was he moaning that it was a pointless task in this wind? No, he was performing his ear-splitting duty bravely and stoically. Like a loyal S.S. man. Thousands of these had completed their tasks regardless of the burden placed on them, even though they could have easily complained, "What are we to do with all these Jews? It makes no sense anymore; they're being delivered faster than we can load them into the gas chambers!"

I was so moved that I dressed swiftly, hurried out to the worker, put a hand on his shoulder and said, "My good man, I should like to thank you. It is for people like you that I will continue my struggle. For I know that from this leaf-blasting apparatus, indeed from every leaf-blasting apparatus in the Reich, blows the red-hot breath of National Socialism."

That is the fanatical will this country requires. And I hoped that I had aroused it in Sensenbrink too.

xí

On the morning I strode into the office put at my disposal, I was reminded again of the long path down which I yet had to travel. I entered a room which was perhaps five by seven metres, with a ceiling two metres fifty high at most. I thought wistfully of my Reich Chancellery. Now *that* place had rooms; the very instant one entered one felt dwarfed, one trembled before such power, such high culture. Not on account of the splendour – the ostentation had always left me cold – but whenever I received someone in the Reich Chancellery, I noticed at once that he felt the superiority of the German Reich, felt it physically. Speer got everything so right. Just take the Great Reception Hall – each chandelier alone must have weighed a tonne; had any one of them come down they would have crushed a man below, turning him to a pulp, a mash of bones and blood and squashed flesh, with maybe some hair sticking out the side. I was almost afraid to stand beneath them myself. I never gave any hint of this, of course; why, I strolled beneath those chandeliers as if it were the most natural thing in the world. It was just a matter of getting used to them.

But that is exactly how things must be.

For how could one spend millions and millions on a Reich

Chancellery, only for someone to come in and say to himself, "Oh, I thought it would be bigger than this"? The point is, this man must not think at all, he must feel it viscerally, instinctively. He is nothing; the German Volk is everything! A master race! The edifice must emit an aura, like a pope, but a pope, of course, who smites the slightest contradiction with fire and sword, like the Lord God himself. The mighty double doors open, out steps the Führer of the German Reich, and foreign visitors must feel like Odysseus before the Cyclops, but this Cyclops has two eyes, over which no man will be able to pull the wool!

And there were no boulders at the Chancellery.

There were escalators. I almost felt as if I were in Kaufhof in Cologne, to which I had paid a visit immediately after its Aryanisation. You have to hand it to him, that Tietz; the Jews certainly know how to build department stores. But here is an important distinction: in Kaufhof the customer should think he is king, whereas when he came to the Reich Chancellery, the customer knew that he had to bow – in spirit at least – to something far greater. I was never in favour of having every Tom, Fritz or Heinrich crawling about, especially not on *that* floor.

The floor of the office at my disposal was made of a dark-grey compound. It was no carpet I recognised, but a type of covering fabricated from a tatty felted substance – but not at all the sort of material from which one would choose to tailor a German soldier's winter uniform. I had seen its like many times in this new world; it was so ubiquitous that I did not need to feel humiliated by its presence in my office. It was plainly a feature of these impoverished times. I vowed that in the future the German worker and his family would have different floor coverings from these.

And different walls.

The walls here were paper thin, no doubt due to a want of raw materials. I had a writing desk, which was manifestly second-hand, and was obliged to share the room with another desk, which must be for the typist I had been promised. I sighed deeply and gazed out of the window. It gave onto a motor park with dustbins in an array of colours, the reason for this being that waste was carefully separated, no doubt another consequence of the raw materials shortage. I shuddered to contemplate from which bin's contents the wretched floor covering had been made. Then I chuckled to myself at Destiny's bitter irony. If only the Volk had made a greater effort at the right time, there would be no need to collect refuse in this manner, given the wealth of raw materials in the East. All kinds of waste could have been happily tipped into just two dustbins, or even a single one. I shook my head in disbelief.

Rats scurried around in the yard below, alternating with groups of smokers. Rats, smokers, rats, smokers, and so it went on. I scrutinised once more my modest, nay pathetic writing desk and the cheap, whitish wall behind it. It would not look any better no matter what one hung up there, even a bronze imperial eagle. One would have to content oneself that the wall did not come crashing down with the weight. Once upon a time I enjoyed four hundred square metres of office; now the Führer of the Greater German Reich sat in a shoebox. What had become of the world?

And what had happened to my typist?

I looked at the clock. It was just after half past twelve.

I opened the door and peered out. Nobody was to be seen save for a middle-aged woman in a suit. She laughed when she caught sight of me.

"Oh, it's you! Are you already rehearsing? We're all terribly excited!"

"Where is my secretary?"

She stopped momentarily, to think about it. Then she said, "They must have given you a part-timer, which means she'll probably only come for the afternoons. Around two."

"Oh," I said, dumbfounded. "What will I do until then?"

"I don't know," she said, laughing as she turned to go. "Touch of Blitzkrieg, perhaps?"

"I will remember that!" I said, frostily.

"Really?" She stopped and turned again briefly. "That's fab. It'd be great if you could use it for your programme! I mean, we're all working for the same firm here!"

I went back into my office and closed the door. On each desk stood a typewriter without a cylinder, in front of a television set which must have been placed there by mistake. I decided to continue my research into broadcasting, but could find no operating box. It was deeply frustrating. I reached angrily for the telephone, but then replaced the receiver. I had no idea with whom the switchboard should connect me. The entire modern technological infrastructure was getting me nowhere. I sighed, and for a moment my heart pounded with an uneasy despair. But only for a moment. Resolutely I banished the temptations of weakness. A politician makes the most of what there is. Or, as in this case, of what there is not. So I might as well go outside for a while and observe the new German Volk.

As I stepped out of the building I looked about me. Opposite was a small park, whose trees were already displaying the most intense autumnal colours. To the left and right stood more houses. Out of the corner of my eye I spied a madwoman on the edge of the park who was gathering up what her dog had just deposited. Had this creature been sterilised? I wondered, but came to the conclusion that she could hardly be representative of Germany as a whole. I headed off in the opposite direction.

An automatic cigarette dispenser hung on the wall, and I imagined it must serve the smokers who shared the motor park with the rats. My uniform seemed not to cause a distraction here, perhaps because it didn't stand out. I encountered two men in passable Wehrmacht uniforms, as well as a nurse and two doctors. Ever since my release from prison, supporters were hot on my heels and their attention was not always welcome. Back then I had to outfox my adherents with small tactical manoeuvres, in the truest sense of the word, so that I could enjoy some brief moments undisturbed by photographers. In this particular environment, however, I was able to wander around as myself and yet remain incognito – ideal for allowing me to study the population. In the presence of the Führer, you see, many people begin to behave unnaturally. In such situations I always say "No fuss, please," but of course the ordinary man pays no heed to this. In my Munich years the common Volk clung to me like mad. This was not what I needed here. I wanted to see the genuine, unadulterated German: the Berliner.

A few minutes later I passed a construction site. Men in helmets were shuffling about; it reminded me of the time in Vienna when I was dirt poor, hiring out my labour to foremen in order to earn my daily bread. Out of curiosity I peeped through the fence, expecting to see the houses rise before my very eyes. But evidently technology had not made great advances in this area. On the upper floor a foreman was excoriating a youth, who may have been a student, a prospective architect, a young man full of hope, as I once was. He, too, had to subject himself to the fierce authority of the worker; the ruthless world of the construction site was still the same as it had ever been. Whatever insight the young man may have into philology and philosophy, it counted for nothing in this universe of steel and cement. On the other hand I could see that the brutal, unsophisticated masses still existed – all I had to do was awaken them. And the quality of the blood seemed acceptable as well.

As I strolled onwards I scrutinised the faces around me. Overall, not much seemed to have changed. The racial measures implemented during my time in government had evidently paid off, even if they had been abandoned by successive regimes. What struck me most of all was the apparent lack of half-breeds. I could see comparatively strong oriental influences, Slavic elements in many of the countenances, but that had always been the case in Berlin. What was new, on the other hand, was a substantial Turkish–Arab element on the streets. Women with headscarves, old Turks in jackets and flat caps. To all appearances, however, there had been no racial mixing. The Turks I saw looked like Turks; I failed to detect any enhancement through Aryan blood, even though such a development must surely be of interest to the Turk. What such a large number of Turks was doing on the streets remained a complete mystery. Especially at this time of day. They did not look like imported domestics; there was no sense that these Turks were hurrying anywhere. Rather their manner of walking suggested a certain leisureliness.

I was jolted from my musings by a ringing, the pealing of a bell, such as would usually signal the end of a school lesson. Looking about I saw that there was indeed a school building fairly close. I quickened my pace and sat on a bench opposite it. It might be recreation, an opportunity for me to examine young people en masse. As it happened, a stream of individuals did pour out of the building at that moment, but it was impossible to tell in more detail what type of school this was. I was able to make out quite a few boys, but there appeared to be no girls of the same age. Those that emerged from the building were either elementary-school pupils or seemed capable of bearing children. It may be that science had discovered a way to circumvent those bewildering years of puberty and to catapult young women straight into reproductive age. A perfectly natural concept, for a process of toughening over the years of one's youth only makes sense for males. The Spartans of Ancient Greece would not have thought any differently. Moreover, the young women dressed in such a way as to emphasise their figure, clearly signalling their intention to find a partner with whom they could start to breed. However – and this I found most remarkable – very few of them were German. It appeared to be a school for Turkish guest pupils. And from the first scraps of conversation I picked up, an extraordinary, even gratifying picture painted itself.

Indeed, from those Turkish pupils I was able to observe how my principles had obviously been acknowledged as correct, and later implemented as directives. Quite clearly the young Turks had been taught only the most rudimentary language. I detected barely any correct syntax; it sounded more like a linguistic tangle of barbed wire, furrowed with mental grenades like the battlefields of the Somme. What emerged from their mouths might suffice for communicating the most basic information, but for organised resistance it would be no use at all. Lacking an adequate vocabulary, most of them supplemented their utterances with expansive gestures – a real sign language, no less, in accordance with ideas that I myself had developed and wished to implement. Admittedly, it had been intended for the Ukraine and the conquered Russian territories, but of course it was just as suitable for any other population group under German domination. And I witnessed a further technological advance: evidently the Turkish pupils had to wear tiny earplugs, to prevent them from picking up extraneous information or unnecessary knowledge. The principle was simple and appeared to work almost too well – some of these young pupil-like characters wore expressions of such intellectual frugality that one could scarcely imagine what useful activity they might one day be able to perform for society. But, as I established with a quick glance, neither they nor anybody else was sweeping the pavement.

When the pupils of both races became aware of my presence, I noticed joyful recognition flash across some of their faces. The pupils of German descent must know me from their history classes, the Turkish ones from the darkest recesses of the television set. Then the inevitable happened. Once again I was falsely identified as "the other Herr Stromberg from *Switsch*", I was asked to sign a few autographs, and I allowed a number of pupils to have their photographs taken with me. Not total confusion, but enough for me to lose track of things momentarily; what is more, I had the absurd impression that the German pupils were speaking the same minced-up smorgasbord. When, out of the corner of my eye, I saw another madwoman painstakingly gather up her dog's stools, one by one, I thought it time to retire to the peace and seclusion of my office.

I had been sitting at my desk for about ten minutes, gazing at the changing of the guard of the smokers and rats, when the door opened and in came a character who quite conceivably had just graduated from that group of indeterminately aged schoolwomen. Her clothes were black, conspicuously so, and her long, dark hair was parted on one side. Well now, there was no-one fonder of dark hues, of black, than I! I had always found it terribly dashing, especially on the S.S. But in contrast to my S.S. men, this young lady looked almost worryingly pale, all the more conspicuously so because she had chosen to wear a strikingly dark, almost bluish lipstick.

"For goodness' sake!" I said, leaping to my feet. "Are you feeling quite alright? Are you cold? Sit down, at once!"

Unperturbed, she looked at me, chewing on a stick of gum.

Then she pulled out two ear plugs on a cord and said, "Hmmm?"

I began to doubt my theory about the Turkish ear plugs. There was nothing Asiatic about this woman; I would have to get to the bottom of the matter another time. Nor did she seem to be cold; at any rate she slid a black rucksack off her shoulder and took off her black autumn coat. Beneath this her clothes appeared normal, save for the fact that they were entirely black, too.

"So," she said, ignoring my questions, "you must be Herr Hitler! L.O.L.!" She offered me her hand.

I shook it, sat back down and said tersely, "And who might you be?"

"Vera Krömeier," she said. "That's sooooooo cool. Can I ask you a question? Is this method acting?"

"I'm sorry?"

"You know, what De Niro does? And Pacino? Method acting? Where you're like, completely immersed in your role?" Each one of her sentences sounded as if it were a question.

"Look here, Fräulein Krömeier," I said firmly, rising from my chair. "I have no idea what you are talking about, but far more importantly, you should know what I am talking about, and—"

"You're right," Fräulein Krömeier said, fishing the chewing gum from her mouth with two fingers. "Is there a bin here? They normally like, forget?" She looked around and, finding no waste-paper bin, said, "One sec," stuck the gum back in her mouth and vanished. I was standing rather pointlessly in the middle of the room, so I sat back down again. She reappeared soon afterwards carrying an empty waste-paper basket. She put it down, plucked the chewing gum from her mouth once more and dropped it with satisfaction into the basket.

"Right," she said. "That's better." Then she turned to me again. "O.K., ready to roll. So, boss, what's on the menu?"

I sighed. Her too. I would have to start from the very beginning.

"First of all," I said, "my title is not 'Boss' but 'Führer'. So please call me 'Mein Führer'. And I should like you to give me the appropriate greeting when you enter!"

"Greeting?"

"The Nazi salute, naturally! With the right arm outstretched."

Her face lit up and she was on her feet at once, firing off more statements dressed up as questions. "I knew it? L.O.L.! That *is* what you're doing? Method acting? Do you want me to start now?"

I nodded. She dashed out of the door, closing it behind her. She knocked, and when I said, "Come in," she strode forwards, thrust her hand into the air and screamed, "GOOD MORNING, MEIN FÜHRER!" Then she added, "You have to shout it, don't you? I like, saw it in a film once?" She paused, seemingly confused, and then bellowed, "OR DOES EVERYTHING HAVE TO BE SHOUTED? DID EVERYONE SHOUT ALL THE TIME WITH HITLER?" Looking me in the eye, she said in an anxious voice, "I got it wrong again, didn't I? Sorry! Are you going to like, get someone else in instead?"

"No," I said, reassuring her. "That was fine. I do not expect perfection from any comrade. All I expect is for him to try his best, each in his own way. And you seem to be very much on the right track. Just one tiny favour, please. No more screaming!"

"Jawohl, mein Führer," she said, adding, "Not bad, eh? L.O.L.!"

"Very good," I said. "But the arm needs to be pointed further outwards. You are not putting your hand up in elementary school!"

"Jawohl, mein Führer. So, what are we going to do now?"

"First," I said, "you can show me how to operate this television set. Then please remove the device from your desk; after all, you are not being paid to watch television. We will have to find you a decent typewriter. You cannot have any old machine; we need the Antiqua 4mm typeface, and I should like you to type everything with a centimetre gap between the lines. Otherwise I cannot read it without glasses."

"Can't do typewriters," she said. "Only Pee–Sees. And if you take that away from me then I like, can't do it at all. Anyhow, with the computer we can get any size font you like. And I can also turn on your computer for you."

Then she introduced me to one of the most extraordinary achievements in the history of human civilisation: the computer.

xii

It never ceases to amaze me how the creative genius of the Aryan race refuses to be suppressed. This is an axiom I recognised long ago, and still I find myself surprised by how it holds true time and again, even in the most adverse circumstances.

Assuming, of course, that the climate is right.

Once upon a time I had to lead unfailingly asinine discussions about the murky pre-history of the forest-dwelling Germanic peoples. And I never denied that, when it is cold, the Teuton does nothing. Apart from light a fire, perhaps. Just look at the Norwegian or the Swede. It came as no surprise to learn of the success the Swede has recently enjoyed with his furniture. In that rotten state of his the Swede is permanently on the lookout for firewood, so it is no wonder that from time to time this might result in the odd table or chair. Or a so-called social system, which delivers heat free of charge into the apartment blocks of millions of parasites. This can only lead to spinelessness and greater sloth. No, besides the Swiss, the Swede displays the worst facets of the Teuton, but – and let us never lose sight of the fact – this is all down to climate. As soon as the Teuton makes his way south, he is seized by an inventiveness, a will to create, and so he builds the Acropolis in Athens, the Alhambra in Spain, the pyramids in Egypt. We know all this, it is so self-evident that it is all too easy to overlook; many fail to see the Aryan for the building. The same is true of America, of course: without German immigrants the American would be nothing. Time and again have I rued the fact that it was not possible to offer every German his own land back then; at the beginning of the twentieth century we lost hundreds of thousands of emigrants to the Americans. A curious development, I should like to point out, for very few of them became farmers over there; they could have just as easily remained here. I expect, however, that most of them imagined the countryside was bigger in America and that it would only be a matter of time before they were allocated their own farm. In the meantime, of course, they had to earn their daily bread in different ways. Thus these men sought out careers, small artisanal activities such as shoemaking, joinery or atomic physics – whatever was going. And that Douglas Engelbart, well, his father had already emigrated to Washington, which is further south than one thinks, but young Engelbart then goes to California, which is even *further* south; there his Germanic blood begins to roil, and he promptly invents this mouse apparatus.

Fantastic.

I have to say that I was never particular taken by this computing stuff. I was only faintly aware of what Zuse was bolting together – I believe his work was being funded by some ministry or other – but in essence it was something for the boffins. Zuse's electronic brain was far too unwieldy to be of any use on the front; I would not have liked to see him trying to wade through the Pinsk Marshes with it. Or parachuting into Crete – the man would have dropped like a stone. One would have had to equip him with a military glider, and what for, ultimately? In essence it was just glorified mental arithmetic. You can say what you like about Schacht, but anything Zuse's machine computed Schacht could have calculated half-asleep after seventy-two hours under enemy fire while buttering a slice of army bread. And thus I was initially reluctant when Fräulein Krömeier put me in front of this screen.

"I have no need to acquaint myself with such equipment," I said. "You are the secretary here!"

"Just sit down here then, mein Führer," Fräulein Krömeier said – I recall the moment as if it were yesterday. "Else you'll be like, 'Can you help me with this?' and 'Can you help me with that?' and I'll be like, so totally busy with you? That I won't be able to get on with my own work?"

I was not especially keen on her tone, but her surly manner reminded me very vividly of when Adolf Müller gave me a rudimentary lesson in the basics of driving. Müller was pretty tough on me, I have to say, although this was less a reflection of his concern for the national question and more down to his fear that if I broke my neck he would lose his print order for the *Völkischer Beobachter*. Müller was not a professional driving instructor, but a businessman first and foremost. Although perhaps I am doing him an injustice; I have since learned that he shot himself soon after the war, and let's face it, there's no profit in suicide. In any event he took me in his automobile to show me how to drive correctly, or more accurately, what to watch out for when one has a chauffeur. Müller's was a tremendously valuable lesson, in which I learned more than

I had from any number of professors over the years. At this juncture I should like to make it quite clear that I do listen to people other than those old-school cretins on the general staff. Many may be better than I at driving a motorcar, but when it comes to tidying up a front line or judging how long to offer resistance when caught in a pocket, then I am still the one who makes the decision and not some Herr Paulus who is starting to get cold feet.

The very thought of it!

Ah well. Next time.

Anyway, on the basis of various reminiscences I declared myself willing to follow Fräulein Krömeier's instructions, and I must say it was worth my while. I had always been put off by typewriters. I never wanted to be an accountant or pen-pusher, and I had dictated my books. The last thing I wanted to do was type away like some pea-brained hack in a local rag, but then this miracle of German resourcefulness arrived: the mouse contraption.

Rarely can there have been a more ingenious invention.

As you manoeuvre this mouse contraption around the table, a small hand moves on the screen in precisely the same way. And whenever you want to touch a place on the screen, you press on this mouse and the small hand actually touches that place on the screen. It is so childishly simple and I was utterly fascinated. Naturally, the computer would have been no more than an entertaining diversion if its sole purpose were to simplify a few office tasks. But this piece of equipment turned out to be an extraordinarily composite tool.

One could use it to write, but through the wiring system

one could also make contact with all the individuals and institutions who had likewise agreed to be part of this network. Moreover, unlike with the telephone, not all participants had to be sitting at their computers, rather they could simply deposit things, allowing one to retrieve them in their absence – all manner of peddlers engaged in this practice. What especially pleased me, however, was that newspapers and periodicals, indeed every possible form of information was accessible. It was like a vast library with unrestricted opening hours. How I could have done with that! How many hard days had I spent making tough military decisions, after which all I wanted was to indulge in a little reading at two o'clock in the morning. Admittedly, Bormann did his best, but how many books can a simple Reichsleiter procure? Besides, space in the Wolf's Lair was not unlimited. This wonderful technology, on the other hand, which is called the "Inter-network", offered absolutely everything all day long and at night too. All one had to do was to search for it in a contraption called "Google" and touch the result with that magnificent mouse. Before long I established that I kept arriving at the same address: a proto-Germanic reference work called Vikipedia, an easily recognisable compound of 'encyclopedia' and those ancient Germans with exploration in their blood, the Vikings.

It was a project which brought me to the verge of tears.

Here, nobody thought of himself. In the true spirit of self-abnegation and self-sacrifice, countless people were compiling all manner of knowledge for the greater good of the German nation, without demanding a pfennig for their labour. It was like a charitable campaign for knowledge, which demonstrated that even in the absence of the National Socialist Party the German Volk instinctively worked to support its fellow man, even if there was a certain question mark hanging over the expertise of these selfless comrades.

For instance, to cite just one example, I was delighted to note that my vice-chancellor, von Papen, had bragged in 1932 that within two months of my accession to power I would be pushed against the wall until I squeaked. But elsewhere in this Inter-network one could read that von Papen believed this would be accomplished within three months rather than two, and in yet another place the time frame cited was six weeks. Frequently he thought that I would be pushed into a corner rather than against the wall. Or even into a tight spot. And perhaps I was not going to be pushed, but squashed, while maybe the goal was not to have me squeak, but squeal. Ultimately, the bemused reader was left to work out the truth for himself – von Papen had wanted to manoeuvre me in some way into some place within a period of time between six and twelve weeks until I emitted some sort of high-pitched sound. Which was still astonishingly close to the actual intention of that self-appointed "strategist" back then.

"Got an address yet?" Fräulein Krömeier asked.

"I am staying in a hotel," I said.

"E-mail – electronic post."

"Send it to the hotel, too!"

"That's like, a 'no' then," she said, typing something into her computer. "What name shall I register you under?"

I frowned at her.

"Under what name, mein Führer?"

"Under my own," I said. "Naturally!"

"I imagine that's going to be like, difficult?" she said, typing away.

"What the devil is so difficult about it?" I asked. "Under which name do you receive *your* post?"

"Vulcania17 at web Dee Eee?" she said. "There we go: your name's not allowed."

"I'm sorry?"

"I can try it with a few other providers, but I doubt it'll make much difference. And even if *were* allowed, I bet one of those nutters has already like, taken it? L.O.L."

"What do you mean, 'taken it'?" I asked in irritation. "There is more than one man called Adolf Hitler, just as more than one man has the name Hans Müller. The postal service does not insist that only one man is allowed to be called Hans Müller. One cannot monopolise a name!"

To begin with she appeared slightly confused, then she cast me a look not dissimilar to one I had often received from the ancient Reich President Hindenburg.

"There's only one of each address," she said firmly and very slowly – without turning it into a question this time – as if she were worried that I should not otherwise be able to follow her explanation. Then she carried on typing.

"Here we are: Adolf dot Hitler's gone," she said. "As is Adolf Hitler all one word and Adolf underscore Hitler, too."

"What do you mean, 'underscore'? There's nothing 'under' about me," I spat. "I am a member of the master race, not some kind of Slav!" But Fräulein Krömeier was already typing again.

"AHitler and A dot Hitler have both gone too," she announced. "Just Hitler and just Adolf as well."

"Then we will simply have to get them back," I thundered.

"You can't get anything back," she said petulantly.

"Bormann could! How else would we have got all those houses on the Obersalzberg? Do you really imagine it was uninhabited beforehand? No! People were living there, but Bormann had his ways and means . . ."

"Would you rather Herr Bormann sorted out your e-mail address?" Fräulein Krömeier asked, sounding anxious and slightly aggrieved.

"I'm afraid Bormann is currently unlocatable," I conceded. Not wishing to demoralise the troops, I added, "Listen, I'm sure you're doing your best."

"O.K. In the meantime I'll just like, go on?" she said. "Do you mind telling me when your birthday is?"

"20th April, 1889."

"Hitler89 – gone. Hitler204 – no, we're not getting anywhere with your name."

"What impertinence!" I said.

"What about like, choosing another name? I mean, I'm not really called Vulcania17."

"But this is an outrage! I am not just any old clown!"

"That's what it's like on the Internet. Like, first come, first served? You could choose something symbolic?"

"A pseudonym?"

"That sort of thing."

"Right . . . I'll have Wolf, then," I said grudgingly.

"Wolf on its own? Someone's bound to have that already. It's too simple."

"Then in God's name make it Wolf's Lair!"

She typed.

"Gone. You can have WolfsLair6."

"But I'm not Wolf's Lair 6!"

"Wait a sec, what else could we do? Hey, what was that thing called: Obersalzbach?"

"Berg! Obersalz*berg*!"

She typed. Then she said. "Oops. I don't suppose you want Obersalzberg6, do you?" And without waiting for an answer she continued, "Let me try ReichChancellery. That would be good. Well . . . you can have ReichChancellery1."

"Not Reich Chancellery," I said. "Try 'New Reich Chancellery'. At least I liked that building."

She typed again. "Bingo!" she said. "It works. L.O.L." In that brief moment I must have seemed somewhat disheartened; at any rate she felt obliged to reassure me, and said in a well-nigh maternal tone, "Don't look so sad! You'll get your e-mail at the New Reich Chancellery. It sounds brilliant!" She paused, shook her head and added, "I hope you don't mind me saying, but I think you like, do that so brilliantly! It's just so totally convincing? L.O.L. I'll have to watch out or I might start thinking you like, really were alive then . . ."

For a minute or so neither of us said a word while she typed more things into the computer.

Then I said, "Who supervises all of this? Surely there is no longer a ministry of Reich propaganda."

"No-one," she said. Then she probed me cautiously: "But –

you know all that, don't you? It's all part of the act, isn't it? I mean, that I've got to explain everything to you? As if you just turned up yesterday?"

"I am not accountable to you," I said, somewhat more harshly than I'd intended. "Answer my question!"

"Well," she said with a sigh. "It's all pretty unregulated . . . mein Führer. I mean, we're not in China. They censor it there."

"Good to know," I said.

xiii

I am relieved that I was not around to see the Allied Powers carve up the Reich after the war; it would have cleft my heart. On the other hand, in view of the state of the country back then, I doubt it would have made a grain of difference. Particularly as grain had been in very short supply, as I was able to glean from a variety of documents that had unquestionably been distorted by propaganda. The winter of 1946 was said to have been especially disagreeable, but I was unable to find anything bad about it: the ancient Spartan ideal of education held that relentless hardship produces the strongest children and peoples. A winter of starvation burns mercilessly in a nation's memory, and ensures that in the future it will think twice before losing another world war.

If one chooses to believe the democratic writers of history, fighting only continued for one pathetic week following my withdrawal from active politics at the end of April 1945. This is a disgrace. Dönitz called off the resistance of the Werwolf partisans, and Bormann's expensive bunker installations were never properly used. I accept that, no matter how many human lives we sacrificed, we would still have had to count on the Russians flooding Berlin with their hordes. But I had relished the prospect of reading about a catalogue of nasty surprises devised for the arrogant Americans – now, to my bitter disappointment, I learned that there had not been a single one.

A fiasco.

What I had written in 1924 had proved true once more: by the end of a major war the most valuable elements of the Volk have fallen selflessly at the front, leaving behind only the mediocre and inferior chaff, who then of course consider themselves too good or, paradoxically, even too refined to go underground and prepare a good old-fashioned bloodbath for the Americans.

And I admit to having made a mental note at this point in my deliberations. It is fascinating how, with the benefit of a certain distance, one can see things from a wholly new perspective. Having already established that the best elements of the Volk die prematurely, how could I assume that things should have been any different in this war? I therefore promised myself, "Next war: inferior specimens first!" Then, when it occurred to me that an initial offensive by inferior warriors might fail to achieve the desired outcome, I amended this mental note to "Mediocre first", then "Best first, but promptly substitute with mediocre and possibly inferior," only to add, "combine with the quite good and very good". In the end I scrubbed everything out, noted "Cleverer distribution of the good, mediocre and inferior!" and decided to postpone solving this particular problem. Contrary to what the petty-minded may assume, the Führer is not obliged to come up with answers immediately – he needs only to have them up his sleeve at the right time. And in this instance let us say that the right time would be at the outbreak of the next war.

I was only faintly surprised by the course of events that followed the miserable surrender by that moron Dönitz. The Allies did in fact squabble over the spoils as fervently as I had predicted – regrettably, however, they did not forget to divide them up. The Russians kept their share of Poland and in return for this generously gifted the Poles Silesia. Led by a group of Social Democrats, Austria broke away into neutrality. Across the rest of Germany, what were essentially puppet regimes – some well-disguised, others less so – were installed by means of democratic-looking processes, under the leadership of such characters as the former convicts Adenauer and Honecker, the corpulent economic soothsayer Erhard or – nor much of a surprise either – Kiesinger, one of those hundreds of thousands of half-hearted fellows who rushed to join the Party in 1933. I must say it gave me a certain satisfaction to read that this bandwagon-jumper was ultimately undone by his joining of the N.S.D.A.P. at the eleventh hour.

Naturally, the victors implemented their old plan of injecting the Volk with an excessive dose of federalism, to ensure perpetual discord within the nation. They created a number of states, called Bundesländer, which from the outset interfered in each other's affairs and picked to pieces all those resolutions passed by the totally inept federal parliament. The most lasting and senseless harm inflicted by this Allied policy was on my beloved Bavaria. Here, where once I had laid the foundation stone of my movement, the population revered the most cretinous thugs, who aspired to hide their sanctimonious piety and incorrigible venality by brandishing and emptying large tankards of beer. Their most honest enterprises were occasional visits to brothels.

In the north of the country, meanwhile, Social Democracy had made great headway, expanding its dominion into a vast social–romantic clubhouse, in the process happily frittering away the nation's wealth. The other characters running this republic were to my mind equally unworthy of mention; they were the usual windbags of sham parliamentary politics, the most nauseating representatives of which – as after the Great War – were appointed chancellor with the greatest urgency. Surely it was one of Destiny's special "jokes" to have selected the most boorish and doughy of these intellectual dwarves and tossed the so-called reunification of Germany into his expansive lap.

I have to concede that this supposed "reunification" was one of the few first-rate lies propagated by the republic. For how could they call it a proper reunification when essential components – such as the aforementioned Silesia granted to Poland, as well as Alsace-Lorraine or Austria – were missing? One can gauge the simple-mindedness of those monkeys in government by the fact that they were in a position to coax a few run-down square kilometres from the wavering Russians, but not a prosperous region from the French arch-enemy, which would have been a real boon for the nation.

But the greater the lie, the more readily it is believed. Out of gratitude for his heroic "reunification" deeds, that stand-in chancellor was allowed to "govern" the country for sixteen years, four years longer than I. Inconceivable. And the man looked like Göring after a double dose of barbiturates. The very sight of him was debilitating. For fifteen years I laboured hard to hone the outward appearance of a powerful party; now I discovered that one could just as easily administer this country in a cardigan. I was only pleased that Goebbels was not here to see this. The poor man would be spinning so rapidly in his grave that smoke would be pouring from the soil.

In the intervening years the French arch-enemy had become our closest friend. The fools in charge of the two countries flung their arms around each other's necks at the slightest opportunity, swearing that never again would they fight each other like real men. This steadfast resolve was cemented in a European alliance, not dissimilar to a gang of schoolboys. The gang seemed to have spent its time arguing over who should be the leader and who had to contribute the most sweets. The eastern part of the continent, meanwhile, had endeavoured to match the inanities committed by the western half, albeit with a difference: arguments were entirely absent in the east, for the be-all and end-all was to drool after the Bolshevist dictators. I felt so ill as I read this that I felt like throwing up on several occasions. The reason the West was able to waste most of its time on childish squabbling was that the American-Jewish financiers, who ruled supreme over there, took care of the more important matters. From the remaining German masses at the end of the war they had secured the services of the acquiescent Sturmbannführer, Wernher von Braun, a highly suspicious opportunist from the day he was born. True to form, he was instantly willing to sell to the highest bidder the knowledge he had gained from developing our V-2 missiles. His rockets enabled the propulsion of American weapons of world destruction and thus world domination, which confusingly led to the bankruptcy of the Judeo–Bolshevist system in the east in scarcely forty-five years. I cannot conceal the fact that, to begin with, I found this utterly baffling.

What sleight of hand was behind this?

Since when did Jew ruin Jew?

For the time being the puzzle would have to remain unsolved. What was indisputable was that, following the collapse of the Bolshevist system of rule, the German puppet regime had been handed a peace treaty as well as independence. Of course, one could hardly call it real independence without our own rocket weapons. On the contrary, governments of all shades strove not for strong armament, but for more intense involvement in European trade, which greatly simplified foreign policy; essentially there were dozens of people stipulating what you had to do – one might as well have entrusted the post to a five-year-old.

The only prevailing ideology was a wholly unchecked expansion of the juvenile alliance, which meant that almost everybody was included, even the most backward inhabitants of peripheral European regions. If you permit all and sundry to join your club then membership ceases to be anything special. Then anybody seeking to gain advantage has to start a new club within the club. Unsurprisingly, efforts in this direction had already been initiated: the stronger members were considering whether to constitute their own club, or to force out the weakest ones, which naturally made a complete mockery of the original club.

The current state of Germany painted a highly distressing picture. Running the country was a chunky woman with all the confidence and charisma of a weeping willow. She had blotted her copybook by having played along with the Bolshevist episode for thirty years, yet no-one in her entourage felt the slightest bit uneasy about this. She had joined forces with the Bavarian beer-swillers, whose party looked to me like a dismally pale imitation of National Socialism. It dressed up its half-baked, socially progressive elements not with nationalist conviction, but with an enslavement to the Vatican which was familiar from the Centre Party of old. Other holes in its programme were stuffed with alpine gun clubs and brass bands; the whole outfit was so wretched it made you want to give these fraudsters a good slap in the face.

But as their support was insufficient to form a workable government, the Eastern lady chose another group made up of clueless and directionless youths, which employed as their mascot an utterly useless foreign minister. Common to all members of this party was the fact that, with each movement the youths made, insecurity and inexperience flowed from their every pore. No sane person would trust such cowards with a box of drawing pins were there even the hint of an alternative. But none existed.

When I contemplated Social Democracy, tears welled in my eyes. I thought nostalgically of Otto Wels or Paul Löbe, unpatriotic fellows, blackguards, no question about it, but at least they were blackguards of *stature*. These days Social Democracy was led by a pushy blancmange and a petit bourgeois hen. Anybody seeking political salvation further to the left was forsaken altogether. There was not a single man on the left who knew how to smash a beer tankard against the skull of his political opponent; the leader of this pigsty was more concerned with the layers of varnish on his sports car than the needs of his supporters.

The sole ray of light in this entire democratic shambles was a splendid party which went by the name of the "Greens". It, too, had its share of unworldly, pacifist numbskulls, but even our movement had needed to offload its S.A. in 1934 – an unpleasant, but necessary affair, in which we had not exactly covered ourselves in glory, but there had been no room for Röhm in our plans. No, what was halfway gratifying about these "Greens" was that they had deep roots, although the N.S.D.A.P. could not possibly have been aware of them back in its day; nevertheless I found them admirable. After the war, major industrialisation and motorisation had caused considerable damage to the land, air, soil and Volk. The "Greens" had committed themselves to the protection of the German environment, including the Bavarian mountains for which I had developed such affection, and where German woodland had evidently suffered great harm. Their rejection of atomic energy, which was capable of such fabulous things, was utter nonsense, and particularly regrettable given that in the wake of incidents in Japan almost every party had now decided to renounce it, thereby also losing access to weapons-grade fissile material. But from a military standpoint the republic was a dead duck anyway.

Over the course of a few decades this catalogue of political failures had run down the greatest army in the world, and to such an extent that one would be tempted to line them all up against a wall. Sure, I had preached again and again that one must never finish off the East for good, that a certain element of conflict must always remain, that a healthy Volk needs a war every twenty-five years for the renewal of its blood. But what was taking place in Afghanistan was no ongoing conflict to harden the troops; it was an outright joke. The exemplary casualty figures were not – as I had at first suspected – a result of massive technological superiority, but of the fact that we had only sent a handful of men over there to begin with. One could see at first glance that, militarily, the whole affair was highly dubious; the number of troops sent was not calculated in relation to any particular goal, but – according to best parliamentary tradition – so as to avoid discontent amongst both the people and our "allies". As one might have predicted, it failed on both counts. The sole outcome of this escapade was that the soldier's heroic death, the most noble way a man can end his life, had been practically eliminated. Funeral services were held where celebrations would have been more appropriate; nowadays the German Volk thought it the most normal thing in the world for soldiers to return home from the front, and better still, unscathed!

Only one thing was gratifying: German Jewry remained decimated, even after sixty years. Around 100,000 Jews were left, a fifth of the 1933 figure – public regret over this fact was moderate, which seemed to me perfectly logical, but not entirely predictable. In view of the uproar which accompanies the disappearance of German woodland, one might have imagined a sort of Semitic "reforestation" to be possible, too. But to the best of my knowledge, new settlements and the nostalgic restoration of the past, especially beloved where buildings were concerned (e.g. the Church of Our Lady and the opera house in Dresden), had failed to materialise.

Without a doubt the creation of a state of Israel had relieved the burden to some extent. Their positioning of this state in the middle of Arabic peoples was an eminently sensible move, as it meant that for decades and centuries all parties involved would be permanently busy with each other. The consequence of the decline of the Jews – no doubt an inadvertent one – was a so-called economic miracle. Democratic history-writing has ascribed this to podgy Erhard and his Anglo-American accomplices, but any normal person can see that this prosperity went hand in hand with the disappearance of the Jewish parasites. If you still refuse to believe this you need only to take a look at the eastern half of the country, where for decades they had – such imbecility! – specifically imported Bolshevism and its Jewish teachings.

One might as well have let a troop of degenerate apes run the country; they would have done a better job. The so-called reunification had brought no improvement; at best one had the impression that apes had been swapped for other apes. There was an army of unemployed people, millions strong, and a silent anger in the population, a dissatisfaction with the prevailing circumstances which reminded me of 1930, except that back then we lacked the felicitous phrase "political apathy" – it implied that there are limits to the deception one can perpetrate against a Volk such as the Germans.

To put it another way, conditions were absolutely perfect for me. So perfect that I resolved at once to examine the international situation in greater detail. Unfortunately I was detained from my research by an urgent communication. Someone with whom I was unacquainted had turned to me with a military problem, and as I was currently without a state to govern I decided to lend my comrade my support. Thus I spent the following three and a half hours engaged in a naval exercise by the name of "Minesweeper".

At this juncture I can hear the chorus of those Reich sceptics howling, "How can the Führer of the National Socialist movement possibly take part in a telecast featuring one Ali Gagmez?" And I can well understand these doubts if they are motivated by artistic considerations, for great art must not be sullied by politics. One would never, after all, seek to embellish the Mona Lisa, not even with a swastika. But the ramblings of an emcee – and Herr Gagmez is no more than that – could never be ranked amongst the expressions of high culture, quite the opposite, in fact. If, however, the doubts are triggered by a fear that the national cause might suffer from being presented in such an inferior milieu, I must refute this by saying that there are things which most people can neither grasp nor judge simply through the application of their reason. This is one of those matters in which the people must have faith in their Führer.

Here I must confess that I was labouring under a slight misapprehension. At the time I still assumed that Madame Bellini and I would work together to implement my programme for the greater good of the German nation. In fact, all that Madame Bellini ever spoke about was my stage programme.

And this is precisely another example of how pure, innate talent – the Führer's instinct – is far and away superior to acquired knowledge. Whereas the scientist with his painstaking calculations, or the highly ambitious parliamentarian, are all too easily distracted by superficial detail, the appointed one feels the subliminal call of Destiny, even though a name like Ali Gagmez might appear to contradict this. And I do believe that Providence has intervened once more, as she did back in 1941 when the early onset of a bitterly harsh winter brought our Russian offensive to a grinding halt before we could push too far, thereby gifting us victory.

Or it would have done if my incompetent generals . . .

But I'm not going to get worked up about this anymore.

Next time I shall proceed quite differently, with a faithful and devoted general staff, bred and raised within the ranks of my S.S. Then it will be child's play.

In the case of Gagmez, on the other hand, Destiny employed misapprehension to expedite my decision. For I would have appeared on his telecast – let the hucksters take note here – even if I *had* known the true nature of the product being peddled. But only after lengthier consideration, which may have robbed me of the opportunity. Very early on I made it quite clear to Goebbels that I was prepared to play the fool if it enabled me to capture the attention of my fellow Germans. You won't win over a single soul if nobody is listening. And that Gagmez had brought me an audience that numbered in the hundreds of thousands.

From a critical perspective, Gagmez was one of those "artists" that only a bourgeois democracy can spawn.

Crossbreeding had paired a southern, even Asiatic appearance with impeccable spoken German, albeit tainted with an excruciating dialect. This combination seemed to be the very thing which made Gagmez's performance possible. It was not dissimilar to those white actors in America who blackened themselves up to win roles playing simple-minded negroes. The parallel was striking, except in this case the fare on offer was not negro jokes, but jokes about foreigners. These appeared to be in such demand that a number of racial comedians were now plying their trade. It was incomprehensible. In my eyes jokes about race or foreigners are a contradiction in themselves. A witticism related to me by a comrade in 1922 may serve to illustrate the point:

Two veterans meet.

"So where were you wounded, then?" one of them asks.

"In the Dardanelles," says the other.

"Ooh, that must be painful!" the first one replies.

A humorous misunderstanding, which any soldier can share without too much difficulty. And by substituting the characters, we can change the degree to which the joke is funny and even enlightening. It is amplified if, for example, the role of the interrogator is taken by a notorious know-all, such as Roosevelt or Bethmann-Hollweg. If, on the other hand, we assume that the brainless questioner is a silverfish, the humour vanishes at a stroke, for every listener will ask, "How can a silverfish know where the Dardanelles is?"

An idiot who does idiotic things is not funny. A good joke needs the surprise element to unfurl its didactic effect to the full. How could it strike anyone as a surprise that a Turk is a nincompoop? Of course, if there were a joke about a Turk playing the role of a brilliant scientist, then the absurdity of this alone would raise a laugh. But neither Herr Gagmez, nor any of his colleagues, told such jokes. What seemed popular in this line of work were farcical anecdotes about poorly educated foreigners who stuttered away in double Dutch. The habitual democratic duplicity of this "liberal" society was manifest: whereas tarring all foreigners with the same brush was generally frowned upon – and thus German political humorists had endlessly to separate out the different varieties – Gagmez and his dubious consorts were able to lump Indians, Arabs, Turks, Poles, Greeks and Italians all together.

I was perfectly happy with the approach, more than happy, in fact. If Herr Gagmez enjoyed a large audience, this would ensure that I, too, received widespread attention. Moreover, by the very nature of his jokes I could assume with confidence that this audience was composed predominantly of true-blooded Germans. Not, regrettably, because German viewers might harbour a particular sense of national consciousness, but because the Turks are a simple, proud people, who may well enjoy watching real burlesque, with all those clowns, but they do not like to be lectured and teased by Turkish émigrés. The Turk needs to be certain that he commands the respect and esteem of the world around him, and this is incompatible with playing the fool.

To my mind this form of humour was as pitiful as it was pointless. If you have rats in the house you don't call a clown, you call the vermin exterminators. But if that was what was necessary then it was essential for me to demonstrate from my very first appearance that an upright German has no need of foreign henchmen to help him make jokes about inferior races.

When I arrived at the studio I was approached by a young lady. She had such an athletic physique that one might have thought she was from an auxiliary unit, but since my experience with that Özlem girl, I had decided to be more cautious. The young woman was wired up to the hilt, wearing something by her mouth which must have been some kind of microphone, and gave the impression she had walked straight out of Luftwaffe control centre.

"Hello," she said, holding out her hand. "I'm Jenny. And you must be . . ." She faltered slightly. "Adolf . . . ?"

For a moment I wondered what to make of this direct, even clumsy familiarity, but nobody appeared to be shocked by it. In fact this was my first encounter with television industry jargon. As it later emerged, people here evidently believed that the broadcasting experience was similar to the common struggle in the trenches, and that henceforth one belonged to a fraternity of veterans whose members swore allegiance to each other until death, or at least until that particular programme was discontinued. Initially I found such an approach inappropriate, but in mitigation one had to consider that Jenny's generation had never had the opportunity to experience life at the front. I intended to change this in the future, but for the time being I decided to meet familiarity with familiarity and said reassuringly to the young thing, "You can call me Uncle Wolf."

She frowned momentarily and then said, "O.K., Herr . . . I mean . . . Uncle . . . will you come with me to make-up?"

"Of course," I said, following her through the broadcasting

catacombs, while she pressed her microphone to her mouth and said, "Elke, we're coming over." We made our way down the corridors in silence.

"Have you been on television before?" she asked. I got the impression that she was being slightly more reserved with me. I expect she felt awed by the Führer's aura.

"On several occasions," I said. "But rather a long time ago now."

"Right," she said. "Might I have seen you in something before?"

"I don't think so," I said. "It was also here in Berlin, at the Olympic Stadium."

"Were you the warm-up for Mario Barth?"

"What?" I asked, but she seemed no longer to be listening.

"You caught my attention straight away, that skit of yours was brilliant. I think it's amazing that you put it all together yourself. But you'll be doing something different now, won't you?"

"Something . . . quite different," I said hesitantly. "The time for games is long past . . ."

"Here we are," Fräulein Jenny said, opening a door behind which was a make-up table. "I'm going to leave you in the hands of Elke. Elke, this is . . . erm . . . Uncle Rolf."

"Wolf," I corrected her. "Uncle Wolf."

Elke, a tidy-looking woman of around forty, knitted her brow, looked at me and then at a note that lay next to her cosmetics. "I can't see any Wolf here. My list says I should have Hitler now," she smiled. Then she offered me her hand and said, "My name's Elke. What's yours, darling . . . ?"

Here once more was the familiar comradeship of the

trenches, although Frau Elke seemed a little too old for Uncle Wolf. So I settled for: "Herr Hitler."

"Right then, Herr Hitler," Frau Elke said. "Take a seat, sweetheart. Any special requests? Or should I just do as I see fit?"

"I have full confidence in you," I said, sitting down. "After all, I cannot attend to everything myself."

"You're not wrong," Frau Elke said, putting a smock over me to protect my uniform. Then she examined my face. "You've got fabulous skin, babe," she said, reaching for a powder compact. "Many people of your age just don't drink enough. You should see the complexion of some of the others I get in here . . ."

"I like to drink a lot of water," I said. "Damaging the vigour of our race is the height of irresponsibility."

Frau Elke snorted, engulfing the tiny room and the both of us in a massive cloud of powder. "Sorry about that, hon," she said. "I'll clear it up in a jiffy." Then she vacuumed away the cloud and cleaned the trousers of my uniform with a small suction device. As she was dusting off my hair, the door opened. In the mirror I could see Ali Gagmez enter the room. He coughed.

"Is the smoke mortar part of the programme?" he smirked.

"No," I said.

"It was my fault," Frau Elke said. "But we'll have him right as rain in no time." I liked that. No prevaricating, no excuses, just an unswerving acknowledgement of one's errors, and a promise to make amends for these autonomously. I never failed to find it gratifying that over the past few decades the German racial inheritance had not been fully swamped by the genetic soup of democracy.

"Excellent," Gagmez said, holding out his hand. "I hear from Frau Bellini that you come out with these firecrackers. I'm Ali."

I worked my unpowdered hand out from under the smock and shook his. Tiny avalanches trickled from my hair.

"Pleased to meet you. Hitler."

"So? How's it going, mate? Everything O.K.?"

"I think so. Frau Elke?"

"I'm almost done, pet," Frau Elke said.

"Great uniform," Gagmez said. "It looks totally authentic! Where do you pick up things like that?"

"Well, it's not that simple," I said, giving the matter some thought. "My most recent visits were usually to Josef Landolt in Munich."

"Landolt," Gagmez pondered. "Never heard of him. But Munich . . . that must be with Pro Sieben. They've got some ace costume designers."

"I expect he's retired in the meantime," I said.

"I can see it's going to work brilliantly – you with your Nazi piece, and me. Even though Nazi routines aren't exactly new."

"And?" I asked suspiciously.

"No, sure, it'll be great anyway," he said. "It always is. Not a problem, mate. Everything's been done before . . . I picked up the foreigner routine in New York, it was all the rage in the nineties. Where do you get your Führer thing from?"

"From the Germanic peoples, ultimately."

Gagmez laughed. "Bellini's right, you really carry your part through all the way. O.K., mate, see you later. Do you need a cue? Should I start on a particular subject before I introduce you?"

"That is quite unnecessary," I said.

"I couldn't do that," Gagmez said. "You know, without any sort of script. I'd be up shit creek. But I've never really had much time for improvisation . . . Anyway, mate – later." And he left the room.

In truth I had been expecting further instructions.

"What now?" I asked Frau Elke.

"Fancy that," she laughed. "I thought the Führer would know which way to go."

"There is no need for arrogance," I rebuked her. "As the Führer of the German Reich my business is to conduct the affairs of state, not tuppenny tours."

With a snort she swiftly removed the powder compact from the vicinity of her nose. "You're not getting me this time," she said, sounding somewhat cooler. She pointed to a corner of the room. "See that? You can follow the programme on the screen. There's plenty of them around the place, in wardrobe and down in the canteen. Jenny will come to collect you, to be sure you make your entrance on time."

The programme was exactly as I had expected, given what I had already seen and heard of it. Gagmez introduced a few film snippets in which he appeared as a Pole or a Turk and translated their various shortcomings into stage routines. This man was no Charlie Chaplin, but in fact that was no bad thing. The audience gave his tomfoolery a sympathetic reception, and if one stretched the concept far enough one might say that at least part of his performance had a political awareness at its core. Which meant it was incontestable that what I had to say would fall on fertile soil.

The handover was effected by means of a fixed phrase,

uttered by Gagmez without further ado: "And now, a topical piece from Adolf Hitler." And so for the first time I stepped out from the wings and into the glare of the spotlights.

It was as if I were returning home to the Sportpalast after years of hardship in a foreign land. The heat from the lights burned into my skin, I could make out the youthful faces of the audience. There may have been several hundred of them, representing the tens of thousands, the hundreds of thousands in front of their television sets. Here was the future of the Reich, here were the people with which I was going to build my Germany. I could feel the tension within me, and the joy, too. If ever I had harboured doubts, these vanished in the rapture of this build-up. I was accustomed to speaking for hours on end; now I had but five minutes.

I stepped up to the lectern and stood there without saying a word.

My gaze wandered from one side of the recording studio to the other. I listened to the silence, eager to discover whether decades of democracy had, as I expected, left behind little more than faint traces in these young minds. Laughter had erupted in the audience as my name was announced, but it quickly subsided; my physical presence unleashed a hush across the assembled crowd. From their expressions I could see that they were trying to compare my countenance with the faces of professional performers more familiar to them; I could see the uncertainty triggered by nothing more than simple eye contact in that breathless silence. My concerns about heckling were unfounded – at each and every gathering in the Hofbräukeller the reception had been more hostile.

I moved forward and readied myself to speak, but then merely crossed my arms – at a stroke the noise level dropped further by one hundred times, one thousand times even. Out of the corner of my eye I could see Gagmez the dilettante starting to sweat as he watched apparently nothing happening. I realised straight away that this man feared silence, and knew nothing of its power. His eyebrows contorted into a grimace, as if I had forgotten my script. An assistant tried to give me a sign, tapping furiously on her wristwatch. I prolonged the silence even further by slowly raising my head. The tension in the room was palpable, as was Gagmez's anxiety. I enjoyed it. I let the air flow into my lungs, straightened up and broke the silence with a barely audible sound. When everyone is listening for cannon fire, a falling pin can suffice.

"My fellow Germans!

What I,

what we

have just seen

in numerous routines,

is perfectly true.

It is true

that the Turk has no creative genius

and nor

will he ever have.

True

that he is a hawker,

a peddler,

a huckster

whose intellectual abilities

will rarely surpass those
of one of our kinsmen.
True
that the Indian
is a garrulous type
befuddled by his religion.
True
that the relationship
between the Pole and property
has been
ruined
for good!
These are all
general truths,
manifest to every fellow German,
man or woman,
needing no further
explanation.
And yet,
it is a disgrace to our nation
that here,
on German soil,
only
a Turkish! follower of our movement
dares to say these things
out loud.
My fellow Germans,
looking at our country today,
this comes as no surprise.

Germans today

keep their waste more thoroughly separated

than their races,

with one single exception.

In the field of humour.

Here,

only

the German makes jokes about Germans,

the Turk makes jokes about Turks.

The house-mouse makes jokes about the house-mouse

and

the field-mouse jokes about the field-mouse.

This has to change

and this *will* change.

From today, at 22.45,

the house-mouse will joke about the field mouse,

the badger about the deer,

and the German about the Turk.

And so

I concur fully

with the criticism of foreigners

expressed by the previous speaker."

I stepped back.

The silence was astounding.

I marched off stage. Still no sound from the audience. Madame Bellini was whispering something into a colleague's ear. I stood beside her and observed the audience once more. People's eyes were deranged; their gaze searched the stage for something to alight on, then darted back to the presenter's desk. Gagmez sat there, his mouth opening and closing like a puppet as he struggled to find a witty line with which to conclude the programme. It was this conspicuous show of impotence which set off a volley of laughter in the audience. Not without some satisfaction I watched his utter helplessness, which ultimately petered out in an indifferent "Till next time – tune in again." Madame Bellini cleared her throat. She seemed uncertain, so I decided to reassure her.

"I know what you're thinking," I told her.

"Oh?" she said. "Do you now?"

"Of course," I replied. "The same happened to me once. We had hired out the Circus Krone building and it was not clear whether—"

"Excuse me," Madame Bellini said. "That's my phone."

She retired to a corner of the backstage area and put her mobile telephone to her ear. She did not appear to like what was being said. As I was trying to make out her expression I felt a hand on my uniform. Gagmez was collaring me. His face had lost all of its earlier cheeriness. As he shoved me against the set and hissed at me through gritted teeth I was once again made painfully aware of how much I missed my S.S.

"What do you think you're playing at, you stupid prick? You and your concurring with the previous speaker can fuck right off!"

Over his shoulder I spotted some stewards rushing towards us. Gagmez pushed me against the wall again, then let go. His face was purple. Then he turned around and screamed, "What the fuck is going on here? I thought this arsehole was going to do his Nazi shit!" He turned to Hotel Reserver Sawatzki and, without lowering the volume, said, "Where is Carmen? Where? Is? Carmen?"

Pale but undiminished, Madame Bellini hurried over. I wondered whether I would be able to count on her loyalty, but could not reach a definitive conclusion. She waved her hands about in an effort to defuse the situation and opened her mouth to say something, but no words came out.

"At last! Carmen! That was one major fuck-up. Did you see it? Did you fucking well *see* it? Where did you dig up this arsehole? You said I'd do my foreigner routine and he'd follow with his Nazi crap. You said he'd disagree with me. He'd get all uptight about Turks on the telly and that sort of shit! And now *this*! What the fuck do you mean by 'follower of our movement'? *What* fucking movement? And how am I a follower? Where the fuck does that leave *me*?"

"I did tell you he was a bit different," Madame Bellini said. She had regained her composure with astonishing rapidity.

"I don't give a fuck," Gagmez frothed. "Let me tell you right here: I want this cunt off my programme *now*. He doesn't stick to his agreements. I'm not having this arsehole shit all over my programme and ruin it."

"Calm down," Madame Bellini said in a curious tone, which was at once soft and energetic. "It didn't go that badly."

"Is everything O.K.?" one of the two stewards enquired.

"Absolutely fine," Madame Bellini said, reassuring him. "I've got it all under control. Calm down, Ali."

"I'm not going to fucking well calm down," Gagmez howled, and then dug his index finger under my shoulder strap.

148

"You are *not* going to fuck me over, matey," he said, hammering repeatedly on my chest with his finger like a woodpecker. "You think you can just swan up here with your ridiculous Hitler uniform and your oh-so-fucking inscrutable manner. But let me tell you: it's nothing new; it's old fucking hat. You're an amateur. What the fuck do you think you're doing here? You turn up and think you've got it all sewn up. But you're not going anywhere, matey, you can fucking kiss this one goodbye! If there's anyone here who's got followers, it's me! This is *my* audience, those are *my* fans – keep your filthy little hands off! You are a pathetic amateur. Your uniform and your routine – it's all a heap of shit. With that toss you might be able to do the odd beer tent or rifle club, but let me tell you: you're never going to be anybody."

"I have no need," I said calmly. "Behind me are millions of fellow Germans, who—"

"Cut the crap," Gagmez shrieked. "You're not on the fucking telly now! Do you think you can wind me up? You're not going to wind me up! Not! Me!!"

"Cool it, both of you," Bellini said, now raising her voice. "Sure, we need to work at it a bit. There's still a little fine-tuning to be done. But it wasn't that bad. Just something new. Now, let's all calm down and wait and see what the critics say . . ."

If I had ever felt certain of my calling since my reappearance in this modern epoch, it was at this moment.

It is in times of crisis that the true Führer is revealed. When he shows his nerve, persistence and sheer determination, though the world be set against him. If I had not been at Germany's helm, nobody would have marched into the Rhineland in 1936. They were all quivering in their boots; there was nothing we could have done if the enemy had decided to attack. We had five divisions at the ready; the French alone had six times as many. And yet I risked it. Nobody else would have dared, and at the time I watched carefully to see who was standing by me, with their feet or their heart, side by side, sword in hand.

It is also in those times of crisis that Destiny reveals the true loyalists. Those moments of doubt when a hazardous venture gives rise to success if – but only if – the fanatical belief remains unbroken. The occasions when one can identify those who lack this belief, but who watch the situation unfold in uneasy expectation, to determine on which side they should fight. A Führer must keep a close eye on these people. Although they can be manipulated, one must never make the success of the movement dependent on them. Sensenbrink was one of their ilk.

Sensenbrink was wearing what these days would probably be called a high-quality suit. He was trying to look casual, but

I could see that he was pale; his face exhibited the pallor of a gambler who knows that he cannot suffer a loss, or worse still, he cannot bear the moment in which it becomes obvious that his loss is inevitable. Such people never focus on their own goal, they always elect to pursue the goal which promises the most rapid success, and yet fail to recognise that this success will never be their own. They hope to achieve success, but they will only ever chaperone it, and because they sense this, they fear the moment of defeat when it becomes manifest that not only is the success not their own, but it is not even dependent on their chaperoning. Sensenbrink was anxious about his reputation, not the national cause. It was patently clear that Sensenbrink would never shed blood for Germany or me in a hail of bullets outside the beer hall in Munich. On the contrary: how winsomely he consorted with Madame Bellini – anyone with half an eye could see that in spite of all his puffed-up self-confidence, he was the one hoping for her moral support. This came as no surprise.

In my life I have met four dominant women. Women who would be unthinkable as a choice of partner. Let us say you have Mussolini or Antonescu over for a visit. If you then tell one of these women to go into the room next door and not come back until invited to, you need to be sure that this is what is going to happen. Eva did it, but I could never have asked it of any of those four. Leni Riefenstahl was one of them. A wonderful woman, but if I had made such a request to Leni she would have smashed me over the head with her camera! And Madame Bellini was of the same calibre as this venerable quartet.

I do not think that anyone besides me noticed how she, too, was aware of the significance of these hours, these minutes. But – my goodness! – this fantastic woman had exceptional control. I noticed she inhaled a touch more deeply on her cigarette than usual, but that was all. She held her wiry, lithe body upright, she was attentive, always prepared to offer helpful instructions, and her reactions were precise and rapid, like a skulking wolf. And not a single grey hair; perhaps she was even younger than I had thought, late thirties – a truly magnificent specimen of womanhood! I also intuited that she found the sudden prox-imity of Sensenbrink disagreeable, not because she found him bothersome, no, but because she despised his unmanliness, because she sensed that rather than putting all his strength at her disposal he was draining her of energy. I felt an enormous urge to ask her how she was planning to spend the evening, and with a certain melancholy I suddenly recalled those evenings on the Obersalzberg. Many a time we would sit up long into the night – three, four, five of us. Sometimes I would talk, some-times not. In fact, sometimes hours would pass in silence, interrupted only by the occasional cough. At other times I would just stroke the dog. I always found these gatherings rather conducive to contemplation. Things are not always easy; the Führer is one of the few people in the state who has to forgo the simple pleasures of normal family life.

And life in a hotel like mine *was* rather lonely; this was one of the aspects of my existence which had changed least over the last sixty years.

Then it occurred to me that in my situation I really ought to ask Madame Bellini, but somehow this felt inappropriate, too familiar, especially as we had not known each other long. I decided to push the thought to the back of my mind. On the other hand, I felt it would only be fitting to have a small celebration to mark my return to public life. Just a glass of sparkling wine or something similar, not for me of course, but I always enjoyed being in the company of others in high spirits who raised a toast. My gaze alighted on Hotel Reserver Sawatzki.

His eyes beamed at me, they were full of unmistakable esteem. I knew this look, one which should not be interpreted the wrong way. Sawatzki was not one of those men in an S.A. shirt, whom one drags from Röhm's bed in the night and then into whose repulsive body one fires a few bullets in disgust, saving the fatal one until last. No, Sawatzki looked at me with a sort of silent reverence, which I had last witnessed in Nuremberg in those hundreds of thousands to whom I had offered hope. Who had grown up in a world of humiliations and fear for the future, a world of procrastinating windbags and war losers, who in me saw the firm hand which would lead them, and who were willing to follow me.

"So," I said, wandering over to Sawatzki. "Did you enjoy it?"

"Unbelievable," Sawatzki said. "Really impressive. I've seen Ingo Appelt, but he's lame compared to you. You've got balls. Do you really not care what people think of you?"

"On the contrary, young man," I said. "I will speak the truth. And they should think: Here is someone who speaks the truth."

"And? Is that what they're thinking now?"

"No. But they are thinking in a different way from before.

153

Sensenbrink eagerly filled glasses with sparkling wine, while Sawatzki returned and handed me a glass of something the colour of apricots.

"What is this?"

"Just try it," he said, raising his glass. "Guys: To the Führer!"

"To the Führer!"

There was sympathetic and jubilant laughter all around and I had a keen struggle to fend off all the congratulations offered to me. "Please, ladies and gentlemen, we still have much work to do!" Cautiously I took a sip of the drink and gave Herr Sawatzki an appreciative nod. It tasted very fruity, was a delight to the palate and yet was not of such overblown complexity. Essentially it seemed to be a simple country-style fruit pulp, enlivened by a little sekt, but only a drop so that having enjoyed the drink one need not fear excessive hiccoughing or similar aggravations. The significance of such details is not to be underestimated; in a situation like mine, one must always take care to behave impeccably.

What I find disagreeable about these informal, yet important gatherings, is that one cannot simply retire when one would like, unless one is waging war at the same time. If one is busy executing the Manstein Plan in northern France, or if one is launching a surprise attack to occupy Norway, then everybody is full of understanding, quite naturally. As they are if one retires to one's study after the toast to look over U-boat designs or help develop high-speed bombers crucial to our final victory. In peacetime, however, one just stands around wasting one's time drinking fruit pulp. Sensenbrink's raucous manner was increasingly testing my nerves, while Gagmez's sour face did not make the evening any more congenial. So I excused myself, temporarily at least, to fetch myself something from the buffet.

An assortment of sausages was being served in heated, rectangular tin vessels, as well as an array of roast meats and large quantities of noodles, none of which particularly appealed to me. I was about to turn away when Sawatzki appeared at my side.

"Is there something I can get you?"

"No, no, don't worry . . ."

"Damn it!" Sawatzki said, slapping his forehead. "You're looking for the stew, aren't you?"

"No, I can . . . take one of these sandwiches . . ."

"But you'd prefer stew, wouldn't you? The Führer loves simple food!"

"That would indeed be my choice," I admitted. "Or something without meat."

"I'm really sorry, we didn't catch on early enough," he said. "I should have thought. But if you wait a moment . . ."

He pulled out his mobile telephone and tapped at it with his fingers.

"Can your telephone cook, too?"

"No," he said. "But ten minutes from here there's a restaurant which is well known for its honest fare and stews. If you like I can order something from there."

"Please refrain from going to any trouble. I quite fancy a bit of a stroll anyway," I said. "I can have the stew there."

"If you don't mind, I'll take you there myself," Sawatzki said. "It's not far."

We absconded from the party and walked through the chilly Berlin night. This was far more agreeable than standing around in that canteen where an entire division of broadcasting types were incessantly lavishing praise on each other. Every so often our feet kicked up a few leaves.

"Can I ask you something?" Sawatzki said.

"Please do."

"Is it a coincidence? I mean, that you're a vegetarian too?"

"Absolutely not," I said. "It's common sense. I have been one for so long, it was only a matter of time before others shared my conviction. It's just those buffet cooks who don't seem to have heard of it."

"No, what I meant was: have you always been one, or only since you became Hitler?"

"I have always been Hitler. Who do you imagine I was before that?"

"Well, maybe you tried a few others first. Churchill, or Honecker."

"Himmler believed in all that esoteric humbug, reincarnation and mysticism. I can assure you I was never that Honecker fellow."

Sawatzki looked at me. "And don't you ever think you take your art too far?"

"One must undertake everything with utter, fanatical determination. Or one will get nowhere."

"But – just to take an example – no-one would notice whether you were really a vegetarian or not."

"First," I said, "it is a question of well-being. And second, there can be no doubt that this is the way nature desires it.

Look, a lion can run two or three kilometres before it is completely exhausted. Twenty minutes, not even – a quarter of an hour. A camel, on the other hand, can keep going for a week. It's the food which does that."

"A nice example of sophistry."

I stopped and glared at him. "What do you mean, 'sophistry'? Right, let's put it another way then. Where is Stalin?"

"Dead, I'd say."

"I see. And Roosevelt?"

"Same."

"Pétain? Eisenhower? Antonescu? Horthy?"

"The first two are dead, and I haven't heard of the others."

"Well, they're dead too. And what about me?"

"You're not dead."

"Precisely," I said with satisfaction, and set off again. "And I am convinced that this is because I'm a vegetarian."

Sawatzki laughed. Then he caught me up. "That's really good. Don't you write that sort of stuff down?"

"Why bother? I know it."

"I'm always worried that I'll forget these things," he said, pointing to the door of a restaurant. "Here we are."

We entered the half-empty restaurant and placed our order with an elderly waitress. She gave me a hard stare and then screwed up her face in confusion. Sawatzki gave her a reassuring wave, and the lady went to fetch the drinks without further ado.

"It's nice here," I said. "It reminds me of the time of my struggle in Munich."

"Do you come from Munich?"

"No, from Linz. Or actually . . ."

". . . or actually from Braunau," Sawatzki said. "I've been doing a bit of reading up."

"Where do you come from?" I asked him in return. "And how old are you, by the way? You cannot be thirty yet!"

"Twenty-seven," Sawatzki said. "I come from Bonn, and I studied in Cologne."

"A Rhinelander," I said with delight. "And an educated Rhinelander to boot!"

"German and History. In fact I wanted to be a journalist."

"It's a good thing you aren't one," I asserted. "Lying vermin, through and through."

"The T.V. industry isn't much better," he said. "It's unbelievable, the crap they churn out. And whenever we get hold of anything good, the stations would rather have another pile of crap. Or something cheaper. Or both." Without pausing he added, "Apart from you, of course. What you do is completely different. For the first time I get the feeling that we're not just flogging any old rubbish. I love your approach. The vegetarianism and everything – you're not faking it; somehow, with you, it's part of the whole concept."

"I prefer the term ideology," I said, but I was overjoyed by his youthful enthusiasm.

"You know, this has been something I've always wanted to do," Sawatzki said. "Not just tout any old thing, but something of quality. At Flashlight we have to peddle so much garbage. Listen, when I was a boy I always wanted to work in an animal sanctuary. Help poor animals, that sort of thing. Or save animals. Do something positive."

160

The waitress placed two bowls of stew before us. I was quite touched; the stew looked excellent. And it smelled as a stew ought to. We began to eat, and for a while neither of us said a word.

"Good?" Sawatzki asked.

"Very good," I said, spooning it from the bowl. "As if it were straight from the field mess."

"Yes," he said. "There's something about it. Simple, but good."

"Are you married?"

He shook his head.

"Engaged?"

"No," he said. "More like interested. There is someone."

"But?"

"She doesn't have a clue. And I don't know if she's interested in me, either."

"You must be bold and go all out for total victory. You are not shy otherwise."

"Sure, but she . . ."

"No wavering. Onward, quick march. Women's hearts are like battles. They are not won through hesitation. One must concentrate all one's forces and deploy them gallantly."

"Is that how you got to know your wife?"

"Well, I could never complain about a lack of female interest. But my approach was generally the other way around."

"The other way around?"

"In the later years especially I won more battles than women."

He laughed. "If you're not going to write it down, I will. If you go on in this vein you really should think about writing a book. Hitler's how-to book. How to have a happy relationship."

"I am not sure that is my calling," I said. "I mean, my marriage was rather short."

"So I've heard. But that doesn't matter. We'll call it *Mein Kampf – With My Wife*. With a title like that it would sell like hot cakes."

I had to laugh too. I looked pensively at Sawatzki, his short hair sticking up cheekily, his alert expression, his buoyant, but by no means foolish words. And in his voice I perceived that this man could have been one of those who accompanied me back then. To prison, to the Reich Chancellery, to the Führerbunker.

XVI

"Ah, Herr Hitler, I've been expecting you!" the newspaper seller said in an enigmatically theatrical voice.

"Really?" I said, amused. "Why?"

"Well, I saw your performance," he said, "and then I reckoned you'd want to read what's been written about you. And that you might look for a place where the selection of papers and magazines is – how should I put it? – a little broader! Come in, come in! Take a seat. Would you like a coffee? What's wrong? Don't you feel well?"

I found it disconcerting that he had spotted this minor weakness in me, and it really was a minor weakness, a surge of joy, the like of which I had not experienced in a long time. I had woken as fresh as a daisy at around half past eleven, partaken of a small breakfast and then decided to read the newspapers, just as the vendor had guessed. Two days previously my suits had been delivered, allowing me something somewhat less official to slip into. The one I was now wearing was simple, dark and traditionally cut, and I had chosen to pair it with the dark hat. As I set off from the hotel I could see at once that I was attracting many fewer glances than usual. It was a crystal-clear, sunny day and wonderfully fresh, as one might expect for the time of year. For now I felt free of all obligations and I marched forth with a sense of purpose. It was so peaceful, it almost felt normal, and because I took the green route along footpaths and through parks there was little to grab my attention, save for a madwoman who was bending down, obviously trying to pinpoint and then gather up her spaniel's excrement in the long, unmown grass. It struck me briefly that this lunacy might be the result of an epidemic, but nobody appeared to be surprised by what she was doing. On the contrary, as I discovered soon afterwards, dispensing machines had been thoughtfully installed here and there, from which these madwomen were able to draw lots of small bags. The provisional conclusion I reached was that these must be women whose fervent wish to have a child had remained unfulfilled, giving rise to a form of hysteria which presented itself in this disproportionate care for all manner of dogs. And I had to concede that providing the poor creatures with bags was an astonishingly pragmatic solution. In the longer term, of course, these women ought to be steered back to their proper duties, but I expect that some party or other had opposed this. It's all too familiar.

My mind full of these less than demanding deliberations, I walked uninterrupted to the kiosk; indeed I was scarcely recognised at all. The situation felt curiously familiar, but it was not until I heard the words of the newspaper seller that I understood why. It was that magical atmosphere I had frequently experienced in those early days in Munich, after my release from prison. I was fairly well known in the city, but at the time I was still a minor party chairman, a speaker who could see into

164

people's hearts. And it was the little people, the littlest people, who, touchingly, lent me their support. I would cross the Viktualienmarkt, where the poorest of the market women would smile and beckon me over, offering me a couple of eggs or a pound of apples. I went home like a veritable forager, to be greeted by a beaming landlady. Their faces used to radiate the same pure joy that I recognised now in the newspaper vendor. This impression of the past washed over me so quickly, before I could even grasp what it was; it was so overwhelming that I had to look away hurriedly. But on account of his long professional experience, the newspaper seller had acquired an impressive understanding of his fellow man such as one might otherwise only find in motor-cab drivers.

I let out an embarrassed cough and said, "No coffee for me, thank you. But I'd love a cup of tea. Or a glass of water."

"Your wish is my command," he said, filling a kettle like the one in my hotel room. "I've put the papers by your chair. There aren't many of them; I think the Internet's the best place to look."

"Yes, this Internetwork," I said in agreement. "A splendid facility. And nor do I believe that my success will be dependent on the goodwill of the newspapers."

"I don't want to spoil your enjoyment," the newspaper seller said, fetching a tea bag from a shelf. "But there's no need to worry . . . Those who saw it seemed to like you."

"I have no worries," I said confidently. "What is the opinion of a critic worth?"

"Well . . ."

"Nothing," I said. "Nothing at all! It counted for nothing in the Thirties and it counts for nothing now. All they ever do is tell people what to think. The wholesome sensibility of the Volk is in no way inferior. Indeed, the Volk instinctively knows what to think, even without our noble critics. A wholesome Volk has a perfectly clear sense of what is good and what is not. Does the farmer need a critic to tell him how good the soil is in which he cultivates his wheat? No! The farmer himself knows better."

"Because he sees his fields every day," the newspaper seller chirped in. "But he doesn't see you every day."

"But he does see his television set every day, so he can make his own judgements. No, the German needs no-one to draft opinions for him. He forms his own opinion."

"Well, you should know," he said with a grin, offering me the sugar. "I mean, you're the expert on forming one's own opinions."

"What is that supposed to mean?"

"I really have to watch out with you," the newspaper seller said, shaking his head. "I can't help talking to you as if you really *were* him." A hand rapped on the sales counter behind him. "I've got customers. Have a read of what the papers say. There's not that much."

I looked at the small pile by the chair. I did not feature on their front pages, but I couldn't have supposed that would be the case. Nor had any of the major newspapers addressed the topic. For example, that formidable *Bild* was not amongst the pile. Seeing as Gagmez's programme had been running for a while now, the press were probably no longer all that interested. In the end it was only covered by the smaller regional papers, which commissioned writers to watch the television set every day in order to compile a short column. Three of these writers had switched on to the programme hoping to be entertained, and all were of the opinion that my speech had been the most noteworthy feature. One found it astonishing that of all people it was a Hitler figure who had identified exactly what Gagmez was serving up every week: a mass of clichés about foreigners. The other two said that, thanks to my "splendidly wicked performance", Gagmez had finally rediscovered his edge, which had been missing for far too long.

"So?" the newspaper seller said. "Happy?"

"I started from the very bottom once before," I said, sipping my tea. "Back then I spoke to an audience of twenty. I suspect a third of them had come by accident. No, I cannot complain. I must look to the future. How did you find it?"

"Good," he said. "Hard core, but good. Gagmez didn't look too thrilled, though."

"Indeed," I said. "It's something I have come across before. Those drunk on success always cry foul whenever a fresh idea makes its mark. At once they start fretting about their livelihood."

"Is he going to let you back on his programme?"

"He will do whatever the production company tells him. He lives off the system; he must follow its rules."

"I can hardly believe it's only been a few weeks since I picked you up off the ground outside my kiosk," the newspaper vendor said.

"The rules are the same as they were sixty years ago," I said. "They never change. The only difference is that there are fewer

Jews to worry about. And so the Volk is in better shape. By the way, I haven't thanked you properly. Did they . . . ?"

"Don't worry," the newspaper seller said. "We came to an agreement. I've been looked after." Then his portable telephone rang. He lifted the device to his ear. I picked up a copy of *Bild* and leafed through it. The newspaper projected a combination of anger and hatred, starting with reports of political ineptitude and building a picture of a clueless, but ultimately benign matron chancellor, shuffling awkwardly through a horde of obstructive dwarfs. Meanwhile, virtually every political decision "legitimated" by democracy was debunked as poppycock. This admirable smear-sheet reserved especial venom for the idea of European union, which it found utterly repellent. But what I liked best of all was its subtle mode of operation. For example, I found the following in a humorous column between jokes about mothers-in-law and cuckolded husbands:

A Portuguese, a Greek and a Spaniard go into a brothel. Who pays?

Germany.

Very, very funny. Of course Streicher would have commissioned a drawing to accompany it, portraying three unshaven, oily southerners pawing at an innocent little thing, while the honest German worker grafts away in the background. On balance, however, that would have spoiled the joke's subtlety.

Otherwise, a colourful hotchpotch of criminal tales filled the pages, followed by that category of reporting which has always been the most effective form of appeasement – sport. And then a collection of photographs showing famous people looking ancient or ugly, a full-blown symphony of envy, resentment and malice. For this very reason I would have been pleased if a brief notice of my appearance had found its way into these pages. But the newspaper seller had been correct not to include *Bild* in his pile; it made no mention of me. I lowered the paper when he put his telephone away.

"That was my son," he said. "The one whose shoes you didn't like. He asked whether you were the bloke from my kiosk. He saw you. On his mate's mobile. He said you were absolutely unreal."

I looked at the newspaper vendor blankly.

"He thinks you're brilliant," the man translated. "I dread to think what kinds of films they've got on their mobiles, but you can be sure they don't watch anything they find dull."

"The sensibilities of young people are unadulterated," I declared. "For them there is no good or bad, they merely think instinctively. If a child is raised correctly, he will never come to make a bad decision."

"Do you have children?"

"Unfortunately not," I said. "I mean, rumours were occasionally spread by those with an interest in the matter that there were some 'off the record', as we say in our neck of the woods."

"I get it," the newspaper seller said cheerfully, lighting a cigarette. "Was it a question of maintenance, then?"

"No, they wanted to ruin me, turn me into a laughing stock. Since when has it been wrong or dishonourable to give a child the gift of life?"

"Try telling that to the ultra conservatives."

"Agreed, one must always take the simple people into

account. You can concoct whatever arguments you like, but for many people it will be one step too far. Himmler tried it once, in the S.S. He wanted to institute the same rights for legitimate and illegitimate children, but it didn't work, not even there. Regrettably so – the poor children. Small boys, little girls, they suffer disapproving glances, they get teased, the other children dance around them, singing cruel songs. And this is damaging to the national spirit, the sense of community. We are all of us Germans, the legitimate as well as the illegitimate. I always say: Children are children, whether in the cot or in the trenches. Of course, one must provide for them. But only the most despicable Schweinehund would do a runner."

I put *Bild* back in its rack.

"So, how did it end up?"

"Nothing. It was pure slander, of course. And nothing ever came of it."

"There you go," the newspaper seller said, sipping his tea.

"I have no idea whether the Gestapo took the matter in hand at any stage, but I'm sure that won't be necessary anymore."

"Probably not. I mean, you brought the press into line, didn't you?" he said, laughing, as if he had cracked a joke.

"Precisely," I nodded. Then "The Ride of the Valkyries" rang out.

Fräulein Krömeier had set it up for me. After we brought the computer into service, we established that the quartermaster had also supplied me with one of those portable telephones. The device was an unbelievable affair, moreover one could use it to navigate this Internetwork, and even more efficiently than with the mouse tool – one steered with one's fingers. I realised at once that I held in my hands a masterpiece of Aryan creative genius, and all it took was a few swipes of the finger to discover that – of course – the superlative Siemens company had been responsible for the technology which brought this miracle to pass. Fräulein Krömeier had to undertake the finger movements for me, as I was unable to decrypt the visual display without spectacles. I wanted to sign the whole thing over to her; after all, the Führer cannot concern himself with too much bric-a-brac, that is what the secretariat is for. Quite correctly, however, she reminded me that I could only be reliant on her labour for half of each day. I rebuked myself for having become too dependent on my party machine. Finding myself again at square one, I would have to confront this contraption myself, for better or for worse.

"Any particular ringtone?" Fräulein Krömeier had asked me.

"Certainly not," I replied sardonically. "After all, I don't work in an open-plan office!"

"So, I'll just give you like, the normal one?"

I then heard a noise which sounded like a drunken clown playing the xylophone. Over and over again.

"What the devil is that?" I asked, horrified.

"That's your phone?" Fräulein Krömeier said, adding, "Mein Führer!"

"And it sounds like *that*?"

"Only when it rings."

"Switch it off! I don't want people taking me for an imbecile!"

"That's why I asked you?" Fräulein Krömeier said. "D'you prefer this one?"

More clowns playing diverse instruments.

"That's appalling," I groaned.

"But I thought you didn't care what people thought of you?"

"My dear Fräulein Krömeier," I said. "Personally I consider short lederhosen to be the most masculine trousers a man can wear. And when, one day, I am once again commander-in-chief of the Wehrmacht, I will supply an entire division with these short trousers. And woollen stockings."

At this point Fräulein Krömeier made an outlandish noise and wiped her nose.

"I know," I continued. "You do not hail from southern Germany; you cannot understand my way of thinking. Just wait until this division is standing there, on parade, then it will become clear that all those jokes about leather shorts are base-less. But – and now I am coming to the point – on my path to power I was forced to acknowledge that industrialists and statesman do not take politicians in these trousers seriously. It is one of my greatest regrets to have abandoned the short trousers, but I did it because it served my cause and thus the cause of the German Volk. And let me tell you, I did not relin-quish these wonderful trousers only for a telephone set to render my sacrifice worthless and leave me looking like a total moron! So don't just stand there; find me a sensible ring."

"That's why I like, asked you?" Fräulein Krömeier sniffed, putting away her handkerchief. "I can leave it so it's like a normal phone? But I can get you any other sound you like, like. Words, sounds, music . . ."

"Music, too?"

"If I don't have to play it myself. It would have to be like, on a . . . a . . . record!"

So then she set up "The Ride of the Valkyries" for me.

"Good, isn't it?" I said to the newspaper seller, confidently raising the device to my ear "Hitler here!"

I could hear nothing but Valkyries riding forth.

"Hitler!" I said. "Hitler here!" And when the Valkyries continued to ride I tried "Führer headquarters!" Just in case the caller was in shock at having got through to me personally. Nothing happened save for the Valkyries getting louder. By now my ear was truly hurting.

"HITLER HERE," I screamed. "FÜHRER HEADQUAR-TERS!" It felt as if I were back on the Western Front in 1915.

"Press the green button!" the newspaper seller said plain-tively. "I can't stand Wagner!"

"Which green button?"

"That thing on your phone," he cried. "You have to swipe it to the right."

I looked at the machine, where indeed I could see a green slider. I pushed it to the right, the Valkyries fell silent, and I shouted, "HITLER HERE! FÜHRER HEADQUARTERS!"

Nothing. The newspaper vendor rolled his eyes, took my hand together with the telephone and gently guided it to my ear.

"Herr Hitler?" I could hear the voice of Hotel Reserver Sawatzki. "Hello? Herr Hitler?"

"Yes," I said. "Hitler here!"

"I've been trying to get hold of you for ages. Frau Bellini wanted you to know that the company is really happy!"

"Well," I said, "that is nice. But I had expected somewhat more."

"More?" Sawatzki asked, confused.

"My dear Herr Sawatzki," I said dismissively, "three newspaper articles are all well and good, but we do have greater goals . . ."

"Newspaper articles?" Sawatzki roared. "Who's talking about newspaper articles? You've made it onto YouTube. And you're getting endless hits!" Then he lowered his voice and said, "Just between you and me, some people here wanted to drop you right after the show. I'm not going to name names. But just take a look! Young people love you!"

"The sensibilities of young people are unadulterated," I said.

"And that's why we've got to produce some new stuff straight away," Sawatzki said excitedly. "They're extending your slot. They want to do some short clips, too! You have to come to the office right away! Where are you?"

"At the kiosk," I said.

"Great," Sawatzki said. "Stay right there, a taxi's on its way!" He hung up.

"So?" the newspaper seller asked. "Good news?"

I held out my telephone. "Can you use this to get to something which goes by the name of U-Tube?"

xvii

What had happened was this. By means of some technical appliance, someone had taken a recording of my appearance on Gagmez's programme and inserted it into the Internetwork, in a place where everyone could exhibit their short films. And everybody could watch whatever they wanted, without being dictated to by the Jewish gutter press. The Jews could offer up their pitiful efforts here too, but one could see directly what was happening: the Volk was watching my appearance with Gagmez over and over again. You could tell this from a figure beneath the film clip.

Now, I do not place undue faith in statistics. I have had sufficient experience of party comrades and industrialists to know that careerists and other shady characters lurk everywhere, always happy to lend a hand when they can present "figures" in a positive light. They embellish them, or compare them with another figure which makes their own look very attractive, while suppressing a dozen other statistics which would reveal a far less favourable reality. For this reason I decided to address the task myself, and I checked the figures of some Jewish submissions. I even bit the bullet — one cannot be squeamish in these matters — and looked at the figures for that

Chaplin film, "The Great Dictator". Yes, the number of visitors here stretched into seven figures, but one had to put this into its proper context. After all, Chaplin's cheap and shoddy effort was more than seventy years old, which translated into approximately 15,000 visitors per year. Still not an inconsiderable sum, but only on paper, of course. For one would have to assume a gradual decrease in interest. It is only natural that human curiosity for current events should be greater than that for dusty old goods. Especially in a case like this: a black-and-white production, whereas people these days are used to technicolour. One may thus assume that this film must have attracted most of its Internetwork visitors in the 1960s and '70s. These days there could only be around a hundred per year at most, very likely film students, some rabbis and other such "specialist viewers". Over the past three days I had easily surpassed this figure by a thousand times or more.

I found it all very interesting, for one specific reason in particular.

Until that point my most positive experiences with public enlightenment and propaganda had been with methods considerably different from those employed today. I had worked with columns of S.A. Brownshirts, who waved flags from the backs of lorries as they drove through the city, smashing their fists into the faces of Bolshevist Red Front fighters, cracking their skulls with clubs and, with my full support, also trying to kick some sense with their jackboots into these bone-headed communists. Now I observed that evidently the mere attraction of an idea, a speech, could induce hundreds of thousands to watch and engage in intellectual debate. In truth, this was very hard to understand. It was even plain impossible. Something was niggling away at me, a hunch, if not a fear, so I immediately called Sensenbrink. He was in great spirits.

"Have you seen the figures?" he rejoiced. "You've just hit 700,000, and the numbers are going north all the time. It's madness. You're out of the ballpark."

"Indeed," I said, not quite understanding everything he had said. "But I find your delight quite overblown. It can't possibly make any sense!"

"What? What do you mean? You're our golden goose, old chap! Believe you me, this is just the launchpad. It's a game changer, a paradigm shift."

"But you still have to pay all the people!"

"Which people?"

"I was myself in charge of propaganda for a while. And I know that to bring 700,000 people over to your side you need 10,000 men. And they have to be fanatical."

"Ten thousand men? What ten thousand men?"

"Ten thousand stormtroopers, theoretically. And that's a conservative estimate. But I don't imagine you have an S.A. yet, do you? So you will need at least 15,000."

"You really are a few sandwiches short of a picnic," Sensenbrink said. I had no idea what he was going on about, although he sounded cheerful enough. I couldn't be sure, but I thought I heard glasses clinking in the background. "But watch out, one day someone's going to take you seriously!" And he hung up.

And so the matter appeared resolved. Sensenbrink clearly had nothing to do with it. The endorsement seemed to be from the Volk itself. Sensenbrink could have been an unscrupulous liar, of course, a charlatan; these doubts still lingered, which is precisely the risk one faces when one has not hand-picked one's subordinates oneself. But overall he seemed to be a trustworthy fellow. And so I embarked on the production of additional material for the programme.

As always when people are overtaxed creatively, they come up with the most dubious suggestions. I was to film bizarre reports such as "The Führer pays a visit to the bank" or "The Führer at the swimming pool". I dismissed such claptrap out of hand. Having to watch politicians engage in sport is little more than an embarrassment for the Volk. My sporting activities were brought to a swift conclusion after my takeover of power. Football players, dancers – they are the ones people want to see, executing their moves to perfection. Their disciplines may even rise to the height of great art. In athletics, for example, a consummate javelin throw is a magnificent sight to behold. But then imagine that someone like Göring comes along, or that matron chancellor. Who would want to watch either of those two whales attempt the sprint hurdles? It would not be a pretty sight.

Of course there are some who will argue, "She ought to show the Volk that she's a dynamic leader. For this she need not venture into show jumping or rhythmic gymnastics, but rather something more harmless, such as golf. Surely that would be feasible." Such would be the discussion in conservative anglophile circles. But anybody who has seen golf played to a high standard would certainly not want to watch a shapeless old trout fiddling about for hours on the course. And what are the

178

other statesmen to say? In the mornings she painstakingly follows the intricacies of economic policy; in the afternoons she is out on the golf course, taking ungraceful swipes at the turf. And as for appearing in swimming trunks – well, that is the most preposterous thing imaginable. You couldn't dissuade Mussolini from doing it. And more recently that suspect Russian leader has been doing it too. An interesting fellow, no question, but as far as I am concerned it is a foregone conclusion: the moment a politician removes his shirt, his policies are dead in the water. All he will say is, "Look, my dear fellow countrymen, I have made the most extraordinary discovery: my policies look better without a shirt on."

What sort of nonsensical proposition is that?

I have even read that a German war minister was lately photographed with a wench in a swimming pool. While his troops were in the field, or at least preparing for deployment. Had I been in charge, this would have been the gentleman's last day in office. I wouldn't have bothered with a letter of resignation – you lay a pistol on his desk, a bullet in the chamber, you leave the room, and if the blackguard has an ounce of decency he knows what he has to do. And if not, the following morning the bullet's in his brain, and he's face down in the pool. Then everyone else in the ministry knows what to expect if you stab your troops in the back while wearing swimming trunks.

No, bathing larks were out of the question as far as I was concerned.

"So, what do you want to do instead, if that's not up your street?"

This question was fired at me by one Ulf Bronner, an

assistant director, in his mid-thirties perhaps, and a strikingly ill-dressed man. Still, he was not kitted out as shabbily as the cameramen; through my recent work for and with broadcasting companies I have discovered that they are the scruffiest-looking individuals in any form of employment, outdone only by press photographers. I have no idea why it should be thus, but as far as I can make out press photographers seem to wear the ragged cast-offs of television cameramen. Perhaps they imagine that nobody will ever see them, because after all the camera is in front of their faces. Whenever I come across an unflattering picture of someone in a magazine – they may be grimacing or similar – I frequently wonder what the photographer must have looked like. This Bronner fellow was better dressed than that, but not much.

"I deal with politics," I said. "As well as with issues that extend beyond politics."

"How on earth is that meant to be funny?" Bronner grumbled. "All politics is crap. But it's not my show, is it?"

Over the years I have learned that fanatical belief in the common cause is not always essential. And in some matters it can even be a hindrance. I have seen directors who for art's sake were incapable of producing a comprehensible film. Ultimately I preferred Bronner's indifference; at least it allowed me a pretty free hand when it came to pillorying the woeful achievements of the democratically elected political representatives. And as one should always simplify things where possible, I plumped for the most elementary topic – literally so. I began one morning by standing outside a kindergarten, next door to the unconventional school I had by now passed on many an occasion. Time and again I had observed the irresponsible behaviour of automobile drivers, who raced past at high speed, carelessly putting at risk the lives and wellbeing of our children. In a brief speech I launched a brutal attack on this speeding frenzy, then we took some film of these asinine would-be child murderers, which could later be cut into the programme. The reactions we elicited were extraordinary.

"Are you doing that hidden camera programme?"

"Absolutely not, my dear woman. The camera is here, do you see?" I pointed to the recording device and my camera comrades, addressing her gently and patiently, for a woman's understanding of technical matters is always somewhat fragile. When I had finished my explanation, I enquired whether the woman was a regular visitor to the area.

"Which means these automobilists may well have come to your attention."

"Y-yeesss," she said slowly. "Why do you ask?"

"Would you agree with me that, in view of the behaviour exhibited by a veritable myriad of automobilists, one must fear for the children who play here?"

"Errm . . . I suppose, sort of, but . . . what are you getting at?"

"Voice your concerns as freely as you wish, my dear woman and comrade!"

"Hold on! I'm nobody's comrade! But seeing as you ask . . . I do sometimes get a bit worked up when I'm going past here with the children . . ."

"Why then does this freely elected government not mete out harsher punishments to such thoughtless racers?"

"I don't know . . ."

"We will change this! For Germany. You and I! Which punishments would you recommend?"

"Which punishments would I *recommend*?"

"Do you think that the existing punishments are adequate?"

"I'm not sure . . ."

"Or are they not dispensed harshly enough?"

"No, no – I wouldn't want that."

"What do you mean? What about the children?"

"I mean it's . . . it's alright. Alright as it is. I'm perfectly happy!"

This was a frequent response. It was like living in a climate of fear, and this under a form of government which was supposed to be so free. The simple, innocent woman from the Volk dared not speak openly in my presence when I approached her in my plain soldier's uniform. I was appalled. And this was the reaction from approximately three-quarters of the people to whom I spoke. The other quarter asked, "Are you the new security guard around here? Finally someone's saying something! It's an absolute disgrace! They should all be locked up!"

"You are calling for imprisonment, then?"

"At the very least!"

"I thought the death penalty had been abolished . . ."

"More's the pity!"

Following that same principle I now lashed out at whatever ills I observed, either with my own eyes or in the press reports. Poisoned food, automobilists who telephoned with their portable devices while driving their vehicles, the barbaric custom of hunting, and much more. And what astounded me was that people either demanded draconian punishments or, as was more frequent, dared not speak their minds. There was one occasion where this was particularly manifest. A large number of people had already gathered in the city centre to demonstrate against the government. Seemingly it had occurred to no-one to opt for the most obvious solution – stormtroopers – but at least they had erected a kind of market stall to collect signatures, aimed at eliminating the sensationally high figure of 100,000 abortions per year in Germany.

Such large-scale extermination of German blood is unacceptable to me too, of course. Any cretin could see that, assuming 50 per cent were boys, this would lead to a loss of three divisions in the medium term. If not four. In my presence, however, these upright, decent people were unwilling to articulate their beliefs, and shortly after we arrived the demonstration broke up altogether.

"What can one say?" I asked Bronner. "All of a sudden these poor people seem changed. So much for so-called freedom of expression."

"Incredible," Bronner gasped. "That was even better than the thing with the dog owners protesting against compulsory leads!"

"No," I said. "You misunderstood. The dog owners who bolted were not decent Germans. They were all Jews. Didn't you see the stars? They knew at once who they were dealing with."

"Those weren't Jews," Bronner protested. "That wasn't 'Jew' written on the stars, it was 'Dog.'"

"There you go, so typical of the Jew," I explained. "All he

does is sow confusion. And then on the flames of bewilderment he cooks up his greasy, poisonous soup."

"But that's . . ." Bronner panted, and then he laughed. "You are absolutely unbelievable!"

"I know," I said. "By the way, have the uniforms for your camera people arrived? In future the movement must appear united!"

Our revelations were greeted with wild enthusiasm back in the offices of the production company. "You could even turn a vicar into an atheist," Madame Bellini laughed as she viewed the material.

"You might think so, but I have already made considerable efforts in that direction," I recalled. "Not even a stint inside a camp does the trick for many of those devil-dodgers."

The short films were included in Gagmez's programme as soon as two weeks after my première, and were in addition to the passionate oration I delivered towards the end. After a further four weeks I was commissioned to provide yet another segment. To all intents and purposes it was like the beginning of the Twenties all over again. With the difference that back then I took possession of a party.

This time it was a television programme.

Moreover, my assessment of that Gagmez character was proved accurate. A certain resentment had fermented within him as he witnessed my increasing influence and sway on his programme, and the Führer principle asserting itself ever more definitively. And yet the man offered no resistance to this development. Although he did not exactly fall into line, his protests were lame, while behind the scenes he would occasionally give those in charge a good earful. In his shoes, I would have gone for broke; from the very start I would have refused point blank to tolerate any interference; my response to that first appearance would have been to threaten to cease all work for the company – what would I have cared for contracts? But Gagmez behaved true to form; in desperation he clung to his sorry achievements, to his doubtful fame, to his television slot, as if it were an accolade. This Gagmez would never have put his neck on the line for his convictions; he would never have gone to prison.

On the other hand, what convictions could he possibly foster? What did he have apart from a shadowy background, apart from meaningless, vainglorious tittle-tattle? I had it far easier; behind me was Germany's future. Not to mention the Iron Cross. Or the Wound Badge, which proved that I had already sacrificed blood for Germany. What had Gagmez ever sacrificed?

Naturally, I was not expecting to see him parading the golden Wound Badge. How could he have acquired one of those without a war? And if he *had* acquired one, it is highly debatable whether he would have been a suitable candidate for his entertainment programme. When one takes a closer look at the men who have been awarded such rare, distinguished honours, one notices that there is not much left of the poor blighters. That is in the brutal nature of things. These are men who were wounded at the front five times or more, by bayonets, grenades, gas; men who have glass eyes or artificial limbs, or whose mouths are contorted, if they possess a lower jaw at all. This is not the wood from which Destiny carves us the best humorists. And while a certain bitterness may well be understandable in their situation, the Führer must also consider the other side. The people in the audience have dressed up for the occasion and are sitting there in high spirits. After a hard day's toil in the shrapnel factory or maintenance hangar, or even a long night of heavy bombing, they wish to relax, and I fully understand that they might expect something more from a comedian than two amputated legs. So let me state here emphatically that, for all concerned, a lethal direct hit from a grenade must be better than a Wound Badge followed by a career as a clown on the home front.

What struck me immediately about Gagmez was that, not only did he lack an ideology to rival National Socialism, he lacked an ideology altogether. And of course without an established ideology, in the modern entertainment industry one hasn't got a chance, nor even a raison d'être. The rest is taken care of by history – or the viewing figures.

xviii

The Führer is nothing without his Volk. That is to say, the Führer *is* of course something, even without his Volk, but nobody can see what he is. Any person sound of mind can be made to understand this; it is as if you had sat Mozart down and not given him a piano – how would anyone have noticed that he was a genius? He would not even have been the performing Wunderkind alongside his sister. True, she would have had her violin, but if we take the violin away too, then what is left? Two children who can at most recite poems in the Salzburg dialect or perform other such displays of cuteness. But who would pay to watch what takes place in any parlour at Christmastime? The Führer's violin, however, is the Volk.

And his cohorts.

Yes, I know, one can already predict the response of the sceptics, those smart alecs who prattle on about how one cannot play two violins at the same time. But let us examine their perspective on reality. That which must not, cannot be. But what if it is? A large number of even truly great Führers have foundered on this very point! Take Napoleon, for example. The man was a genius, no question about it. But only on his military "violin". He foundered on account of his cohorts. And so of every genius one must ask: what sort of cohorts has he chosen? Take Frederick the Great. He had Kurt Christoph Graf von Schwerin, a general who was shot from his horse for his country, banner still in hand. Or Hans Karl von Winterfeldt, chopped to bits by sabres in 1757. My goodness, those were cohorts! But Napoleon?

It must be said he was dealt an unfortunate hand, and that is putting it politely. Nepotism of the worst sort; his relations were queuing up for jobs. His halfwit brother Joseph sits there in Spain, Bernadotte marries his sister-in-law, Jérôme acquires Westphalia, the sisters are furnished with an array of principalities in Italy. And does anybody thank him? But the most egregious parasite of all was Louis, whom Napoleon had installed as King of Holland, and who spent his time there honing his royal career to his heart's content, as if he had conquered the place himself! With leeches such as these, how can one possibly wage war or rule the world? Not only have I always set great store by having impeccable cohorts, for the most part I have found them too.

I mean, just look at the Siege of Leningrad!

Two million civilians trapped without food. A certain sense of duty was required to drop thousands of bombs each day, especially targeting the food stores. In the end the burghers of Leningrad reached the point where they smashed in each other's skulls, only to be able to gobble up the soil into which the burned sugar had melted. Naturally, from a racial standpoint, these civilians were not worth preserving, but the simple soldier might easily have thought, "Those poor, poor people!"

Especially as many of these soldiers are so terribly fond of animals.

I experienced this at first hand in the trenches, where men would dash into the most violent barrage of fire just to retrieve "Maunzi", or share the rations they had been saving up for weeks with stray little "Bello". This is just another example of how wartime stirs not only the harshest emotions in men, but the softest, warmest ones too. In many respects, armed conflict chisels out the best in people. The simple man goes into battle an unhewn chunk of stone, emerging as a flawless animal-lover with the implacable will to do what is necessary. And one knows one has the right cohorts when these simple people, these hundreds of thousands of soldiers and cat-lovers do not say, "Let's go more gently on them; if it comes to the worst at least the Leningraders will starve more slowly," but rather, "Let's get going with these bombs! The Führer knows what he's doing with his orders."

The right consorts, I pondered again, as I observed Fräulein Krömeier typing up my latest Führer speech. I was entirely satisfied with Fräulein Krömeier's efforts overall. Her work could not be faulted; her commitment was exemplary, and of late she had been at my disposal for the whole day. The only area where there was room for improvement was her appearance. Not that she looked dishevelled or unkempt, but this outwardly sombre impression – which flew in the face of her affability – this deathlike pallor was hardly conducive to such a joyous and life-affirming movement as National Socialism.

On the other hand, a Führer must have the capability to see beneath the surface. Von Ribbentrop, for example, was in appearance a model example of the master race – a perfect chin, first-class genetic material – but ultimately the man was a perennial twit. And that is no use to anybody.

"Very good, Fräulein Krömeier," I said. "I think that is all for today."

"I'll like, just quickly print it out for you?" she said. She typed something into her computer. Then she took a small mirror from her bag, together with a dark lipstick, and started painting over her lips. This seemed an appropriate opportunity to broach the subject.

"What does your fiancé say about this?"

"What fiancé? About what? Mein Führer!"

Her Führer address still needed some practice.

"Well, I suppose there's a young man . . . there *must* be a young man . . . an admirer, let's say."

"No," Fräulein Krömeier said as she applied her lipstick. "There's no-one."

"Well, I should not like to be indiscreet or insistent," I reassured her. "But you can tell me. I mean, we're not amongst Catholics here. I can see no objection if two young people like one another – why should a marriage certificate be necessary? True love ennobles itself!"

"That's all well and good," Fräulein Krömeier said, pressing her lips together as she looked into the mirror. "But at the moment there isn't like, anybody? Because four weeks ago? I personally told him where to get off? He was a right douche-bag, let me tell you!"

I must have appeared somewhat taken aback, for Fräulein Krömeier immediately said, "O.M.G.! That just like, totally slipped out! L.O.L. We can't have that in Führer Headquarters! What I meant to say, of course, was that the man was an absolute Schweinehund! Mein Führer!"

I did not really understand the point of this rephrasing, or how it constituted an improvement. At any event, the expression on her face radiated honest effort and now a certain pride, too, at having come up with the second formulation.

"First of all," I said sternly, "we are not in Führer Headquarters, strictly speaking, because I am not commander-in-chief of the Wehrmacht – not yet, at any rate. And second, I do not think that such words should spring from the mouth of a German girl! And definitely not from the mouth of my secretary!"

"But's that what it was like! You should have been there, you'd've said something similar! I could tell you a few tales . . ."

"Such tales mean nothing to me! All that is important here is the appearance of the German Reich, and in these rooms the image of the German woman, too! If somebody walks past I want him to gain the impression of a well-ordered state and not . . ."

That was as far as I got, for a tear ran from one of Fräulein Krömeier's eyes, then from the other, followed by a great many tears all round. These are the very moments which the Führer must avoid in wartime, as empathy may rob him of the concentration urgently required for the victorious execution of cauldron battles and carpet bombing. When the situation is less favourable, so I discovered, it is somewhat easier: you give the order that every metre of ground must be defended until the last drop of blood is spilled, and then the job of waging war is effectively finished for the day – one might as well go home. All the same, one must never allow oneself to get bogged down in other people's emotions.

Admittedly, we were not in the middle of a war. And I had the highest regard for Fräulein Krömeier's faultless output. So I handed her a paper handkerchief, which seemed to be in widespread manufacture once more. "There's no real damage done," I said soothingly. "All I wanted was that in future you . . . I mean, I do not doubt your ability; indeed I am highly satisfied with your work . . . You should not take the admonishment to heart . . ."

"Oh," she sniffed, "it's not because of you. It's just that, well, I like . . . I like, really loved him? I thought we were going places? You know, like, totally serious?" She rifled through her rucksack and retrieved her telephone. She tapped around on it a few times until it showed a photograph of the Schweinehund, then held it out to me.

"He was so totally good-looking. And he was like, always so . . . so . . . special?"

I looked at the picture. The man did indeed look handsome. He was tall, blonde, if a good dozen years older than Fräulein Krömeier. The photograph showed him on the street, in an elegant suit, but there was nothing dandyish about him; rather he looked extraordinarily dignified, as if he were the manager of a wholesome small business.

"I should not wish to offend," I said, "but now I am not at all surprised that this relationship came to an unhappy conclusion . . ."

"No?" Fräulein Krömeier sniffed.

"No."

"Why?"

"Look, naturally you think that you ended the relationship. But, in all honesty, have you not recognised that you are not the right partner for this man?"

Fräulein Krömeier sniffed and nodded. "But we were like, so good together? And then – I never imagined . . ."

"Of course," I said, "But you can see it at once!"

She crumpled the handkerchief in her fist as she looked up at me. "What? You can see it?"

I took a deep breath. It is astonishing how, in the struggle for the future of the German Volk, Providence can drive one to the most far-flung secondary theatre of war. Yet it is also amazing how Providence brings some things together and combines them: the problem of Fräulein Krömeier and the dignified representation of racial policy.

"Look, a man, precisely a racially untarnished man such as he, surely wants a cheerful, life-affirming partner, a mother for his children, a wife who exudes the wholesome spirit of National Socialism . . ."

"But that's what I am! Like, totally!"

"Yes, of course," I said. "You know that, and I know it too. But just look at yourself through the eyes of a man in the prime of his life! This black wardrobe all the time. This dark lipstick, this face which you always make up to look so pale, or at least that is the impression I get . . . I – now, Fräulein Krömeier, please do not start crying again, I beg you – in 1916 I saw corpses on the Western Front that looked jollier than you!

Those dark eyes, and set against your black hair. You are such a charming young lady, why don't you wear some cheerful clothes for a change? A gay blouse, or a pretty skirt? Or a bright summer frock? Then you will see how gentlemen turn their heads!"

Fräulein Krömeier stared at me, as still as a statue. Then she let out a hearty laugh.

"I just had to picture it," she explained. "Me like, going around in a little dress like Heidi of the Alps? L.O.L. With flowers in my hair? And then like, bumping into him in the pedestrian zone? Him and his fancy lady? And then finding out that the . . . the *shit* is married? O.M.G. I must say, I would look even sillier than usual. No, it's a really funny image. That's so sweet of you to like, cheer me up?" she said. "And now I'm off home." She stood up and put her rucksack over her shoulder.

"I'll fetch the speech from the printer and put it in your pigeon hole," she said, her hand already on the door handle. "Have nice evening, mein Führer! Me in like, a little dress. L.O.L. . . ." She left.

I wondered what I might get up to that evening. Maybe I should return to the hotel and have that new device connected which Sensenbrink had ordered for me. It was supposed to allow you to play films via the television set, films which for practicality's sake were no longer preserved on spools, but on little plastic discs. The Flashlight company had shelves full of them. I always enjoyed films, and I was curious to discover what I may have missed in the intervening decades. My other thought was to get started on my design for the future space airport in Berlin. After all, experience had shown that when

194

one is actively waging war one scarcely gets the time to attend to such matters. And thus it seemed wise to pursue my former passion with increased vigour now. The door opened again and Fräulein Krömeier put a letter on my desk.

"I found this in your pigeon hole?" she said. "It didn't arrive with the post; someone must have just slipped it through the letterbox. Have a good evening again, mein Führer!"

The letter was indeed addressed to me, but the sender had written my name within inverted commas, as if it were intended as the title of a television programme. I gave it a good sniff; in the past it had quite often transpired that women had wanted to express a certain reverence for my person. The letter smelled of nothing. I opened it.

Even now I can clearly recall the enthusiasm I felt on seeing an immaculate swastika at the top of the letter. I had not counted on such positive reactions so soon. Apart from that there was nothing to see.

I unfolded the letter. Below, in fat, black, clumsy handwriting, it said:

"Stop all yur shit, you fukking Jewish barsturd!"

I hadn't laughed so much in ages.

xix

It was a minor triumph, and very satisfying, when the young lady at the hotel reception greeted me with the Nazi salute. I was on my way to the breakfast room, and by the time I answered her greeting by flipping back my arm she was already lowering hers.

"I can only do that because you get up so late and there's no-one about." She winked at me. "So don't give me away!"

"It's difficult at the moment, I know," I said in a hushed tone. "But the time will come again when you, too, will be able to hold your head high and display your pride in the Fatherland." Then I hastened into the breakfast room.

Not all the serving-folk had seen the signs of the times as clear-sightedly as the young lady at the reception. There was no clicking of heels and the only greeting I received was a hollow "Good morning". On the other hand, since I had switched to wearing suits more often, the looks people cast me were more friendly than before. Conditions here were similar to those in the Weimar era, after my release from prison. Here, too, I needed to begin from the very bottom, with the difference that the influence and mores of the effete bourgeoisie had eaten more deeply into the proletariat – in order to establish a certain level of trust Uncle Wolf had to attire himself in the sheep's clothing of the bourgeoisie even more so than in the past. And in the mornings, as I partook of my müsli and orange juice with linseeds, I could palpably sense an acknowledgement of my past achievements in the looks people afforded me. I was just debating whether to get up and fetch another apple when I heard the Valkyries galloping on their steeds. With a confident movement I had seen performed by a number of young businessmen, I brought out the telephone and raised it to my ear.

"Hitler!" I said in a commendably discreet voice.

"Have you read the paper yet?" the voice of Madame Bellini asked straight away.

"No," I said. "Why?"

"Then take a look. I'll call you back in ten!"

"Wait!" I said. "What do you mean? What newspaper are we talking about here?"

"The one with your picture on the cover," Madame Bellini said.

I stood up and went over to the pile of newspapers, where there were a few copies of that *Bild.* On the cover was a photograph of me together with the headline: "Loony YouTube Hitler: Fans go wild for his tirades!

I took the paper back to my table and sat down. Then I started to read.

Loony YouTube Hitler

Fans go wild for his tirades!

The nation is stumped: Is this humour?

Once upon a time he murdered millions – now millions have made him a YouTube sensation. With his tasteless routine and bizarre catchphrases, a "comedian" dressed up as "Adolf Hitler" is venting hatred against foreigners, women and democracy in Ali Gagmez's show, *Epic, Guys*. Youth protection workers, politicians and the Central Council of Jews are appalled.

Fancy a sample of his "art"?

– *The Turks have no creative genius.*
– *100,000 abortions per year are intolerable; later this will cost us four divisions for the war in the East.*
– *Cosmetic surgery is racial defilement*

This Nazi rabble-rousing is awakening bad memories amongst older Germans. Pensioner Hilde W. (92) from Dormagen said, "It's terrible. That man did so much harm!" Politicians can scarcely believe his success. According to C.S.U. minister, Markus Söder, the whole thing is "sheer madness. It's got nothing to do with humour!" S.P.D. health expert, Karl Lauterbach, told BILD, "It's extremely borderline and offensive." Green leader, Claudia Roth: "Dreadful. I turn off whenever I see him." Dieter Graumann, president of the Central Council of Jews: "Incredibly poor taste; we're considering lodging an official complaint."

Particularly bizarre is the fact that no-one knows the real name of this "comedian", who bears a terrifyingly close resemblance to the Nazi monster.

In an attempt to find out more, BILD questioned the boss of MyTV, Elke Fahrendonk.
BILD: "What has any of this got to do with humour and satire?"
Fahrendonk: "Because 'Hitler' shows up the extreme contradictions in our society, his controversial approach is justified from an artistic point of view."
BILD: "Why won't the loony TV Hitler tell us what his real name is?"
Fahrendonk: "Atze Schröder's no different in this respect. He has every right to a private life, too."

BILD promises to monitor the case closely.

198

I have to admit that I was astounded. Not by the paper's outlandish take on reality, something I have encountered only too often in the past – it is well known that the biggest fools are generally to be found on the editorial boards of the national press. But because I sensed this *Bild* newspaper was an institution which might turn out to be a secret ally. A little uptight, maybe, with a typical petit-bourgeois subservience which recoiled from speaking its mind. But on many issues the position it took was not dissimilar to my own. When I heard the daughters of Wotan soar across the skies once more, I reached for the telephone.

"Hitler."

"I'm disgusted," Madame Bellini said. "They didn't give us any warning!"

"What do you expect from a newspaper?"

"I'm not talking about *Bild*, I'm talking about MyTV," she said in a state of high excitement. "They interviewed Fahrendonk. At the very least I thought we might have been told in advance."

"What difference would that have made?"

"None," she sighed. "You're probably right."

"In the end it is only a newspaper," I said. "It is of no interest to me."

"Maybe not to you," Madame Bellini said. "But it is to us. They want to bring you down. And we've invested rather a lot in you."

"What is that supposed to mean?" I asked curtly.

"It means," Madame Bellini said in a cooler tone, "that we have arranged an interview with *Bild*. And that we need to talk."

"Why do we need to talk?"

"Because once they've got it in for you they'll leave no stone unturned. I'd like you to tell me if there's anything they might dig up."

It is always exhilarating to watch our business leaders take fright. When the deal appears sufficiently tantalising, they hurry over with beaming smiles, scarcely able to throw enough money at you. When everything goes well, they are at the front of the queue to increase their share, suggesting that they would have borne the whole risk. But the moment something looks perilous, they are the first to foist this lucrative risk onto others.

"If that is your concern," I mocked her, "then it has come too late. Do you not think you ought to have asked these questions earlier?"

Madame Bellini cleared her throat. "I'm afraid I have something to confess."

"Which is?"

"We ran a check on you. Listen, don't get me wrong, we didn't have you tailed or anything like that. But we did hire a specialist agency. I mean, one needs to find out whether one is actually employing a devoted Nazi."

"Well," I said peevishly, "I imagine the results will have reassured you."

"On the one hand, yes," Madame Bellini said. "We didn't find anything bad."

"And on the other?"

"On the other hand, we didn't find anything at all. It's as if you didn't exist."

"I see. So now you would like me to tell you whether I existed before?"

Madame Bellini paused a moment.

"Please don't get the wrong end of the stick. We're all in the same boat here; all we want to do is avoid the sort of situation where . . ." Here she let out a rather forced laugh. ". . . we end up – without knowing it, of course – having someone like the real Hitler on our books." She paused again before adding, "I can hardly believe what I'm saying here."

"Me neither," I said. "It's high treason!"

"Can't you be serious for a minute?" she asked. "I want you to answer just one question for me – hand on heart, are you sure that the hacks at *Bild* won't unearth anything they could use against you?"

"Frau Bellini," I said, "I have done nothing in my life of which I am ashamed. I have neither sought any unwarranted financial gain, nor have I ever acted purely in my own interest. This will be of little use in our dealings with the press, however. In this instance we must assume that *Bild* will concoct a whole heap of ugly lies. I expect they will falsely attribute an array of illegitimate children to me once again – we know this is the worst thing the scurrilous petit-bourgeois press can think of. But I can live with such accusations."

"Illegitimate children? Nothing else?"

"What else do you imagine there might be?"

"What about your political background, Nazi affiliation and that sort of thing?"

"My political background is above reproach."

"So you were never a member of a right-wing party?" she probed.

"What are you talking about?" I laughed at her clumsy

trick question. "I was practically one of the party's founders. Member number 555!"

"I'm sorry?"

"I don't want you to go around thinking I was just some hanger-on."

"Was that a youthful indiscretion, perhaps?" Once again Madame Bellini made an awkward attempt to undermine my unimpeachable convictions.

"What are you saying? Think about it. In 1919 I was thirty. I even helped come up with the ruse. We invented the first 500 to make the numbers look better! It is a stunt I'm awfully proud of. Let me reassure you, the worst that this newspaper will be able to print about me is that Hitler falsified his membership number. I think I can live with that."

There was another pause on the other end of the line. Then Madame Bellini said, "1919?"

"Of course. When else do you think? You can only join a party once, unless you leave it. And I certainly never left mine!"

She laughed and sounded relieved. "I can live with that, too. 'YouTube Hitler fudged party entry in 1919!' I'd almost pay to see a headline like that."

"Return to your post, then, and hold your position. We will not surrender a metre!"

"Jawohl, mein Führer," I heard Madame Bellini laugh before hanging up. Dropping the newspaper onto the table I suddenly found myself staring into gleaming blue eyes set beneath a mop of blonde hair. A boy, with his hands clasped timidly behind his back.

"Well, well," I said. "Who do we have here? What is your name?"

"My name is Reinhard," the whippersnapper said. Really a delightful little chap.

"How old are you?" I asked. Tentatively, he brought forth a hand and put up three fingers before eventually adding a fourth. Adorable.

"I knew a Reinhard once," I said, gently stroking his hair. "He lived in Prague. Such a beautiful city."

"Did you like him?" the lad asked.

"I liked him very much indeed," I said. "He was a very good man! He made sure that lots of wicked people can't harm people like you and me anymore."

"How many?" the boy asked. I could see he was becoming more trustful.

"A huge number! Thousands! A very good, brave man!"

"Did he put them in prison?"

"Yes," I nodded. "That, too."

"I bet they got their bottoms smacked," this enchanting scallywag chortled, taking his other hand out from behind his back. He held out a copy of *Bild*.

"Did you bring this for me?" I asked.

He nodded. "From Mummy! She's sitting over there," he said, pointing to a table in the distance. Then he pulled a felt-tipped pen from his trouser pocket. "Mummy said I have to ask you if you'll draw a auto on it."

"A auto," I laughed. "Are you sure? Or did Mummy say an autograph?"

The boy pulled the sweetest frown imaginable and thought

hard. Then he cast me a look of consternation: "I don't know anymore. Will you draw me a auto?"

"Why don't we ask Mummy?" I stood up, took the little fellow by the hand and brought him back to his mother. I signed the newspaper for her and also drew on a piece of paper a picture of a beautiful automobile – a magnificent twelve-cylinder Maybach. As I returned to my seat the telephone rang. It was Madame Bellini.

"You do that very well," she said.

"I like children," I said. "I was unable to start my own family. But please stop watching everything I do!"

"What do you mean, 'children'?" she asked, sounding quite astonished. "No, I mean you argue well, you're quick-witted. You're so good that Herr Sensenbrink and I thought we could offer them an interview right away. The *Bild* people!"

I pondered this for a few seconds, then said, "No, we're not going to do that. And by not doing it we'll feature more frequently on their front page. We will grant them their interview when it suits *us*. And on our terms."

XX

I am not often mistaken. On the contrary, I am very seldom mistaken. This is one of the advantages of not entering the political fray until one has had some proper experience of life – and let me emphasise here the word "proper". These days there seems to be no end of self-styled politicians who, having stood behind a shop counter for a whole quarter of an hour, or once peered through an open door into a factory hall, now think they know what real life looks like. To take an example I just have to think of that liberal Asiatic minister, who abandoned his medical studies to concentrate on his career as a political nonentity. This begs the question: Why? If, instead, he had said he was concentrating on completing his medical studies, then aiming to work as a doctor for ten or twenty years, fifty to sixty hours per week, so that afterwards, schooled by harsh reality, he could gradually form his own opinions and develop these into a view of the world, allowing him to embark on meaningful political work with a good conscience, he might have been somebody, given favourable enough circumstances. But no: this fellow is one of those ghastly modern types who think they should enter politics first and the ideas will somehow piece themselves together along the way. And indeed, this is precisely what it looks like. Today they state the case for Jewish finance; tomorrow they're chasing after Jewish Bolshevism. This stripling is no different; he is like the class dunce, forever running after the bus. All I can say is: ugh! Had he waited until his first experience on the front line, unemployment, the men's hostel in Vienna, rejection by those professorial oafs of the academy, then he would know what he was talking about today. Errors would be committed only in exceptional circumstances. As with this *Bild* affair, in which I confess I had misread the situation.

I had assumed that the press vermin would be all over me, my policies, my speeches. In fact they sent a horde of photographers. Two days later a large picture appeared of me drinking tea from a paper cup at the newspaper kiosk. The vendor stood beside me holding a bottle of lemonade, which might have resembled a beer bottle. Above the photograph in large type was written:

Loony YouTube Hitler:

Hanging out with his drinking buddies

In the evenings he rails on telly against foreigners and our politicians; by day he hangs out with his drinking buddies: Germany's most unsavoury "comedian", who calls himself "Adolf Hitler" and still refuses to tell the country his real name (as reported in BILD). Having spruced himself up and put away his uniform, the Nazi "humorist" (left) is acting the innocent man on the street. Is he planning his next distasteful tirade?

Watch this space.

True, the newspaper vendor had not been having his best day sartorially. This was due to the fact that he had decided to undertake some renovations to his sales window, for which he had been wearing some decommissioned fatigues under a smock that he removed in his cigarette breaks. He had looked no shabbier than one would expect from someone in the middle of a painting job – nobody can judge this better than I. But the vendor was no "drinking buddy" of mine, not by a long shot; I had never sought the company of drinkers. I found the whole business most unpleasant; I mean, the newspaper seller really did not deserve to be treated like that. Fortunately he seemed to know how to deal with it. I had set off late morning to offer my apologies for the distress caused by the article. But he could barely spare me the time of day.

I found him standing in front of the kiosk serving an extraordinarily large number of people, despite the cold, wet weather. A large sign hung above the sales window: "Buy *Bild* – today featuring me and the loony YouTube Hitler!"

"Great timing!" he called out when he saw me.

"I had come to apologise," I called back. "But now I no longer know what for."

"Me neither," the newspaper seller laughed. "Grab a felt tip and get signing! That's the least you can do for your drinking buddy."

"Are you really him?" asked a labourer, thrusting his newspaper at me.

"Indeed I am," I said, signing my name.

"When I saw it I ordered another batch of copies straight away," the newspaper vendor told me, selling papers over people's heads. "Yes, by all means go over. Herr Hitler will be glad to sign for you."

In truth I do not particularly like signing my name. You never know what people will do with a signature. You can sign a piece of paper in all innocence, but the next day someone else will paste a declaration above it, and suddenly you find you have given away Transylvania to some corrupt Balkan entity. Or surrendered unconditionally, even though your bunkers are still full of weapons of retaliation with which you could turn around the war whenever you fancied. In the end, however, my signature on a newspaper seemed harmless enough. I was delighted, moreover, that for the first time nobody was complaining that I wasn't writing Herr Stromberger, or whoever, but my own name.

"There, please, across the photo!"

"Could you write 'For Helga'?"

"Could you say something bad about the Kurds next time?"

"We should have gone to war together back then! We would have won!"

A small girl was pushed to the front with her newspaper, and I took deliberate care to sign it slowly. Let them photograph this; young people trust the Führer as much now as they did in the past. And not only the young. An ancient woman approached me with one of those modern walking frames on wheels and a twinkle in her eye. She held out her newspaper and said in a quivering voice, "Do you remember? 1935, in Nuremberg. I was in the window, watching you march by! I always thought you were looking at me. We were so proud of you! And now – well, you haven't changed one bit!"

"Nor have you," I gaily fibbed, shaking her hand. I felt touched. Not that I could remember this woman, obviously, but her sincere loyalty had a charm all of its own. At any event, when a nervous Sensenbrink telephoned me I was calmly able to allay his concerns by describing to him this demonstration of trust by the Volk, and could rebuff the demands that we make a legal response. Nor was I daunted the following day. Naturally, the paper had suppressed the photographs of the public's affirmation; instead they printed the utterly irrelevant headline: "Loony YouTube Hitler: now Germany votes". Beside this were several photographs from concentration camps, showing the unattractive, but alas necessary work of the S.S. This made me rather indignant.

A thorough investigation of major operations should never focus on those petty isolated instances where the overall plan has caused a minor inconvenience; such an analysis lacks all gravity. Wherever there is a large motorway enabling the transport of tonne after tonne of German goods, you will inevitably find a sweet little rabbit trembling by the roadside. Or you build a canal, thereby creating hundreds of thousands of jobs, and of course you will encounter the occasional small farmer who sheds bitter tears because he has to relinquish his land. But for this I cannot, I must not ignore the future of the Volk. And when the need to eradicate millions of Jews – and there really were that many back then – has been recognised, you will always find the odd naïve, compassionate German who thinks, "Well, that Jew wasn't so bad after all, surely we could have put up with this or that one for a few more years." For this reason it is terribly easy for a newspaper to appeal to people's sentimental side. It is an old refrain – everybody agrees that the rats must be exterminated, but when it comes down to it, sympathy for the individual rat is huge. Only sympathy, mind you; there is no desire to keep the rat. The two must not be confused. But it was precisely this confusion which knowingly underpinned the paper's questionnaire. The poll, which I doubted was going to be an honest and fair one, offered three choices, eliciting from me a grim smile. I could have dreamed this up myself. The options were:

1. Enough! Get the YouTube Hitler off our screens!
2. No, he's not funny, and MyTV doesn't think so either.
3. Never seen him. Not interested in that Nazi rubbish.

This was entirely to have been expected. Such claptrap is the slanderous bread and butter of the bourgeois gutter press, which quite clearly is still infected by the spirit of the Jews. It was something I would have to live with, particularly as the necessary facilities to accommodate these lying vermin were lacking. From a cursory piece of research I had been able to establish that only two barracks were still standing in Dachau. A scandalous state of affairs – the crematoria would have to be fired up again after the first wave of arrests.

Sensenbrink, of course, was in a high-velocity spin. It is always those "great strategists" whose nerves start to flutter first. "We're toast," he wailed repeatedly. "We're toast. MyTV'll be sweating bullets. We've got to give them an interview!" I signalled to Hotel Reserver Sawatzki that he should keep an eye on this loose cannon. By contrast, Madame Bellini was positively blooming. Nobody since Ernst Hanfstaengel had managed so successfully to sweet-talk the important and not-so-important people on my behalf. And she was a damn sight better looking, too, a thoroughly attractive woman.

On the fourth day, however, I gave in.

Even now it is the only thing I reproach myself for. I ought to have shown unyielding steeliness, but perhaps I was some-what out of practice. And yet, in my wildest dreams I could never have imagined what might happen.

They had published a large photograph showing me accom-panying my respectable secretary, Fräulein Krömeier, to the door of the offices. The photograph, snapped in the bright light of early evening, had – as I was able to conclude thanks to long conversations with Heinrich Hoffmann back in the day – been wantonly and deliberately distorted. The image was unneces-sarily blurred, as well as greatly enlarged, and it was presented as if the services of a highly experienced spy had been engaged to take the picture. Which was utter nonsense, of course. On the day in question I had decided to take a short walk and had gone with Fräulein Krömeier to the exit, from where she caught the bus. In the photograph I was holding open the door. Printed in bold above the image was the following:

Who is the mysterious woman at his side?

They furtively creep out of a side door and then look around: the Nazi "comedian" and his mysterious beauty. The man, who still refuses to tell Germany his name and who rails against foreigners, this self-proclaimed champion of decency, is conducting his sordid affair at twilight.

Who is the mysterious woman he is courting?
From a close acquaintance, BILD learned the following:

"That is punishment by association," I said coldly. "And poor Fräulein Krömeier is not even related to me!"

We were sitting in the conference room, Madame Bellini, Sensenbrink, Hotel Reserver Sawatzki and myself. Inevitably it was the great strategist Sensenbrink who asked, "Come on, open the kimono . . . is there anything going on between you and the Krömeier girl? Are you dipping your pen in company ink?"

"Don't be ridiculous," Madame Bellini cut in. "Herr Hitler has opened the door for me too on occasions. Do you intend to ask me the same question?"

"We just need to proceed carefully," Sensenbrink said with a shrug.

"Proceed carefully?" Madame Bellini retorted. "With what? I'm not going to waste a moment's thought on this distasteful business. Fräulein Krömeier can do as she pleases. Herr Hitler can do as he pleases. We're not living in the Fifties."

"Nonetheless he mustn't be married," Sensenbrink insisted.

212

"At least, not if there's something cooking with Fräulein Krömeier."

"You still haven't understood," Madame Bellini said, and then turned to me. "Well? *Are* you married?"

"Actually, I am," I said.

"Great," Sensenbrink moaned.

"Let me guess," Bellini said. "Since 1945? April?"

"Absolutely," I said. "It's extraordinary that the press release got out. At the time, you see, the city was teeming with Bolshevists, alas!"

"Without wishing to intrude on your personal life," Hotel Reserver Sawatzki said, "I think Herr Hitler can rightly be considered a widower." You can say what you like, but even under fire this Sawatzki fellow was quick witted, clear, reliable, pragmatic.

"I cannot be one hundred per cent sure," I said, "but I'm assuming Herr Sawatzki is correct."

"Well," Madame Bellini said, turning to Sensenbrink. "Satisfied now?"

"It's my job to throw curve balls," Sensenbrink said stroppily.

"The question is: What are we going to do?" Bellini said.

"Do we have to do anything?" Sawatzki said in a sober voice.

"I agree with you, Herr Sawatzki," I said. "Or I would agree if this was just about me. But if I do nothing those around me will be affected even more. It may not do Herr Sensenbrink any harm," I said with a mocking glance, "but I cannot expect you and the company to put up with it."

"I would always expect us as a company to put up with it,

but not our shareholders, not for five minutes," Madame Bellini answered drily. "Which means no interview on our terms. But on their terms."

"I will hold you responsible for ensuring that it does not turn out like that," I said, and as I sensed that Madame Bellini was not as happy to take orders as Sawatzki, I added quickly, "But in this case you are absolutely right. We will grant them an interview. Tell them it will be in the Adlon. And they can pay."

"Your ski-brain has gone totally off-piste," Sensenbrink teased me. "In this situation we can hardly get them to agree to a fee."

"It's all about principle," I said. "I refuse to squander the Volk's money on this press scum. If they pay the bill I'll be happy with that."

"So when?"

"As soon as possible," Madame Bellini said, quite correctly. "Let's say tomorrow. Then they might leave us in peace for a day."

I agreed. "In the meantime we ought to intensify our own propaganda efforts."

"Which means?"

"We must not allow our political opponents to enjoy control over reporting. This must never happen to us again. We need to publish our own newspaper."

"So . . . maybe the *Völkischer Beobachter*?" Sensenbrink sneered. "We're a production company, not a newspaper publisher! Stir-fry that in your think-wok!"

"Guys, it doesn't have to be a newspaper," Hotel Reserver

214

Sawatzki interjected. "Herr Hitler's strength is his on-screen appearance. We've already got the videos, so why don't we post them on our own website?"

"All his appearances so far in H.D., which will offer more than the clips already up on YouTube," Madame Bellini reflected. "And it will give us a platform if we want to put out any particular bits of information. Or our own view on things. Sounds good. Have the digital media department prepare a few designs."

We concluded the conference. Noticing a light still burning in my office as I left the room, I went to turn it off. Until the Reich has converted fully to regenerative energies, one must be sparing with one's resources. One seldom thinks of it at the time, but imagine the misery thirty years later when just outside El Alamein one's tank lacks that very last drop of fuel to achieve the final victory. As I looked in I could see Fräulein Krömeier sitting absolutely still at her desk. It was only then that I realised I had not enquired how she was bearing up. Birthdays, bereavements, personal calls – these were all things which Traudl Junge used to remind me of, and more recently Fräulein Krömeier. But in this case, of course, it had not happened.

She was staring at the desktop in consternation. Then she looked up at me.

"Do you know what sort of e-mails I'm getting?" she said weakly.

I was deeply moved by the sight of this poor creature. "I'm terribly sorry, Fräulein Krömeier," I said. "I can easily stomach this sort of thing; I'm used to enduring such hostility when standing up for the future of Germany. I bear full responsibility – it is unforgivable when one's political opponents choose to attack lesser employees."

"But it's got nothing to do with you," she said, shaking her head. "It's just the usual *Bild* crap? You appear once in that shitty rag with tits plastered on every page and then everyone's got it in for you. I'm getting like . . . photos of men's dicks? I'm getting really nasty mail? People saying what they'd like to do to me? I stop reading after the first couple of words. I've been Vulcania17 for seven years, but now I can forget it. That name's contaminated and now," she said, sorrowfully pressing a key, "now it's like . . . history."

Being unable to make a decision is not a pleasant feeling. If Blondi had still been alive, at least I would have been able to stroke her; in such moments an animal, particularly a dog, is always good for relieving some of the tension.

"And it doesn't stop with the Internet, either," she said. She stared blankly into the distance. "At least on the Internet you can read what people are thinking? But you can't do that on the street. You can only have a guess? And I'd rather not guess?" She snivelled.

"I ought to have warned you in advance," I said after a moment's silence. "But I underestimated the enemy. I am really very sorry that you are having to pay for my error. Nobody knows better than I do that sacrifices have to be made for the future of Germany."

"Couldn't you just put a sock in it for a couple of minutes?" Fräulein Krömeier said, looking rather exasperated. "F.Y.I., this is not about the future of Germany! This is real! This isn't a joke! It isn't a performance, either! It's my life these arseholes are messing up with their lies!"

I sat on the chair facing her desk.

"I cannot stop for a couple of minutes," I said seriously. "Nor do I wish to stop for a couple of minutes. I will defend to the very last what I believe to be right. Providence put me in this post, and here will I stand for Germany until the last round is fired. You might well say, 'All the same, can't Herr Hitler let up for a couple of minutes, just for once?' In peacetime I would be prepared to, for your sake, dear Fräulein Krömeier! But I do not wish to. I will tell you why. And then I'm sure you will no longer wish me to, either!"

She gave me a quizzical look.

"The very moment I start making concessions, I am not making them for your sake; ultimately I am doing it because this lying rag is forcing me to. Is that what you want? Do you want me to do what this newspaper demands of me?"

She shook her head, slowly at first, then in defiance.

"I am proud of you," I said. "And yet there is a difference between you and me. What I demand of myself, I cannot demand of everyone. Fräulein Krömeier, I would perfectly understand if you were to cease working for me. I am certain that Flashlight would accommodate you somewhere else, where you would not be confronted with such unpleasantness."

Fräulein Krömeier sniffed again. Then she sat up straight and said with determination, "Like hell I will, mein Führer!"

XXI

Che first thing I saw was large lettering in the Gothic script. The word on the screen was "**Heimatseite**". At once I picked up the telephone and called Sawatzki.

"So . . . you seen it yet?" he asked. And without waiting for an answer he said gleefully, "Come out well, hasn't it?"

"Heimatseite?" I asked. "What's that supposed to mean? What Heimat are we talking about?"

"Well, we can't exactly put 'Homepage' on your website, can we?"

"Really?" I said. "Why ever not?"

"But the Führer doesn't know foreign words . . ."

I shook my head energetically. "Sawatzki, Sawatzki, what do you know about the Führer? This uptight Germanness is the worst attitude one can have. You must not confuse racial purity with cultural isolation. Don't be ridiculous; a homepage is a homepage! One doesn't call R.A.D.A.R. *Funkortung und -abstandsmessung* just because the English invented it."

"O.K.," Sawatzki said. "'Homepage' is fine. I'll sort it. How do you like it otherwise?"

"I haven't really had time to look," I said, inquisitively pushing the mouse device across the table. On the other end of the line, Sawatzki was tapping away at his keyboard. Suddenly, a large "**Homepage**" appeared on my screen. "Hmm," he said. "That doesn't really make sense anymore. Why should 'Home-page' be in that old font?"

"Why must you make everything so complicated?" I upbraided him. "Just make it into 'Führer Headquarters'."

"Aren't you always saying that you're not commander-in-chief of the Wehrmacht just at the moment?" Sawatzki said with a hint of irony.

"Top marks for paying attention," I praised him. "But this is symbolic. As with my e-mail address. After all, I'm not the New Reich Chancellery, either." I hung up and set about exploring my site.

Right across the screen ran a bar, via which one could pay a visit to specific departments by manoeuvring the mouse. One was "Latest Dispatches", where we were planning to announce items of news, but which as yet contained little to read. Then came "Film Reel", where a small window showed visitors my previous appearances. Then a short biography of me, in which it said that during the period from 1945 to my return I had been "On Extended Leave". This had been Sawatzki's suggestion, and I had chuckled to myself at the thought that I had slept through the intervening years beneath the Kyffhäuser hills, like the great Kaiser before me. On the other hand, given that I was unable to provide any better or more detailed information on the time that had elapsed, I agreed to this formulation. Another department was "Ask the Führer!" – this was to serve as a channel of communication between me and my followers. Out of curiosity I checked to see whether anybody had asked a question yet. And one gentleman had indeed sent me a communiqué:

> Dear Herr Hitler,
> I read with interest your theory about the relative values of different races. I have been breeding dogs for many years and now I'm worried that I might be breeding an inferior strain. So my question is: Which is the best breed of dogs and which is the worst? And what is the Jew of the dog world?
> Yours,
> Helmut Bertzel, Offenburg

I was delighted. A good question, and an interesting one, too! Especially as I had been posed so many military questions of late – I had almost had enough of them. Moreover, military topics have limited entertainment value if one only ever receives bad news. In the early years of the war we would often have stimulating discussions around the table on the most diverse of subjects. Latterly I had really started to miss these. The dog-related question reminded me of this wonderful time! Eager to give the man an answer, I reached for my miracle telephone right away and searched for the somewhat complicated dictation function.

"Dear Herr Bertzel," I began. "Dog breeding has in fact advanced further than the reproduction and development of human beings." I paused briefly to consider whether I should provide Herr Bertzel with a succinct answer, but my enthusiasm took over and I decided to approach the subject with a thoroughness becoming the Führer of the German Reich. I would treat the question at length and produce a comprehensive, definitive response. But where to begin?

"There are dogs which are so intelligent that it is alarming," I spoke into the machine, in a measured way at first, then with increasing fluency. "Dog breeding is thus an interesting example of where human beings could already be. It also shows us, however, where unrestrained racial mixing leads, for if they are left unattended, dogs will mate indiscriminately. The consequences of this are to be seen predominantly in southern Europe, where mangy and feral mongrels roam and maraud, each more degenerate than the last. But where the hand of order intervenes, pure breeds develop, each one progressing towards perfection. Around the world there are – and I cannot help but put it as bluntly as this – more elite dogs than elite humans, a deficit which might have been eliminated by now had the German Volk shown greater perseverance in the mid-Forties of the previous century."

I paused, wondering whether I was not being excessively harsh on my fellow Germans, but then again my comments had only been aimed at those who were by now quite old. The younger Germans, on the other hand, should have an inkling of the demands which would be made of them at a later date.

"Naturally, the reproduction and development of dogs are not subject to the same laws as those of human beings. Dogs are under the authority of humans, humans control their nutrition and reproduction, which means that dogs will never have a problem with Lebensraum. For this reason the aims of breeding are not always oriented towards a future battle for world domination. Consequently, the question of what dogs might look like had they been fighting for global supremacy over millions of years must remain pure speculation. What goes without saying is that they would have larger teeth. And better weaponry. I consider it more than a mere possibility that dogs such as these would be able to use simple devices today, such as clubs, catapults, possibly even bows and arrows."

I paused again. Would these superior master dogs indeed have primitive firearms by now? No, I concluded, that would be unlikely.

"Nevertheless, the racial differences are not so dissimilar to those of human beings. Which justifies the question as to whether the canine world has its own Jew, the Jewhound, so to speak. The answer is: Of course there is a Jewhound."

I could already imagine what the hundreds of thousands of readers would be thinking at this stage, and thus I needed to pre-empt them: "But this is not, as many might suspect, the fox. A fox can never be a dog, nor can a dog ever be a fox, so it follows that the fox cannot be a Jewhound. If anything, foxes have their own identifiable Jewfox, to my mind most readily seen in the fennec, which in typical Jewish fashion even denies its foxiness in its name."

I had dictated myself into a mild rage. "Fennec," I muttered darkly. "What impudence!" Then I said quickly, "Fräulein Krömeier, please cross out 'fennec' and 'what impudence'. This was one thing I did not like about my miracle telephone. There must be an eraser function, but I could not work out how to use it.

"We must conclude, therefore," I continued, "that the Jewhound is to be sought amongst dogs. How to proceed here is quite clear. We must look for a grovelling dog, one which ingratiates and salivates, yet is poised to perform a cowardly ambush at any moment. It can be none other than the dachshund. Yes, I can hear many dog owners, especially those from Munich, protesting, 'How can this be? Isn't the dachshund the most German of all dogs?'

"The answer is: no.

"The most German of all dogs is the Alsatian, followed in descending order by the Great Dane, the Dobermann, the Swiss mountain dog (but only those from German-speaking Switzerland), the Rottweiler, all schnauzers, Münsterländers and – why not? – the spitz, which even finds a mention in Wilhelm Busch. Un-German dogs, on the other hand – apart from those foreign introductions such as terriers, bassets and other canine riffraff – are the Weimaraner (nomen est omen!), the vain spaniel, the unsporty pug, as well as all types of degenerate ornamental dogs."

I switched off and then back on again at once: "And those scrawny greyhounds!"

I pondered whether I had forgotten something important, but nothing came to mind. Excellent. I was eager for the next question, but unfortunately none had been submitted. I pushed the mouse contraption along to the final department: "Obersalzberg – be the Führer's guest". Its function was similar to a hotel guest book, and it had already attracted a fair few messages. Even if not all were comprehensible.

The serious comments were not a problem. I read: "All respect to you for your straight talking" or "I watch every programme. At last, here's someone prepared to dismantle the fossilised structures." This seemed to be a pressing concern of the German Volk; several people had mentioned the existence of such fossilised structures, or the dismantling of them. One fellow – a farmer, I presumed – spoke of "tructors"; another seemed to imagine these structures were as entangled as embroidery thread when he referred to them as "flossilised". In the end it became clear what they were trying to say. And there are more essential skills in which a German should be proficient than orthography, which has a tedious tendency towards bureaucratic hair-splitting.

Equally pleasing was the message "Führer rulez". This implied that I now had followers in France too, unless this was a typographical error, for I also saw the comment "Fuehrer RULZ!" but maybe a certain Herr Rulz was trying to achieve prominence at my expense. Several well-wishers exhorted me to "Keep at it!" or demanded "Führer for President". I was about to terminate my visit, when further down the list I caught sight of half a dozen absolutely identical entries, sent by someone who signed himself "blood&honour".

To my surprise the message was rather critical: "Stop yor lyes, you Jewturk!"

Shaking my head I called Sawatzki to have someone remove this nonsense. Jewturk – what was that supposed to be? He promised to sort it out and said I should make my way to the first page again. Across the screen were the words "𝕱ü𝖍𝖗𝖊𝖗 𝕳𝖊𝖆𝖉𝖖𝖚𝖆𝖗𝖙𝖊𝖗𝖘".

It looked splendid.

xxii

Press work is a tiresome affair when the newspapers have not been "brought into line". Not only for politicians like me, whose mission it is to save the German Volk – no, I find it absolutely incomprehensible that such a thing should be foisted on the people. Let us take business reports as an example. Every day another "expert" tells us what needs to be done, then the following day a different, even more expert "expert" explains why this is wholly wrong and why the contradictory solution is the correct one. This is a classic case of that Jewish strategy – albeit these days largely without the involvement of Jews – the sole purpose of which is to disseminate the greatest possible chaos, which is why people in search of the truth have to buy even more newspapers and watch even more television broadcasts. In the past no-one paid the slightest interest to the business sections, but now everybody feels obliged to devour them, only to be alarmed all the more by this financial terrorism. Buy shares, sell shares, now gold, now bonds, then property. The simple man is pressed into a secondary occupation as a financial expert; what this boils down to is that he is driven to gamble using his own carefully saved money as a stake. How preposterous! The simple man should work honestly and pay his taxes; in return a responsible state should take away his financial worries! That is the very least it should do. Especially as this government, for preposterous reasons (no atomic weapons of their own and a host of similar excuses), doggedly refuses to let the people have free farmland on the Russian Plain.

It is, of course, the height of idiocy that the political elites should permit such scaremongering in today's press. Amidst this chaos their own cluelessness is thrown into even sharper relief, and as the general worry and panic increases, so does the sheer incompetence of these political jokers. This is fine by me, for it makes the Volk more aware by the day that these are rank amateurs dabbling in positions of the highest responsibility. But what baffles me most of all is that millions didn't march on this parliamentary gossip chamber ages ago, wielding torches and pitchforks and chanting, "What are you doing with our money???"

But the German is no revolutionary. One must not forget that, in German eyes, even the most reasonable and justified revolution of 1933 was only possible by means of an election. A revolution on prescription, so to speak. Now, I can assure you that I shall do my utmost this time, too.

I had wanted to take Sawatzki with me to the Adlon. Not that I expected any significant inspiration from him, but it seemed appropriate to turn up with an entourage, and useful, in the case of any controversial utterances, to have a witness with me – *a* witness, please note, but Sensenbrink insisted on coming too. I do not know whether Sensenbrink supposed he might be able to make some helpful contribution, or whether his intention was to monitor what I had to say. As I have come to realise, deep down Sensenbrink is one of those subordinate business leaders who believe that nothing can work unless they themselves are involved in some form or another. I cannot warn enough against such nonsense. A truly universal genius emerges at most once every hundred or two hundred years – a man who, besides countless other activities, has to assume supreme command of the Eastern Front as well, else all is lost. In general, however, these indispensable people turn out to be wholly dispensable as well as useless, or worse. For very often they cause a mountain of damage too.

I had chosen to wear a sober suit. Not that I was ashamed of my uniform, but I am of the opinion that occasionally it is no bad thing to present a bourgeois image, particularly as I am the ambassador for uncompromising opinions. We contested the Olympic Games in 1936 along these lines and, as I have read, they recently tried to copy this overwhelming propaganda triumph in Peking, with very favourable results.

When we arrived at the hotel, which had been decorated for Christmas, we were taken to the appointed conference room. And although I had endeavoured to arrive slightly late, it was somewhat annoying to find we were the first ones there. It may have been a deliberate strategy on the part of those press scribblers, but equally it could have been a coincidence. In any event, the door opened soon afterwards and I was approached by a blonde woman in a suit. At her side was a corpulent photographer, who in the tattered clothing particular to his profession began to take pictures without being invited to. Before Sawatzki or Sensenbrink could come up with any absurd ideas of making introductions like a head teacher, I stepped forward, removed my peaked cap, jammed it under my arm and, with a "Good afternoon", offered my hand to the lady.

"Pleased to meet you," she said coolly, but not uncordially. "Ute Kassler from *Bild*."

"The pleasure is all mine," I said. "I've read much of your writing."

"I was expecting you to give the Nazi salute," she said.

"Then I know you better than you know me," I replied, leading her to a table around which chairs had been arranged. "I had not been expecting a Nazi salute from *you* – now, which one of us was right?"

She sat and carefully placed her handbag on a vacant seat. This handbag culture, this positioning of the object immediately after sitting down, as if they were taking their assigned place with luggage in a train compartment, I bet that will not change for another sixty-five years.

"I'm delighted you've finally found time for us," she said.

"You're not suggesting that I have favoured other newspapers over yours, are you?" I replied. "After all, you have . . . how shall I put it? . . . been making the greatest efforts to engage with me."

"Well, you're worth writing about," she said. "Who are these gentlemen with you?"

"This is Herr Sensenbrink from Flashlight. And this," I said, pointing to Sawatzki, "this is Herr Sawatzki, likewise from Flashlight. An excellent man!" Out of the corner of my eye I saw Sawatzki's face beam, partly a result of my praise, but perhaps also on account of the attention he was receiving from the reporter, a handsome woman after all. Sensenbrink wore an expression which one could interpret either as competent or clueless.

"You brought along two minders," she smiled. "Do I look that dangerous?"

"No," I said, "but without these two gentlemen I look completely harmless."

She laughed. As did I. What drivel. My utterance made no sense from start to finish. But I admit that I slightly underestimated the young blonde woman, and at the time assumed that I would be able to satisfy her with a few cheerful platitudes.

She took her telephone from the handbag, showed it to me and said, "You don't mind if we record the interview, do you?"

"Not if you don't," I said, bringing out my own telephone and passing it to Sawatzki. I had no idea how to record entire conversations with it. Sawatzki acted smartly, as if he had a jolly good idea. I decided to praise him again when the opportunity arose. A waiter came to the table to take our order, and then departed.

"Well?" I said. "What would you like to know?"

"How about your name?"

"Hitler, Adolf," I said, and my answer was enough to bring forth beads of sweat on Sensenbrink's forehead. It was as if I had never introduced myself before.

"What I mean, of course, is your real name," she said, narrowing her eyes.

"My dear young lady," I said, leaning forward. "As you may have read, some time ago I decided to become a politician. How dumb must any politician be who gives the Volk a false name? How should people vote for him in such a case?"

A vexed frown appeared on her face. "Precisely. So why aren't you telling the German people what your real name is?"

"But I am," I sighed. This was very tiring. Particularly as on the previous evening until late I had watched with interest a documentary which had drivelled on about my own miracle weapons. A highly amusing piece of twaddle, which broadly came to the conclusion that any of these weapons could have decided the war in our favour if I hadn't kept on ruining our chances. It is extraordinary what these history fantasists dream up without letting the facts get in their way. It hardly bears thinking about that even one's own knowledge of important men, such as Charlemagne, Otto I or Arminius, has strictly speaking been passed down by some historian who has felt himself called to the vocation.

"In that case would you be so kind as to show us your passport?" the young woman asked. "Or your identity card?"

From the corner of my eye I could see Sensenbrink wanting to say something. The chances are it would be poppycock. One never knows when and why such people start talking; frequently they only open their mouths because they realise they haven't said anything yet, or because they're worried that if they continue to remain silent they will be regarded as insignificant. This behaviour must be halted with every mean at one's disposal.

"Do you ask to see the passports of all your interviewees?"

"Only those who claim to be called Adolf Hitler."

"How many would that be?"

"I'm pleased to say you're the first."

"You are young and perhaps badly informed," I said, "but throughout my life I have always refused special treatment. And I have no intention of changing this now. I eat from the same field kitchen as any other soldier."

She said nothing for a short while, pondering a different approach.

"On television you speak about highly controversial topics."

"I speak the truth," I said. "And I say what the simple man is feeling. What he would say if he were in my place."

"Are you a Nazi?"

This was rather vexing. "What sort of a question is that? Of course!"

She leaned back. In all probability she was not used to talking to someone who was not afraid of speaking his mind. It was remarkable how calm Sawatzki remained, especially compared to Sensenbrink who was now sweating almost embarrassingly.

"Is it true that you admire Adolf Hitler?"

"Only in the mirror in the morning," I joked, but she impatiently ignored this.

"O.K. Let's be more precise: Do you admire the achievements of Adolf Hitler?"

"Do you admire the achievements of Ute Kassler?"

"We're not getting anywhere here," she said indignantly. "Look, I'm not dead, am I?"

"You may be sorry to hear this," I said, "but nor am I."

She pursed her lips. The waiter returned and handed round

the refreshments. Frau Kassler took a sip of coffee. Then she tried a new ruse.

"Do you deny the deeds of the Nazis?"

"On the contrary. I'm the first to refer to them – I never tire of it."

She rolled her eyes. "But do you condemn them as well?"

"How idiotic would that be? I am not as schizophrenic as our parliamentarians," I grinned. "This is the marvellous thing about the Führer state. Not only is there someone responsible before and during it, but afterwards too."

"For six million dead Jews as well?"

"For them especially! I wasn't keeping count, of course."

A spark of triumph glinted in her eyes, until I said, "But that's hardly anything new! If I've understood correctly, not even the press of the victors has disputed my accomplishment of having obliterated these parasites from the earth."

Her eyes flashed at me.

"And nowadays you're making jokes about it on the television," she hissed.

"That's a new one on me," I said seriously. "The Jews are no laughing matter."

She took a deep breath and leaned back once more. After a gulp of her coffee, she tried again.

"What do you do when you're not making your programme? What do you get up to in your spare time?"

"I read a lot," I said. "In many respects this Internetwork is a pure delight. And I like to draw."

"Let me guess," she said. "Buildings, bridges, things like that?"

"Absolutely. I have a passion for architecture . . ."

"Yes, I've heard about that too," she groaned. "Some of your stuff is still standing in Nuremberg."

"Still? How nice," I said. "I did my bit, but the glory really belongs to Albert Speer."

"Let's stop there," she said icily. "We're not getting anywhere. I don't get the impression that you came here today in a particularly cooperative frame of mind."

"I do not recall that our negotiations in advance of this meeting included a secret protocol."

She signalled to the waiter for the bill, then turned to her photographer. "Need any more pictures?" He shook his head. She stood up and said, "You'll read about this."

I stood up as well, and Hotel Reserver Sawatzki and Sensenbrink followed my lead. Manners maketh man. The poor young creature could not help it that she had grown up in a world in disarray.

"I'm very much looking forward to it," I said.

"Look forward all you like," she said as she left.

Sensenbrink, Sawatzki and I sat down. "So . . . that was a pretty short interview," Sawatzki said cheerfully, filling his cup. "No reason to let the coffee go to waste, guys. They make a damn fine cup here."

"Oh dear," Sensenbrink fretted, "Those two left with a warm bowl of nothing."

"They will write what they want anyway," I said. "What I'd like them to do is to leave Fräulein Krömeier alone."

"How is she?" Sawatzki asked with concern.

"Like the civil population of the Reich: the more the enemy

drops his despicable bombs, the more fanatical the resistance becomes. A tremendous girl."

Sawatzki nodded, and for a moment it appeared as if his eyes gleamed a touch too brightly. But I may have been mistaken.

xxiii

The problem with these parliamentarians is that they simply haven't understood a thing. I mean, why did I wage this war, for goodness' sake? Not because I enjoy waging war! I hate waging war. If Bormann were still around you could ask him; he'd back me up on the spot. It is a dreadful affair and had there been a better candidate for the job I would have gladly handed him the task. And now, well, I don't have to concern myself with it now, not in the short term, but in the medium and longer term I expect the onus will fall on me once again. Who else would do it? Indeed who else would do anything like it? Ask any parliamentarian these days and he will tell you bluntly that wars are no longer necessary. That is the argument people were peddling back then, too, and it was as nonsensical as it is today. Our planet is not growing, that is incontestable. But the number of people living on it is. And if the world's natural resources become too scarce for the global population, which race will get hold of them?

The nicest one?

No, the strongest. And for this reason I did my utmost to strengthen the German race. And to kibosh the Russians before they overran us. At the last possible moment, or so I thought.

Back then there were, after all, 2.3 billion people alive on this earth. Two point three *billion*!

Nobody could possibly have imagined that this would increase threefold.

But – and here is the key point – one needs to draw the right conclusion from this statistic. And the right conclusion is not that, because there are now seven billion of us, then all my efforts back then were unnecessary. The right conclusion is: If I was right in those days, then I am three times more right today. This is simple arithmetic, as any elementary school pupil could tell you.

Since my return the issue has yet again become most evident. Why are there seven billion people now living on earth?

Because I waged a war, which was entirely – to use this new-fangled word – sustainable. If all those people had since reproduced, we would now be at eight billion. And it is beyond doubt that most of those would be Russians, who would have overrun our country, harvested our fruits, driven away our live-stock, enslaved those of our men fit for labour and slaughtered the rest, thus leaving themselves free to abuse our innocent young women with their filthy hands. Providence thus first charged me with the task of wiping out the excess Bolshevist population. And henceforth my brief is to complete this mission. The intermezzo was necessary to preserve my strength over those decades, and now this strength is needed to see through the final outcomes of the war. Namely: discord amongst the Allies; collapse of the Soviet Union; loss of Russian territory; and of course reconciliation with our closest ally,

England, so that some day in the future we can act as one. It remains a mystery to me why that relationship never worked out. How many more bombs would we have had to drop on their cities before they realised that they were our friend?

Looking at more recent figures, however, it is hard to understand why one might need England at all. That sick island is barely a world power anymore. Well, not all questions need to be answered at once. However, the last possible moment for taking drastic measures is gradually approaching. And for this reason I was horrified at the state of the so-called nationalist forces of this country.

To begin with I had assumed that I was more or less on my own. But Fate had already put one or two allies in place. The fact, however, that it took me months to discover that someone had felt called to continue the work of the N.S.D.A.P. was proof of their inadequacy. I was so disgusted by their pathetic efforts at propaganda that I engaged the services of Assistant Director Bronner, together with a cameraman, and went to Berlin–Köpenick, home to the largest of these associations which went by the name N.P.D. And, I have to say, I was almost sick on the spot.

I grant that the Brown House in Munich had not exactly set the world on fire, but at least it was serious and representative. Or Paul Troost's administrative building, just a stone's throw away – that would have induced me to join any party in a jiffy. But this snow-covered dump in Berlin–Köpenick? It was a disgrace.

There stood a miserable hovel, freezing in a gap between two tenement blocks, like a child's foot in his father's too-large slippers. Even the building looked hopelessly overburdened, which may have been the result of some birdbrain having come up with the great idea of giving this frightful shack a name and screwing it onto the façade in large, classically ugly letters: "Carl Arthur Bühring House". This was akin to a child's bathing ring being christened the "Duke of Friedland". On the nameplate by the doorbell was written N.P.D. PARTY HEADQUARTERS, so small that it smacked of cowardice in the face of the enemy. Unbelievable – it was just like the Weimar era; yet again the racial principle, the national question, was being dishonoured, devalued, subjected to ridicule by a bunch of numbskulls. In a fury I pressed the bell, and when there was no immediate reaction I thumped it several times with my fist. The door opened.

"Can I help you?" asked a pimply boy with a confused expression.

"What do you think?" I said coldly.

"Have you got a permit to film?"

"What sort of dreadful whining is that?" I shouted at him. "Since when has a national movement ever hidden behind such oily, southern tricks?" I forced the door wide open. "Get out of my way, boy! You are a disgrace to the German Volk! Where is your superior?"

"I, er . . . hang on a sec, I'll go and fetch someone."

The youth disappeared, leaving us in some sort of reception room. I looked around. The place could have done with a paint and it smelled of stale smoke. A few party programmes were lying about, bearing absurd slogans. "Step on the gas" read one in inverted commas, as if one were in fact being urged to do the exact opposite. One sticker said: "Millions of foreigners are

238

costing us billions". Of course it failed to mention who would then manufacture the bullets and grenades for our troops, or who was supposed to excavate the bunkers for the soldiers at the front. Not the boy that I had seen, at any rate; he would have been just as useless with a shovel as he would in the field.

Never have I felt so ashamed of a nationalist party. I had to brace myself at the prospect of the camera filming all this, to prevent tears of rage from welling in my eyes. Ulrich Graf would not have taken eleven bullets to the body for these vermin; von Scheubner-Richter would not have fallen under the fire of the Munich police so that these scoundrels in their squalid dump could exploit the blood of outstanding men. I heard the bewildered youth stammering into a telephone next door. The camera recorded everything, all the incompetence. It was a bitter experience, but there was nothing for it but to muck out this cesspit once and for all. In the end I could bear it no longer; seething with wrath, I marched into the next-door room.

". . . Yeah, I would've chucked him out, but somehow . . . He looks like Adolf Hitler, he's got the uniform . . ."

I tore the receiver from the urchin's hand and screamed down the line, "Which lame duck is in charge of these premises?"

It was astonishing how nimbly Assistant Director Bronner managed to slip around the table and with unashamed delight press a button on the telephone. Now, thanks to a loudspeaker on the device, one could hear the answers perfectly well in the room.

"Please allow me . . ." the loudspeaker said.

"If I allow anything here, you'll know about it," I bellowed. "Why is there no supervisor in the office? Why is this four-eyed pipsqueak holding the fort? Get here at the double and account for yourself!"

"Who on earth is that?" the loudspeaker said. "Are you that madman off YouTube?"

I admit that certain recent events may not be easy for the man on the street to comprehend. But we need to apply different standards in this instance. Anybody wishing to lead a nationalist movement must be able to react to the most unpredictable turns of fate. And when Fate comes knocking at his door, he cannot ask, "Are you that madman off YouTube?"

"Right," I said. "I'm assuming that you haven't read my book."

"No comment," the loudspeaker said. "And now you're going to leave the offices or I'll have you thrown out."

I laughed.

"I marched into France," I said. "I marched into Poland. I marched into Holland and into Belgium. I encircled hundreds of thousands of Russians before they could even make a peep. And now I find myself in your so-called offices. If you had a residue of sympathy for the nationalist cause then you would get down here at once and explain why you are frittering away our magnificent racial heritage."

"I'm going to—"

"You would have the Führer of the Greater German Reich removed by force, would you?" I asked with great composure.

"But you're not the Führer."

For reasons I could not wholly comprehend, Assistant

Director Bronner clenched his fist at that moment and gave a very expansive grin.

"What I mean, of course, is: Hitler," the loudspeaker stammered. "You're not Hitler."

"I see, I see," I said calmly, extremely calmly, so calmly that Bormann would have been handing round the protective helmets. "But if," I continued politely. "But if I were, then would I have the honour of being able to count on your unconditional loyalty to, and support for, the National Socialist movement?"

"I . . ."

"I expect to see the appropriate Reichsleiter. At once!"

"At the moment he . . ."

"I have time," I told him. "Whenever I glance at my diary I see that I have an inordinate amount of time." I hung up.

The youth gave me a look of utter bafflement.

"You're not being serious, are you?" asked the worried-looking cameraman.

"I'm sorry?"

"Well, I don't have an inordinate amount of time, mate. I'm off at four."

"It's O.K., it's O.K.," Bronner reassured him. "If necessary we'll find a replacement. We're getting some great material here!" He took his portable telephone from his pocket and set about making arrangements.

I sat on one of the empty chairs. "Do you have any literature I could read?" I asked the youth.

"Er . . . I'll have a look, Herr . . ."

"The name's Hitler," I said soberly. "I must say, the last time I found it such an effort to introduce myself was in a Turkish dry cleaner's. I say, are you related to these Anatolians in any way?"

"No, it's just that – we . . ." the youth babbled.

"Listen. I do not see a great future for you in this party!"

The telephone rang, interrupting the boy's hunt for reading material. He picked up the receiver and braced himself.

"Yes," he said into the receiver. "Yes, he's still here." Then he turned to me. "It's the national party chairman for you."

"I'm not free to talk. The time for telephone conversations is over. I want to see the man in person."

The scrawny youth looked no better bathed in sweat. This was no graduate from one of the boarding schools we had established, nor could the weed have been anywhere near a military training ground; in fact sport seemed to have passed him by altogether. Even a cretin would find it hard to fathom that such a racial reject had not been sifted out in the party's admission process. The youth whispered something into the telephone receiver, and then hung up.

"The chairman asks for your patience?" the boy said. "He'll be here as soon as he can? This is for MyTV, isn't it?"

"This is for Germany," I set him straight.

"In the meantime, can I offer you a drink at all?"

"In the meantime you can take a seat," I said, giving him a long, concerned look. "Do you play any sport?"

"I'd rather not . . ." he said. "And the chairman's going to be here any moment now?"

"Cut the whimpering," I said. "Swift as a greyhound, tough as leather, hard as steel. Ring a bell?"

He gave a tentative nod.

"Then all is not lost," I said, somewhat indulgently. "You may be afraid to talk. But all you have to do is use your head. Swift as a greyhound, tough as leather, hard as steel – would you say that these are advantageous qualities when pursuing one's targets?"

"I'd say they couldn't hurt?" he said guardedly.

"Well," I asked. "Are you as swift as a greyhound? Are you as hard as steel?"

"I . . ."

"No you are not. You are as slow as a snail, as fragile as an old man's bones, and as soft as butter. Behind the front line that you are purportedly defending, women and children need to be evacuated at once. The next time we meet you will be in better shape! Dismissed."

He walked away sheepishly.

"And stop smoking," I yelled after him. "You smell like cheap ham!"

I picked up one of the amateurish brochures, but could not bring myself to read it.

"We're no longer alone," Bronner said, peering out of the window.

"Eh?" the cameraman said.

"God knows who tipped them off, but there's a whole gaggle of T.V. crews out there."

"I bet it was a copper," the cameraman conjectured. "That's why they're not slinging us out. You don't look like a good Nazi if you throw out the Führer when the cameras are running."

"But he's not the Führer," Bronner pondered.

"Not *at present*," I corrected him harshly. "The first task is to unite the national movement and dispose of these harmful imbeciles. And here," I said, glancing over at the youth, "we are in a veritable nest of harmful imbeciles."

"Ooh, now someone's here, guys!" Bronner said. "I think that's the big cheese."

The door opened and a wimpish-looking figure entered. "How nice," he said, short of breath, and offered me his chubby hand. "Herr Hitler. My name is Apfel, Holger Apfel. Federal Chairman of the National Democratic Party of Germany. I watch your programmes with great interest."

I looked this bizarre figure up and down. Bombed-out Berlin had not presented a sorrier picture. His voice sounded as if he were permanently chewing on a salami roll, and he looked like it too. I ignored his hand and asked, "Can't you salute me like an upstanding German?"

He gave me a confused look, like a dog to whom one has issued two instructions simultaneously.

"Take a seat," I told him. "We need to talk."

Huffing and puffing, he sank into the chair opposite me.

"So," I said, "you represent the national cause here, do you?"

"I have to," he said with a half-smile. "I mean, it's a long time since you were looking after things."

"I have to manage my time carefully," I said brusquely. "The question is: What have you been doing in the interim?"

"I don't think we have to hide our achievements," he said. "Now we represent Germans in Mecklenburg–Western Pomerania and Saxony, and our comrades in—"

"Who?"

"Our comrades."

"We call them fellow Germans," I said. "A comrade is some-one beside whom one fought in the trenches. Apart from my humble self I see nobody here to whom that applies. Do you?"

"For us National Democrats . . ."

"National Democracy?" I sneered. "What is that supposed to be? National Socialist policy requires a concept of democracy that does not lend itself to being named. When the Führer is appointed, democracy is brought to an end, but there you are still going around with the word in your name! How stupid can people be?"

"As National Democrats we are of course fully committed to the constitution . . ."

"You do not appear to have been in the S.S.," I said, "but have you at least read my book?"

He looked a little unsure, then said, "Well, I think you have to read as broadly as possible, and although the book is not easy to come by in Germany . . ."

"What is that supposed to mean? Are you apologising for having read my book? Or for not having done so? Or for not having understood it?"

"Come on, this is going too far now. Couldn't we just turn off the cameras for a bit?"

"No," I said stonily. "You have frittered away too much time already. You are a fraudster trying to cook his soup on the neglected embers of Greater German nationalism and love of Heimat, but each word that falls from your inept mouth throws the movement back decades. It would come as no surprise to me if in the end you were nothing more than a hostel for national traitors, infiltrated by Bolshevists."

He attempted to lean back so as to cast me a superior smile, but I was not going to let the man get off that easily.

"Where," I said icily, "in your 'brochures' is there any mention of the racial idea? The idea of German blood and racial purity?"

"Look, only recently I was stressing that Germany should be for the—"

"Germany?! This 'Germany' is a dwarf of a state compared to the country I established," I thundered. "And even the Greater German Reich was too small for its population. We need more than Germany. How are we going to get it?"

"We, er . . . we dispute the, er . . . legitimacy of the treaties recognising the borders, imposed on us by the victorious powers . . ."

I could not suppress my laughter, although I grant you it was the laughter of despair. This man was a joke, pure and simple. A hopeless idiot who was leading the largest national association on German soil. I bent forward and snapped my fingers.

"Do you know what that is?"

He gave me a quizzical look.

"That is the amount of time needed to quit the League of Nations. 'We dispute the legitimacy blah blah blah' – what snivelling nonsense! Quit the League of Nations, arm yourself, then take what you need. And if you have a racially pure German Volk ready to fight with a fanatical will, then everything will come to you on this earth. So, let's hear it again. Where do you stand on the racial question?"

"O.K. then. Having a German passport doesn't make you a

German; you're German by birth, that's what it says in our—"

"A true German does not wriggle around in legal formulations; he talks straight! The racial idea is the fundament for the preservation of the German Volk. If this is not impressed on the Volk time and again, in fifty years we will no longer have an army, but a bunch of layabouts like the Habsburg Empire." Shaking my head, I turned to the youth.

"Tell me, did you vote for this so-called democratic dumpling?"

The youth made an uncertain movement with his head.

"Was he *really* the best man available?"

The youth shrugged. I stood up in resignation. "Let's go," I said bitterly. "I'm not surprised this party doesn't spread any terror."

"What about Zwickau?" This was Bronner.

"What do you mean, 'Zwickau'?" I said. "What has that got to do with terror? My, we knew how to bring terror to the streets back then! In 1933 we exploited it to enormous success. But there was a reason for that. The S.A. drove around in trucks, breaking bones and flourishing banners. Did you hear me? Banners!" I yelled so wildly at this doughball that he recoiled.

"Banners! The most important things of all! When a deluded Bolshevist nincompoop is sitting there in his wheel-chair he ought to know who knocked the stuffing out of him, and why! And what does that trio of idiots in Zwickau do? They kill one foreigner after another – without any banners. Everyone thinks these must be random attacks or the Mafia. So what is there to be frightened of? The only reason we know these damp squibs existed at all is by the fact that two of the buffoons killed themselves." I threw my arms skywards in dismay. "If I had got my hands on these gentlemen in time I would have rolled out a euthanasia programme just for them!"

In a rage I turned to the doughball. "Or I would have trained them for as long as it took for them to work effectively. Did you at least offer assistance to any of the three cretins?"

"I had nothing to do with the matter," he said hesitantly.

"And I expect you're proud of that!" I screamed. If the man had been wearing epaulettes I would have torn them from his jacket in front of the camera. I marched to the door in disgust and stormed outside.

Before me lay a sea of microphones.

"What have you been talking about?"

"Are you going to stand for the N.P.D.?"

"Are you a member?"

"A bunch of sissies," I said disappointedly. "I'll just say one thing: this is no place for an upstanding German."

xxiv

"That's pure gold!" Madame Bellini said when, heavy-hearted, I showed her the report on the "National Democrats" alongside others we had filmed. "That's quite special," she gushed. "It'll only need the lightest of edits. This will be the next step on the path to consolidating the Hitler brand! We'll put it out at New Year! Or Epiphany, when everyone's lounging around at home, desperate to find something to watch other than 'Die Hard 64', or the hundredth repeat of 'Star Wars'." This was our last meeting prior to what they called the Christmas break. For now there was nothing to do but wait for the broadcast dates, for the *Bild* interview to appear, and for this time of peace and goodwill to all men to pass.

I have never been a great advocate of Christmas. In the old days many Bavarians found this hard to understand; there they celebrate the run-up to it with what they call "Yuletide". Had it been down to me, I would have eliminated the lot of it, including Advent and St Nicholas. Nor am I an advocate of this roast goose business, not on St Martin's Day, not at Christmas and definitely not at Candlemas. In any case, during my first tenure as Führer I had no time to waste as I prepared for the final victory. In fact, I was willing to give Christmas a miss altogether, but Goebbels always held me back and said we had to take the needs of the Volk into consideration. At least in the beginning.

Well, Goebbels was a family man. And I think it's no bad thing to have at least one man in the party who is able to bury his antennae deep into the soul of the Volk; one shouldn't ignore such currents of feeling. Although, in retrospect, perhaps the idea of using golden swastikas as tree decorations was a touch excessive. It is never a simple undertaking to put a new gloss on an old idea – one should rather offer up something entirely new, something of one's own creation. Although I never checked, I don't imagine that Goebbels used the swastika baubles himself; at most he may have hung up the odd one out of politeness or good manners. Himmler, on the other hand . . .

What I did cherish, however, were the possibilities Christmas afforded. All the books I was able to get through in that period. And the designs I managed to draw. Half of Germania came into existence! For this reason I did not mind spending the time around the turn of the year more or less alone in my hotel room. Hotel management had given me a small gift of a bottle of wine and a few chocolates. They couldn't have known that I don't much care for alcohol.

For me, the only unhappy aspect of the Christmas period has been the constant reminder that I was never blessed with my own family. Reorganising a Reich, cultivating the national movement amongst the Volk, ensuring my order not to surrender a centimetre in the East was carried out with due fanaticism and an iron will – these are not the sorts of matters one can attend to with children, not even with a wife. It was difficult enough with Eva; a certain consideration of her needs was essential, but ultimately the increased or sometimes extreme demands on my time and person from party, politics and the Reich meant one could not rule out the possibility that in her distress she might once again try to . . .

I will concede, however, that on those days when in theory I had comparatively little to do, Eva's company would have been most pleasant. Her happy disposition. Oh well: the strong man is mightiest alone. This also holds true at Christmas, especially so, in fact.

I looked at the bottle the hotel had given me. I would have preferred a sweet Beerenauslese.

Recently I had become accustomed to taking the occasional stroll to the kindergarten playground. I loved to watch the children romp around and squeal with excitement, and found it cleared my mind. But I discovered that the kindergarten was closed for Christmas. There are few gloomier sights than a deserted playground.

Then I took to the drawing board; after all, one never knows when one might find the time to sketch again. I drew a motorway network and a railway system – this time for the Lebensraum beyond the Urals – a few main train stations and a bridge over to England. They've dug a tunnel there now, but lately I've been more taken by solutions above ground. Perhaps I spent too much time in bunkers. Unsatisfied with my blueprint, I then designed two new opera houses for Berlin, each with 150,000 seats. But this task was executed more out of a sense of duty than any real desire – who would address these matters if I didn't take care of them? In the end I was delighted when I was able to resume work for the production company at the beginning of January.

XXV

I had not expected anything different. In fact I was almost satisfied, for at least they had left Fräulein Krömeier alone this time. It was not, however, what one might call good journalism. On the other hand, I regard the term "good journalism" as an oxymoron. All the same, I had expected that my accommodating attitude towards the paper might have been better rewarded than with the headline:

Loony YouTube Hitler tells BILD:
"I am a Nazi"

Wearing an inoffensive lounge suit, he pretends to be the honest citizen: the Nazi "joker" who calls himself "Adolf Hitler", while refusing to reveal his real name. All of Germany is discussing this "comedian" who parades as a monster. BILD interrogated the immigrant-baiter in an exclusive interview in Berlin's €400-a-night Hotel Adlon.

BILD: What is your real name?
Adolf Hitler.

BILD: Why will you not tell the German people what your real name is?
It is my real name (he grins smugly).
BILD: Would you show us your passport?
No.
BILD: Are you a Nazi?
Of course! (He cynically takes a sip of his mineral water. Giving him no slack, we elicit from this wicked man his most outrageous confession.)

BILD: Do you condemn what the Nazis did?
No, why should I? I'm the one who's responsible.
BILD: For the murder of six million Jews as well?
For them especially.

BILD says: This is no longer satire, it's incitement to hatred. It's high time we unmasked this bigot!

When is the law going to get involved?

"Are you *insane*?" Sensenbrink said, firing the newspaper onto the table. "If we go on like this we'll end up in court in no time! Come on, guys, you were all here when Frau Bellini said that the Jews were no laughing matter!"

"That's exactly what he told them," Sawatzki interjected. "Literally. But they didn't mention that."

"Calm down," Madame Bellini said. "I listened to the recording again. Everything Herr Hitler said he said as Adolf Hitler."

"As I always do," I added in astonishment, to emphasise just how ridiculous that comment was. Madame Bellini frowned at me briefly and then continued, "Er . . . yes, precisely. No-one can lay a finger on us legally. I want to stress once again that you've got to be careful when talking about the Jews. But I don't see what's false about the statement that Hitler was responsible for the death of six million Jews. Who else do you think was?"

"Don't let Himmler hear you saying that," I chuckled. I could see Reich Sceptic Sensenbrink's hair stand on end, even if I couldn't be sure why. I toyed with the idea that Himmler might also have woken up somewhere in Berlin, and that Sensenbrink was planning a television programme with him, too. But that was nonsense. Himmler did not have the face for television, and he never received a single letter from an admirer, or at least not to my knowledge. A decent administrator when needed, but his expression always harboured a slyness – pure treachery in spectacles, as it ultimately turned out. Nobody wants to see that kind of thing on their television set. Even Madame Bellini looked annoyed for a moment, but then her face relaxed and she said, "I hardly like to say it, but you're already an expert at this sort of thing. Other people would need at least half a year's media training."

"That's just great," Sensenbrink ranted. "But it's not just a legal thing. If they keep firing from both barrels our ratings could go south. Rapido. And there's nothing else they can do."

"Oh yes there is," I said. "But they choose not to."

"No," Sensenbrink bellowed. "There isn't. This is the Axel Springer Verlag we're talking about! Have you seen their mission statement? Point two: "To bring about reconciliation between Germans and Jews, including supporting the right of the Israeli people to exist." This isn't any old tittle-tattle, it comes from Springer himself. It's their Bible; every editor is given a copy when they're appointed and Springer's widow makes a point of checking that these principles are being adhered to!"

"And you're only telling me this now?" I asked acidly.

"It's not necessarily a bad thing if they give you no let-up," Sawatzki butted in. "We could do with all the attention we can get."

"Exactly," Bellini said. "But we mustn't let it go the wrong way. We must make sure that all our viewers know who the baddie is."

"So who is the baddie, then?" Sensenbrink groaned. "Himmler?"

"*Bild*," Madame Bellini and Hotel Reserver Sawatzki said in unison.

"I will clarify the situation in my next Führer address," I promised. "It's time that these parasites were named."

"Do you really have to call them 'parasites'?" Reich Sceptic Sensenbrink whimpered.

"We could accuse them of duplicity," Sawatzki said, "if we had a little more in our budget. Have you looked at Hitler's mobile?"

"Sure, he's got the recording of the conversation," Madame Bellini said.

"Not only that," Sawatzki said. He bent forwards, picked up my telephone and fiddled about with it for a moment. Then he held the device in front of us so we had a good view of the screen. It showed a photograph.

This was the moment I first realised I no longer missed that genius Goebbels.

xxví

There are always advantages to having reached a certain time in one's life. I am most pleased that I did not come to politics until I was thirty, an age when a man finds his peace physically and sexually, and thus can focus all his energies on his actual goals, without his time and steel forever being purloined by the impulses of physical love. It is also true that age determines the sorts of demands people will make of one. If the Volk elects a Führer who is twenty, let's say, and he displays no interest in women, people will start talking right away. What a queer Führer, they'll soon be saying, why doesn't he take a wife? Has he no wish to? Isn't he able? But if, like me, the Führer is forty-four and does not choose a wife immediately, the Volk will say, "Well, he doesn't have to, maybe he's got one already." And, "How nice that he's thinking only of us." And so it continues. The older one becomes, the more one assumes the role of the wise man, without, incidentally, having to do anything oneself. Take Schmidt, that ancient "Federal Chancellor" from some years back. This man has no shame whatsoever; he goes on and on spouting utter rot. They sit him in a wheelchair, where he ceaselessly puffs on one cigarette after the other, and delivers the most cretinous platitudes in an intolerably monotonous

257

tone of voice. This man has understood nothing at all, and by consulting a few books I have discovered that his fame is based on two silly deeds. One: when a storm surge hit Hamburg he called out the army to help – you don't need to be a genius to do that. Two: he let the communist criminals keep the kidnapped industrialist Schleyer, which surely was no great sacrifice for him; indeed he may even have been broadly sympathetic to the end result, as Schleyer was for many years in my S.S. and no doubt a thorn in the side of the Social Democrat Schmidt. And now, barely forty years later, this chimney on wheels is paraded about the country as an all-knowing oracle. You would think the Lord God himself had descended from the heavens.

But back to my point: naturally nobody expects this man to be womanising anymore.

The advantage of being older than one hundred and twenty is chiefly tactical. One's political opponent is not anticipating it, and so is completely ambushed. He expects one's appearance or physical constitution to be quite different. So the truth of the situation is denied outright, because what must not cannot be. This has very "unpleasant" consequences. For example, shortly after the war, the deeds of the National Socialist regime were declared to have been crimes. This was highly perplexing, seeing as my government had been a legitimately elected one. And it was established that there would never be a statute of limitations for these "crimes", which always sounds good to the ears of those sentimental parliamentary curs. But I'd like to see which of today's scoundrels in government will be remembered in three hundred years' time.

The Flashlight company had in fact received an official communication from the public prosecutor's office, saying that they had been telephoned by a number of nitwits, and that several complaints had been lodged relating to the alleged crimes. The investigations were stopped dead in their tracks, of course, because I could not possibly be who I purported to be, they said, and as an artist I naturally had more licence, and so on and so on . . .

Once again we see that even simple souls in the public prosecutor's office have a greater understanding of art than those professors at the Vienna Academy. Although public prosecutors today are like the blinkered legal experts of yesteryear, at least they recognise an artist when they see one.

Fräulein Krömeier informed me of all this when I arrived at my office just before lunch, and I construed it as a good start to the day on which I intended to bring my conflict with *Bild* to an end.

Irritatingly, I'd had to discuss my speech with Madame Bellini in advance, a state of affairs I found most objectionable, particularly as she had the company lawyer in tow, and we all know what we think of lawyers. To my great surprise the pedant had no reservations, or only very tiny ones, and these Madame Bellini swept from the table with a dynamic "We'll do it anyway!"

I still had a little time afterwards, so I headed for my office and bumped into Sawatzki, who was just leaving. He had been looking for me, he said, he'd left some manufacturing prototypes on my desk, and was thoroughly looking forward to the day of reckoning and so on and so forth. What he said came across as surprisingly inconsequential. Especially as I had already seen the prototypes the previous day – coffee cups, stickers, sports jerseys which were now called T-shirts, following the American usage. Sawatzki's enthusiasm, however, was one hundred per cent trustworthy.

"We will return fire at 22.57," he said, full of vim.

Intrigued, I said nothing.

And then he added, "Henceforth syllable will be met with syllable!"

I gave a smile of satisfaction and went into my office, where Fräulein Krömeier was diligently trying out new typefaces for my speech. Then I wondered whether I ought not to develop my own typeface. After all, I had already designed medals and the N.S.D.A.P. flag, a swastika in a white circle on a red background. Logically, therefore, I should invent the ideal typeface for a national movement. Then it occurred to me that before long graphic designers in printers' workshops would be discussing whether to set a text in "Hitler Black", and I scrapped the idea.

"Is there anything new about the prototypes?" I asked casually.

"Which prototypes, mein Führer?"

"The ones Sawatzki just delivered."

"Oh, I see!" she said. "Not really, there's only a couple of cups?" She quickly grabbed a handkerchief and blew her nose very, very thoroughly. When she had finished her face was quite red. Not tear-stained, but certainly rather animated. Well, I wasn't born yesterday.

"Tell me, Fräulein Krömeier," I speculated. "Is it possible

that you and Herr Sawatzki have got to know each other rather better of late?"

She smiled uncertainly. "Would that be a bad thing?"

"It is none of my business . . ."

"Well, seeing as you asked, it's my turn to ask a question: What do you think of Herr Sawatzki, mein Führer?"

"Enterprising, enthusiastic . . ."

"You know what I mean, L.O.L. He's been really friendly recently? And popping in a lot? But what do you think of him – as a man? Do you think he's right for me?"

"Well," I said, and Frau Junge momentarily came to mind. "It would not be the first time that two hearts have come together in my anteroom. You and Herr Sawatzki? I'm sure the two of you have a great deal of fun together . . ."

"So true!" Fräulein Krömeier beamed. "He's a real sweetie! But O.M.G., don't go telling him I told you that."

I assured her that she could count on my discretion.

"What about you?" she asked, sounding a little concerned. "Aren't you nervous?"

"Why should I be?"

"It's so unbelievable?" she said. "I've seen some of these telly people? But you're defo the coolest?"

"In my profession one must have veins of ice."

"Give it to them," she said firmly.

"Will you be watching?"

"I'll be right behind the set," she said. "And I've already got one of them T-shirts, mein Führer!" Before I could say a word she jauntily opened the zipper of her black jacket and proudly showed me the shirt.

"I beg you!" I snapped, and when she rapidly zipped up her jacket again, added more kindly, "Just for once wear something that isn't black . . ."

"Whatever you say, mein Führer!"

I left the office and was brought to the studio by the chauffeur. Jenny was already waiting and greeted me with a sonorous "Hi, Uncle Ralf!" By now I'd given up correcting her, in part because I knew she was turning it into a running joke. Over the past few weeks I had been Uncle Wolf, Uncle Ulf, Uncle Golf, Uncle Hoof and Uncle Woof. I was not sure I should be able to depend on her when it came to the crunch; it was indisputable that her frivolity would undermine morale in the long term, and so I had made a mental note. If this sort of thing did not cease after the first wave of incarcerations, then I had her earmarked for the second wave. But for now, naturally, I wasn't giving anything away as she led me to wardrobe and Frau Elke.

"Put the powder away, Herr Hitler's here!" she laughed. "Today's the big day, pet, so I've heard."

"Yes, but perhaps not for everyone," I said, taking a seat.

"We're counting on you, my love."

"Hitler – our last hope," I said dreamily. "As it used to say on the placards . . ."

"That's laying it on a bit thick," she said.

"Well, take some off then," I said anxiously. "I don't want to look like a clown."

"No, treasure, what I meant was . . . Forget it. You don't need much. The man with the dream skin. Go on, honey, out you go and show them who's boss."

I went behind the set and waited for Gagmez to announce

me. He now did this with increasing reluctance, although I had to admit that no outsider would have been able to detect it.

"Ladies and gentlemen. To preserve the multicultural balance, I give you Germany from the perspective of a German – Adolf Hitler!"

I was greeted by rapturous applause. With each programme I had found it easier to appear in front of the audience. A sort of ritual had evolved, as it had all those years ago in the Berlin Sportpalast: incessant cheering, which I subdued to absolute silence by not saying a word and looking deathly serious for minutes on end. Only then, in this tension between the expect-ation of the crowd and the iron will of the individual, did I begin to speak:

"Recently . . .

and on more than one occasion . . .

I have been obliged . . .

to read *things* written about me . . .

in the newspaper.

Of course . . .

I am used to that.

From the lying scum . . .

of the liberal press.

But now, too, in a paper . . .

which has lately printed some . . .

very pertinent comments about the Greeks.

Or about certain Turks.

And idlers.

Now it is I who am criticised

in that paper

for a number of remarks which . . .
were in the same vein.
Then 'questions' were raised,
such as who am I?
To cite only the most inane of the lot.
It was enough to make me ask:
What sort of newspaper is this?
What sort of rag?
I have asked my colleagues.
My colleagues know of it,
but do they read it?
No!
I have asked people on the street.
Do you know this paper?
They know it,
But do they read it?
No!
No-one reads this rag.
And yet . . . millions of people buy it.
Well . . . nobody knows better than I
that there can be no greater praise for a newspaper.
This was the case
with the *Völkischer Beobachter*."

Here the audience signalled their passionate approval for the first time. Appreciatively, I let them continue for a while, before I called for silence with a wave of my hand.

"By contrast . . .
the *Völkischer Beobachter* had a boss
who was a real man.

A lieutenant.

A fighter pilot

who lost his leg for

the Fatherland.

Who is running this *Bild*?

A lieutenant too.

Well, well, well!

So . . . what is wrong with this man?

Perhaps he is lacking in ideological leadership.

When the lieutenant and editor-in-chief

of the *Völkischer Beobachter*

was ever in doubt,

he would ask me

what *I* thought.

But no-one from this *Bild* paper

has ever solicited my opinion.

At first I thought the man might be one of those principled
    idealists,

who keep all politics at arm's length.

Then I realised.

He does indeed call when he needs moral support.

But he does not call me.

He calls Herr Kohl.

Another politician.

If one can call him that.

The very Herr Kohl who was a witness at his wedding.

I have made my enquiries at the lieutenant's publishing
    house.

They said it was all above board

and there was no comparison with the *Völkischer*
    Beobachter.

And yet,

this politician was the former chancellor of united
    Germany.

And *that*

is precisely what I cannot understand.

For after all, I am an even more former chancellor of
    united Germany.

But I doubt that the united Germany of this Herr Kohl

is as united as mine was.

Quite a few pieces are missing.

Alsace.

Lorraine.

Austria.

The Sudetenland.

Posen.

West Prussia.

Danzig.

East Upper Silesia.

The Memel Territory.

I have no desire to go into too much detail here.

But there is one thing I should like to say:

If the editor wants well-informed opinions

he ought to seek out the organ grinder

rather than the monkey."

Once more the studio exploded with applause, which I acknowledged with a solemn nod of the head before continuing.

    "But perhaps

this editor is not in search of well-informed opinions.

As people say so beautifully these days,

I 'googled' this man.

I found a photograph of him.

Then everything fell into place.

You see, this is the advantage of having a thorough
    grounding in racial theory.

One glance is enough.

This 'editor'

goes by the name of Diekmann.

Of course, this is not a real editor at all,

but a walking suit with a pound of lard in his hair."

A further blast of cheering told me that in Editor Diekmann I had hit upon exactly the right target. I gave the audience less time to show their elation this time, to draw out the tension.

"But ultimately, it is the deed which determines

the truth

and the lie.

The lie is: this newspaper is trying to convince its readers that it is my bitter enemy.

The truth you can see here."

I imagine it had taken all manner of photographic skill to process the detail of the image on my telephone, but nothing had been manipulated and the facts remained unchanged. One could clearly see Frau Kassler paying the bill at the Adlon. And then the picture was overlaid with Sawatzki's headline:

"*Bild* financed the Führer."

I have to say, I had not been applauded like that since the Anschluss of Austria in 1938. But the real show of support was seen in the visitor numbers to my special address on the Internetwork. At times my speech was not accessible – such bungling incompetence; in the past I'd have had Sensenbrink dispatched to the front for that. His skin was saved by the fact that Sawatzki's slogan had ensured excellent sales of "*Bild* financed the Führer*" sports jerseys, coffee cups, key rings and many such items. And the shops had been more than adequately stocked in advance.

Which made me adopt an even more conciliatory attitude towards Sensenbrink.

xxvii

It took three days for them to surrender.

On the first day they failed with their temporary injunction. The court rejected it on the perfectly reasonable grounds that *Bild* did not exist at the time of the Führer, which meant that the only possible reference was to the T.V. Führer. And the fact that the newspaper had financed him was incontrovertible. The court remarked, moreover, that the embellishment of facts in the headline was a stylistic device often employed by the paper, and thus *Bild* could not complain if such a tactic were used against it.

On the second day they realised that all revisionist aspirations were hopeless, and they were obliged to acknowledge the sales figures of sports jerseys, stickers and cups bearing the slogan. Some upstanding young Germans even staged a protest outside the publisher's offices, albeit in a far more avuncular mood than I would have considered apt.

For the time being I could no longer complain that other publications were ignoring me. When it began, the quarrel had got me onto the occasional gossip page, but now I was starting to make inroads into the arts sections. Sixty years ago I wouldn't have set the slightest store on being discussed cheek by jowl with all those unattractive and unintelligible contrivances of so-called "culture". In the meantime, however, a movement has evolved, according to which virtually anything can pass for culture or is extolled as such. Hence my appearance in these pages was to be welcomed as part of a transitional process stamping me with a seal of political seriousness that exceeded the norms of broadcast entertainment. The intellectual gobbledygook of this writing had not changed in sixty years, suggesting that readers still regarded as highbrow only material which they themselves found incomprehensible, and surmised the basic substance of these articles from the discernibly positive tone.

And there was no doubting the positive tone. The *Süddeutsche Zeitung* praised the "Potemkin-like retrospective" which "behind the apparent refraction of neo-fascist monostructures" suggested "the vehemence of an ardent plea for pluralistic or direct democratic processes". The *Frankfurter Allgemeine Zeitung* welcomed the "superb manipulation of inherent paradoxes in the sheep's clothing of the nationalist wolf". And the *Mirror Online* word-games section referred to my causing a "Führ-ore", which no doubt was meant well.

On the third day, as I later learned, the editor received a call from the widow of *Bild*'s publisher, who demanded to know how much longer the paper was going to put up with this violation of her late husband's memory. She thought it had gone on far too long already and insisted that this harrowing affair be brought to a swift conclusion the following day.

How he would achieve this was his own business, she added.

When I arrived at my office in the early afternoon, I could

see Sawatzki in the distance, bounding down the corridor towards me. In a rather adolescent gesture he was shaking his fist and shouting "Yes! Yes! Yes!" in English. I found his manner somewhat unbecoming, but could understand the enthusiasm. The surrender had been virtually unconditional. The negotiations, personally conducted by Madame Bellini in constant contact with me, first brought a ceasefire in reporting of several days, during which I was twice feted on the front page as that day's "mover and shaker" or "winner". After every retreat of theirs we would in response withdraw one item of merchandise from the market.

For the next edition of the programme the paper duly sent their best scribe, a sycophantic old soak by the name of Robert or Herbert Körzdörfer, who stuck to his task impeccably when he pronounced me the funniest German since a certain Herr Loriot. I read that behind the mask of the Nazi leader I "articulated intelligent ideas and was a true representative of the Volk". From Herr Sawatzki's unorthodox gymnastics I could infer that this was an excellent result.

But best of all I instructed the paper to do me a small favour and exploit some of its contacts. Just for once the idea came from Sensenbrink, who until then had been at his wits' end. A fortnight later there appeared a tear-jerking story about the bitter fate of my official documents, which had perished in some conflagration. Before another fortnight went by I was the proud owner of a passport. I have no idea by which legal or illegal channels this was acquired, but now I am lawfully registered in Berlin. I merely had to change my date of birth, which is now officially 30 April, 1954. Here Fate intervened once more by getting the numbers the wrong way round. I should have written 1945, of course, but 1954 is far more appropriate, given my age.

The only concession I made was that I had to forgo my intended visit to the *Bild* editorial board. My original demand was for the entire team to greet me with the Nazi salute while singing the Horst Wessel song in a round.

Ah well. You can't have it all.

Otherwise, everything turned out splendidly. The visitor numbers to the "𝕱ü𝖍𝖗𝖊𝖗 𝕳𝖊𝖆𝖉𝖖𝖚𝖆𝖗𝖙𝖊𝖗𝖘" Internetwork site necessitated ever more technological resources, requests for interviews mounted up, and on the recommendation of Sensenbrink and Madame Bellini, the visit to the "National Democratic" ne'er-do-wells was produced as a special trans-mission to satisfy the huge popular demand.

By the end of that day I was in the mood to clink glasses with Sawatzki again; maybe he would be able to conjure up some of that very agreeable Bellini drink. But Herr Sawatzki was nowhere to be found, even though he could not have left the building. And nor was Fräulein Krömeier, as I established when I returned to my office.

I decided against seeking out the two of them. This hour belonged to the victors, of which Herr Sawatzki was one; truly, he had made a not insignificant contribution to our triumph. And oh, how a warrior drunk on victory can enchant a young woman. In Norway, in France, in Austria, hearts flew to our soldiers. I am convinced that in the first few weeks following our invasion of each country, between four and six divisions were begotten from the loins of first-rate purebloods. How many new soldiers would we have produced had the older, not so pure-blooded generation been able to withstand the enemy for a paltry ten or fifteen years more?

The youth is our future. Which is why I made do with Madame Bellini and another glass of sour sparkling wine.

xxviii

I had never seen Sensenbrink look so ashen. Sure, the man had never been a hero, but his face now bore a colour I had not witnessed since the trenches in 1917, in that rainy autumn when stumps of legs stuck up out of the muddy earth. It might have been the result of unaccustomed exertion, for instead of telephoning me the man had come to my office in person to request my presence in the conference room. But Sensenbrink looked like the sporty type.

"It's unbelievable," he said repeatedly. "It's unbelievable. This has never happened in the entire history of the company." Reaching for the door handle with a sweaty hand, he turned round and said, "If I could have known when I met you at that bloody kiosk . . ." and then he smacked his head on the door frame as he made to leave the office.

Helpful Fräulein Krömeier jumped to her feet at once, but Sensenbrink staggered into the corridor, holding his head as if in a trance and interspersing several more "unbelievables" with a couple of "It's fine, I'll be O.K.".s. Fräulein Krömeier cast me a look of such shock, as if the Russians were suddenly back at the Seelow Heights, but I gave her a reassuring nod. The past weeks and months had taught me not to take Herr

Sensenbrink's fears especially seriously. Some anxious bureau-crat, or democrat, had probably sent another letter of protest to a state prosecutor; even now such complaints were being filed on a daily basis, and each time the investigation was aban-doned as inconclusive and preposterous. Maybe this time it was a little different and they would send an official to the office, but I doubted there was anything to worry about. In any case I was always prepared to go to prison for my convictions.

I must admit, however, that a certain curiosity gnawed at me as I made my way to the conference room. Not only were Herr Sawatzki and Madame Bellini also striding towards the room, but a general sense of nervousness or tension was palp-able in the corridors. Colleagues were huddled in doorways in small groups, chatting in hushed tones and casting me furtive, quizzical or unsettled looks. I decided to take a minor detour and pay a visit to the in-house cafeteria to acquire some glucose. Whatever was going on in that conference room, I resolved to strengthen my own position by making them wait.

"I say, you've got balls," said Frau Schmackes, who ran the cafeteria.

"I know," I said amicably. "That's why no-one but I was able to enter the Rhineland."

"Oooh, stop exaggerating! I've been there too, you know," Frau Schmackes said. "But I can't stand that Cologne lot. What can I get you, love?"

"A packet of your glucose, please."

"That'll be 80 cents, love," she said before bending forward almost conspiratorially. "Kärrner's come in specially, you know? He's already in the meeting room, so I've heard."

"I see," I said, paying. "Who is this Kärrner?"

"Let's put it this way," Frau Schmackes said. "He's the big cheese, the boss of the whole set-up. You don't see him much, because normally it's Bellini running the show, and if you ask me she's got a better handle on things. But when there's a major disaster, Kärrner comes in himself." She pushed my 20 cents change across the table. "Also when there's some special announcement, of course. But it has to be pretty big, I mean Flashlight's not doing bad, you know."

I carefully took out a tablet of glucose and placed it in my mouth.

"Shouldn't you be on your way, love?"

"That's what they all said in winter 1941," I told her, and then finally headed with measured step in the right direction. I didn't want to give the impression that I was trying to avoid the conference.

The groups of people in the corridors had grown. It was almost as if my colleagues were standing on parade and I was inspecting them. I gave a friendly smile to a few young women and jerked my arm back in greeting. There was the occasional giggle, but also a "You'll do it!"

Of course. The only question was: What?

The door to the conference room was ajar and Sawatzki was standing in the entrance. When he saw me approaching from a distance he gestured with his hand, urging me to hurry. And yet this was clearly no reprimand; his expression of confidence immediately signalled that he desperately, really desperately wanted to know what it was all about. I slackened my pace ever so slightly again to pay a passing compliment to a young woman for her pretty summer dress. My speed reminded me of the paradox of Achilles and the tortoise he can never overtake.

"Good morning, Herr Sawatzki," I said firmly. "Is this the first time we've seen each other today?"

"Go in," he beseeched, gently pushing me. "In, in, in. Or I'll die of curiosity."

"There he is," Sensenbrink said from inside the room. "At last!"

A few other men were seated around the conference table. More than at my first conference, and sitting beside Madame Bellini was apparently that Kärrner character. A slightly corpulent, but definitely sporty type of around forty years old.

"You all know Herr Hitler, of course," said Sensenbrink, who was still as white as a sheet, but at least no longer bathed in sweat. "But the converse is not necessarily true, despite the fact that he's been working with us for quite a while now. So, as we've got the top brass – if I may put it like that – of our company around the table today, I'd like just to introduce you guys briefly."

Sensenbrink reeled off a list of names and functions, a colourful array of Senior and Vice Account Managing Executives and whatever else they have these days. The titles and faces were all so interchangeable that I knew at once that the only name worthy of note was Kärrner's. Accordingly, he was the only man I acknowledged with a discreet nod of the head. "Fine," Kärrner said. "Now that we all know who we are, could we please throw some light on this surprise? I've got another meeting straight after this one."

"Sure thing," Sensenbrink said. I realised that I had not been offered a seat. And yet there was no rehearsal stage as there had been on my first visit to the company. One might assume that my position was unchallenged. I looked over at Sawatzki. He had balled his right hand into a fist and was nibbling away at his knuckles.

"This isn't official yet," Sensenbrink said. "So I'd ask you to keep the cone of silence on it for the moment. But I have it from an absolutely reliable source. Or, more accurately, from two absolutely reliable sources. It's because of the N.P.D. special, the extra programme we put on straight after the *Bild* coup."

"Well, what about it?" Kärrner asked impatiently.

"Herr Hitler's getting the Grimme Prize."

A deathly silence enveloped the room.

Then Kärrner spoke.

"And you're sure of that?"

"One hundred and ten per cent," Sensenbrink said, turning to me. "I thought the deadline had passed, but someone called you in as a late nomination. They tell me you've steamrollered the rest of the field. Someone used the word 'tsunami'."

"A lightning victory!" Sawatzki called out in excitement.

"Are we doing culture now?" I overheard one of the numerous executives say; everything else was drowned out by vigorous applause. Kärrner stood up, Madame Bellini got to her feet almost simultaneously, and then the entire assembled company rose. The glass door opened and two women led by Sensenbrink's receptionist, Hella Lauterbach, stepped in carrying several glasses of sour sparkling wine. Without the need for verification I could be confident that, at this very moment,

Sawatzki was issuing an order for that fruity Bellini drink. All kinds of people shuffled in from outside: typists, assistants, trainees and helpers. The words "Grimme Prize" alternated continually with "really?" and "unbelievable!" With difficulty Kärrner made his way towards me through the throng, his hand outstretched and a strange expression on his face.

"I knew it," he cried in sheer excitement, darting glances between me and Sensenbrink. "I knew it! We can do more than just comedy! We can do much more!"

"Superlative!" Sensenbrink cried back, and again even more loudly: "Superlative!"

I concluded from his comment that the prize must be a prestigious seal of quality for broadcasting.

"You're just fantastic," a soft, female voice said close to my ear. I turned around. Standing in another group with her back to me was Madame Bellini.

"I can but repay the compliment," I said over my shoulder, without conspicuously turning towards her.

"Ever thought of doing a film?" she murmured.

"Not for a long time," I replied. "When you've worked with Riefenstahl . . ."

"Speech! Speech!" roared the crowd.

"You've got to say something!" Sensenbrink urged. And although I don't tend to speak at those sorts of social occasions, now it was unavoidable. The crowd retreated a couple of paces and fell silent, apart from Sawatzki who swished through the throng to pass me a glass of the Bellini drink. I took it gratefully and surveyed the assembled company. Having nothing prepared, I had to fall back on some tried and tested phrases.

"My fellow Germans!
In this hour of victory
I turn to you
to clarify two things.
This triumph is unquestionably gratifying,
it is well deserved,
long deserved. We have driven larger productions
from the battlefield,
more expensive,
and even international ones.
But this victory
can only be a step
on the way
to the final victory.
Most of all we have your sincere and confident efforts to
     thank!
Your unconditional, fanatical support.
But in this hour
we also wish to remember the victims
who have sacrificed their blood for our cause . . ."

"I'm sorry," Kärrner said suddenly, "but I know nothing
about this."

Only then did it occur to me that I must have absent-
mindedly slipped into the routine I used after the Blitzkrieg
triumphs, which was perhaps a touch inappropriate, given the
circumstances. As I was weighing up whether I ought to offer
an apology or something along those lines, a voice interjected:

"It's lovely you should be thinking about her in a moment
like this," said a colleague I had never met, an expression of

"Good morning," I said.

"I've got to tell you something right now, mein F—" she said somewhat stiffly. "I can't salute you anymore. And I can't work here anymore either? I just can't do it anymore." Then she sniffed and bent to pick up her rucksack. Placing it on her lap, she opened the zipper and then closed it again without taking anything out. She returned the rucksack to the floor, stood up, opened a drawer in her desk, peered in and closed the drawer again. She sat back down and continued typing.

"Fräulein Krömeier, I . . ."

"I'm like . . . really sorry, but I can't do it anymore," she said as she typed. "It's such crap!" She looked at me and cried, "Why can't you do that stuff the others do? Like Klamaukheiner, who always plays the postman? Or that Bavarian, Mittermeier? Why couldn't you just strut about and – I dunno – put on a funny accent? That would be much better!"

I fixed my gaze on Fräulein Krömeier and asked, somewhat awkwardly, "You want me to strut about?"

"Yes. Or just insult people? It doesn't even have to be funny! Why do you always have to be Hitler?"

"It is not something one can choose," I said. "Providence sets us in our place and there we perform our duty!"

She shook her head. "I'm typing up the advert for internal recruitment," she sniffed. "You'll get a replacement nice and quick. It'll be as quick as a flash, just you wait. I bet there's tons of people ready to jump on the bandwagon."

Lowering my voice, I said quietly but firmly, "Stop your typing this instant and tell me what is wrong. Now!"

"Look, I can't work here anymore," she said defiantly.

"You can't? And why not?"

"Because I was at my nan's yesterday!"

"Sorry, but I'm none the wiser."

Fräulein Krömeier took a deep breath.

"I love my nan. I lived with her for almost a year when my mum was ill. And I went to see her again yesterday? And she was like, 'What are you up to?' And I was like, 'I'm working for a real star?' I was so proud? And then she was like, 'Who is it?' And I was like, 'Guess.' And she didn't have a clue, so I was like, 'Adolf Hitler?' And she was so pissed off? My nan absolutely flipped, she lost it. And then she starts crying? And she's like, 'What that man does is not funny. It's nothing to laugh about. We can't have people like that around.' And I'm like, 'But Nan, it's satire? He's doing it so it doesn't happen again?' But she's like, 'That's not satire. He's just the same as Hitler always was. And people laughed then, too.' So I'm sat there, thinking, 'For goodness' sake, she's just an old woman exaggerating? She's never said much about the war, I expect she's just in a tizz because she went along with a lot of it?' And then she goes over to her desk and takes out an envelope with a photo inside."

She paused briefly and gave me a searching look. "You should have seen how she took that photo out. Like it was worth a million euros? Like it was the last photo in the world? I made a copy of it. I had to spend half an hour persuading her to give it me to copy."

Fräulein Krömeier bent to take a photograph from her rucksack and handed it to me. I examined the picture. It showed a man, a woman and two young lads somewhere in the countryside. They may have been beside a lake; they were lying on a blanket or a large beach towel. I surmised that this was a family. The man in his bathing trunks was perhaps a little over thirty. He had short dark hair and looked athletic; the blonde woman was decidedly attractive. The lads were sporting paper hats – made from a newspaper, I expect – and posing with wooden swords, broad smiles across their faces. My assumption about the lake proved correct; at the bottom of the picture someone had written in dark pen: "Wannsee, summer 1943". All in all, this appeared to be an impeccable family.

"What about it?" I asked.

"It's my nan's family. Her dad, her mum, her two brothers."

I did not wage war for six years without a sense of the tragedies that war can unleash. The wounds that untimely death can hack into people's souls. "Who died?" I asked.

"They all did. Six weeks later."

I looked at the man, the woman, the two lads, especially the two lads, and I had to clear my throat. One can expect the Führer of the German Reich to be relentlessly harsh with himself and with his Volk too, and I am always the first to impose such severity upon myself and on others. I am sure I would have been steely and indomitable had I been scrutinising a more recent photograph, let's say of a soldier in this new Wehrmacht, even if he had been a victim of hopelessly incompetent political machinations, a sacrifice of this ineffable Afghan venture. But this photograph, dating so evidently from that time to which I still felt very close, this picture touched my heart.

I surely cannot be reproached for having been prepared at any moment, and without hesitation, to sacrifice hundreds of thousands on the fronts in the East and West to save millions.

For having sent men to their deaths, men who took up arms in full confidence that I would commit and – if the worst came to the worst – give up their lives for the welfare of the German Volk. Maybe the man in the photograph was one of these; it was very possible that he had been on leave. But the woman. The boys. Indeed, the civil population as a whole . . . It still made me sick, this impotence, the fact that I had not been able to protect the Volk on home soil. That dipsomaniac Churchill ought to have been ashamed of himself for having allowed the most innocent of the innocent to perish miserably in the flames of the firestorm, living torches of his all-consuming hatred.

All the wrath and ire of those years came to the boil again, and with moist eyes I said to Fräulein Krömeier, "I am so terribly sorry. I will – and here I give you my word – I will spare no effort to prevent any English bomber from even daring to come near our borders and cities again. Let nothing be forgotten, and mark my words, one day we will meet each bomb a thousandfold . . ."

"Please!" Fräulein Krömeier stuttered. "Please, cut it out for a second. For just a *single* bloody second. You haven't got a clue what you're talking about."

This would take some getting used to. It's been a long time since the Führer was rebuked, even unjustly so; the Führer should be far too high up in the national hierarchy to be rebuked. Moreover, one ought never to rebuke the Führer; one must have trust in him. In this respect any and all rebuking of one's superiors is unjustified, and of me especially so, and yet . . . and yet Fräulein Krömeier seemed genuinely troubled. Thus I glossed over her remarks, delivered in anger, for her objection was of course utter nonsense. There is barely a person alive who knows better than I what they are talking about, most especially on this score.

So I held my tongue for a moment.

"If you should like to have the day off . . ." I then said. "I believe you are in a difficult situation. I just wanted you to know that I have nothing but the very highest regard for your work. And if your grandmother is unhappy about it, maybe it would help if you explained to her that she's directing her ire at the wrong target. The bombing was Churchill's idea."

"It's not aimed at the wrong target, that's what's so awful," Fräulein Krömeier shrieked. "Who's talking about a bombing? These people weren't bombed. They were gassed!"

I paused and took another look at the photograph. The man, the woman, the boys – none of them looked like criminals, or Gypsies, certainly not like Jews. Although in their facial features, if you looked closely enough – no, that could also be my imagination.

"Where is your grandmother in this picture?" I asked, but I'd already guessed the answer.

"She took the photo?" Fräulein Krömeier said in a voice that sounded like green, untreated wood. Motionless, she stared at the wall opposite. "It's the only photo she has of her family. And she's not even in it herself." A black tear ran down her cheek.

I offered her a handkerchief. At first she did not react, but then she took it and smeared kohl across her face.

"Perhaps it was a mistake?" I said. "I mean, these people don't look at all like . . ."

"What kind of argument is *that*?" Fräulein Krömeier asked.

289

"Are you telling me that if they were killed by mistake then everything's O.K.? No, the real mistake is that someone came up with the idea that all the Jews had to be killed! And the Gypsies! And the gays! And everyone else whose face he didn't like the look of. Let me tell you something. The answer is, if you don't kill everyone you don't kill the wrong ones either, do you? It's that simple!"

I stood there, somewhat at a loss. Her outburst had taken me quite by surprise, even though I am attuned to the more sensitive emotional realm of women.

"It was a mistake then . . ." I declared, but I was unable to finish my sentence for she leaped to her feet and howled, "No! It wasn't a mistake. They were Jews! They were gassed totally legally! Just because they didn't wear their stars. They kept a low profile and took off their stars, because they hoped they wouldn't be recognised as Jews? But unfortunately a policeman tipped off the authorities? So they weren't just Jews. But illegal Jews. Happy now?"

In fact I was. It was utterly astounding. I might well not have arrested these people myself; they looked German through and through. I was so taken aback that my first thought was to congratulate Himmler once more on his thorough, incorruptible work when I got the chance. But at this particular moment it seemed inadvisable to give a direct and truthful reply.

"Sorry," she said all of a sudden, breaking the silence. "It's not your fault. It doesn't matter. I can't go on working for you; I can't do it to my nan. It'd be the death of her. But why can't you just say, 'I'm sorry about your grandmother's family, it was horrid what went on back then, sheer lunacy'? Just like any normal person would do? Or that you're trying to make people finally understand what bastards that lot were? With me, with all of us here, trying to make sure that nothing like that ever happens again." Then she added, almost in supplication, "I mean, that's what we're doing here, isn't it? Just say that! Just for me?"

The 1936 Olympic Games came to mind. Perhaps not purely by coincidence, for the blonde woman in the photograph reminded me distinctly of Helen Mayer, the fencing Jewess. Consider the following scenario: You're hosting the Olympic Games; you have a fantastic opportunity for excellent, nay, the very best possible propaganda. You can make a positive impression on the world outside, you can win time for rearmament if you are still weak. And you have to decide whether during all of this you are going to continue to persecute Jews, thereby forfeiting all the advantages you have gained. In such a situation it is imperative to set crystal-clear priorities. Thus you allow Helene Mayer to compete, even if she only gets a silver medal. And you must tell yourself, "Fine. I shall persecute no Jews for a fortnight. Alright, let's make it three weeks." And just as in the past, now it was essential to win time. Sure enough, I had obtained a certain acceptance amongst the Volk. But did I have a movement behind me yet? I needed and liked Fräulein Krömeier. And if Fräulein Krömeier had an undetected portion of Jewish blood running through her veins, I had to find an accommodation with this.

Not that it would have bothered me. If the rest of the genetic material is of sufficiently high quality, the body can sustain a certain portion of Jewish blood without its having an effect on the person's character and racial features. Whenever Himmler disputed this, I reminded him of my splendid Emil Maurice. Having a Jewish great-grandfather did not prevent him from being my key man in dozens of brawls, faithfully at my side, in the front line against the Bolshevist brood. I intervened personally to ensure that he remained in my S.S., for fanatical, granite conviction can override everything, even one's genetic constitution. Moreover, I actually saw how Maurice, over time and with an iron will, killed off more and more Jewish elements within himself. A kind of mental self-Aryanisation – it was phenomenal! But loyal Fräulein Krömeier, still so very young, had not yet reached that point. Her awareness of these minor Jewish elements in her make-up was causing her resolve to waver. This had to be halted. Not least on account of the positive influence she was having on Herr Sawatzki, and vice-versa. The 1936 Olympic Games. It presented the perfect opportunity to conceal our aims.

I was offended, however, by Fräulein Krömeier's criticism of my life's work. Or at least of my former life's work. I decided to take the straight path. The path of eternal, unadulterated truth. The upstanding path of the Germans. In any case, we Germans cannot lie. Or at least not very well.

"What bastards are you talking of?" I said, as calmly as I could.

"The Nazis, of course!"

"Fräulein Krömeier," I began. "I don't imagine that you'll thank me for saying this, but you are mistaken in many things. The mistake is not yours, but it is a mistake all the same. These days people like to assert that an entire Volk was duped by a handful of staunch National Socialists, unfaltering to the very end. And they're not entirely wrong; an attempt did in fact take place. In Munich, 1924. But it failed, with bloody sacrifices. The consequence of this was that another path was taken. In 1933 the Volk was not overwhelmed by a massive propaganda campaign. A Führer was elected in a manner which must be regarded as democratic, even in today's understanding of the word. A Führer was elected who had laid bare his plans with irrefutable clarity. The Germans elected him. Yes, including Jews. And maybe even your grandmother's parents. In 1933 the party could boast four million members, after which time we accepted no more. By 1934 the figure might otherwise have been eight million, twelve million. I do not believe that any of today's parties enjoy anything approaching this support."

"What are you trying to say?"

"Either there was a whole Volk full of bastards. Or what happened was not the act of bastards, but the will of the Volk."

Fräulein Krömeier looked at me in disbelief. "You . . . can't say that! It wasn't the will of the people that my nan's family should die! Come off it, it was the idea of those who were found guilty. In, what's it called, in . . . Nuremberg."

"Fräulein Krömeier, I beg you! This Nuremberg spectacle was nothing more than a deception, a way to hoodwink the Volk. If you are seeking to find those responsible you ultimately have two options. Either you follow the line of the N.S.D.A.P., and that means the man responsible is precisely the one who bears responsibility in the Führer state – i.e. the Führer and no-one else. Or you must condemn those who elected this Führer, but failed to remove him. They were very normal people who decided to elect an extraordinary man and entrust him with the destiny of their country. Would you outlaw elections, Fräulein Krömeier?"

She looked at me uncertainly. "I might not understand as much about it as you do, no doubt you've studied and read it all, but you do think it's bad, don't you? What happened? Surely you would want to prevent it . . ."

"You are a woman," I said indulgently. "And in emotional matters women are very impulsive. This is nature's way. Men are more objective; we do not think in categories like bad, not bad and suchlike. Our task is to deal with problems, and to identify, establish and pursue goals. But these questions do not permit of any sentimentality! They are the most important questions for our future. It may sound harsh, but we cannot look back at the past and complain; instead we must learn from it. What happened has happened. Mistakes are not there to be regretted; they exist so that they are not repeated. In the aftermath of a fire I will never be that man who spends weeks and months crying over an old house! I am the man who builds a new house. A better, a stronger, a more beautiful house. But in this I can only play the modest role which Providence has assigned to me. I can only be a small, modest architect for this house. The master builder, Fräulein Krömeier, the master builder is, and must always remain, the German Volk."

"And it mustn't ever forget . . ." Fräulein Krömeier said, wagging her finger.

"Exactly! It must never forget the strength that lies dormant within it. The capabilities it has! The German Volk can change the world!"

"Yes," she said. "But only for the better! We must never let the German people do anything dreadful again!"

This was the moment when I realised just how much I cherished Fräulein Krömeier. For it is astonishing how some women can take a tortuous path and nevertheless end up at the right destination. Fräulein Krömeier had understood that history is written by the victors. And any positive appraisal of German deeds naturally requires German victories.

"That, precisely that must be our goal," I lauded her. "And we will attain it. If the German Volk prevails, then in one hundred, two hundred, in three hundred years you and I shall find only hymns of praise in our history books!"

A faint smile darted across her face. "In two hundred years someone else'll have to read it? You and I'll be long gone by then."

"Well," I said thoughtfully, "at least that is what we must assume."

"I'm sorry," she said, pressing a button on her keyboard. I knew this sound by now, the sound Fräulein Krömeier made when printing on the communal machine in the corridor. "I'd have loved to go on working here."

"And what if you didn't tell your grandmother?"

Her answer pleased me as much as it pained her: "No. I can't lie to my nan."

But I could see to it that she receives special treatment, I thought instinctively, albeit only briefly. It is unrealistic to think one can arrange special treatment if one is lacking a Gestapo. Or a Heinrich Müller.

"Please, don't rush into anything," I said. "I understand the position you're in, but good secretaries are not exactly ten a pfennig. If you have no objections, I will personally have a word with your grandmother about your staying on in my office."

She looked at me. "I don't know about that . . ."

"I'll be able to clear up any misgivings she may have, you mark my words," I assured her. I could see the relief blossom on Fräulein Krömeier's face.

Few people would have embarked on such an undertaking. Personally, I have never had cause to doubt my powers of persuasion. And not only because I am aware of the rumour spread behind my back that whenever I am in the vicinity of Frau Goebbels you can hear her ovaries rattling or clattering, or whatever noise the soldiers' crude humour deems appropriate. No, such mockery falls short. What we are talking about here is the self-assured charisma of the victor, the charisma of the man who precisely does *not* doubt. Used properly, it works just as well on the youngest women as on the eldest. The Jewesses were no exception in this regard; on the contrary, in their urge for assimilation, for normality, I found them even more susceptible. Why, Helene Mayer, our fencing Jewess at the Olympic Games, even gave the Nazi salute as she received her silver medal. Or if I think of those tens of thousands who believed they could feel like Germans just because they had spent some time shirking at the front in the previous war, some even lying their way to an Iron Cross.

Anyone who can behave so deceitfully while his own racial comrades are being bludgeoned, while their shops are being boycotted and demolished, can be effortlessly hoodwinked sixty years later, particularly by – and I say this not out of any false vanity, but because it represents the profound truth – a seasoned expert in the strengths and weaknesses of this race.

And to all you romantics and gullible souls, who imagine that these devious parasites possess an extraordinary astuteness to match their allegedly superior intelligence – well, I'm afraid I have to disappoint you. Even back then, passing off a gas chamber as a shower room was not exactly the height of subtlety. And in this specific instance all it needed was the usual dose of polite courtesy in tandem with honest, yet effusive praise for the excellent work of her talented granddaughter. When I explained how indispensable Fräulein Krömeier was for my work, the glint in the old wench's eye told me I would not need a new right-hand woman. As for any misgivings she might harbour regarding ideological matters, from that point on the lady only heard what she wanted to hear.

But it helped, of course, that I did not visit her in full uniform.

XXX

I was nervous, but only slightly. I find there is something comforting about a mild flutter of nerves; it shows that I am focused. We had been working on this for four and a half months. I had outgrown Gagmez's programme, as heretofore I had the Hofbräukeller; I had moved into a studio for my very own show, as heretofore I had into the Circus Krone. We learned that the advertising revenue from German industry had already reached a level comparable to the donations we were receiving shortly before my takeover of power in 1933. I was struck by the thrill of anticipation of what was to come, but I maintained my iron concentration. I checked myself once more in the looking glass. Immaculate.

The opening titles played across the studio screen. They had been getting better and better; my esteem for former Hotel Reserver Sawatzki had only grown. The titles were introduced by the opening melody, a simple arrangement of bass notes. Old film recordings were played, such as my watching an S.A. parade in Nuremberg. Then some short sequences by Riefenstahl from "The Triumph of the Will", over which there sang a most delightful voice: "*Look who's back, look who's here.*"

Now they showed some good scenes from the Polish

campaign. Stukas over Warsaw. Artillery in action. Guderian's raging tanks. Then a few excellent sequences of me visiting troops at the front.

"*Look who's back,*" the sweet female voice sang. "*But not for me.*"

This was followed by a number of more recent recordings. They showed me strolling across the new Potsdamer Platz. Buying some rolls at the bakery and – a scene I treasured above all – patting the heads of two small children in a playground, a boy and a little girl. The youth is our future, pure and simple.

"*He hasn't been round,*" the voice lamented, "*he hasn't come by. I don't understand it – why, oh why?*"

I had found this song extremely moving when I heard it for the first time; we had been meeting to decide on the title melody. If the truth be told I didn't understand it either, what had happened to me. The images now showed me in the back seat of a black Maybach, on the way to the disused picture house in which we were recording. As I alighted and walked into the building, the camera behind me panning onto the large lettering outside announcing the name of my programme – "The Führer Speaks" – the woman sang the last bars of her song, skilfully spliced to finish in time with the title sequence: "*Look who's back, look who's he-e-e-e-re.*"

I could have watched the opening titles again and again, but I had to be in position by no later than the bakery scene. As the song ended I would be sitting at my desk, receiving the applause with a serious expression. It was certainly more relaxed than at the Sportpalast, but the introduction lent it a good degree of solemnity.

They had built me a wonderful studio, a vast improvement on the simple rostrum on Gagmez's programme. It had been modelled on the Wolf's Lair, as a compromise. My initial suggestion had been the Obersalzberg. Madame Bellini said that was too cheerful and cosy and proposed instead the Führerbunker. So we settled on the Wolf's Lair. I even went there on a reconnaissance mission with a squad from Flashlight, out of curiosity more than anything, for I could have drawn the entire structure of the complex in detail, and from memory, including the guards. But Madame Bellini rightly insisted that the production team should visit the place to get their own impression.

I had assumed that within their sphere of influence the Russians would have razed everything which bore witness to our past, but of course they didn't stand a chance with the Todt Organisation's reinforced concrete. They even had to leave the flak towers in Vienna standing because they were unable to blow them up. Of course they could have stuffed them to the rafters with T.N.T., but Tamms – that devil of a fellow – had cunningly placed the towers bang in the heart of residential areas. And they are still standing there, impressively sombre, and testament to the art of German fortification.

The Poles, on the other hand, had turned the Wolf's Lair into a sort of leisure park. It pained me to see the naïve indifference with which these clueless peasants dragged themselves around the site. The place lacks the necessary gravity; ultimately I prefer those documentation centres they're building everywhere these days. True, such centres ideologically bombard the people who visit them, but the seriousness and aims of the movement are by and large accurately conveyed, including the Jewish problem. A little distorted by these do-gooders, of course, but only a little. As a precaution they still have to scribble everywhere how "inhuman" our policies were. Goebbels would have ordered them to cross that out forthwith. "If you have to refer to it specifically the text sounds weak. With a good text the reader can think nothing else but 'That was inhuman'. Then, and only then, you see, he believes he has come to this conclusion himself!"

Good old Goebbels. I adored his children; in the Führer-bunker they were always my favourites.

So, the Wolf's Lair. They have a hotel there now, with a canteen that serves up Masurian food, and nearby is a shooting range for air rifles: a woeful set-up. If I had been in charge of the premises I would have used our original weapons: the Gewehr 43, the Pistole 35, the Luger, the Walther army pistol or even the P.P.K. – on second thoughts, maybe not the P.P.K., because whenever I think about the good old P.P.K. it gives me these bothersome headaches. Perhaps I should consult a doctor about it, but that is something I have found difficult of late. It was very practical back then, with Theo Morrell always on hand. Göring didn't like him, but Göring was not an expert in all matters.

I waited until the applause had died down completely, which was usually a sheer test of nerves between the broad-caster, the audience and myself, for I wanted absolute silence. I have succeeded in this with every audience so far.

"My fellow Germans!

We know that
a nation lives
off
its land.
Its land
is its
Lebensraum.
But, in what
state
do we find
this land
today?
The 'chancellor'
says:
'Excellent.'
Well, well.
Once upon a time in this country
the land could boast a healthy soil.
Now the land is simply soiled.
I put it to this 'chancellor',
where is the healthy soil of yesteryear?
I will have an eternal wait for my answer, for
the 'chancellor' knows as well as I do
that German soil is contaminated
with the poison of big capital,
of international finance!
German land is full of rubbish,
German children need the refuge of high chairs
to sit in safety.

The German man, the German woman
the German family are fleeing as far as they can
to skyscrapers;
the small German dog,
called Struppi
or maybe Spitzl,
he steps with his sensitive paw onto
a bottle top,
or laps at a dioxin and dies
excruciatingly
and with cramps!
Poor, poor Struppi.
And *this*
is the land
which our 'chancellor'
proclaims to be excellent.
Our guest today is an expert on German soil.
The Green politician,
Renate Künast."

She was led in by a tall orderly in S.S. uniform. Werner, his name was, blonde and with impeccable manners. Even if it was clear that the lady found his uniform distasteful, her countenance also betrayed a certain appreciation of his physical assets. Women will always be women.

Werner was one of Sawatzki's ideas too. The general opinion amongst the ranks at Flashlight was that I needed an adjutant.

"It's important," Sensenbrink had said. "It gives you someone else to interface with. If you've got a guest who's dead wood, if a remark fails to trigger a discussion, then at least you're not fire-fighting on your own against the audience."

"You mean I could push the blame onto someone else?"

"In a manner of speaking."

"I will not do that. The Führer may delegate operations, but never responsibility."

"But when the bell rings the Führer's not going to open the door himself," Madame Bellini demurred. "And you'll be having more than enough guests."

That was certainly true.

"In the past you must have had an adjutant. Who used to open the door for you?" She stopped to think, then added, "I don't mean you, but the real Hitler."

"It's alright," I said. "The door? That would have been Junge. Or towards the end one of Schädle's chaps . . ."

"Mamma mia!" Sensenbrink had sighed. "C'mon guys, let's eat a reality sandwich here. Who the hell's going to know who they are?"

"What on earth did you think? That Himmler personally ironed my uniform every morning?"

"At least he's a name!"

"Let's not get too complicated," Madame Bellini had said. "Now, you weren't talking about any old S.S. man, were you, but . . . Schäuble?"

"Schädle."

"Exactly. A name. So let's go one step up. I mean, it's only symbolic."

"I have no objections," I said. "I suppose that means Bormann."

"Who?"

"Bormann! Martin! Reichsleiter."

"Never heard of him."

I was about to give Sensenbrink a piece of my mind, but Madame Bellini grabbed my arm.

"Your knowledge of the subject is superb," she said in a honeyed voice. "It's fantastic that you know all these details, no-one else could do that! But if we want to win over the masses, get *really* big viewing figures . . ." And here, quite skilfully, she paused. ". . . then your adjutant can only be one of a really small bunch. Let's be realistic about this, we could have Goebbels, Göring, Himmler, at a pinch Hess . . ."

"Not Hess," Sensenbrink objected. "With him you've always got the sympathy vote. Poor old man, banged up for ever because of the evil Russians."

". . . Yes, you're right. I agree," Madame Bellini continued. "So that's that as far as our candidates are concerned. Otherwise, thirty seconds into the show, everyone will wonder who that strange bloke is next to the Führer. Confusion is not good. You're confusing enough yourself."

"Goebbels would never open the door for me if the bell rang," I said somewhat defiantly, but I knew, of course, that she was right. And of course Goebbels *would* have opened doors for me. Goebbels would have done anything for me. A bit like my Fuchsl back in the trenches. But even I understood that it couldn't be Goebbels. They would turn him into a Quasimodo figure, like Fritz the hunchback in that sensationalised motion picture adaptation of "Frankenstein" with Boris Karloff. They would transform him into a grotesque creature, exposing him to derision each time he shuffled across the stage. Goebbels did not deserve that. Göring and Himmler, on the other hand . . . True, each had his merits, but a justifiable fury still smouldered within me at their betrayal. And they would have stolen the show. After all, I'd seen what had happened to Gagmez.

"Hey guys, what about using the unknown soldier?" This suggestion came from Hotel Reserver Sawatzki.

"What do you mean?" Madame Bellini asked.

Sawatzki sat forward. "Tall, super-blonde," he said. "An S.S. type."

"Not bad, not bad at all," Madame Bellini said.

"Göring would get more laughs," Sensenbrink said.

"We don't want cheap laughs," Bellini and I said in unison.

We looked at each other. I liked this woman more and more with every meeting.

"Good evening and welcome," I said to Frau Künast, offering her a seat. She sat down confidently, like someone accustomed to the camera.

"I'm delighted to be here," she said mockingly, "sort of."

"You may well be wondering why I invited you."

"Because no-one else said yes?"

"Not at all. We could have had your colleague, Frau Roth. Which reminds me, could you do me a favour?"

"That depends."

"Please expel that woman from your party. How could anybody form an alliance with a party that accommodates something quite so gruesome?"

"Well, that's never stopped the S.P.D. or the C.D.U. in the past . . ."

"Indeed; aren't you a bit surprised?"

For a moment she looked perplexed.

"Just for the record I'd like to say that Claudia Roth makes an indispensable contribution to . . ."

"Maybe you're right, perhaps all you need to do is keep her away from the cameras, in a windowless, sound-proofed basement – but now we've arrived at the subject I wanted to discuss. I invited you here because I have to plan for the future, of course, and if I understand it correctly I will need a parliamentary majority for a takeover of power . . ."

"Parliamentary majority?"

"Yes, just as in 1933, when I needed the support of the D.N.V.P. Things might develop in a similar fashion in the foreseeable future. But, alas, the D.N.V.P. no longer exists, so I thought I'd look into potential candidates for a new Harzburg Front . . ."

"And of all the parties you see the Greens as a substitute?"

"Why ever not?"

"I don't see many opportunities here," she said with a frown.

"Your modesty does you great credit, but don't hide your light under a bushel. Your party is more suitable than you might think."

"Now I'm curious."

"It is my assumption that we have compatible visions for the future. Pray tell me, where do you see Germany in five hundred years' time?"

"Five hundred?"

"Or in three hundred years?"

"I'm no prophet, I prefer to focus on the realities."

"But surely you have a plan for Germany?"

"Not for three hundred years. Nobody knows where we'll be in three hundred years."

"I do."

"Oh really? Where will we be, then?"

"In devising their plans for the future, ladies and gentlemen, the Greens are seeking advice from the Führer of the German Reich – I did tell you that cooperation is not so inconceivable . . ."

"You can keep your alliance," Künast backtracked hastily. "The Greens will get by perfectly well without you . . ."

"I see. In that case, how far into the future *does* your planning stretch? One hundred?"

"That's nonsense!"

"Fifty? Forty? Thirty? Twenty? I know, I'll count down from twenty and you can say 'Stop!'"

"In all seriousness, nobody can predict future developments further ahead than, what? Ten years?"

"Ten?"

"O.K. Fifteen."

"Alright, then. Where do you see Germany in a quarter of an hour?"

Künast sighed.

"If you absolutely insist, in the future I see Germany as an environmentally friendly high-tech country – especially as far as environmental technology is concerned – with a sustainable energy policy, embedded in a peaceful Europe under the umbrella of the E.U. and U.N. . . ."

"Did you get that, Werner?" I asked my adjutant.

". . . embedded in a peaceful Europe under the umbrella of the E.U. and U.N.," Werner dutifully jotted down.

"But can you be sure there will still be an E.U. by then?" I asked.

"Of course."

"Will the Greeks still be in it? The Spaniards? The Italians? The Irish? The Portuguese?"

Künast sighed again. "Who can say for certain?"

"But you're sure about your energy policy! There you are thinking along the same lines as I am! Few or no imports, total autarky from renewable raw materials, water, wind – energy security in one hundred, two hundred, even one thousand years. There you are – you *can* see into the future after all. And this – how shall I put it? – is precisely what I was always calling for . . ."

"Hang on one minute! For completely the wrong reasons!"

"What have these reasons got to do with a sustainable energy industry? Are there good and bad windmills?"

She looked at me crossly.

"If I understand you correctly," I followed up, "for species-appropriate husbandry of dolphins, it is fine to use good, wholesome solar energy, but if you settle Ukrainian farmland with Germanic peasant soldiers, all they get is electricity from lignite? Or atomic energy?"

"No," Künast protested. "You settle it with Ukrainians. If you settle it at all!"

"May the Ukrainians use wind energy? Or do you have specific ideas about this, too? Do you, in fact, have a directory of the different forms of energy and their correct use?"

She leaned back. "You know perfectly well that's not what I meant. The way you're arguing you might just as well ask whether the murder of millions of Jews would have been better with solar energy . . ."

"Interesting," I said. "But the Jews are no laughing matter."

For a moment not a sound was to be heard in the studio.

"Silence on television is a waste of expensive Volk airwaves," I said. "So in the meantime, let us take a commercial break."

The lights were dimmed slightly. A few people came and reapplied our make-up. Künast covered her microphone with her hand.

"What you do sails very close to the wind, let me tell you!" she said in a hushed voice.

"Of course I'm very aware of your party's sensibilities," I said. "But you cannot deny that you were the one who brought up the Jews."

She pondered. Then the lights went up again. I waited for the applause to die down, then asked, "Would you mind accompanying me to the map table?"

On the far right of the studio we had reconstructed the old map table from the Wolf's Lair. I had commissioned a beautiful, large relief map of the world. "Why," I asked as we strolled over to it, "has your party in recent times been forgoing the experience and knowledge of Fischer, the former minister of war?"

"Joschka Fischer was never minister of defence," Künast retorted brusquely.

"You're right," I agreed. "I never saw him as a minister of defence, either. One can only defend Reich territory, and Kosovo is not an integral part of that. Given how far away it is, an annexation wouldn't have made any sense either. Or do you think otherwise?"

"There was no question of annexing Kosovo! It was all about ethnic cleansing . . . Listen, I'm not going to start talking about the intervention in Kosovo. It was simply that we couldn't turn a blind eye!"

"No-one understands that better than I do," I said in all seriousness. "You are absolutely right, there was no alternative. This I remember well from 1941. So what is that Fischer fellow up to at the moment, then?"

I could see her eyes oscillating between Herr Fischer's current circumstances and a comparative study of Balkan policy over the past seventy years. She opted for the former.

"The most important thing is that the Greens have no concerns about the talent in our ranks. Joschka Fischer was and still is an important figure in the history of the Green movement, but now it's the turn of others."

"Like you, for example?"

"Amongst many others, yes."

We had arrived at the map table. With flags I had marked the places where the "Bundeswehr" was currently deployed.

"May I ask how the Greens would bring the operation in Afghanistan to a victorious conclusion?"

"What do you mean, 'victorious conclusion'? The military operation there must be brought to a *speedy* conclusion. It's only leading to more violence . . ."

"I take the same view – there's nothing for us to gain in Afghanistan. What is our objective there?"

"Hold on," she said, "but—"

"Please don't say you have fresh misgivings about my motives," I said. "Please don't tell me *you're* allowed to withdraw from Afghanistan, whereas I have to stay there!"

"I'm not sure I'm going to say anything," she said, her eyes darting around the studio. Her gaze came to rest below the map table.

"There's a briefcase," Künast said superciliously. "Is that meant to be there?"

"Someone must have forgotten it," I said absently. "Where is Stauffenberg, by the way?"

The briefcase had been another idea of mine. In fact, the whole incident had come back to me in sharp detail when we visited the Wolf's Lair. I suggested we could include it as a permanent feature in the programme. That and the visit to the map table. I thought we should hide the briefcase anew for each guest.

"Seeing as we've agreed on a withdrawal from Afghanistan," I said, leaning over the table, "please tell us, to conclude: If the Greens took power in this country, which would be the first state they would annex?"

"The briefcase is ticking," Künast said, dumbfounded.

That had been Sensenbrink's idea. He had hit on it moments before I did.

"Don't be daft," I said. "Briefcases don't tick. A briefcase is not an alarm clock. Which state, did you say?"

"Is confetti going to come out of it? Or flour? Or soot?"

"For goodness' sake, why don't you take a look?"

"That's exactly what you want me to do, isn't it? Come off it, I'm not stupid!"

"Then you will never find out," I said. "We, on the other hand, have found out many interesting things about your most congenial party. Many thanks for having spent the evening with us – Frau Renate Künast!"

During the applause I glanced backstage, where Sensenbrink and Madame Bellini were standing. They clapped and then stuck out their fists with thumbs pointing upwards.

It felt wonderful.

xxxi

The most important skill I have acquired during my career as a politician is the ability to judge one's public obligations shrewdly. Essentially I have always despised the dependence on benefactors, and yet for the sake of his country the politician frequently has to compromise. It may be that public handshakes and deference to the cream of society is an attraction for that caste of political artistes who confuse life *in* the public sphere with a life for the public sphere, for the nation, for the small man who scrimps and saves to put bread on his table and clothe his children. And anybody who spends even a quarter of an hour watching the news on his television set will, with grim certainty, see at least half a dozen of those bootlickers, toadying up to some important person or other. Such behaviour has always repelled me, and I myself have only suffered various courtesy visits for the sake of the cause. Pure torture, but I undertook these for the sake of the party, for the German Volk, for the preservation of our race, or for a new Mercedes.

And for the four-hundred-square-metre apartment on Prinzregentenplatz.

And I suppose for the Obersalzberg too.

All these were acquisitions, however, which increased the

appeal of the party and thus the movement, besides that of the Führer. When I think of the flood of visitors to the Ober- salzberg, it astonishes me that anybody can maintain that it was a place where I could relax! And then there was Mussolini's visit – ghastly! The point is, a Führer cannot withdraw from public life, or only intermittently. If his Reich capital is lying in ruins, then he may hole up for a while in his Führerbunker. Otherwise, the Führer belongs to his Volk. Which is why I was delighted to receive the invitation from Munich.

Back in late August a renowned society magazine had written me a letter, in which the editor requested that I pay her publication a visit during the Greater German Volksfest, which had reverted to its original name of "Oktoberfest". Everybody at Flashlight encouraged me to accept the invitation; for my part I was hesitant at first. I had never been there during the first period of my life, but times had changed and with them the significance of this fortnight-long tradition. As several people reassured me, the Oktoberfest had now become a Volksfest which took place without involving a particularly large proportion of the population. Anybody wishing to sit and partake of food and drink in one of the tents had to reserve a place months, sometimes years in advance, or else reschedule their visit to a time of day when no decent German would ever dream of going there.

Well, no person sound of mind would plan an innocent affair such as a visit to a Volksfest months or years in advance. As a consequence, so I learned, the place teemed in the morning and early afternoon with indecent Germans as well as foreigners and tourists attracted by the aura of the famous festival. Already by lunchtime these people tried desperately to make an evening of the day. Both Madame Bellini and Sensenbrink warned me against making an appearance too early, as it implied that one was an insignificant, peripheral figure. The evenings were not for the local population either, but for businesses from every branch of industry imaginable. Practically any firm with half a name for itself felt obliged to arrange visits to the "Wiesn" for its clients or the press. Some organs of the press, however, dissatisfied with what was on offer or with the guests present, had taken it upon themselves to tailor a more congenial visit to the "Wiesn". To my mind this was a terribly smart, indeed positively Goebbels-like course of action.

Some of these gatherings, I was assured, were now as important as the opera balls of old. And this magazine's soirée was amongst the most important. My acceptance, moreover, turned out to be a particularly effective propaganda coup; in the past I had kept my distance from the festival, and now several tabloid newspapers were able to write on their front pages, "Führer's First Fest". The smooth relationship I now enjoyed with these papers, I reflected with no little satisfaction, meant that the need to establish a new *Völkischer Beobachter* was dropping down my list of priorities.

I had arrived in the city around noon and used the time to call in on some much-loved old haunts. I lingered for a while at the Feldherrnhalle, remembering the blood spilled by loyal comrades there; I wandered nostalgically past the Hofbräukeller; then, with some apprehension, I walked to Königsplatz. But how my heart beat for joy when I saw all the magnificent buildings still standing unscathed: the Propylaea, the Glyptothek, the State Collections of Antiquities! And – this I had scarcely dared to hope – not only were the Führerbau and the N.S.D.A.P. Administrative Building still standing, but they were in use, too! It had not escaped even those opinionated and cocksure democrats that Königsplatz was only complete with the addition of these highly refined constructions. Feeling gay, I continued my stroll through Schwabing; my feet took me as if of their own accord to Schellingstraße, and to an unhoped-for reunion. It would be hard to convey the sheer magnitude of my delight when I spied the sign for the Osteria Italiana, behind which hid none other than my old hangout, the Osteria Bavaria. I would have loved to have gone in and partaken of something small, a glass of mineral water perhaps, but time was marching on and I had to return to my hotel, from where an automobile was to fetch me that evening.

My arrival at the Theresienwiese, site of the Oktoberfest, was sobering. Police had cordoned off the vast site, but they were making no efforts to ensure security or order. Barely had I got out of the automobile than two exceedingly drunken individuals staggered towards me and fell into the back seat.

"Brrralleeiiiinschraaasse!" one of the two slurred, while the other seemed to be dozing already. The chauffeur, a powerful man, expelled the two drinkers at once with the words, "Oi! Out! This isn't a taxi!" He then accompanied me to the venue. "Sorry about that," he said. "It's always like this at the bloody Oktoberfest."

We walked the short distance across the street to the festival site. It was hard to believe that anybody could have struck upon the idea of holding a soirée of any social importance in this godforsaken place. Endless lines of drunkards leaned with their heads against temporary fences, urinating through them. Waiting for a number of these characters were women in a similarly precarious state; it was quite evident that they would have liked to do the same, but dared not due to some subconscious residue of decency. Propped against an advertising column, a couple were engaged in an act of courtship. The man's intention was to thrust his tongue into her mouth, but because she slipped downwards he missed his target and had to make do with her nose. Responding to his intrusiveness, she opened her mouth and poked her tongue aimlessly in the air. The two of them slid, slowly at first, then more rapidly, down the column until they hit the ground. They shrieked with laughter and tried to say something, but a lack of consonants rendered their babble unintelligible. Lying beneath the woman, the man wriggled about, sat up briefly and then silently plunged a hand into her cleavage. Although it was uncertain whether the woman noticed this at all, three Italians, on the other hand, watched with interest and decided to follow events at closer quarters. These ignominious endeavours failed to attract the attention of anybody else, and certainly not that of the police, who were busy picking unconscious bodies, of which there were plenty, from the ground.

In spite of its name, the Theresienwiese – "Theresa's Meadow" – possesses very little grass; the only patches of green are to be found around the trees which encircle the site. In this respect, nothing had changed since my first time in Munich. As far as I could make out, drunkards – some of them comatose –

occupied almost every one of these patches of grass. Whenever I eyed a vacant spot, I could already see someone reeling towards it. Once at his temporary resting place he would either collapse, throw up, or both. "Is it always like this?" I enquired of the chauffeur.

"Friday's worse," he replied calmly. "Bloody Oktoberfest!"

I cannot explain why, but all of a sudden the reason for this human devastation hit me like a bombshell. It must have been down to a decision taken by the N.S.D.A.P. in 1933 to increase further the party's popularity amongst the Volk: we fixed the price of beer. Since then, other parties had evidently tried to secure their popularity by the same means.

"How typical of these fools," I blurted out. "Haven't they raised the price of beer? These days ninety pfennigs for a litre is a joke!"

"What do you mean, 'ninety pfennigs'?" the chauffeur asked. "It's nine euros a litre, mate! Ten if you include a tip."

As I walked past I saw the extraordinary wreckage of beer-corpses. Somehow, despite all their economic mismanagement, these parties must have brought about an unexpected level of prosperity. Well, not having to wage war certainly saves the odd cost. Looking at the state of the Volk here, however, even the most deluded individual would have to admit that in 1942 or 1944, yes, even in the most harrowing nights of bombardment, the Germans were in better shape than on this September evening at the beginning of the third millennium.

Physically, at least.

Shaking my head, I followed the chauffeur, who delivered me to a blonde woman at the entrance to a tent and then returned to his vehicle. With cables around her head and a microphone in front of her mouth, she said with a broad smile, "Hi there, I'm Tschill – and you are?"

"Schmul Rosenzweig," I said, feeling irritation rise again. Was I really that difficult to recognise?

"Thanks. Rosenzweig . . . Rosenzweig . . ." she repeated. "I haven't got any Rosenzweigs on the list."

"Heavens above," I cursed. "Do I look like a Rosenzweig? Hitler! Adolf!"

"You could have said that in the first place," she wailed with such a quiver in her voice that I almost felt sorry for my remark. "Have you got any idea of how many people we get here? I can't be expected to know them all! Especially not if they start giving false names. Earlier I got Becker's wife mixed up with his ex-girlfriend – he gave me a right roasting for that . . ."

I am no stranger to sympathy. A true Führer feels for each and every one of his fellow Germans as if they were his own children. But pity never helped anyone.

"Brace yourself," I said sharply. "You are at this post because your superior officer is depending on you! Do your best and he will not fail to lend you his support!"

She gave me a look of bewilderment, but – as often happens in the trenches – my harsh words must have sparked some courage in her. She nodded and led me to the party in the upper section of the tent, where I was immediately introduced to the editor. This was a seasoned blonde lady in a dirndl, with shining blue eyes. Her vivacity convinced me that she would have made a perfect office supervisor in party headquarters. I might not necessarily have entrusted her with a newspaper, although . . . a gossip sheet with health tips and knitting patterns . . . that might work, who knows? She was probably very keen to talk; she looked as if she had already raised four or five children, and she must be terribly lonely at home.

"Ah!" she beamed. "Herr Hitler!" The corners of her eyes twinkled mischievously, as if she had just cracked an hilarious joke.

"Correct," I said.

"I'm so delighted you're here."

"Madam, the pleasure is all mine," I said, and before I could add another word her face broke into an even more radiant smile. When she turned to the side I assumed that a mandatory photograph was about to be taken. Adopting a serious expression, I turned in the same direction, there was a flash, and my audience was at an end. In my mind I rapidly sketched a four-year plan according to which this editor would spend at least five minutes talking to me here next year, and twenty the year after that – only in theory, of course, because by that stage my intention was to be able to say a polite "No, thank you" to these sorts of invitations. Then she would have to make do with someone like Göring.

"Catch you later," the editor said silkily. "I hope you can stay for a while." At which a young woman dressed in folk costume dragged me over to a gaggle of women similarly dressed.

This was one of the most frightful regional customs I had ever had the misfortune to experience. Not only the editor and this young woman, but every last damsel in the locality had felt obliged to squeeze herself into dresses which were zealously styled on those worn by country wenches, but which even at first glance revealed themselves to be hideous imitations. We had gone down the same path in the League of German Girls, I admit, but there, as the name implies, we were dealing with *girls*. Assembled here, by contrast, were predominantly women whose girlhood lay at least a decade in the past, if not several. I was led to a beer table where a number of people were already seated.

"What can I get you?" asked a waitress, whose dirndl at least bore the authenticity of an honest work uniform. "A litre?"

"Still water, please," I said.

She nodded and vanished.

"Hey, a pro," said a large coloured man sitting next to a blonde at the other end of the table. "But you gotta get that in a large tankard! Looks better in the photos. Believe me, I've been doing this for fifty years now." He gave me an unbelievably broad grin, exposing a staggering number of teeth. "Doesn't look so good to be at the 'Wiesn' with a water glass."

"Rubbish! Still waters run deep," said a rather raddled dirndl-clad woman opposite me. I later heard on the grapevine that she earned her livelihood in one of those amateurish drama series. That is, when she wasn't featuring in another transmission which, if I understood it correctly, consisted of equally third-rate personalities being taken to ancient woodland where they allowed themselves to be observed wading through worms and excrement.

"You do funny stuff, I've seen some of your programmes," she said, taking a sip from her tankard and bending forward to afford me a view of her cleavage.

"Pleased to meet you," I said. "I've seen a couple of your things too."

"Should I know you?" a young blonde man asked from the other side of the table.

"Of course," the negro said, signing a photograph for another man with a thick felt pen. "That's Hitler from Gagmez. Fridays, MyTV! No, hang on, he has his own programme now. You gotta watch it, it'll crack you up."

"But it's different from the usual, it's kind of political too," the raddled cleavage said. "It's almost like the Harald Schmidt show!"

"Not my cup of tea, I'm afraid," the blonde man said, turning to me. "Sorry, mate. Nothing personal, but politics – I just think nothing ever changes. All those parties and that, it's just a mess."

"A man after my own heart," I said as the waitress placed my mineral water on the table. I took a sip and looked down into the main room of the tent, expecting to see people swaying to and fro in time to the music. But no-one was. Everyone was standing on tables and benches, with the exception of those who had just fallen off. People were wailing and shouting for someone called Jude. I tried to remember whether Göring had ever mentioned this mass debauchery after one of his visits, but my memory harboured no such recollection.

"Where do you come from?" the raddled woman asked. "South Germany, right?" Once more her cleavage was held up to me like a offering bag.

"From Austria," I said.

"Like the real one!" the cleavage said.

I nodded and allowed my gaze to wander around the tent. There was a shriek, then some of the women in their ludicrous dresses attempted to clamber onto the benches and persuade others to join in. There was a hint of desperation about these unappealing women with their affected high spirits. But perhaps appearances were deceptive, and it was merely a consequence of their heavily swollen lips, which despite every effort gave their mouths a sulking, even offended expression. I took a casual glance at the lips of the raddled cleavage opposite me. They, at least, looked normal.

"I don't like all that injecting either," the cleavage said.

"I'm sorry?"

"Well, you were looking at my lips, weren't you?"

She took a sip of beer. "I won't let a doctor near them. Even though I sometimes think I'd have an easier time of it. I mean, none of us are getting any younger, are we?"

"A doctor? Are you feeling poorly?"

"You're very sweet," the cleavage said, bending over the table, tempting one to gather up the contents. Grabbing my shoulder, she turned me so that we were both looking in the same direction. She gave off an odour of beer, albeit not yet at a disagreeable level. Then, with slight twitches of her index finger, she pointing from right to left at the array of women: "Boob job. Nose job. Boobs. Arse. Dunno. Lips. Arse. Boobs – a while ago now. Dunno. Dunno. Nose. Lips. Boobs. Arse. Boobs *and* arse, paid for by the telly channel or production company; she did it for a special report." She sat down again and looked at me. "You've had something done, though, haven't you?"

"I've had what done?"

"This similarity, pur–lease! The whole industry's scratching their heads, wondering who did it. Although . . ." Here she took another gulp of beer. ". . . if you ask me, you should sue the bastard."

"My good woman, I have not the faintest idea what you are talking about!"

"Operations, for God's sake," she said with a tone of irritation. "Don't pretend like you've not had one. That's plain silly."

"Of course there were operations," I said, confused. She was a likeable woman in her own way. "Sea Lion, Barbarossa, Cerberus . . ."

"Never heard of them. Were you pleased?"

Down below they were playing "Pilot, Give a Wave to the Sun", which put me in a pleasantly nostalgic mood. I sighed. "To begin with everything was fine, but then there were complications. Not that the English would have done any better. Or the Russians . . . But still."

She scrutinised me. "I don't see any scars," she said with the air of a professional.

"I'm not going to complain," I said. "The deepest wounds are those that Fate inflicts upon our hearts."

"You're right there," she said with a smile, holding her beer towards me. I matched her gesture with my mineral water, then continued in my attempts to determine the nature of this strange company. Youth was poorly represented here, and yet most people seemed to be behaving as if they were not a day older than twenty. I dare say this was the reason behind the parade of décolletés, as well as the behaviour of one or two individuals. It was disconcerting. The impression it made upon me was so strong that I could not shake it off. All these men who were unable to tolerate their physical decline or compensate for this with cerebral work, or at least a certain maturity; all these women who refused to sit back contentedly, having bred and reared their children for the Volk, but conducted themselves as if this were their one and only opportunity to reclaim their withered youth for a few precious hours. I would have loved to take these characters by the scruff of the neck and shout, "Pull yourselves together! You are a disgrace to yourself and to your Fatherland!" I was ruminating on such matters when a man approached the table and rapped on it with his knuckles.

"Evening," he said in that unmistakable dialect which always reminded me of Streicher's beautiful city. He was in his midforties or older, with long, dark hair, and was accompanied by what must have been his daughter.

"Lothar!" the raddled cleavage said, shifting to one side. "Take a pew!"

"No, I'm not staying. I just wanted to say I think what you're doing is brilliant. I saw the show on Friday – I nearly wet myself, but also what you say is so true. All that Europe stuff and that! And the week before, that stuff with those social whatsits . . ."

"Social parasites," I said.

". . . Exactly," he said, "that, and all that stuff about kids. Kids really are our future. You really hit the nail on the head. I just wanted you to know."

"Thank you," I said. "I am most pleased. Our movement

needs your support. And I would be delighted if I could count your dear daughter amongst our supporters too."

All of a sudden he looked incensed, then he burst out laughing and turned to his daughter. "There he goes again. Utterly ruthless! Gets you where it really hurts." Then he rapped his knuckles on the table once more and said, "Ciao!"

"You do know that's not his daughter, don't you?" the cleavage said when this Lothar had left.

"I assumed as much," I said. "Of course it couldn't be his biological daughter; racially it just doesn't work. I assumed he'd adopted the girl. I've always been a strong advocate of adoption; much better than having such a poor young thing grow up in an orphanage . . ."

The cleavage rolled her eyes.

"Can't you say anything normal at all?" she sighed. "I need to go to the little girls' room! Don't run away! You might be awful, but at least you're not boring."

I took a sip of water. I was still wondering what to make of the evening when I was aware of a commotion behind me, a lady enveloped by a throng of journalists. The lady appeared to be one of the principal attractions of the event, as she was pursued by photographers and television cameras almost without pause. She had a southern complexion, which made her dirndl look particularly odd, and the arrangement of her décolleté was grotesque. This notwithstanding, if her overall appearance could be described as respectable in a vulgar sort of way, such an impression was shattered the moment she opened her mouth. She spoke at a pitch higher than that of any mechanical saw I ever heard. But the photographers and reporters were indifferent to the noise. She was just about to squeak into a camera when a photographer caught sight of me in the background and steered her to my table for a picture of the two of us. The lady appeared unenthusiastic.

I know that look. Behind the eyes laughing superficially, I could detect a merciless machine calculating whether or not this photograph would prove advantageous to her. What helped me to see through her expression was that I was making the same calculation myself, albeit much more rapidly and, moreover, producing an answer in the negative. Her hesitation told me that she, on the other hand, seemed not to have arrived at a conclusion. For her the consequences were uncertain and hence a risk, which she would rather have evaded with a witticism. By now, however, one of the photographers had surged forward and tossed into the fray the slogan "Beauty and the Beast", from which moment the baying pack of press hounds was no longer stoppable. So the exotic reckoning machine took the bull by the horns and rushed towards me shrieking with laughter.

This type of woman is not a new phenomenon; she existed seventy years ago too, although she was not then as prominent. Her craving for recognition knows no bounds and her self-esteem is low. She endeavours to assuage this by trying to conceal each one of her supposed deficiencies. For unfathomable reasons this type of woman considers only one method to be suitable: turning everything into ridicule. She is the most dangerous type of woman a politician can meet.

"Wow, it's you!" she whinnied, trying to throw herself at me. "How fab! Can I call you Adi?"

"You may call me Herr Hitler," I told her soberly.

That is sometimes all it takes to put people off. She was undeterred, however. Sitting on my lap, she said, "Cool, Herr Hitler! So what are the two of us going to do for those cheeky old photographers? Eh? Hmm?"

In such a situation one has nothing to gain and everything to lose. Ninety-nine out of a hundred men would have lost their nerve at this point and beaten a retreat on the pretext of "readjusting the front line" or "redeploying units". I had seen it often enough in the Russian winter of 1941, which at minus 30, even minus 50 degrees descended so suddenly on my troops. There was no lack of people who said, "Retreat, retreat!" I alone held my nerve and said, "On no account, not one metre backwards! Any man who yields will be shot." Napoleon failed, but I held the front, and in the spring we harried those bandy-legged Siberian bloodhounds like hares, over the Don, to Rostov, to Stalingrad and so on – I don't wish to go into unnecessary detail now.

At any rate, there was no question of a retreat back then, nor now in this unpleasant beer tent. The situation is never hopeless if one possesses a fanatical will to victory. One only need think of the miracle which blessed the House of Brandenburg in 1762. Tsarina Elisabeth dies, her son, Peter, concludes peace, and Frederick the Great is saved. Had Frederick surrendered beforehand, there would have been no miracle, no Kingdom of Prussia, nothing at all, just a dead Tsarina. Many people say one cannot count on miracles. I say one can. One need only wait for them to appear. Until that time one must hold one's position. For an hour, a year, a decade.

"You know, madam," I said, winning myself some time, "I'm so pleased to be back here again, in beautiful Munich, the capital city of my movement – did you know that?"

"No, how interesting," she squeaked cluelessly, and ran her fingers through my hair. For bints like this it is the simplest matter in the world to belittle a figure of authority by upsetting his appearance. If Providence had a miracle up her sleeve, then now was the time to unveil it.

All of a sudden one of the photographers thrust a fat, black pen under my nose.

"Why don't you sign the dirndl?"

"The dirndl?"

"Of course!"

"Yeah! Fab idea!" This comment was fired from one his colleagues.

The basest human instincts are the most reliable of allies, especially if one lacks any others. The wench had not the slightest interest in having her dress signed. The photographers were most insistent, however; they must have scented a variation on the usual lewd cleavage photo. And she could offer only limited resistance to their entreaties. He who lives by the sword, dies by the sword, even if the sword is no more than a camera. In any event I spied an opportunity to stall the enemy, maybe even bring up some reinforcements.

"May I, madam?"

"But only on the material," she squealed hesitantly. "And don't make it too big."

"Of course," I said, and got down to business. Every second of time I won here counted double, so I augmented my signature with a few embellishments. I felt quite foolish, and after a while had to stop; I was beginning to resemble one of those little girls doodling in her friendship book.

"Finished," I said regretfully.

One of the photographers said "Flipping heck!" The woman followed his gaze.

I watched with surprise as her horrified eyes widened to the size of saucers.

"Do excuse me, I know it's a bit messy in the folds. That wouldn't have happened, of course, with a normal drawing block. Did you know I used to be a painter once . . . ?"

"Are you off you head?" she screeched, leaping off my lap. I could scarcely believe it. The Oktoberfest miracle.

"I'm sorry, madam?" I said. "I'm not sure I quite understand you."

"I can't go wandering around the Oktoberfest with a swastika on my chest!"

"But of course you can," I reassured her. "This isn't 1924, you know. This country may not have a sensible government, but the parliamentary windbags absolutely swear by freedom of expression, and . . ."

She was no longer listening; instead she was rubbing so furiously around her décolleté that it almost looked indecent. And even if I could not fully grasp her despair, the situation seemed to have been saved. She was the one who ended up not looking so good in the photographs. And in fact the television reports were even better; she could be seen springing up, her face hideously contorted and issuing a volley of insults. Most of the reports concluded with her driving off a few minutes later in

331

a taxicab, looking livid and firing off the most astonishing expletives.

When all is said and done I would have preferred a more dignified appearance. But given the circumstances the outcome was more than respectable. At any rate I considered my own losses to have been lower than those of the enemy. The Volk always loves the watchful victor, he who knows how to defend himself, he who wastes no more effort on such a person than he would on a fly.

I was about to order another mineral water when one was set on the table before me. "From the gentleman over there, with his compliments," the waitress said, pointing into the distance. Peering through the throng of people, I saw, several tables away, a blonde figure whose face was the colour of a farmyard hen. His wrinkles gave him the appearance of an ancient Luis Trenker, all in all making him look as if he were pulling a bizarre grin. When he caught my gaze, the gentleman raised an arm in greeting, his fist balled and his thumb sticking upwards. He tried desperately to broaden his leathery smile, but to no avail.

I rubbed my eyes and resolved to decamp as soon as I could. It was conceivable that the drinks here were being adulterated. For right beside that gentleman sat a carbon copy of the wench who had just left the tent with a swastika on her chest.

xxxii

It is amazing the paths that Providence will find to reach her goal. She allows one man to die in the trenches, and another to survive. She guides a simple corporal to the conference of a tiny splinter party, which he will later lead as it attracts millions of members. Some who are destined for greatness she sentences to a year of incarceration in the very middle of their life's undertaking, so that they can find the time to write an illustrious book. She also makes provision for an indispensable Führer to fetch up on the programme of a Turkish imp, only to surpass the latter with such ease that he has his own programme thrust upon him. And I am also sure that it was down to Providence that Fräulein Krömeier knew nothing about razor blades.

Once more it was time to pause for thought. Although I had always believed in the significance of my return, in the onslaught of current events my quest to ascertain this significance had temporarily taken a back seat. And for the time being there were no other urgent matters to attend to; at present the Volk seemed to be free of the grosser hardships and humiliations. But now Fate resolved to open my eyes, as once it had in Vienna.

Hitherto I had engaged in minimal contact with everyday

life; Fräulein Krömeier had relieved me of any minor chores. It was only when I decided to run a few errands myself that I discovered the extent to which many things had changed. Of late I had been missing my good old safety razor. Until now I'd had to familiarise myself with a makeshift plastic apparatus, the purported virtue of which was that it combined several inadequate blades which scraped the skin simultaneously, but unpleasantly. As I was able to discern from the packaging, this was regarded as major progress, especially in relation to the former version, which contained one fewer blade. But I could see no advantage vis-à-vis a single blade. I attempted to describe to Fräulein Krömeier what one of these looked like and how it functioned, in vain. And so I was forced to make the trip myself.

The last time I had properly gone shopping was back in 1924 or 1925. In those days one would go to a haberdashery or soap shop. To purchase a razor nowadays, one had to frequent the chemist's; Fräulein Krömeier had told me how to get there, Rossmann was the name. Upon arrival I realised that the appearance of the chemist's had changed out of all recognition. Once upon a time there was a counter, and behind this counter were the goods. Although there was still a counter, now it was situated close to the entrance. Behind it was nothing but a window display. The actual goods were stacked on an endless succession of shelves, for every man to help himself. My initial supposition was that there were dozens of sales assistants, all in informal dress. But it turned out that these were the customers, who wandered about collecting their items and then took these to the counter. It was most disconcerting. Rarely had I felt so impolitely treated. It was as if I had been told on the way in to look for the paltry razor blades myself, as the chemist had better things to do.

Gradually, however, I grasped the logistics inherent here. There were indeed a number of advantages to this system. First of all the chemist could make large sections of his sales depot accessible, thus affording him greater selling space. Furthermore, it was obvious that one hundred customers would serve themselves quicker than ten or even twenty shop assistants could have done. And, last but not least, one could save money by dispensing with these shop assistants. The benefits were crystal clear. I made a swift estimate that by introducing this principle across the board, 100,000 to 200,000 troops could be freed up for immediate deployment at the front. This was so impressive that I intended to congratulate the ingenious chemist straight away. I hurried over to one of the counters and asked for Herr Rossmann.

"Which Herr Rossmann?"

"For goodness' sake, the man who owns this chemist's!"

"He's not here."

This was a great shame, but I soon discovered my congratulations would have been premature, for clever Herr Rossmann did not, regrettably, sell my razor blades. I was sent to another chemist's, one belonging to Herr Müller.

To be brief, Herr Müller had likewise implemented Herr Rossmann's inspired idea. But he didn't have my blades either, nor did Herr Schlecker, whose frightfully squalid premises were run according to an even more extreme principle: even the cash desk was unmanned here. Which in a way was perfectly logical

335

because I couldn't find my razor blades. The conclusion I drew from my dismal experience was that fewer shop assistants in Germany were selling no razor blades. It may not have been a happy state of affairs, but at least it was efficient.

At a loss, I continued to wander past parades of shops. Once again my decision to have worn a simple lounge suit had proved to be the right one. I was able to acquire at close quarters a genuine impression of the circumstances of the German Volk, their fears, their concerns and their razor-blade hardships. And now that I had been made aware of the fact, I realised that not only the chemist's, but the whole of society had been organised according to this curious work principle. Every clothing shop, every bookshop, every shoe shop, every department store, even grocers and restaurants – all of these were virtually unstaffed. And money, it turned out, was no longer obtained from the bank, but from machines. Exactly the same was true of tickets for travel, and stamps – they were liquidating the post offices one and all. Packages, too, were pushed into a machine, from which they had to be fetched by the recipient. Given all this, the new Wehrmacht ought to have had an army of millions at its fingertips. In reality, however, it had with difficulty scraped together only twice the number to which we had been restricted by the scandalous Treaty of Versailles. It was puzzling.

Where were all those people?

My initial assumption had been that they must be building autobahns, draining swamps and suchlike. Yet this was not the case. Swamps were a rarity these days and tended to be refilled rather than drained. And autobahns were still being built by

Poles, White Russians, Ukrainians and other foreign workers, for wages that were more cost-effective for the Reich than any war. Had I known back then just how cheap it was to employ Poles, I might as well have leapfrogged their country.

One lives and learns.

The thought did occur to me that the German Volk might have shrunk, with the result that all these extra people simply didn't exist. The statistics, however, showed that there were 81 million living Germans. I expect you are wondering why I had not considered the possibility of unemployment. The reason being that my mind had a very different recollection of what unemployed men looked like.

The jobless man I remembered from the past went out onto the street with a placard around his neck that read "Looking for any type of work". When he'd had enough of drifting fruitlessly around in this manner, he would remove the placard, grab a red flag handed to him by a loitering Bolshevist, and return to the street. An army of millions of angry jobless men was fertile ground for any radical party, and I was fortunate enough to have led the most radical of them all. But in the streets of today I could not see any unemployed men. Nor was there any evidence to substantiate the hypothesis that they had been rounded up for some labour service or sent to a camp. Instead, as I later discovered, the country had chosen the capricious solution of a certain Herr Hartz.

This gentleman had established that one does not earn the favour of the workers only through higher wages and suchlike, but also by supplying their representatives with money and Brazilian lovers. By means of a number of laws this formula had been extended to the workers themselves, albeit with lesser inducements, of course. Rather than running to the millions, the sum was considerably more modest, and rather than real Brazilians, there were pictures of Hungarian or Romanian ladies of pleasure on the Internetwork, which presupposed that every jobless man was in possession of one or more computer. In this way, Herr Rossmann and Herr Müller were able to go on filling their pockets in their staff-less and razorblade-less trade without having to fear that the unemployed might smash their shop windows. The whole scheme was paid for out of the taxes of the small man from the munitions factory. And for the experienced National Socialist, everything pointed to a conspiracy of capital, of Jewish finance. Using the money of the poor, the even poorer were placated to the benefit of the rich in such a way that their businesses could happily continue to profit from the crisis. Politicians on the left never tired of pointing this out, although by neglecting to mention the Jewish element their explanations fell short. There could be no question that not only Jewish finance, but world Jewry as a whole must be involved here. Only now was the true villainy of the plot revealed. And this – it struck me like a thunderbolt – was the task Providence had reserved for me. In this liberal–bourgeois world of make-believe, I alone was able to recognise and expose the truth.

Superficially, one could make a strong case that Herr Hartz and his social-democratic accomplices had achieved their purported objectives. A White Russian woman on the computer, a warm, dry apartment and sufficient food – did all these not represent redistribution in the socialist sense?

No. The truth could only be understood by the man who knows the Jews, the man who knows that with them there is no left and no right, and that both sides work hand in hand in perpetuity. And only the perspicacious spirit who sees through all the disguises could recognise that in their aim to eliminate the Aryan race, nothing had changed. The final struggle for the earth's scarce resources would come – far later than I had prophesied – but it would come nonetheless. And the aim was so clear that only a fool could deny it: the Jewish hordes were planning once more to flood the Reich with their repulsive masses. But they had learned from the last war. Because they realised their inferiority, they resolved to undermine, reduce and annihilate the valour of our Volk. So that when the day came, the Asiatic millions would be met only by effeminate Hartz-men, helplessly waving their mouse devices and television control boxes.

I was chilled to the bone with horror. And the nature of my mission was transparent.

I must resolutely follow this path. I elected at once to look for somewhere else to live. The hotel was no longer to be my home; I needed a proper base.

xxxiii

I had in mind something similar to where I had stayed in Prinzregentenplatz in Munich. An apartment large enough for me, guests, staff, preferably an entire, self-contained floor. But not a house. A villa with a garden, even with dense shrubbery, is far too easy a target for one's political opponent to monitor or raid. No, a large apartment, close to the centre of town in a lively area – this still has its advantages. And if it were right next door to a theatre, I wouldn't mind.

"Don't you like it here anymore?" asked the receptionist, who by now was totally uninhibited and saluting me correctly. There was a jocular undertone to her question, but also a perceptible and sincere regret.

"I thought about taking you with me," I replied. "My sister used to keep house for me, but she's no longer alive I'm sorry to say. Were I able to pay your hotel salary I would very happily offer you a job."

"Thanks," she said. "I like the variety here. Still, it's a shame."

In the past someone else would have taken care of finding an apartment; now I had to take the matter in hand myself. In one respect this was interesting, because it brought me into

340

contact with contemporary life. On the other hand it also brought me into contact with agency riff-raff.

It soon became evident that without an estate agent one could not acquire a halfway decent apartment between 400 and 450 square metres. What became evident only later was that it was unlikely even with the assistance of these agent vermin. It was quite shocking how little these envoys of the rental inferno knew about their own properties. Even after sixty years' absence from the market I was on every occasion able to locate the fuse box in less than half the time that it took the "expert" they sent. After the third firm I started insisting on more experienced colleagues, for otherwise I only got sixteen-year-olds in suits too large for them. These ignorant youths looked as if they had been dragged straight from their school desks into the front line of property broking.

At the fourth attempt I was actually offered something suitable in the north of Schöneberg. A decent walk from there would take me to the government district, another factor in this property's favour. After all, one never knew how soon my proximity to that area would become essential.

"Do I know you?" the older agent asked as he showed me the servant's quarters beside the kitchen.

"Hitler, Adolf," I said tersely, adeptly inspecting a few empty cupboards.

"Of course," he said. "That's it! Without your uniform on – excuse me. And anyway, I thought you'd take the moustache off."

"Whatever for?"

"Well, you know. When I get home the first thing I do is take off my shoes."

"And I take off my moustache?"

"That's what I thought . . ."

"I see. Is there a room here for physical exercise?"

"A fitness room? The last tenants didn't have one, but before them there was someone from the jury of a talent show – he used the room over there."

"Is there anything I should know?"

"Like what?"

"Bolshevist neighbours?"

"There may have been in the Thirties. But then . . . then you . . . how should I put it?"

"I know what you're trying to say," I said. "Anything else?"

"Well, let's see . . ."

I thought melancholically of Geli. "I don't want another suicide apartment," I said firmly.

"Since we've been managing this property, no-one's killed themselves. Not before that, either," the agent said hastily. "At least I believe that's the case."

"It's a fine apartment," I said drily. "The price is unacceptable, however. Lower it by 300 euros and we have a deal." I turned to go. It was half past seven. After my successful première, Madame Bellini had surprised me with some opera tickets. "The Mastersingers of Nuremberg" was being performed and she had immediately thought of me. She had even said she would come with me – for my sake, she emphasised, as normally she didn't care for Wagner.

The agent promised to get back to me about the rent. "There's not really any provision for discounts," he said warily.

"It is always possible to reverse such a policy if you can count Hitler amongst your customers," I reassured him before leaving.

It was unusually mild for late November. The sky had long since darkened; the city hummed and rushed all about me. For a brief moment I was seized by the frenzy of old, the fear of the Asiatic hordes, the urgent desire to increase our level of armament. Then this turmoil gave way to the pleasant feeling that catastrophe had not engulfed us over the past sixty years, that Providence had certainly chosen the right moment to summon me to action, without leaving me too little time to enjoy a spot of Wagner now and again.

I buttoned up my coat and wandered through the streets. Some shops were taking delivery of large quantities of fir and spruce branches. When I found the hustle and bustle a little too overwhelming I ducked into the smaller side streets. I pondered a few changes to certain details in my programme, and strolled past an illuminated sports centre. Large sections of the population were in tip-top physical condition – too often, however, these were women. A well-trained body may make childbirth easier; it improves the resilience and health of the mother. But ultimately the aim was not to breed hundreds of thousands of female partisans. The proportion of young men in these sports facilities had to be raised markedly. Such were my musings when two men blocked my path.

"Oi, you. Jewish bastard," one said.

"Do you think we're just going to sit back and watch you insult Germany?" the second said.

343

Slowly, I removed my hat and showed my face in the light of a streetlamp.

"Step back into the ranks, you vermin," I said, unruffled. "Or you'll end up like Röhm!"

For a while neither of them said another word. Then the second man hissed, "What sort of a sick bastard are you? First you get that face operated on, then you use it to stab Germany in the back!"

"A sick, vile bastard," the first one said. Something glinted in his hand. With incredible speed his fist hurtled towards my face. Attempting to maintain my poise and my pride, I did not evade the blow.

It was like being hit by a bullet. There was no pain, only speed, only a powerful impact. Then the wall of the building rushed silently towards me. I tried to keep my footing, but something hit the back of my head hard. The building shot past above me, my hand felt in my coat pocket, I grabbed the opera tickets and took them out, while the blows around me increased. The English must have new artillery, a murderous barrage, it became so dark, how could they aim with such accuracy, our graves, like the end of the world, I didn't even know where my helmet was, or my faithful dog, my Foxl, my Foxl, my Foxl . . .

xxxiv

The first thing I saw was a glaring neon light. "I hope some-body's been looking after Wenck's army," I thought. Then I looked around the room and when I caught sight of the appar-atus it soon became clear that there was no pressing need for Wenck's army just for now.

Beside me was a type of coat stand, to which several plastic sacs had been attached. The contents of these dripped slowly into my right arm; the left was in a rigid plaster mould. This was not so simple to observe, for I was unable to open the eye on the non-plaster side. I was baffled: it all looked mightily painful, and yet I could feel no pain save for a permanent thudding in my head. I turned my head to afford a better reconnaissance of my situation, then raised it carefully, trigger-ing a sudden and sharp pain in my chest.

I could hear a door open on the other side of the room, but decided not to look over. The face of a nurse appeared cautiously above the bridge of my nose.

"Are you awake?"

". . ." I said. This was intended to be a question about the date, but my mouth issued no more than a sound somewhere between a grunt and a rasp.

"Good," she said. "Now, don't go back to sleep, will you? I'm going to fetch the doctor."

". . ." I wheezed in reply. I could already tell that in all likelihood I had suffered no permanent damage, just a slight rusting of the vocal chords as a result of their not having been used for some time. I rotated my functioning eye. In my field of vision was a small table on which sat a telephone and a bouquet of flowers. I saw a device which must be monitoring my pulse. I tried to move my legs, but soon abandoned the attempt as it was probable that this would incur further pain. Instead I essayed some short speaking exercises; I presumed, after all, that I would have a question or two to put to the doctor.

In fact nothing happened for a considerable length of time. I had forgotten how things tended to be in hospital if one is not Führer and Reich Chancellor. The patient is supposed to recover, but in fact all he does is wait. He waits for nurses, treatment, doctors – ostensibly everything is going to happen "soon" or "straight away", whereas "straight away" means "in half an hour to forty-five minutes" and "soon" means "in an hour or more".

I was overcome by an acute urge, and I sensed at once that a certain provision had been made for this too. I would have liked to have taken a look at the television for a while, only the operating of this machine was as perplexing to me as it was physically impossible. So I stared motionlessly at the wall opposite and tried to reconstruct recent events. I recalled a moment in a patient transport vehicle and Fräulein Krömeier's screams. Confusingly, my mind played that short sequence over and again in which I greeted France's surrender with a spontaneous leap or dance for joy. And yet I wasn't wearing a uniform but a turquoise tutu. Then Göring came up to me, leading two saddled reindeer, and said, "Mein Führer, when you're in Poland please get me some curd cheese. I'll cook us something fabulous this evening!" I looked at him incredulously and said, "Göring, you fool! Can't you see I don't have any pockets?" At this Göring burst into tears and someone was shaking my shoulder.

"Herr Hitler? Herr Hitler?"

I woke with a start, jerking up as far as my body would allow.

"The ward doctor's here."

A young man in a white coat offered me his hand, which I was barely able to shake.

"Here we are," he said. "I'm Doctor Radulescu."

"Considering your name, you speak remarkably fluent German," I croaked. "No trace of an accent."

"Considering the state you're in, you're remarkably talkative," the imported doctor said. "Do you know how I perfected my German accent?"

I shook my head wearily.

"Thirteen years of school, nine semesters studying medicine, two years working abroad, then I married my wife and took her name."

I nodded and coughed; assaulted by pain, I tried to avoid coughing again, at the same time attempting to exude an element of strength and Führer-like leadership qualities. The outcome of not coughing, however, was that a number of small and unlovely bits and pieces shot out of my nose. All in all I felt miserable.

"Let's get one thing out of the way first. You're in better physical shape than you look. There's nothing that won't heal or get working again properly in time . . ."

"My vo–ice?" I moaned. ". . . I'm an or–ator."

"There's nothing wrong with your voice, it's just out of practice, hence the dry throat. What you must do is keep drinking. All the time. If I'm not mistaken," he said, glancing down beside my bed, "you don't even have to worry about waste disposal for the time being. Let's see, what else have we got? A nasty fracture of the cheekbone, severe concussion, several ugly bruises on the jaw, but the most puzzling thing is that it's not broken. The guys in casualty immediately put money on a knuckleduster. If they're right you can thank your lucky stars ten times over. Your swollen eye might not be pretty, but it'll work again. And then we've got a broken collarbone, broken arm – a clean break, which is perfect – five broken ribs, and we had to open you up to put that rupture of your liver right again. While we're on the subject, might I say that you've got one of the finest livers we've ever seen? Am I right in thinking you don't drink?"

I nodded weakly. "Vegetarian, too."

"Your results really are excellent. You might make it to one hundred and twenty."

"Won't be enough," I said dreamily.

"Now, now," he laughed. "You've got plenty of time ahead of you. I can't see any problems; you're just going to have to be patient."

348

"You really ought to report this to the police," the nurse said.

"That would suit those villains down to the ground! What would Röhm have given to have been reported to the police?"

"I'm not your lawyer," said the doctor with the Roumanian name. "But with injuries like this . . ."

"I shall strike back in my own way," I coughed, and it occurred to me that rarely in my life had I uttered such an empty threat. "I'd rather you tell me how much longer you intend to keep me here."

"A week or two, if there are no complications, maybe a little longer. Then you can recuperate properly at home and let everything fuse together again. Right now you should get some more sleep. And do think about telling the police, the nurse is absolutely right. I know you should turn the other cheek, but that doesn't give people the right to administer beatings like that."

"And have a think about your menu." This was the nurse, showing me a list of meals. "We need to know what you'd like to eat during your stay with us." I pushed the list away. "No special treatment. Simple soldier's rations. Vegetarian. Like the Ancient Greeks."

She looked at me, sighed, ticked a dozen or so boxes and gave me back the list. "You have to sign it."

Fcebly, I signed with the hand I could move. Then I passed out again.

I was standing at a bus stop in the Ukraine, holding a huge bowl of curd cheese.

Göring wasn't there, and I remember just how much that irritated me.

XXXV

I did, in fact, briefly consider reporting the matter to the police, but then dismissed the idea. It contradicted all my principles. The Führer cannot assume the role of victim; it is not right. He is not dependent on the intercession or assistance of such wretched characters as state prosecutors or police officials; he does not hide behind them, he grabs the law with his own fist. Or, rather, he offers it to the burning hands of the S.S. and then they grab it with their many fists. If I'd had an S.S. at my disposal this obscure "party headquarters" would have gone up in flames the very next evening and, within a week, each one of its cowardly members would have had the opportunity to ponder the true principles of the racial idea while bathed in a pool of their own blood. But from whom could I demand such brutality in these peaceable times, in which people had been weaned off violence? Sawatzki was a man for deft punchlines rather than punches; he worked with his brain, not his brawn. All I could do at this juncture was to defer the matter to an unspecified time in the future and take great care that no press photographer would have the opportunity to take some unfavourable pictures of me when I availed myself of the sanitary facilities at the hospital. The incident itself could not be kept secret, however, and only a few days later it was reported in the newspaper that I had been the victim of "far-right violence". It was, of course, the usual journalistic incompetence to exalt these feeble-minded stooges as "far-right", a label they did not merit. But every cloud has its silver lining, and within a few days, even hours, I had quite a number of extraordinary telephone exchanges with people to whom Fräulein Krömeier – at the suggestion of Herr Sawatzki and with his blessing – had given the number of my mobile telephone.

The first conversation, other than those with Flashlight colleagues wishing me a speedy recovery, was conducted with Frau Künast, who enquired about my well-being and wanted to know if I did actually belong to any party.

"Of course," I said. "My own."

Künast laughed and said that the N.S.D.A.P. was, for the time being at least, dozing or in hibernation. Until it awoke, she continued, I ought to consider whether the Green Party couldn't offer a home to me, the man who had risked life and limb in opposition to right-wing violence. "At least for a while," she said, repeating her invitation with a laugh.

I digested the telephone call with a shake of my head, and would most likely have dismissed it as another curious figment of the democratic–parliamentary imagination, had not another call come the following day along surprisingly similar lines. I had a gentleman on the telephone who, as I dimly recollect, was either just completing an apprenticeship as minister of health, or had already done so. Even after much thought I no longer recall his name; in any case I gave up trying to keep a track of this party long ago. After all, rumours are frequently aired on the relevant broadcasting slots that the only remaining elderly gentleman of the alliance is an out-and-out dipsomaniac. In my opinion this is unfair on the man; I rather take the view that it must be utterly impossible to last for even an hour in this bizarre game of political ring-a-ring o'roses without appearing inebriated.

The apprentice health minister told me how sorry he was about the assault. Especially on someone like myself who, as he put it, was a standard bearer for the broadest freedoms of opinion and speech, and needed all the support he could get at this difficult time. I scarcely had the opportunity to emphasise that the strong man is mightiest alone, for the apprentice was already insisting that he would do his utmost to ensure I was back on the television screen as soon as possible. For a moment I was terrified that he would take my treatment in his own notoriously soft-fingered and incompetent hands. Instead he asked me with feigned casualness about my party affiliation and I answered him truthfully.

The apprentice roared with boyish laughter. Then he said I was hilarious and suggested that as the N.S.D.A.P. was currently at rest in the graveyard of history, maybe the F.D.P. could become my new political home. I told him that he and his colleagues should finally stop insulting my party and that I had no interest of any sort in his crowd of liberal maggots. The apprentice laughed once more and said he loved it when I was like this; he could tell I would soon be my old self again. Before he hung up he promised to have an application for membership sent to me. Unsolicited. The telephone, it struck me at that moment, is the wrong means of communication for people without ears. And barely had I put the darned thing down than it rang again.

It turned out that the apprentice health minister and Künast the Green were by no means the only ones who had decided to put their own individual interpretations on my unflinching blood sacrifice. A number of callers from different parties congratulated me on my unequivocal championing of non-violence, which in their view was manifested by my demonstrative refusal to resort to self-defence. These callers included a man from the only grouping whose name aroused any sympathy in me: the Animal Protection Party. I had a very pleasant conversation with this fellow, during the course of which he generously brought my attention to some atrocities perpetrated against Roumanian street dogs, which were beyond belief. I resolved in the near future to devote particular attention to the outrageous goings-on in that country.

Recent events were also interpreted quite differently in the eyes of those "professional" politicians. The "Solidarity Civil Rights Movement" declared me to be a fellow sufferer of their party founder Larouche, who had been persecuted somehow or other. Meanwhile, a strange foreigners' party by the name of B.I.G. assured me that in a country where the beating up of foreigners was outlawed, the beating up of Germans was, of course, outlawed too, to which I gave the emphatic response that I should not wish to live in a country where the beating up of foreigners was outlawed. This produced another outburst of raucous laughter at the other end of the line. For others I was not a symbol for freedom of opinion, but *against* it, at least against the wrong opinions; I was not only regarded as a

353

champion against violence, but by several parties as a champion *for* it (C.S.U., two gun clubs and a manufacturer of firearms) and once as a victim of violence against the elderly (the Family Party). I was particularly struck by the dilettantism of an appeal by the Pirate Party, which thought it had identified in my refusal to press charges a protest against the surveillance state. It saw me as an advocate of extreme independence from the state and what they termed "total pirate thinking". Those that came closest to the truth were a grouping called "The Violets", who saw in my case evidence of a world beyond the purely materialistic, and in me a man who "under the banner of total peaceableness had subjected his return to the harshest tests with the greatest possible forbearance". I laughed for so long that I had to ask for extra painkillers for my ribs.

Fräulein Krömeier brought me more post from the office. She too had been called on the telephone several times, mostly by individuals from the same parties or groupings, but new were the communications from diverse communist organisations. It has now slipped my mind why they got in touch, but I do not suppose the reason was much different from Stalin's in 1939, when he concluded our non-aggression pact. What united these callers and scribes was that they were all soliciting my membership of their respective associations. Only two parties, in fact, failed to contact me. Simpletons would probably put this down to indifference, but I knew better. Which is why, when an unknown Berlin number flashed on my telephone the following day, I hollered speculatively, "Hello? Is that the S.P.D.?"

"Er, yes . . . Am I speaking to Herr Hitler?" a voice at the other end of the line said.

354

"Indeed you are," I said. "I've been waiting for you to call!"

"For me?"

"Not specifically. But for someone from the S.P.D. Who's speaking, please?"

"Gabriel, Sigmar Gabriel. It's fantastic that you can speak on the phone again. I'd heard and read the most awful things. You sound back on form."

"That's purely on account of your telephone call."

"Really? Are you that pleased I phoned?"

"No, not as such. I'm pleased because it took you so long. In the time it takes for German Social Democracy to conceive of an idea one could cure two severe cases of tuberculosis."

"Hahaha," Gabriel sniggered, and it sounded exceedingly natural. "You're right, sometimes that's certainly the case. Look, this is exactly why I'm calling . . ."

"I know! Because my own party is in hibernation at present."

"What party?"

"You disappoint me, Gabriel! *What* is the name of my party?"

"Erm . . ."

"Go on!"

"Excuse me? I'm not exactly sure what you're . . ."

"N. . . . S. . . . D. . . . A. . . . ?"

"P.?"

"Precisely. P. It's having a rest at the moment. And you would like to know whether I might just be looking for a new home. In your party!"

"Well, I was actually . . ."

"By all means send your forms to my office," I said chattily.

"Listen, have you just taken some painkillers? Or a few too many sleeping tablets?"

"No," I said, and was about to add that I wouldn't need any after this conversation. Then it occurred to me that Gabriel might be right. One never really knows what on earth doctors and nurses administer via those bags with tubes. And it also struck me that in its present form, this S.P.D. was no longer a party to be rounded up and incarcerated in a concentration camp. Its sluggishness might even render it useful in some matters. I therefore made immediate reference to some of medicines I was taking and took my leave very cordially.

I leaned back on my pillow, wondering who might be the next person to call. In fact all that I was missing was a telephone conversation with someone from the chancellor's electoral union. Who might that be? The lumpy matron herself was out of the question, of course. But I wouldn't have minded speaking to the employment minister. I was dying to know why she had stopped procreating only one child away from receiving the Gold Mothers' Cross. That Guttenberg would have been interesting too. Even though he had emerged from a centuries-deep swamp of aristocratic incest, here was a man who had the capacity to think in a wider context, without allowing professorial objections endlessly to get in the way. But his political heyday seemed now to be past. Who else? The ecological fellow with the spectacles? The drip of a whip? The wheelchair-bound aspiring-conservative Swabian in charge of finances?

And there were the Valkyries, scouring the battlefields for

fallen heroes once more. The number was unfamiliar to me, but the area code was Berlin. I concluded it must be the windbag.

"Good day, Herr Pofalla," I said.

"I'm sorry?" This was indisputably the voice of a woman. I put her as a bit older, maybe mid-fifties.

"I do beg your pardon – who is speaking?"

"My name is Golz, Beate Golz," and she uttered the name of a well-known German-sounding publishing house. "And to whom am I speaking?"

"Hitler," I said, clearing my throat. "I'm terribly sorry, I was expecting somebody else."

"Is this a bad time? Your office said it would be fine for me to phone in the . . ."

"No, no," I said. "It's perfectly alright. But kindly, put no more questions about how I'm feeling."

"Is it that bad?"

"No, but I'm beginning to sound like an old gramophone record."

"Herr Hitler . . . I'm calling to ask whether you'd like to write a book?"

"I already have," I said. "Two, in fact."

"I know. More than ten million copies. We're very impressed. But someone with your potential ought not to leave a gap of eighty years."

"Well, look, that gap was not entirely within my control . . ."

"You're absolutely right. I can well understand that writing doesn't come so easily when the Russians are rolling over your bunker . . ."

"Indeed," I said. I could barely have put it better myself.

I was pleasantly surprised by Frau Golz's ability to empathise.

"But now the Russians are no longer here. And however much we enjoy your weekly round-up on the telly, I think it's time the Führer produced another report on his view of the world. Or – before I make a total fool of myself here – do you already have other contractual commitments?"

"No, I'm usually published by Franz Eher," I said, but then realised that by now he must be in retirement too.

"I'm assuming you haven't heard from your publisher in a while?"

"In point of fact, you're right," I mused. "I wonder who's cashing in my royalties at this moment?"

"The state of Bavaria, if I'm rightly informed," Frau Golz said.

"What impertinence!"

"You could sue, of course, but you know what the courts are like . . ."

"You're telling me!"

"I'd be delighted, however, if you took the somewhat simpler route instead."

"Which would be . . . ?"

"You write a new book. In a new world. We'd be happy to publish it. And as we're all professionals here I can offer you the following." Then she set forth a schedule of major marketing strategies and mentioned a sum as an advance payment, which even in this suspect euro money elicited my approval – though of course I kept this to myself for the time being. I would also be allowed to choose my own colleagues, whose remuneration would likewise be covered by the publishing house.

"Our one condition: it must be the truth."

I rolled my eyes. "I suppose you'll be wanting to know what my real name is."

"No, no, no. Your name is Adolf Hitler, of course. What other name would we put on the book? Moses Halbgewachs?"

I laughed. "Or Schmul Rosenzweig. I like you."

"What I'm trying to say is that we're not after a humorous book. I assume you'd be thinking along the same lines. The Führer doesn't make jokes."

It was astonishing how simple everything was with this woman. She knew exactly what she was talking about. And with whom.

"Will you have a think about it?"

"Give me a little time," I said. "I will be in touch."

I waited for five minutes, precisely. Then I called her back. I demanded a substantially higher sum. In retrospect I have to presume that she was expecting this.

"O.K. then: Sieg Heil!" she said.

"May I take that as a deal?" I asked.

"You may," she laughed.

"Then a deal it is!"

xxxvi

It is quite extraordinary. For the first time in ages I am not bothered by the snow, even though it has come so early this year. Large flakes are falling outside the window; in 1943 this would have driven me mad. Now I know that everything has a deeper significance, that Destiny does not expect me to win a world war at the first or second attempt, that she is giving me time and has trust in me; now I can properly enjoy this mellow pre-Christmas tranquillity once more, after some arduous years. And I am enjoying them almost as much as I did when I was a child, huddled up in a cosy corner of the parlour with Homer's account of the Trojan War. There is still pain in my ribcage, but it is heartening to feel that it is abating.

The publishing house has supplied me with a dictation machine. Sawatzki wanted me to use my mobile telephone, but in the end I've found the dictation machine easier to operate. Press a button – it records; press a button – it stops. In general I'm very much against this multiplication of tasks. The wireless has to play these silver disks too, the razor machine has to work for both wet and dry shaving, the petrol pump attendant doubles up as a grocer, while the telephone has to be a telephone, a calendar, a camera and everything else besides. This is dangerous nonsense, the only possible consequence of which is that thousands of our young people will be mown down on the roads because they cannot stop staring into their screens. One of my first undertakings will be to outlaw such telephone devices or allow them only for those inferior racial elements remaining in our society – for the latter I may even make them compulsory. Then they will litter the main thoroughfares of Berlin like squashed hedgehogs. So they do have their practical uses. But otherwise: utter nonsense! Certainly, it would be far more advantageous for the state finances if the Luftwaffe could also assume the task of refuse collection. But what sort of a Luftwaffe would we have then?

A good idea. I will dictate it immediately into the device.

In the corridor outside they have stuck up voluminous quantities of Christmas decorations. Stars, fir branches and much more. On Sundays in Advent there is Glühwein, of which they have now developed a most pleasant non-alcoholic variety, although I have my doubts that it will ever find acceptance amongst the troops. Ah well, a private will always be a private. On reflection, I cannot say that Christmas decorations have become more tasteful with the passing of the years. A most disagreeable industrialisation has taken hold. I am not concerned about whether something is kitsch or not, for every example of kitsch harbours a residue of the feelings of the simple man, and since that is the case there will always be the possibility of a development towards real art. No, what really bothers me is that the importance of Father Christmas has grown disproportionally, doubtlessly as a result of Anglo-American cultural infiltration. The candle, meanwhile, has fallen in significance.

Perhaps it only seems like this because candles are not permitted here in the hospital, for fire safety reasons. And much as I appreciate the careful handling of Volk property, I cannot recall large numbers of buildings having been damaged during my time in government, despite the generous use of candles. But I do concede that, from 1943 onwards, the statistics become rather less meaningful given the increasing absence of buildings. Nonetheless, a Christmas like this has its own charm. Free from the burden of governmental responsibility, which in the longer term will be inevitable, I ought to enjoy it while it lasts.

I can say that the personnel are making great efforts to take care of me. I talk to them a lot, about their working conditions, about the social services which – as I am learning more and more – are in such a wretched state that it is well-nigh a miracle anybody can be cured at all. I get many visits from doctors. Coming to me off-duty, they sit down and tell me about the latest example of effrontery from the current blunderer masquerading as the health minister. There are just as many incidences of absurd behaviour involving his predecessor, they say, and no doubt the same will be true of his successor. I must address the matter in my programme, they urge me, and announce in no uncertain terms that change is urgently required. I promise that soon I will tackle this with all my energies. Occasionally I comment that it would help if fewer foreigners were treated here on the ward. They laugh, say, "Well, of course you could see it that way," followed immediately by a "but joking aside", after which comes a tale of the next outrage. Of which there seems to be no shortage.

There is also a strikingly charming nurse, a fiery character, bright and cheerful. Her name is Irmgard, in fact . . . but I definitely need to pace myself. Were I twenty years younger, maybe . . .

Herr Sawatzki has just been to visit with Fräulein Krömeier, or should I say the former Fräulein Krömeier. I still find it hard to get used to saying Frau Sawatzki. The two of them have a happy event looming, and she's already as round as a ball. She insists she can still manage, but it cannot be very long before her belly starts to become a real burden. She has taken on a little colour – or maybe taken off a little white. I still find all that difficult to understand. But I have to say that they make a marvellous couple, and when they look at each other, I know that in nineteen or twenty years a strapping grenadier will be at their side: impeccable genetic material for the Waffen-S.S., and later for the party. They asked me where I was spending Christmas and then invited me over, which delighted me, but I don't think I shall bother them. Christmas is a family celebration.

"But you're practically part of the family?" Fräulein, I mean Frau Sawatzki said.

"Just at the moment," I said, for Schwester Irmgard was coming through the door, "just at the moment Schwester Irmgard is my family."

Schwester Irmgard laughed and said, "Over my dead body. I'm just popping in to check he's alright."

"He is fine," I grinned, and she let out such a hearty laugh that I almost considered putting off the next stage in my political career for a year or two.

"Frau Bellini and Herr Sensenbrink send their best wishes,"

Sawatzki said. "Frau Bellini's going to come tomorrow or the day after, with the outcome of the meeting about the new slot, the new studio . . ."

"You must have seen it," I said. "What is your impression?"

"You won't be disappointed, I can tell you. There's a pile of money behind it! You've not heard this from me, but there's still plenty left in the budget. Plenty!"

"That's enough," Frau Sawatzki said, cutting him off. "We've got to go and buy a pram? Before I can't move anymore?"

"O.K., O.K.," Sawatzki replied. "But do think about my suggestion." I could have sworn that as the two of them left he said something like, "Have you told him what the baby's going to be called?" But I may have been mistaken.

Yes, his suggestion. He is absolutely right, it is a perfectly logical step. If a handful of parties are inviting one to become a member, one would be well advised not to give one's valuable self to causes other than one's own. In 1919 I would have foundered in another party. Instead I took over a tiny, insignificant party and shaped it according to my wishes, which was far more effective. In this case, with the impetus of a book publication and a new programme scheduled, I could launch a propaganda offensive and then start a movement. He has already sent to my mobile telephone some designs for placards. I like them. I really like them.

They are of me and they're modelled closely on the old ones. They're more striking with the old typeface, Sawatzki says, and he's right. I should listen to him; he has a knack for this. He has also devised a new electoral slogan. It will be plastered at the bottom of all the placards, giving them a common thread. The slogan addresses old virtues, old doubts, and for good measure has a humorous, conciliatory element to win over those pirate voters and other young people. The slogan reads: "It wasn't all bad."

I think we can work with that.

Translator's Note

Timur Vermes' cutting satire offers a unique perspective on our modern, media-bloated world, in which celebrity is worshipped above all else. The rapid progress of globalisation over the past two decades means that the most of the material in the novel will resonate with audiences in all Western societies rather than just in Germany. But for those readers who feel they may have missed some or many of the cultural and historical references, what follows is a brief résumé.

Adolf Hitler (1889–1945), we dare assume, is sufficiently well known for no introduction to be necessary. A few biographical notes up to his takeover of power in 1933, however, may serve to clarify some of the observations made in the book. Having left school at sixteen, Hitler moved to Vienna where he supported himself by working as a casual labourer and selling his watercolours. Twice rejected by the Academy of Fine Arts, Hitler fell into poverty, living in a shelter for the homeless, then a men's workhouse. He volunteered immediately to fight in 1914 and was awarded the Iron Cross for bravery. After the end of World War I, Hitler moved to Munich where he joined the embryonic National Socialist party and soon gained a reputation as an orator. After the failed Beer Hall Putsch of 1923,

Hitler was sentenced to five years' imprisonment, but served only one, during which time he wrote *Mein Kampf.* Following his early release he rebuilt the party, became its undisputed leader, and the meteoric rise of the Nazis began. **Eva Braun (1912–45)** was his long-term partner who only became the Führer's wife for the last couple of days of their life. Having already undertaken a couple of unsuccessful suicide attempts in the 1930s, she finally managed it together with Adolf in the bunker.

One of the great ironies of the Third Reich was that neither its Führer nor his three leading henchmen were the embodiment of the Aryan ideal as propagated by National Socialism. **Hermann Göring (1893–1946)**, the portly, arrogant head of the Luftwaffe – one of his many roles – was addicted to morphine as well as fine clothes. Sentenced to death at Nuremberg, he cheated the hangman by swallowing cyanide on the eve of his execution. **Heinrich Himmler (1900–45)**, weaselly head of the S.S. and one of the key figures of the Holocaust, also committed suicide after capture by British forces, having failed in his attempt to negotiate a peace treaty with the Allies behind Hitler's back. The physically frail **Joseph Goebbels (1897–45)**, Hitler's greatest fan and Nazi Germany's propaganda chief, killed his children before he and his wife took their own lives in Hitler's bunker.

Martin Bormann (1900–45), who gets frequent mention in the novel, became very close to Hitler in later years; as the Führer's trust in him grew, so did his power within the regime, while his relationship with Himmler, amongst others, became increasingly antagonistic. For many years after the war, uncertainty prevailed over Bormann's fate, and the West German government did not officially abandon the hunt for him until 1971. It was later accepted that he was killed while trying to escape from Berlin at the end of the war. **Heinrich Müller (1900–45)**, chief of the Gestapo, was another leading Nazi whose death has remained a matter of mystery. It is assumed that he died in May 1945, but no physical remains have ever been found.

Of the other Nazi figures referred to here, perhaps the best known is **Rudolf Hess (1894–1987)**, Hitler's deputy from 1933 to 1941, at which point he took the madcap decision to pilot a plane to Britain in a solo attempt to negotiate with the government. Hess's Messerschmitt crashed in Scotland and his peace efforts came to naught. He was sentenced to life imprisonment at Nuremberg, and he lived out the rest of his life at Spandau prison in Berlin, where for more than twenty years he was the only inmate, guarded by soldiers and warders from the four victorious Allied Powers. **Albert Speer (1905–81)** is best known for his role as chief architect of the Third Reich, although he also became minister for armaments during the war. Speer was responsible for the New Reich Chancellery, which Hitler refers to in the novel, as well as the Nuremberg parade grounds. After the war Speer was imprisoned for twenty years for his complicity in the crimes of the Third Reich. **Ernst Röhm (1887–1934)** was on the radical wing of the Nazi Party that was pressing for social revolution. Head of the S.A., Röhm was executed as part of the Night of the Long Knives in summer 1934. **Reinhard Heydrich (1904–42)**, referred to in the novel by first name only, was the brutal and ruthless deputy protector of occupied

Bohemia and Moravia, as well as one of the main instigators of the Holocaust. Heydrich was assassinated in Prague by a group of Czech and Slovak officers following orders from their government-in-exile. **Julius Streicher** (1885–1946), "the Jew Baiter of Nuremberg", founded the newspaper, *Der Stürmer*, which Hitler recalls in the kiosk. A virulent anti-Semite, his behaviour was condemned as excessive by other leading Nazis, and his star waned after 1938, in spite of his close relationship with the Führer. Streicher was hanged for his incitement of the Holocaust, even though he had not been directly involved. Another leading Nazi executed at Nuremberg was **Joachim von Ribbentrop** (1893–1946), wine salesman turned foreign minister, via a spell as ambassador to London. An incorrigibly vain man, Ribbentrop added the "von" to his name through his aunt's aristocratic connections. **Robert Ley** (1890–1945) was head of the German labour front, which established the "Strength through Joy" leisure organisation for the masses. He committed suicide while on trial at Nuremberg. **Walther Funk** (1890–1960) served as a propaganda minister in the Third Reich, later becoming economics minister. He was imprisoned after the war, but released in 1957 due to poor health. **Ernst Hanfstaengl** (1887–1975) was an early supporter of Hitler who introduced him into Munich society and later worked as chief of the foreign press bureau for the Nazis. He fell from favour in the mid-1930s and later fled Germany. **Franz Schädle** (1906–45) was the commander of the Führer's S.S. bodyguard; he shot himself the day after Hitler committed suicide. **Ulrich Graf** (1887–1950) and **Max Ernst von Scheubner-Richter** (1894–1923) were both shot during Hitler's Beer Hall Putsch of

1923. The former survived, despite having taken eleven bullets to the body.

A number of leading military figures are cited throughout the book. Chief amongst these is **Grand Admiral Karl Dönitz (1891–1980)**, commander-in-chief of the German navy from 1943. Hitler nominated Dönitz head of state after his death; there was little left for him to do but authorise Germany's unconditional surrender on 7 May, 1945. Sentenced to ten years' imprisonment at Nuremberg, Dönitz lived almost another twenty-five years following his release in 1956. **Wilhelm Keitel (1882–1946)**, supreme commander of the armed forces, and his deputy **Alfred Jodl (1890–1946)**, likewise played leading roles in the surrender. Both were tried and hanged as war criminals at Nuremberg. **Heinz Guderian (1888–1954)** and **Walther Wenck (1900–1982)** were both army generals during the war, as was **Felix Steiner (1896–1966)**, whose failure to launch an offensive from Berlin in April 1945 was the trigger for Hitler's fit in the famous scene from *Downfall*, endlessly parodied on YouTube. **Friedrich Paulus (1890–1957)** commanded the German forces in the Battle of Stalingrad, after which he spent ten years in Soviet captivity. **Walter von Brauchitsch (1881–1948)** was commander-in-chief of the German army at the beginning of the war and one of the key players in the Blitzkrieg against France. When the army failed to take Moscow, however, Brauchitsch fell from favour.

Of the other historical figures referred to in the novel, the best known may be **Wernher von Braun (1912–77)**, the "father of rocket science", who took the decision to surrender to the Americans rather than Russians in 1945, and whose work was partially responsible for the moon landings in 1969. **Konrad Zuse (1910–95)** was another German engineer, who is often credited with being the inventor of the computer. The wily **Franz von Papen (1879–1969)** was surprised to find himself on trial with Göring et al. at Nuremberg, as he was a representative of Germany's old conservative elite rather than a Nazi, one of the faction which believed it could manipulate Hitler and use the mass appeal of National Socialism to further its own ends. A key player in smoothing the way for Anschluss in 1938, von Papen then spent most of the war as ambassador to Turkey. Acquitted at Nuremberg, von Papen did a short spell in prison after being convicted by a German court. **Hjalmar Schacht (1877–1970)** was likewise acquitted at Nuremberg, having been ousted as minister of economics in 1937. A decade earlier, Schacht's efforts had helped put an end to the hyperinflation in Germany. **Erich Kempka (1910–75)** was the Führer's chauffeur from 1934 to 1945, and one of those tasked with burning Hitler's and Eva Braun's bodies after they committed suicide. **Adam Müller (1884–1945)** was a publisher and also ran a printing firm, which was responsible for both *Mein Kampf* and the official Nazi paper, the *Völkischer Beobachter*. He hanged himself in his cell after being arrested by the Americans. **Josef Stolzing-Cerny (1869–1942)** was a journalist who wrote for the *Völkischer Beobachter* and who read a draft of *Mein Kampf*. **Fritz Todt (1891–1942)**, who died in a plane crash during the war, was an engineer involved in the building of the German Autobahnen (motorways) after 1933. Later, his Todt Organisation, whose staff included **Friedrich Tamms (1904–80)**, built the defensive line in the West, as well as Hitler's military H.Q.

on the Eastern Front, the Wolf's Lair. The Jewish **Tietz** family introduced the department store to Germany and established the Kaufhof chain, which is still going strong. **Theodor Morrell** (1886–1948) was Hitler's personal physician, known for his unconventional treatments. Morbidly obese, he died from a stroke. **Leni Riefenstahl** (1902–2003) has been called the greatest female filmmaker of the twentieth century. She became mesmerised with Hitler in the early 1930s and produced a number of impressive propaganda films for the Nazis, most famously *Triumph of the Will*. Also a photographer, dancer and actress, she went on to have a long and successful career after the war, although to many her legacy is tainted by her association with the Nazi regime. **Heinrich Hoffmann** (1885–1957) met Hitler in 1919 and soon became the Nazi Party's official photographer. Eva Braun worked in his studio, which is how she came to know Adolf. **Geli Raubal** (1908–31) was Hitler's half-niece with whom he lived from 1929 until her suicide two years later. Hitler adored Geli and was a domineering presence in her life, keeping a close watch on her every move. **Traudl Junge** (1920–2002) was the Führer's secretary from December 1942 until his death. The film *Downfall* was based on her recollections of the last days of the Reich.

The conversation between the teenage boys in the dry cleaner's will probably leave the non-German reader as much at a loss as it does Hitler, and some clarification here may be helpful. "Stromberg" is a popular German comedy which has so far run to five series. Inspired by the B.B.C. hit "The Office", it stars Christoph Maria Herbst, who for his performance as Bernd Stromberg won the same Adolf Grimme Prize that Hitler is awarded in the novel. Coincidentally, Herbst also narrated the German audiobook of *Look Who's Back*. The "**other Stromberg**" refers to a send-up that was a regular feature on "Switch reloaded", a parody show on German television. In it, the Stromberg character becomes a rather ineffectual Hitler figure, trying to solve the problems of the Third Reich from his "office" on the Obersalzberg in the Bavarian Alps. **Stefan Raab**, **Harald Schmidt** and **Hape Kerkeling** are mentioned in the same breath early in the novel. All three are well-known figures of television comedy and recipients of the Adolf Grimme Prize. Amongst other things, Raab has hosted a German talent show; he also composed and performed the forgettable "Wadde hadde dude da" at the 2000 Eurovision Song Contest, somehow finishing fifth. Schmidt hosted a late-night chat show on German television where he would occasionally do Hitler impersonations. Kerkeling has appeared in many comedy shows and once almost succeeded in gaining entrance to the official residence of the German president when he dressed up as Queen Beatrix of the Netherlands. **Mario Barth** and **Ingo Appelt** are both veterans of the German comedy scene, while **Atze Schröder** is a fictitious character whose performer refuses to reveal his true identity and has successfully defended his right to remain anonymous in court.

Finally, a guide to the acronyms dotted liberally throughout the book. The full name of the Nazi Party was the Nationalsozialistische Deutsche Arbeiterpartei (National Socialist German Workers' Party) or **N.S.D.A.P.** Readers may well be familiar with the Nazi organisations of the **S.A.** (Sturmabteilung) and particularly the **S.S.** (Schutzstaffel). The former, under Ernst Röhm, was the original paramilitary wing of the Nazi party, its thuggish stormtroopers in their trademark brown shirts regularly beating up political opponents on the left. After the 1934 purge, however, the organisation was eclipsed by Himmler's S.S., which became one of the most powerful entities in Nazi Germany and was in great measure responsible for the worst humanitarian crimes committed in the Third Reich. The **D.N.V.P.** (Deutschnationale Volkspartei) was another nationalist party in inter-war Germany with a more conservative and thus smaller following than the Nazis. Believing it could piggy-back on the mass appeal of National Socialism, the D.N.V.P. was one of the factions responsible for helping Hitler to power in 1933. **I.G. Farben** was a vast pharmaceutical conglomerate, which notoriously produced the Zyklon B used to gas millions in the Holocaust.

Modern German political parties love acronyms too. The **C.D.U.** (Christian Democratic Union) is the centre-right party of Angela Merkel; in Bavaria, the same movement is represented by its more conservative sister party, the **C.S.U.** (Christian Social Union). On the left is the **S.P.D.** (Social Democratic Party of Germany), while the **F.D.P.** (Free Democratic Party) is the German liberal party which has frequently been a coalition partner in government. The **N.P.D.** (National Democratic Party) is the home of the far right in Germany, while **B.I.G.** (Alliance for Innovation and Justice) is a minority party representing Muslims and their integration in Germany.

JAMIE BULLOCH

375

TIMUR VERMES was born in Nuremberg in 1967, the son of a German mother and a Hungarian father who fled the country in 1956. He studied history and politics and went on to become a journalist. He has written for the *Abendzeitung* and the *Cologne Express* and worked for various magazines. He has ghostwritten several books since 2007. This is his first novel.

JAMIE BULLOCH is the translator of novels by Daniel Glattauer, Katharina Hagena, Paulus Hochgatterer, Birgit Vanderbeke, Daniela Krien and Alissa Walser.

LOOK
WHO'S BACK